# Last of the Pistoleers

## Books by Mark Warren

*Two Winters in a Tipi*
*Wyatt Earp, an American Odyssey* (a trilogy)
*The Long Road to Legend*
*Born to the Badge*
*A Law Unto Himself*
*Secrets of the Forest* (4 volumes)
*Wild Plants & Survival Lore*
*Fire-making, Storytelling, & Ceremony*
*Stalking, Tracking, & Playing Games in the Wild*
*Archery, Projectiles & Canoeing*
*Indigo Heaven*
*Librarians of the West*
*Last of the Pistoleers*
*The Westering Trail Travesties*
*Song of the Horseman*

# Last of the Pistoleers

Mark Warren

SPEAKING VOLUMES, LLC
NAPLES, FLORIDA
2021

Last of the Pistoleers

Cover design by Hannah Linder

ISBN 978-1-64540-750-8

*To my grandfather, James D. Bazemore,*
*former sheriff of Fulton County, Georgia*

# Chapter One

The sound of the gunfire ballooned inside the small space and then seemed to be swallowed up by the open sky above them. Both men welcomed the quiet interlude that followed. Even though they did not speak, each man felt the connection of their friendship gel in the silence. This was how they visited now. Two men with guns making lots of noise and trying to relive some part of their past.

They stood inside a false box canyon of plastic cartons, steel cans, wrecked furniture, abandoned appliances, and every other imaginable item of household waste you'd expect to find in a county landfill. It was a depressing place for Harte, probably the *last* place he ought to be spending the *last* of a weekend in which his soon-to-be ex-wife had asked him to pick up the *last* of his things from the house before she deposited them here in the dump.

As a high school history teacher, Harte Canaday had always felt some hostility toward the waste facility. It was the double entendre of "waste" that ate at him. Here amid the county's refuse was proof positive that rural north Georgia still held to a diehard resistance to recycling.

Truth be told, now with his marriage fallen apart, he didn't care much one way or the other about recycling. In fact, feeling used up and discarded himself, he had begun to entertain a nagging admission that this dump was probably the perfect place for him.

It was Sunday and a typically hot day for late summer in Southern Appalachia. With the facility closed, Harte and Sheriff Jim Raburn had the mountains of garbage all to themselves. Closed to all except, of course, the sheriff, who could on short notice produce a key to any municipal lock in Lumpkin County. Between them, they had probably fired off a hundred rounds of ammo at makeshift targets. Harte removed his earplugs to hear what Jim was mumbling.

"Man!" Jim complained. He hissed a stream of air like a fast leak from a punctured tire. "Something here stinks to high heaven, don't it?"

Harte considered remarking on Jim's penchant for stating the obvious, but instead he just watched his friend look for a new target by emptying a black plastic bag of its sundry contents.

"Gotta be a dead dog in here somewhere," Jim went on, looking around and scowling.

Standing amid all this stench and clad in his sheriff's uniform, Jim Raburn looked ludicrous, Harte thought. Like a well-dressed beggar going through a Dumpster in an alleyway, hoping for something that might pass for a meal. Jim laughed as he held up a white plastic bleach bottle.

"Always knew we'd make it big one day," he said, and then injected a little melody into his performance. "Ah, boy . . . Sunday afternoon at the dump!"

Harte ejected the spent shells from the old Colt pistol he had owned since he was a boy of fourteen. By habit he pocketed the brass, though the practice seemed pointless considering where he was standing.

"Always good to have friends in high places," Harte said straight-faced. "Who else could have gotten me into this oasis on the spur of the moment?"

Jim set the empty *Clorox* jug on top of a junked television set with a shattered screen. He weighted it on the sides with pieces of cinder block and stepped back to where Harte waited.

"By the way," Jim said and began nodding, "I read your magazine article . . . the one on Jesse James. Good insights, as usual." He turned to Harte. "A pretty cold snake, wasn't he?"

Harte finished loading cartridges into his gun and snapped shut the loading gate. Considering the question, he pushed up the flat brim of his "Montana" hat with his forefinger, something he'd been doing since he was a seven-year-old kid after seeing Gary Cooper make the same subtle hat adjustment in a Saturday matinee. He gazed up into the clean blue slate of the near cloudless sky and worked his way back through a century and a half of history.

"I'll say this," Harte said plainly, "I wouldn't have wanted to target practice with Jesse. They say he was an unpredictable cuss." Harte made the practiced twist of his wrist and holstered his gun butt-forward. Then he crossed his arms over his chest, the tacit semaphore that he was waiting for Jim to shoot first.

Jim perched his drugstore reading glasses on his nose and then slid the Plexiglas goggles over the glasses. Next, he stretched the ear protector headset from around his neck and hooked it over the crown of his head with the padded cups covering his ears. Peering downrange at the white plastic bottle, he set his teeth as if he were trying to intimidate the *Clorox* bottle.

"All right," Jim said, his voice a little too loud. "Let's see if I can hit at least *one* damned thing today."

Harte smiled and pushed the foam plugs into his ears.

Taking his typical two-handed grip on his blocky automatic, Jim squinted over the sights of the outstretched weapon. He fired once, absorbing the recoil with a show of impatience. He exhaled his disgust and leveled out his aim again. Each shot came after a long thoughtful interval, but his face never lost its indignant glare at the untouched target.

"Well, shit!" he said and laughed, but there was no humor in it. He turned to Harte, propped his free hand on his hip, and waited, as if some ribbing might be in order. But Harte was a long way from offering criticisms. His thoughts had drifted again to his forthcoming marital status.

"Good thing I'm in a managerial position," Jim said. "I guess a sixty-somethin' sheriff can afford to let his deputies do all the shootin'."He lowered the goggles and the glasses and narrowed his eyes at the *Clorox* bottle. "Did I at least wing one o' the cinder blocks?"

Harte pretended to study the target. "Could be."

Jim's forehead wrinkled. "What?" he asked too loudly.

Harte tapped his own left ear, and Jim jerked off the ear protection with an annoyed look.

"Think you probably did," Harte said. "The one on the right, maybe."

Jim stared at the target. Finally, he just shook his head.

"Hell, you know's well as I do, I didn't hit nothin'," he said, his voice settling down to an acceptance of his faltering marksmanship. He took in a lot of air through his nose and then purged it. "It's my damn eyes," he complained. "I wear my glasses, and I can see my sights just fine . . . only the damn target's a blur. I take 'em off, I can see the target, but my sights are swimmin' around in a fog." Jim gave Harte his beleaguered shrug of the eyebrows. "It's damned if I do and damned if I don't." He shook his head and scowled downrange at the target. "Can't win, pard."

Jim stepped aside, and Harte slid the Colt from its holster, setting his right foot forward to turn his body sideways to the target like a duelist. He stood like that for a time, the gun hanging down by his leg, his head turned so that his chin almost touched his right shoulder.

"Happens to all of us," Harte said matter-of-factly. "No way around it. The eyes go, and so goes the accuracy."

They were quiet for a time, each trying to face the infirmities of aging with some dignity.

4

"So, what do *you* do?" Jim said, nodding toward the target.

Harte thought about it for a few seconds. "Well . . . personally . . . I need to see the target. Doesn't make much sense if you can't see what you're shooting at. So, I just try to get the front sight on it. Don't even worry about the rear sight."

"Yeah," Jim sighed, "that's the way they're trainin' us now at the seminars." He shook his head again. "Guess I'm too old school. Can't seem to get the hang of it."

Raising his right arm, Harte brought up the old .45 Peacemaker, cocking it on the rise and then steadying the long barrel as if it were suspended by invisible wires. The gun roared and kicked up, and part of a cinder block shattered in a spray of gray dust. He leveled the gun again, and this time when he fired, the jug made a sudden jerk, showing a nickel-sized hole like a single dark eye in the white plastic. He cocked again and aimed. This shot clipped the bottle cap, but the next two tore holes through the jug, enough to see daylight through the plastic.

Jim chuckled. "Well . . . if I'm old school, you're ancient with that old thumb-buster, but you're shootin' a hell of a lot better'n me." He slapped Harte's shoulder and squeezed. "Hell, *I* should'a been the schoolteacher and *you* the sheriff."

Harte opened the loading gate on the Colt and began ejecting the cartridges. "You just keep hiring those young guns to do your shooting, Jim. You're doing exactly what you're supposed to be doing. That's why the county keeps voting you back into office. You're good at it. They like you."

Jim rammed a loaded magazine into the butt of his gun and tamped it down with the heel of his palm. "Well, they'd better start likin' somebody else real soon. I'll be doin' good to finish out this term."

Harte studied his friend's lined face. "You're retiring?"

The sheriff adjusted glasses, goggles, and ear cups again, stepped up, and took his shooting stance. "Need to spend more time with Lauren," he said, the words quiet as an overdue confession.

Harte just nodded. He knew there was no need to belabor that topic any more than they already had. That the county sheriff's daughter was fighting a drug addiction was common knowledge in Lumpkin, but no amount of talk was going to change it.

"Besides," Jim went on, "I'm plumb wore out." He relaxed and turned to look at Harte, his face as vulnerable as Harte had ever seen it. "I'm tired of dealing with all these meth labs and coke-heads and heroin addicts . . . from families I've known all my life."

The sheriff shook his head and then rocked on his feet as he readied himself to shoot again. But then his body just wilted, his shoulders slumping and his eyes flat as dull pennies.

"Hell, I'm done here," Jim said, exhaling in a long sigh. "I'm just wasting ammo." He turned again to Harte. "Wanna call it quits?"

"Sure," Harte answered. They holstered their guns—Jim's Glock in-to his minimal nylon harness attached to his trouser belt and Harte's antique Colt into the same cracked, leather holster that he had acquired with the original purchase of the gun half a century ago.

"Where's it all coming from?" Harte asked. "The drugs, I mean."

Jim Raburn propped both fists on his hips, looked off toward the trees to the west, and spewed air, his lips fluttering like a horse's. "Hell, you name it . . . Mexico, Guatemala, Vietnam, Afghanistan . . . and if the local dealers can't get it that way, they try and cook up the damn stuff themselves. Meth is the new moonshine, you know."

They started for their vehicles, moving at the same easy pace they had perfected when they were just boys rambling toward home from school on the county's backroads.

"You remember Ronnie-Mac Rydell?" Jim asked.

"Sure," Harte said without hesitation. "Vernon Rydell was his granddaddy . . . ran the lumberyard where I worked as a kid."

"Well," Jim went on, "Ronnie-Mac, you'll remember, was one o' the best shot-putters to come outta Lumpkin County. Now he weighs about a hun'erd and ten pounds and is missin' most've his teeth. Looks like his skin came unglued from his skull. He was runnin' a meth lab in the old root cellar behind his house, where his forebears stored potatoes and onions and turnips and such." As they crossed the lot, Jim leaned away, spat, and then shook his head. "Guess I'm mostly tired o' bein' disappointed, if you wanna know the truth."

Harte watched the weariness settle into his friend's face, knowing that most of that disappointment had started with Jim's first divorce, escalated with the second, and then snowballed with his daughter's collision with cocaine.

"Lot of that disappointment going around, Jim."

The sheriff turned at the wistful timbre in Harte's voice. "Students?"

Harte shrugged his head to one side, knowing there was nothing else to do but take on every heartache in life as it came at you. "There are always *some* good ones . . . but most are just doing their time, waiting to be handed a diploma."

Jim huffed a laugh. "Ain't that what we did?"

Harte gave him the same sidewise glance he might present to an unprepared student. "I seem to remember us working our butts off, and then working afternoons in the field or the lumberyard."

Jim shrugged, conceding the point.

"These kids these days," Harte continued, "a lot of them don't have chores at home. Even some of the ones living on a farm."

Jim kept his eyes angled to the ground as they walked. "Speakin' o' 'home' . . . I saw Elmer Dowdy the other day. He said he's seen you camped out up at Cooper Gap for the last couple o' weeks. What's that all about? Who goes campin' in August?"

Harte knew that Jim would already know about his separation. Everybody in town would be privy to it by now. Callie would have told a friend or two in confidence, and then they would have passed it along to their husbands. From there it was a wildfire. That was the nature of a small town, where everybody knew everybody. But Harte also knew that Jim needed to hear all this from him.

"Callie and I are calling it quits," he said quietly. They kept walking, the sound of their boots in the dirt marking their time like the tick of a heartless clock.

" 'Quits'!" Jim said, turning his head.

Harte kept looking straight ahead as they walked. "She says I'm uncommunicative . . . and that I keep some kind of anger smoldering inside me."

Jim almost laughed. "You? Angry? Nobody will ever call you a blabbermouth, but, hell, Harte, you're the biggest teddy bear I've ever known. I ain't never seen you really get angry, 'xcept when some bully was pickin' on someb'dy back in school."

When they reached the big black GMC with "*SHERIFF*" painted in luminescent silver across the side panel, their momentum stalled, and Jim spun, leaned back against his driver's door, and folded his arms over his chest. Seeming to chew on a problem, he frowned up at the only cloud moving across the sky.

"Well, damn," he said, trying to sound surprised. He pressed his lips into a thin line and studied Harte. "Listen, I got plenty o' room at my place if you need somewhere to hang your hat. Got to be better than sleeping on the ground . . . 'specially at our age."

Now Harte focused on the same cloud. "Remember that good camping place we found up in the gap? We'd taken a couple of horses up the mountain and ended up staying overnight."

Jim was already nodding. "Yeah, I remember gettin' my butt tanned by my daddy the next day. He thought we'd taken off for Old Mexico or somewhere." Jim chuckled at the memory, but then his face sobered. "I'm serious. Come and stay with me. This can be a hard time for a man."

Harte looked down at the ground, where a bottle top was half-buried in the hardpan. He unearthed it with the toe of his boot and then kicked it away.

"I'm all right," he said. "It's been coming for a while." He looked pointedly at Jim. "*You* know how it is."

"Damn *right*, I know." Jim picked at a thin scroll of chrome peeling off the side mirror. "You reckon this is temporary?"

Harte shook his head. "Guess I'll be signing papers before too long."

Jim's mouth crimped with a false smile. "You know there's only so many problems you can duck in a marriage. Finally, I guess you just run out o' duck."

Harte narrowed his eyes. " 'Run out of duck'," he said in a flat tone. "How is it you and I grow up in the same town, but we each speak a different vernacular?"

Jim huffed an airy laugh. "Look at who I hang out with . . . the worst the county has to offer. 'Bout everybody I arrest has run out of luck and duck . . . everything but pluck." When Harte made no reply, Jim gave his voice a little bounce. "Hey, y'all lasted longer'n most do these days. I mean, look at me. Emily had enough o' me after twelve years. Then it only took Sarah two. You and Callie made it to what . . . twenty?"

"Twenty-one," Harte said.

"Well—," Jim began, but he didn't finish. He raised one boot, wet his finger on his tongue, and rubbed at something above the heel. Letting the boot drop, he looked off toward the sun sinking into the trees. Shadows stretched across the lot, creeping toward them like a dark tide. "Hey," Jim said, plucking the ear-protection headset from around his neck. "You oughta think about gettin' you one o' these. Really keeps the sound out. Want me to order you one? Might be we can hold onto our ears, even if our eyes are goin' to hell."

Harte shook his head and dug the soft rubbery plugs from his ears. After pocketing them, he touched the brim of his "Montana" hat with his forefinger.

"Wouldn't work with the hat," he explained.

Jim tried for a stony countenance. " 'Course not . . . what was I thinkin'? How the hell could Harte Canaday shoot without that damned hat?"

They watched the sun fracture into stained glass shards of light inside the tree canopy. Heat lifted off the hardpan dirt, but a breeze was finding its way out of the forest from the creek.

"Hey," Jim chirped, breaking the silence, "you figure ol' Jesse had the same kind o' problems . . . with his eyes, I mean?"

Harte shook his head. "Didn't live long enough to get old like us."

"Ran out of duck, huh?"

Cracking a smile, Harte had to concede that one. The phrase was just about perfect for Jesse.

Jim tossed his ear-protection headgear into his truck and laughed deep in his chest. Harte knew *that* sound. Whatever came next would be about the golden days of their childhood.

"Hell, when it was cap guns, we *never* used the sights," Jim reminisced. "Just whoever could get off the first shot. Never missed, did we?"

Harte closed his hand around the smooth walnut grips on his old Colt Peacemaker and felt the history of the antique gun telegraph up his arm into the core of him. He had never learned the weapon's story, but he knew it was too old not to have one.

"Ever figure back in those days you'd end up being sheriff, Jim?"

Jim pursed his lips and shook his head. "Nah . . . figured on just keepin' on with the farm. That was Daddy's plan, anyway." He wrinkled his forehead. "Hell," he said, but he let it go.

With their target practice over, the land was quiet all around them, making it seem as if everyone else in the county was indoors waiting out the heat. Between the two of them, they'd shot a lot of rounds. For Jim, who had been Lumpkin County sheriff off and on for twenty-something years, there was no question about the pragmatism of the session. The county paid for every bullet.

For Harte it was something else. There was an art to handling a gun—an esoteric equipoise of explosive power and grace. *And* there was the romance of history, which was his stock and trade as a high school teacher. For Harte, these shooting sessions were expensive. Every time he fired off a round, it amounted to throwing a handful of loose change out into the county's refuse.

Jim made a point of eyeing the holstered Colt on Harte's hip. "I remember the day you bought that hogleg from that ol' goat lived up behind the Blackshear Mill? Hell, we had no idea what that thing was worth, and neither did he. What'd you pay . . . twenty dollars?"

Harte smiled at the memory. "Thought I was paying an arm and a leg for it back then. I was working at the sawmill after school stacking fourteen-foot rough-cut two-by-tens for six bucks an afternoon and seven on Saturdays. But one look at that gun—" He looked down at the outdated revolver at his side, and for just a moment he remembered the exhilaration of buying it.

"Somebody took care o' that thing in the ol' days," Jim said.

Harte nodded. "Somebody's doing that *these* days, too." he said.

Jim opened the door to the GMC. He sat, shut the door, leaned an arm on the open windowsill, and let his eyes take in the whole of Harte, from his boots to the crown of his hat.

"Now tell me again, how is it that's your 'Montana hat' . . . when you bought it in Tucson?"

The jibe was rhetorical. Jim was the only person to whom Harte had confided his dream of Montana. Harte waved away the question and stepped back from the cruiser.

"Hey," Jim said, "how 'bout we go and get somethin' to eat . . . talk about things a little bit?"

Harte knew the invitation was about taking the edge off his marital problems. They had never talked about their marriages—neither of Jim's two attempts at it nor Harte's first and only.

" 'Preciate it," Harte said and gritted his teeth. "I've got a load of papers to grade tonight. Summer school, you know." He offered the sheepish expression that had always served as his apology for a lie.

Jim nodded. "Open invitation," he said and started the cruiser. "You take 'er easy, pard. Lock up when you leave."

The sheriff's cruiser eased out through the gate and passed into the shadows of the trees that swallowed the road as it dipped down to the creek. After the cruiser had climbed the far side, all was quiet again but for the chirr of a cicada that droned from somewhere high in one of the pines.

From where he stood by his truck, Harte could still see the *Clorox* jug. He remembered a day—maybe fifty-five years ago—when Jim had used half a bottle of bleach, trying to convert a tan wide-brimmed hat into a white one to match some movie idol's headgear. The felt had come apart like rotting flesh. Harte smiled at the memory. As boys in those cap gun days, he and Jim had alternated being lawman and outlaw, and even then, before having shot a real pistol, Harte had handled the toy gun with a kind of reverential respect. He knew he was hitting what he was aiming at. He knew it for a fact, simply because his instincts had told him as much. Later, when they started using real bullets, the proof was in the shooting.

When he'd purchased the antique Colt, it had seemed like a rite of passage. At the time Harte had believed that being proficient with the gun was tantamount to being a man, and so he had worked hard at it, and that meant using the sights. Now with his eyes getting worse by the year, those sure-shot days were sliding behind him . . . forever, he guessed. If the *Clorox* bottle had not been such a bright white, he doubted he could have pulled off the few hits he had made.

He stared at the jug long enough to feel the wound to his pride, until finally he convinced himself that the plastic bottle was mocking him. Walking with purpose, he returned to the alcove where he and Jim had finished their shooting. Along the way he picked up a smaller yellow bottle—an empty quart-sized jug of *Pennzoil*. Tossing the *Clorox* jug aside, he raised the swivel antenna on the junked TV and perched the inverted oil bottle on it. Then he stepped back fifteen yards to the spot where Jim's spent casings littered the ground. Turning, he stared at the yellow target, letting his body relax, feeling the butt of the gun nudge his forearm as a point of orientation.

Then, exhuming the style of the fictitious gunfights of his boyhood, he drew deliberately, thrusting the gun forward, righting it in a smooth and fluid twist of his wrist, cocking the hammer on the rise—all this in one practiced motion. This time he brought up the gun only to the level of his chest, his arm bent slightly at the elbow, his eyes fixed on the bottle but peripherally engaging the alignment of the gun barrel. The childhood technique must have been permanently ingrained into his muscles, because it came back to him as a single, flawless move . . . easy as throwing a ball.

The gun gravitated to the vector that defined unmitigated accuracy, hovering loosely to allow for recoil, as if the Colt were floating before him of its own volition. This was the paradox that he remembered—"graceful deliberation"—and all of it compressed into the single beat of a heart.

He fired five times, thumbing back the hammer for each shot, returning the barrel to its appointed level. The shots rang out in a steady rhythm, each explosion connecting to and building on the one before it. The bottle jerked and twisted with each round. Five for five.

As the echo of gunfire came apart and dissipated into the open sky above, only then did he realize he'd forgotten to plug his ears. He stood for a time, letting the silence gather around him like the closing of a forgotten ritual. Lowering the gun, he listened to the cicada begin to chirr again, and Harte knew that something of value had just entered into his otherwise lackluster day.

"Well," he said to the mute weapon, "I can still do one damned thing half-decent."

# Chapter Two

It was dark by the time Harte pulled onto the dirt road that led to his house. Halfway down the hill his headlights illuminated a new sign that had been erected in the middle of the road. *No Trespassing,* it read. *Violators Will Be Prosecuted to the Fullest Extent of the Law.* In the direct beam of his lights, the neon orange letters jumped off the black background like a slap in the face.

Without hesitation he plowed over the sign, hearing the post snap and rake the undercarriage of the truck, but he touched the brakes when his lights carved out the figure of Earl Sandifer pushing away from his locust rail fence. Earl carried a long shotgun gripped in both hands, the weapon's dark pitted metal so old it barely reflected any light from Harte's low beams. Stepping with a measured stride, Earl appeared full of purpose, as though he had been waiting here for anyone who might challenge his claim. The slouch in his tall gaunt frame disappeared when he assumed a stiff defensive position in the road.

"I reckon you can read, cain't you?" barked Sandifer as he squinted into the headlights.

"Earl," Harte said by way of a greeting. "Problem?"

"Damn right there's a problem. This here road is closed. I'm gatin' it off tomorr'. You can start usin' the road runnin' through the Holt property." A hostile gleam blazed in Earl's eyes.

Harte exhaled heavily and rested an arm on the windowsill. He said nothing, just looked at Earl. It was something Harte did with people he deemed either inane or problematic.

"I don't want to use the Holt road," Harte finally said. "Holt probably feels about the same."

Mark Warren

Harte could see that Earl had been working himself up to this state of agitation. He wondered how long Earl had been out here waiting. There were cattle out in the field, a dozen dark shapes scattered against the lighter shade of the grass, but the only sound was the ratchety rhythm of katydids at the edge of the forest.

"I own both sides o' the road," Earl ranted on. "So just turn 'round right now and start usin' t'other way in."

Harte remained as low key as the idle of his truck as he watched Earl's eyes dart about with the kind of nervous energy that Harte had seen develop into monumental mistakes. "I've got ingress and egress rights on this road," Harte explained calmly. "Don't have that on the Holt property. You know all this. It's in your deed just like it's in mine."

"I own both sides o' the road here," Sandifer repeated. "I'm closing it off to the public."

Harte felt his patience start to dwindle, but he managed to keep his face neutral. "You have some kind of trouble, Earl?"

"Damn right I did." Sandifer pointed to the crudely built shed that stood back fifty feet from the fence. The airy, stacked-log outbuilding was a throwback to nineteenth century homesteads. "Somebody's gone and made off with half my damn tractor parts. Got my spreader and rake and steel plow and my goddamned new wood-splitter and who knows what. Ain't had time to sort it all out." Sandifer leaned and spat a thin dark stream into the road ditch. "Sonzabitches might as well 'a taken my tractor. Got 'bout ever'thing that hooks up to it."

Harte looked at the road up ahead. His house lay a quarter mile up the hill. He had not slept there for a month, but Earl Sandifer didn't know that and didn't need to. Sandifer had never accepted a kindness proffered by Harte or his wife. They'd brought down a pound cake when he had moved in, but he'd never said "thank you" or returned the plate.

16

He'd just glared at the couple as though to show that such gifts would reap no favors with him.

"We're the only ones living back here, Earl. Seems to me you're singling us out."

"I'm singlin' out anybody tryin' to use this road! And you're the one on it right now!" He gestured toward Harte briefly with the muzzle of the shotgun, and Harte felt the heat that had already begun to smolder at his core now threaten to ignite the fuse that resided there.

Harte closed his eyes, took in a deep breath, pinched the bridge of his nose, and listened to the weariness in his own words. "You're not thinking straight on this, Earl. I might be the one person who can be helpful to you on this. I can keep an eye out for you."

"Don't need nobody to keep a eye out for nothin'. I'm gatin' off this road. Period!"

Harte decided to put some iron into his voice, just like he did with students who tended to forget who ran his classroom. "Legally, this is my road to use. It's immutable."

"It's what?" Sandifer's face wrinkled, but it only took him a second to recover his righteous anger. "It's *mine* is what it is!"

Harte shut off his engine. The sound of the katydids became a flood of rhythmic scratches and chirrs. Even with this din of insect chatter, a new quiet enveloped the two men. Sandifer moved into the grass beside the truck and reestablished his sentry pose. Harte heard movement behind the fence, and for a moment he believed Sandifer had enlisted reinforcements in this mission of madness. But it was only a wide-eyed cow, curious about the nocturnal parley.

Harte nodded to the shotgun. "This is not the way to talk to me, Earl. I'm going to step out of my truck, and we'll talk about how I can help you with all this."

Sandifer's knuckles paled from his stranglehold on the gun. "Ain't no need fer that. Might as well get use to the other way around . . . startin' right now."

Harte stepped out into the cool of the night, the crunch of gravel under his boots like the dare of crossing a line drawn in the dirt. His six-foot, two-inch frame had the effect of instantly altering the potential of the situation. Sandifer was tall, too, but his stature lacked something more than the slump of his spine. Like most farmers he moved about with a well-oiled economy, but outside of farm work he lost all sense of physical grace. Harte had seen this awkwardness often enough in the last two decades, because Earl was always complaining about something. Every time they'd spoken, Earl came out the victim.

At sixty-three Harte was ten years older than Sandifer and ten pounds past the lithe and light-of-foot that he once had been. But if the years had given Harte anything of value, it was the steadiness of how to handle a crisis. After twenty-six years of teaching teenagers and twenty-one years of marriage—even though that marriage appeared to be coming to its natural end—Harte felt capable of resolving just about anything that the world threw at him, as long as it was not Callie doing the throwing.

"Earl," Harte began, "I want you to set that shotgun against the fence so we can talk."

"Like hell I will. You can git back in your goddamn truck and back out o' here. I don't know you any better'n I know a jackrabbit."

Harte set his jaw. "That's sounding a little like an accusation, Earl. That about right?"

"You can take it any goddamn way you want to."

They stood facing one another in the dim yellow glow spreading from the interior light of the truck. Sandifer's face was almost comdletely lost in shadow, but Harte could hear the uneasy mix of fear, frustration, and rage in his neighbor's voice. Harte took two steps forward.

"I can't talk to you if you keep holding that shotgun in my face, Earl."

"Ain't no need fer talkin'," Sandifer complained, raising his voice. "You just git in your truck and back the hell out o' here." He bobbed the shotgun's muzzle toward the truck and then past Harte in the direction of the paved road. "I got no problem with shootin' a man."

Harte snatched the gun and twisted it propeller-style until it was free. It happened so fast that the farmer lost his footing and stumbled backward, almost falling in the ditch. The cow near the fence crow-hopped, its great mass shifting more quickly than seemed plausible for its size.

The lanky farmer worked at getting his footing in the clumps of grass beside the ditch. Now with his hands empty, he made fists down by his sides and tried to replace his startled expression with one of resentment.

Harte broke open the shotgun, an old double-barreled twelve-gauge with side-by-side hammers. It looked like something that might have been carried on a Wells Fargo coach a century and a half ago. He removed the two shells, pocketed them, and snapped the barrels back in line with the receiver.

"Earl, you think you can calm down enough to have a—"

Sandifer lurched forward and took a swing at Harte, but Harte's reflex brought the shotgun up to fend off the blow. Earl's knuckles rang out on the dark metal, and he swore so loudly that several cattle made a surge away from the fence, their sound in the grass like a wave breaking and receding on a sandy beach. Earl hunched over with his eyes clamped shut above bared teeth, his hand sandwiched between his thighs. He lifted his face to deliver a wordless curse and then turned and strode up his driveway, slinging his hand loosely at the wrist and mumbling. Harte propped the shotgun against the fence, tossed the two fat shells in the grass, got into his truck, and started up the hill to his former house.

Halfway up the mountain he felt the pall of his last conversation with Callie weigh upon him. He knew he should have called before dropping by, just as she had insisted. That ultimatum had irked him upon its delivery, and now it was like a knife in his back, because it probably had something to do with Layland Childers.

Rumors in a town as small as Dahlonega came pretty close to gospel, and the rumor was that Callie had been seeing Layland, the town's richest, glad-handing hound dog, who courted women like they were demos at a car dealership. Some of those women were married, but somehow Layland seemed never to run afoul of the husbands. Jim Raburn had once said that Layland could talk his way out of the Asian flu. In an all-male gathering at the hardware store or barber shop— depending upon which men were present—Harte had more than once heard Layland tally up his female conquests, counting them off on his fingers as easily as a man quoting the number of acres he owns.

Callie's car sat alone in the loop driveway. He parked, got out, and studied the house. Only the upstairs bedroom showed a light. In the quiet of the night the house seemed to hum a silent dirge. He walked to the front door and knocked. Within seconds the porch light clicked on, and the top of Callie's head bobbed up in the glass pane. When the door swung open a few inches, her face seemed to sag with sadness . . . or dismay. He could not tell which.

"Harte?" she said, pinching her robe at her throat. "What are you doing here?"

He was surprised at the makeup caked on her face. All the years with Harte, she had rarely used it. Now she seemed intent on pushing back as many years as possible.

"I just need to get my black wool coat," he announced quietly.

After hesitating for a moment, she stepped back, opening the door wider. If there had been any warmth in her expression seconds before, it was now gone.

"You're supposed to call first, Harte," she said, her voice suddenly tired and flat.

"I'm not here for all my things, just the coat. Should be by the laundry room door."

He thought she might put up resistance, but she turned and strode back to the kitchen. He listened but heard nothing in the house other than her movements in the laundry room. If Layland was here, he was being quiet as a mouse.

When she brought the coat, it was folded in her arms, and she passed it to him like a flag bestowed to a spouse at a military funeral. He took the coat under one arm and stared over her shoulder as he continued to listen for sounds in the house.

"You had any trouble with Earl Sandifer?"

Callie tightened her mouth—her impatient look. "What kind of trouble?"

"He was standing guard in the road with a shotgun, trying to keep me from passing through." He waited for her to reply, but Callie seemed not to hear what he had said.

"Harte—" she whispered wearily and sighed. "There's a lot of anger in you. You just never show it." Her features softened enough to allow that she could still be concerned for him.

"Callie, that doesn't make any sense. If I don't show it, how do you see it?"

She looked away, and by the hardness in her eyes he knew he had once again sabotaged any possibility for a conversation. He slipped his arms into the coat and occupied himself with the buttons. When he looked up at her, she was wearing her expression that said: *Anything else?*

"Never thought we'd be part of the divorce epidemic," he offered as gently as he could. "Feels depressingly common."

Callie closed her eyes for a long three seconds. Then she looked through him like an x-ray. Her disappointment was the last thing he saw as she shut the door.

Earl Sandifer had not returned to take up his post on the road. The shotgun was gone. As soon as he reached the paved road, Harte punched the accelerator to get a rush of air through the windows, letting up only when the road went to dirt and gravel at the bottom of the climb up to Cooper Gap. Weaving ever upward through the endless S-turns of the switchbacks in the dark, he felt the rest of the world retreat behind him as the mountain and surrounding forest became his refuge. Breathing in the elixir of cooler air, he spoke aloud against the jolt and rattle of the truck.

"There's always Montana," he said.

That was his mantra. Montana was the place he'd tucked away in his head for someday in the future. It was big and remote, a place of possibilities, and a long way from Georgia. He'd never been that far west, just to Tucson that one time the high school had paid for a history conference. The only thing worthwhile he had brought back from that trip had been the hat.

The dream of Montana had been planted in his mind by a postcard he had once received from an uncle who had flown out there to hunt elk. Harte didn't think much of buying an airplane ticket, hauling your hunting gear across the country, and hiring a guide to keep you from getting lost, all to kill some poor animal. But he did like that postcard, and the image of that place had not suffered over the years. Montana, he told himself, just might be heaven.

With the divorce and retirement closing in, he had half a mind to go there now. Just take off and start again. Just like that. But if he made that diagonal migration across the continent, what would be his first step once there? What would he actually do every day as a paradigm for living?

"Maybe I could teach those elk how to shoot back," he muttered aloud.

The banging of the truck drowned out his little joke, and he felt a twinge of embarrassment that he was becoming one of those old men who talked to himself. When his headlights carved out the little turnout where his camp was located, he pulled in, killed the engine and the lights, and sat listening through the open window as the high-country wind sleaved through the evening trees like a symphony of toneless strings and woodwinds.

When he had set up here a month ago, there was something refreshing and novel about the hideaway. Like an outlaw's lair. For a time, he had enjoyed the raw life of sleeping on the ground, being open to the elements, and hearing the yowl of coyotes intertwine with the throaty notes of a hoot owl. He especially favored the soporific murmur of the creek that tumbled over stone and root. But now the romance was wearing thin. His joints had begun to complain of the outlaw life.

The moon was up but hidden behind the spine of the Appalachians. That was just as well. In the last weeks that moon had seemed like the eye of God looking down on him, if not condemning, at least accusatory. He wondered if the moon looked different in Montana. Probably not, he thought, but he kept an open mind. God might look down leniently on a man willing to move to Montana.

After lighting a fire in the circle of stones outside his tent, he stood at his tailgate under the stars and prepared an entrée of *Bran Flakes*, half an overripe banana, and the last of the milk from his cooler. Settling at the fire, though he could see no farther than the dull halo of light thrown off by the flames, he ate like an exiled king who had been reduced to overlooking a realm of darkness.

# Chapter Three

He was up at first light, slowly limbering up his aching joints against the morning chill of the mountains. The moon was still up, just past full and skewed from its roundness, sitting in the saddle of a gap to the west as if it had rolled down the slope and settled in the notch with nowhere else to go. Even as he watched over the span of a few minutes, the color of the orb dissolved into the bluing sky, like a light azure marble at the bottom of a swimming pool.

Harte spread a hand over the still-warm ashes and smiled, but when he lifted the coffee pot the old kettle was light as a dried gourd. Upending it he discovered a hole burned through the bottom. He had liked that old pot, its white speckles on blue enamel and the worn-out spots where the gray metal showed through. He liked it because he had considered it part of his back-up Montana gear. Proof that he could head west any time he wanted, and no matter where he ended up at the end of a day, he could brew up some hot coffee for company. Now, without that pot, Montana seemed a little farther away.

He checked his watch. There was time to pick up some coffee and then stop by the hardware store to look for a kettle. He zipped up the tent, pushed his hat onto his head, and slid into the truck, all the while wondering if they still made kettles coated with speckled blue enamel.

"Got to be blue," he said. "For the big sky country."

He fired up the engine and started down the mountain, promising—silently—not to talk to himself out loud anymore. Twenty minutes later he turned onto Highway 60 toward town and eyed the long gray scab of concrete laid over the freshly graded red clay across from the funeral home. The construction strip ran perpendicular to the road, extending back into a butchered swath of woods, where the smell of pine sap still hung in the air. Ten yards back from the street a large white sign announced the future of the enterprise:

*New home of "Mountain Storage," 72 personal cubicles, environmentally controlled, 24-hr. access, a Layland Childers Construction project bringing employment and convenience to Lumpkin County.*

"Second homes," Harte mumbled and shook his head. "People got so much damn junk now they've got to have an extra house where *it* can live."

As if to justify this breach of promise about one-sided conversations, he glanced behind him where the sum of his belongings was jammed behind the seats. He couldn't help but gloat a little. With the separation from Callie complete, his number of possessions was monastic.

After picking up a coffee at the Golden Pantry, he pulled into the hardware store lot, where he saw Layland Childers's anachronistic pickup parked at the door. It was a forty-eight Ford, fire-engine red, and so radiantly restored that it looked like it had just rolled off Henry Ford's assembly line. Layland and Elmer Dowdy were in conversation by the bales of wheat straw, each man with a tan work boot propped up on the tailgate of Elmer's truck. Elmer's boots were stained and cracked. Layland's looked like they had just come out of the box.

Both men turned to watch Harte step from his truck, but then Elmer began hoisting bales of straw into the bed of his truck. Layland smiled at Harte's approach, his eyes amused as though he expected Harte to break into song and dance right there in the parking lot.

"Harte Canaday, how the hell are you?" Layland called out, as if just this morning he had decided to run for governor. Layland looked freshly washed and groomed for the day—a wrinkle-free turquoise shirt that would stand out in any crowd and jeans with a crease but just enough wear to convey a look of utilitarian pride. His golden-brown hair was combed straight back, the perfectly spaced furrows made by the teeth of his comb looking like they might remain in place all day.

"How the hell are you, Harte?" Layland tried again.

Without pausing in his work, Elmer glanced furtively at Layland's performance. Shaking his head he inflated his cheeks, lifted his eyebrows, and let the air seep from pursed lips. Elmer nodded to Harte and walked to the stack of wheat straw and lifted another bale.

When he came alongside Layland's showy Ford, Harte noticed for the first time a man in the passenger seat reading from a manila folder. With his dark complexion and narrow features, the man appeared to be a Latino. Wrap-around sunglasses hid his eyes, but his stillness suggested an imperturbable nature. He brought a slender hand to his mouth and licked his fingertips before turning a page, the movement fluid and calculated, as though the man had settled in to read for hours. His white silk pullover and light gray suit jacket were expensive, and Harte wondered what business scheme Layland was cooking up with this man.

Since they'd been in high school, Harte had barely tolerated Layland's overblown opinion of himself. Now all that was changed. Toleration had been replaced by pure acrimony since one of the teachers at school had informed Harte that Layland had taken Callie to lunch twice last week.

Harte walked past the wheelbarrows tilted against one another in a long chain of metallic orgy. He couldn't help but imagine Layland taking his place there, sweet-talking his way up to the last barrow in line.

"What's up, big guy?" Layland persisted. With his boyish smile and white flash of teeth, he was like a neon sign, glowing all day to bring in business. Harte cut his eyes to Elmer and nodded.

"Good to see you, Elmer."

The diminutive farmer had two sons, one of whom—Lamar—was in Harte's summer class. Lamar was slow and surly, and though twice the size of his father, would never be half the man.

Harte kept walking toward the front door until Layland tried again. "How 'bout it, Mr. C?"

At the sound of his school nickname, Harte stopped and stared into the door glass at the reflection of Layland's luminous smile. Something about Layland Childers's eternal bliss had always needled into Harte's skin, but now with Callie thrown into the equation, the prickly sensation had escalated to tenpenny nails. He turned and approached Layland, stopping just inside the man's cloud of aftershave.

"Around the middle of the nineteenth century," Harte began, his voice as quiet and steady as if he were in private conference with a student, "some of the Plains Indians out West hung around the military forts and started raising a hand like this and saying 'how.' " Harte raised his open palm, like a man taking an oath in court.

Layland, smiling, planted both feet on the ground, crossed his arms over his chest, and rocked back and forth on his feet, as though he were about to hear the best joke coming his way all day. Elmer tossed a bale onto the stack in his truck, paused, and watched Harte from a cautious angle, his eyes fairly begging for some kind of good will in the telling of this story.

"The white soldiers were puzzled," Harte continued, frowning in storyteller fashion. "They started asking each other what the Indians meant by it. No one knew, so someone finally asked."

Layland was chewing up every word. Probably memorizing the story for a later telling.

"So," Harte went on, "this chosen Indian answers: 'Every morning the white man greets us with a question: *How are you doing? How's it going? What's new?*' " Now Harte made a point of mimicking Layland's

28

last inane query. " '*How 'bout it?* ' " Layland's smile only widened, as if he might have somehow contributed to this story.

"So," Harte went on, "the Indian explains: 'This here is our sign for question.' " Harte rotated his raised hand at the wrist. " 'It can mean *who* or *where* or *what* or *how*. We're trying to be like the white man in every way. We ask a question as a greeting, just as he does. It doesn't matter the question. Or, for that matter, the answer.' "

Harte stared at a grinning Layland, who, apparently, was waiting for the punch line. Elmer pinched the bridge of his nose, ballooned his cheeks again, and exhaled quietly.

"Are you seeing my wife?" Harte said, his voice carrying the dull impact of a sledgehammer.

Surprised a little, Layland straightened and uncrossed his arms. He tried to hold on to the smile, but it fought against him.

"Well, wait a minute now, old buddy, the two o' you are—"

Harte's left foot took a half-step toward Layland, and his right shoulder rotated back an inch. Layland looked like a man who had mistakenly opened the stall gate on an angry bull. Retreating, he caught the backs of his legs on Elmer's tailgate, where his knees buckled, and he sat down hard. Then Elmer was suddenly taking hold of Harte's upper arm with the kind of grip that sank a posthole-digger into hard dry clay.

"Whoa there, Harte!" Elmer said. "Good thing I caught you. You just about tripped!" Elmer's face was just inches from Harte's when he delivered the coded message. The two stood there like boxers frozen in a clench. "Wouldn' want you to fall and get hurt, Mr. C." Elmer's whisper, Harte knew, related more to falls from grace and into lawsuits rather than to bruises. "Got your balance now?"

Harte relaxed, but he kept his eyes on Layland. Out of some irritating instinct of being watched, he glanced at the man in Layland's truck. The Latino was holding a slender cigar and looking his way, blowing a stream of smoke from a tight smile. His eyes were still hidden by the dark glasses, but his face radiated an amused glow. Harte turned back to Layland, who remained seated, trying to resurrect his meaningless smile.

"Callie and I are still married," Harte said, letting his eyes convey the force of his message.

Layland tried to look taken aback. "Well, sure, old buddy, I know that. We just talked some business over lunch, that's all. She's considering some investments." He started to push himself up from the tailgate, but then thought better of it and eased back down.

Elmer began walking Harte toward the store entrance. "He ain't worth it, Harte," Elmer mumbled and clapped a hand to Harte's back. "Just let it go." Elmer's hand slid off his back as Harte allowed his momentum to carry him into the store.

"Well, hey there, Mr. C." Behind the checkout counter, one of Harte's former students smiled at him from behind a magazine.

"Lorena," Harte said, trying for a new start on his day.

"I just saw Mrs. C," Lorena said, flipping a page and scanning its contents. Closing the magazine, she smiled. "She came in for a collar for your new cat."

" 'New cat'," Harte repeated, being careful not to frame the phrase as a question.

Lorena held the smile and nodded. Apparently, she was the only person in Lumpkin County who knew nothing of Harte's separation.

"Got any blue coffee pots?" he said.

Lorena's smile disappeared. "Blue?"

"Blue enamel. With little white speckles. A camp kettle."

Lorena frowned at the rows of goods that marched to the back of the store. "Look back there on aisle nine on the right, next to those big pots and pressure cookers. We used to have one."

Harte walked toward the back of the room with less than a modicum of hope, but when he turned the corner, he found a smaller version of his burned-out kettle dwarfed by two big silver pots on either side. The blue metal was rimed with a patina of dust. When he wiped it with his hand the pot gleamed with newness, its virgin white spangles like a snow flurry against a deep blue sky. He lifted it by its coiled wire handle and found that the diminished size appealed to him. He didn't plan on visitors, and he didn't need to drink more than a cup or two of coffee at any one time.

At the back of the shelf was an identical kettle still in its box. The artwork on the packaging jumped out to him, and his hand went to his shirt pocket to dig out his glasses. The picture showed a cowboy rendered in black silhouette as he reclined by his campfire at night, his Stetson-capped head propped on his saddle. Above him the night sky arched like a curtain of diamond-studded black velvet. It was as if this kettle had waited here for him out of some kind of fated, arcane devotion.

When Harte left the store, Layland's truck was gone. Elmer was tying down the bales of straw in the bed of his truck. Harte checked his watch, set down his purchase on one of the enraptured wheelbarrows and helped with the lashing, crisscrossing a long hemp rope back and forth through the cargo hooks.

"How're your classes goin'?" Elmer asked, as if nothing had transpired between them earlier.

Harte pushed out his lower lip to make a doubtful face. "Nobody wants to be in school in summer, Elmer. And nobody cares about history anymore. It's like teaching a cat how to fetch a stick. Even on a good day, most of the students seem like they're in a coma."

Elmer frowned. "I believe my oldest boy is in your class. Lamar?"

Harte nodded. "One of the braindead."

31

Elmer took the assessment with a sideways tilt of his head. "Well, least he got his mother's looks," he said, as if he believed it.

They stood for a time watching the morning traffic. A new silver Corvette sped by, looking strikingly out of place in rural America. Thirty seconds later, as though to add some kind of balance to the morning, a rusted pickup pulling a horse trailer cruised past them. The trailer was filled with tattered furniture, a portable basketball goal, and an enormous toy stuffed animal that might have been a rhinoceros. The two men looked at one another, but neither commented.

Harte retrieved his new kettle and propped the box between arm and hip. "Layland say anything to you about my wife, Elmer?"

Elmer pivoted his head toward Harte a little too quickly. "Callie? No, not to me. Hell, no."

Harte believed him, but he could read from Elmer's reaction that Callie's contact with Layland was common knowledge even to the farmers in the county. Elmer frowned for a time at the box wedged under Harte's arm and then looked away. The highway was painfully quiet now.

Harte checked his watch. "Well," he said and nodded toward the school across the street. "Off to the trenches."

"You hang in there, Harte. Ever'body says you're the best thing we got over there at the high school." Elmer plucked at a rope, testing the tautness with his thumb.

Harte turned, got in his truck, and fired the engine.

"Hey!" Elmer called out. "Slap that boy o' mine upside the head, if you need to. He tends to drift, and even when he don't, he ain't the sharpest knife in the kitchen drawer."

Harte checked his watch again. He still had time for a shower in the gym before his first class. He pulled the truck closer to Elmer and idled there with his arm resting on the windowsill.

"Thanks, Elmer," Harte said.

Elmer Dowdy made a little one-fingered salute above one eye and continued checking his ropes.

## Chapter Four

"Mr. C, do we have to read all these footnotes or just the main text?"

The room had been quiet for a full ten minutes, and Harte had already lost himself in working on the Hickok article he was writing as a followup to the Jesse James piece published in *The American West Magazine*. He looked up enough to peer over his glasses and give Lonny Grizzle his best, no-nonsense teacher's glare, but when he scanned the classroom, it was apparent that most of the students were awaiting his answer.

It was the coming night's homework he was giving them a chance to complete, so that they could have their evening free for something more suited to a summer night. He set aside the book on Hickok and exhaled a long slow sigh as his eyes tracked across the room. Knowing that no one wanted to read a word more than was required, Harte removed his glasses and stalled long enough to choose his words with care.

"Footnotes are the backbone of a history book," he said, mustering patience. "They reference the primary research and let you know you can believe what you're reading."

Lonny looked at his book the way a six-year-old studies a plate of vegetables. "Okay . . . but does that mean we gotta read 'em?"

Harte stared at him with a deadpan expression as he invented some numbers. "Seventy-five per cent of the test will come from the footnotes," he said, then let his smile put a crimp on their day before returning to his book on Hickok.

"Mr. C?" It was Lonny again. "So . . . if we just read the footnotes and forget the other stuff, we could maybe make a C on the test, right?"

Harte stacked his forearms on his desk and tried for Hickok's cold gunman-eyes. "Lonny, what else do you have to do right now?"

"Mr. C," Lonny persisted, "this is the most God-awful book I've ever read in my life."

Harte smiled and cocked his head. "Share that life list with us, would you, Lonny?"

Lonny's forehead furrowed with deep horizontal lines. "What list?"

Harte opened his hands, palms up. "My point exactly."

Lonny sat up in his desk and cleared his throat. "All right, Mr. C, just listen to this." The entire class turned to Lonny. " 'State hegemony over the native tribes took its template from its colonial subordination under England, in effect, reverberating like an expansionist precept during the Crown's rule, all of which rendered Georgia's trade relations with the natives far from egalitarian.' "

When Lonny looked up from his book, his face compressed as his shoulders shrugged and froze up around his neck. "Mr. C, that's, like, ear-torture." Everyone laughed.

Harte couldn't argue it. The text was dry and awkward. He looked down at his desk. His book was open to a color illustration of the famous Hickok-Tutt shootout in Springfield, Missouri—Hickok as cool as a breeze, taking aim seventy yards across the town square. Harte casually covered the picture with his forearms.

"That's your textbook, Lonny. I won't pretend it's a page-turner. But it's what we have, until someone writes a better one." He took in the class with a sweep of his eyes. "Might be wise to keep a dictionary handy."

"What I need is an alarm clock, Mr. C," Lonny quipped, getting more laughs. "They oughta be selling this book in the drug store next to the sleeping pills." Lonny pointed his chin at Harte's desk. "I bet whatever you're readin' ain't as hard to swallow as this stuff." He raised his closed textbook and backhanded it with a hollow sound.

"What *are* you reading, Mr. C?" This from Streak Pendergrass in the front row. His eyes angled down at Harte's book with interest, and Harte knew he was caught.

"Just another history book," he said, shrugging. "A biography."

"Okay," Lonny said, now charged with a new energy, "I tell you what." He propped an elbow on his desk and repeatedly poked the air with a finger toward Harte. "Pick out any page of your book . . . without looking . . . just a random place, okay? Then read one paragraph, and I'll make a bet with you." Lonny counted off the terms of the wager on his fingers. "One, that your book makes sense. Two, that I can tell you what it means. And three, that it's not half as boring as this stupid book." He raised his textbook and slapped it down on his desk.

Streak turned to face Lonny. "So, what's the bet, Lon? You gotta have stakes."

Lonny frowned. "I don't know." He looked out the window and thought for a moment. "Okay, Mr. C, I lose . . . I wash your truck. I win . . . you paraphrase our homework assignment."

"Yeah," Streak said, squirming in his desk. "You always tell a good story, Mr. C." Streak cocked his head and waited. Harte looked around the room and saw that all eyes were expectant.

"Come on, Mr. C," Lamar Dowdy prodded. "That truck o' yours can use a wash."

"We'll all pitch in," said Verdelle Rogers, getting a nod from the other three black girls behind her. "We'll turn that dust-mobile into new, Mr. C."

"We'll throw in the works," Streak announced. "Tire polish, full detail inside, vacuum the carpet, *Armor-All* the dash, *Windex* the windows—"

Harte studied their faces and marveled in the moment. The students' usually lackluster eyes shone with a visceral hunger.

"All right," he said. "I'll take the bait and read one paragraph. But it's just a short break. I'm not agreeing to your terms. You've got to do your own reading."

Holding his eyes on Lonny, Harte opened his book and pinned his finger to a page. He looked down, adjusted his glasses, and inhaled a slow breath. His reading voice kicked in with a measured pace, enunciative and loud enough for all in the room to hear.

" 'Abilene was typical of the Kansas cowtowns that would boom into prominence over the coming of the railroad. The town merchants needed the Texas drovers to patronize their shops, but the wild and woolly end-of-the-trail celebrations regularly produced a volatile combination: young men just paid for three months on the trail, free-flowing alcohol, prostitutes aplenty, and guns openly carried on public streets. The town-mortality rate rose whenever a new cattle outfit arrived. One barroom killing often spawned another retaliatory one. It was common practice for such a community to hire a peace officer who ranked high in violence by his own right. Hickok, a man-killer, carried this kind of reputation. Tall and imposing, he knew how to carry himself as a visible threat. His pair of guns were stuffed butt-forward in a red sash—a rather showy accoutrement for the drab life on the frontier. And most importantly, he would back down from no man, and every cowhand knew this.' "

His obligation complete, Harte whipped off his glasses and looked up to find the class mesmerized. He could not recall a time this summer within these four walls when all movement had ceased as it had now. He had to chuckle.

"Are you telling me that this sinks its hooks into you? It's still history."

"Keep going!" Streak said.

Then Lonny snapped out of his reverie. "Yeah, read the rest! Is this *Wild Bill* Hickok?"

Harte gave them a crooked smile. "You sham artists. You'd listen to me read from the telephone book, if you thought it would keep you from doing your assignment."

"No, really, Mr. C! Read more!" Streak was like a child pleading for another bedtime story.

Harte checked the other faces. To his surprise they *did* want more. He sat forward, settled his glasses in place, and read for another twenty minutes, covering Hickok's early career as a lawman, including the duel on the square at Springfield. Everyone wanted to see the illustration.

There were no school bells in the summer, but the clock on the wall behind Harte held the silent power to unleash a stampede from the room. Usually, it did. But when three o'clock came on this afternoon, no one bolted.

"School's over for the day," Harte announced. "Get that reading done tonight. Friday's the exam. If you don't pass, those of you who were supposed to have graduated last spring are going to have to register in fall. Read the text, read the footnotes. And don't just memorize names and dates. Think about what you're reading. Put yourself into the place of the people you read about. Think how you might have behaved had you been alive then."

Lauren Raburn was the first to get up, looking agitated as she collected her things. Her movement broke the spell in the room, and others began sliding from their seats. She walked to the door without any sign of parting—just as she had done all summer—no longer acknowledging the social connection Harte had enjoyed with her when her parents had been married.

"See you all tomorrow," he said to the room at large, not wanting to single her out. "And by the way, there'll be nothing on the exam about Hickok." Harte was the only one to smile. A few more girls made their exit, but a crowd of boys began to gather in front of Harte's desk.

Streak spun the book around to see its cover. "So, was Hickok, like, the fastest dude on the draw back then?" Lonny and Lamar appeared at his sides, both wanting to hear Harte's answer.

Harte picked up the book and dropped it in his briefcase. "Hickok was deliberate and deadly. But all that stuff about a fast draw . . . that's mostly the invention of Hollywood."

Most of the class had filed out, leaving the three boys and, to Harte's surprise, Collette Devereaux, who remained seated quietly in her desk. When she saw Harte looking at her, she turned her head to gaze out the window at the parking lot.

"Com'n, Mr. C," Streak goaded, "he had to be pretty fast or we'd a' never heard of him."

Harte shrugged. "It wasn't about a fancy draw from those low-slung, tied-down holsters you've seen in the movies. It was *being willing* to kill without hesitation. Men wore their guns high and snug to keep from losing their hardware from a bounce in the saddle."

With such a rapt audience, Harte's words rolled off his tongue. "That said . . . Hickok raised the bar on getting a weapon into action. He carried two, one on each hip, butt-forward. Two guns were showy and threatening. It meant instant backup. And he *was* good with them." He patted the briefcase. "Face to face shootouts—like this one in Springfield—were rare."

"So, how come his butt was forward?" Lonny sniggered. The trio of boys laughed.

"The guns were worn backward," Harte explained. "The butt is the bottom of the handle."

Lamar frowned. "Why carry your guns backward?"

"Hickok's guns were fairly long-barreled. With the conventional set-up—butt to the rear—the elbow has to come up high because the gun is pointed straight down."

He opened his middle drawer and pulled out a foot-long plastic ruler. Pushing back his chair, he stood, positioned the ruler at his hip, and went through a slow, vertical drawing motion.

"See how high my elbow has to rise?" Then he repositioned his hand by his side, this time his wrist turned so that the palm faced out, the ruler angled backward, and the elbow forward. "This way, all that upward movement is unnecessary." He demonstrated the practiced technique that he, himself, used with his Colt. His elbow moved forward but no higher than its original position.

As the three boys struggled with the concept, Collette quietly collected her things and started out. "Collette?" Harte said, stopping her. "Did you need to talk to me?"

She glanced at the boys crowding Harte's desk and then looked away. Wearing her guarded expression, she shook her head, hitched up her books, and left the room.

"I still don't get the butt-forward thing," Lamar said.

"Me neither," seconded Lonny.

Streak took the ruler and tried the motion for himself. "Yeah, if you gotta, like, twist your wrist around . . . it seems like it complicates everything."

"Yeah, that doesn't make sense," Lamar complained, looking almost angry now.

"Just take my word for it," Harte said. "It *is* easier." He lifted the briefcase and plucked his hat off the coatrack. "You boys may have already permanently damaged your reputations by lingering nine minutes after school is out."

On the walk down the hallway, Streak sidled up to Harte with a big grin. "So, what's this I hear about you writin' an article for some magazine, Mr. C?"

They pushed through the exit door into sunlight and started across the parking lot. "It's a history magazine," Harte explained. "I doubt it would interest you." When he reached his truck, the boys were still with him. "What!" he said, turning to their anxious faces.

"I heard it was an article about outlaws," Lonny said through a sly smile.

Harte conceded with a nod. "Jesse James. Do you know who he was?"

"Sure," Streak laughed. "Everybody's heard of him."

Harte spotted Collette standing in the shade of the big oak at the edge of the lot, her books cradled in both arms and held flat against her stomach. When he smiled at her, she looked down at her feet. Harte unlocked the truck, climbed inside, and set his hat in the passenger seat.

"Mr. C?" Streak called through the windowglass. "Read the article to us tomorrow?"

Harte cranked down the window. "Son, do I really look that gullible?"

"No, really!" Streak insisted. "We're interested." Lonny and Lamar nodded in unison.

Harte chuckled. If they weren't being genuine, he decided, they were damned good actors.

"Then why don't you pick up a copy and read it? It's in *The American West Magazine*."

"They don't carry it at the drug store," Streak said. "I already tried."

He stared at the three boys for a full ten seconds. "All right, you can borrow my copy tonight. But I want it back tomorrow. Fair enough?"

The trio nodded like a team of trained seals.

Harte reached for the glove box, and as he did, he saw Collette staring his way. His hand paused at the button, and he turned back to his new fan club.

41

"Let me ask you something," he said, taking time to look into each boy's eyes. "Why is it you fellows don't pay much attention to her?" He nodded covertly toward Collette. "You don't consider her a friend?"

"I wish," said Lamar and rolled his eyes. Lonny backhanded Lamar's arm in a cryptic, male message that made both boys snicker.

Streak leaned in closer and lowered his voice. "She's about two tiers up on the food chain, Mr. C. We wouldn't stand a chance."

"And she's smarter'n the three of us put together," Lamar added.

Lonny repeated the backhand to Lamar, this time harder. "Speak for yourself, idiot."

Lamar gave Lonny his flat stare. "I just did, dumb ass!"

Harte stared through the windshield at the girl. Her dark hair and eyes made her all but disappear in the dappled shadow under the oak.

"So, you're afraid of her," Harte said, not posing the comment as a question.

"Hell, no," Lonny growled. "We're not afraid of any girl."

"*I* am," Lamar said, and the other two turned to stare at him.

Harte leaned back to the glove box, popped the door, and removed the magazine.

"Whoa!" Streak breathed. He leaned his head into the truck. "Is that your gun?"

Holding the furled magazine, Harte looked at the now exposed antique Colt. Dark and brooding, it lay wrapped in its equally old leather holster and belt next to his cell phone.

"Holy frijole!" said Lonny. "Looks like a cannon."

Lamar frowned. "I thought there was a law about bringin' a gun onto the campus."

Harte sat back. "That's true, but right now I can't leave it at my—" He'd almost said "campsite," but he didn't want to explain that. ". . . At the place I'm staying."

Streak kept his voice to a whisper. "That's an old one, isn't it, Mr. C?"

Harte leaned and slapped the glove box door shut. "Yep. It's old."

Streak's face filled with new energy. "Can we see it, Mr. C?"

Harte shook his head. "Nope, you outlaws need to go home and read your assignment."

Recognizing the tone of finality in Harte's voice, the three boys waved and jogged across the lot toward the student parking area. Occasionally, they stopped and crouched in gunfighter poses and fired at one another with their index fingers, mouthing whispery bursts of gunfire and feigning minor flesh wounds to arms and shoulders.

Chuckling to himself, Harte picked up the box with the new kettle and again admired the painting of the cowboy stretched out beside his campfire beneath a showcase of stars. That was what he wanted to do now. Drive the switchbacks up to Cooper Gap to his camp, sit in solitude by his fire, and sip some coffee.

"Mr. Canaday?"

Harte turned to see Collette standing beside his window, her books pressed against her like a shield. Her dark eyes lowered to the pavement. When she raised her head, her shyness melted something at the core of him. He looked away at the box in his hands.

"Burned out the bottom of my old kettle," he laughed, but his words came back to him as a feeble attempt at filling the empty space around her. He set the box aside and turned to her. "But I guess you don't need to hear the confessions of an inept cook. What can I do for you?"

"Mr. Canaday, I have a favor to ask."

Up close like this, the severe angles of her cheekbones suggested a certain gauntness in her face, as if she might not be eating well. In the classroom she held her own, but here in the near empty lot there was about her an air of vulnerability. He guessed that she did not ask favors often.

"All right . . . shoot."

"I won't be in class Friday," she said evenly. "I wondered if I could stay late Thursday and take the test." She spoke calmly, rationally, making no attempt at over-wrought diplomacy or any other manipulative device that would have been more typical of other girls her age.

Harte looked out his windshield at the school. "That'll work," he said and nodded to her.

As she met his gaze, nothing changed in her expression. Some of the students' cars were revving now. They could hear Streak and Lonny laughing over the rumble of modified mufflers. Then they tore out of the lot as if making good their escape from a bank robbery.

"Thank you, Mr. Canaday," Collette said quietly.

"You bet. See you tomorrow."

Collette started toward the exit drive, moving in a perfect straight line, her shoulders so level she might have been transported along a conveyor belt. Harte watched her until she turned the corner of the building and disappeared from sight. Her introversion was painfully acute when experienced up close, less a personality trait, he guessed, than some unalterable condition of her life.

He fired up the truck and pulled around the building where he spotted her at a distance walking the school's long driveway toward the highway.

"Mr. Canaday!"

Coming out of the front door the school principal waved, tapped down the front steps, and stopped at the curb. Morris Blackadar appeared uncharacteristically upbeat as he held up a manila folder as a signal to parley. Smiling, he half-squatted with his hands on his knees. The bald spot on his head caught the light from the summer sky and shone like a light bulb.

"Well, Mr. C, are you keeping them awake this summer?"

Harte rested his arm on the window flashing and pretended to think about his answer. "Well, their eyes are open . . . most of the time."

The principal made a perfunctory laugh. Twenty years younger than Harte, Morris Blackadar had assumed a certain deference to the veteran teachers when he'd moved into the county seven years ago, and, to his credit, he still did. Harte checked the highway and saw Collette walking along the right of way headed north, her books still clutched to the front of her body.

"We'd like to get a hundred per cent passing this time," Blackadar announced. Behind his thick lenses a gleam of encouragement flashed in his eyes but quickly snuffed out. "Our ranking on the state's list is nothing short of embarrassing." He pulled a newspaper clipping from the folder and thrust it through the window. "Georgia is forty-second in the country on SAT's. And *we* are fourth up from last place in state history." He pushed his glasses higher on his nose and winced. "That affects our state funding, you know. We need that hundred per cent, Harte."

Harte stared out the windshield and felt the principal's eyes hold on the side of his face. "Well, you know, Morris, I'd like to see that, too." He turned to Blackadar. "But if this is a pep talk, shouldn't it go toward the students?"

"Harte, we all benefit when our student record is improved."

"Really?" Harte said, giving the word some melody.

"So how are they doing?" Blackadar asked.

Harte considered the drudgery of the past summer weeks, knowing that, on most days, many textbooks had not gone home with the students. "Today was good. Lots of questions." He smiled. "Some of the students even stayed late . . . by choice."

45

"There you go," Blackadar said, now hopeful. "That's what we want. But it's those scores that will talk for us. I want to see them pass, Harte. It's just the state history, for God's sake. It's not like any student's future is going to depend on it."

"Well, actually, Morris, it *is* like that." Harte gave his principal the same deadpan look he had used on Lonny over the footnote question. "There's a reason we teach history, you know."

Blackadar raised both palms and closed his eyes—the see-no-evil monkey. Waiting until the administrator opened his eyes, Harte raised his eyebrows, an expression asking: *Are we done here?*

"When's the final exam . . . Friday?" Blackadar asked. When Harte made no response, the principal forged ahead. "Well, I see no need to make it too tough for them . . . do you?" He slipped a paper from the folder and held it out until Harte took it. "Just read over those standings for our school, would you?" The principal straightened and patted the roof of the truck as he turned. "Okay, see you tomorrow," he said and bounced back up the steps with the spring of optimism in his legs. He was whistling as he passed through the door.

Harte stared at the typed page, making the face he should have shown to Blackadar. "Thanks, Morris. I'll tack this to a stump and use it for target practice," he muttered. Jamming the stick into first gear, he pulled down the driveway and decided that talking out loud in the truck was all right as long as he was addressing someone else.

At the end of the drive, he stopped and stared across the highway at the hardware store. "Ammunition," he reminded himself. Then he snorted. "So much for the talking out loud rule," he said.

Coming out of the store with a new box of cartridges rattling in each hand, he walked into an ambush. Streak, Lonny, and Lamar stood at his cab, each wearing the same impish smile.

"Can you show us your gun here, Mr. C?" Streak said. "We're not on school property."

Harte gave the boys a doubtful look. "I wish you three were this persistent about history."

"This *is* history, Mr. C!" Streak pressed. "Right?"

Harte recognized a perfect response when he heard one. He couldn't refuse. He got into his truck, set the boxes of shells in the passenger seat, propped his arm in the window, and gave his three overtime students his inspecting eye. Each boy appeared to be holding his breath.

"If I show you, will you read tonight's lesson with this same kind of enthusiasm?"

They nodded as if they had choreographed their response. Harte laughed and started his truck.

"Meet me behind the store." As he backed out, the boys were already running.

They were waiting wide-eyed and talking a mile a minute. Turning off his engine, Harte pulled gun and holster from the glove box. Slipping the old Peacemaker from the leather, he checked the cylinder, rotating it to assure empty chambers, the parts ticking like an antique clock that had just come alive. Through the window they watched it all, their eyes glued to the gun.

Getting out, Harte began talking his audience through a tour of the weapon, parsing its working parts, explaining how each mechanism contributed to the whole. But he could see that no one was listening. The mere presence of the gun was enough.

"Mr. C?" Streak said, "where'd you, like, learn all this stuff about guns?"

Harte stuffed the revolver back into its holster. "Guess I grew up with it," he said. "You boys have got all these reality shows on TV now.

In my day, it was Westerns." He looked back at the gun. "It's what got me interested in history."

Lonny frowned at the holster. "So, you shoot left-handed, Mr. C?"

Harte shook his head. "This is the butt-forward setup I was telling you about."

Streak's eyes widened. "So now you can show us how that works . . . right?"

After eyeing the building for onlookers, Harte strapped on the belt. The boys went still and quiet.

"All right, this is a one-time-only deal. I don't want you talking this up, understand?"

"Sure, Mr. C," Streak promised. With solemn faces, Lonny and Lamar nodded.

"See how the holster tilts?" Harte began. "So, the handle is slanted forward in front, the barrel up in the rear. That positions it for an easier draw."

"So . . . it's, like, covering your back for you," Lamar ventured. He looked so certain of himself that Harte, for the sake of time, decided against rebuttal.

"Just watch my elbow," Harte instructed and went through a slow extraction of the gun, rotating his wrist in the draw. The Colt corkscrewed through the air and righted itself. He checked their faces for signs of comprehension, but it was obvious that they were waiting for more.

He holstered the gun and unbuckled the belt so that he could flip the rig around, butt to the rear. Reaching across with his left hand, he held the holster vertically against his right hip.

"Watch what my elbow has to do to clear leather now."

In another slow demonstration, he pulled the gun straight up, hesitating at the apex for the change in direction to thrust the gun forward. Harte looked at each face again. They were getting it.

"Really, Mr. C, how'd you learn this stuff?" Streak asked, admiration muting his voice.

Harte hefted the gun in the flat of his hand. "Like you said, this is history. History is what I do." He smiled, knowing that he could not adequately explain it. "Ever noticed the word that sits inside the word 'history'?" He checked each boy's face, giving them a few seconds.

" 'Story'?" Streak said.

Harte nodded. "Exactly." He rubbed his thumb along the dull finish of the vintage metal. "This gun has a story," he said, hearing the curiosity in his own voice. "If only it could talk." He smiled as he took in the boys' rapt faces, knowing that he had turned the key that all teachers wished for their students. "The trick to history," Harte said in a quiet, intimate tone, "is making it real in your mind, so you can see it as what actually happened. Like these lessons you're reading." He pointed down at the gravelly ground on which they stood. "Right here beneath us, there are bones and arrowheads and cartridge shells and the shards of broken household goods . . . all of it buried. It's our history." When he stopped talking, they seemed just as interested in his silence.

"Can I try it?" Streak said, grinning at the gun.

Harte shook his head. "Not a good idea."

"Are you fast, Mr. C?" Lonny said. "Can you hit anything with it?"

"Have you ever shot anybody?" This from Lamar.

Harte turned dead eyes to Lamar. "I'm a history teacher." He coiled the belt around the holster and climbed into his truck. "Let's all go home," he said, hearing his suggestion come back to mock a man without a home. "In two days you boys have a test that determines whether or not you've wasted your summer and mine." He fired up the engine and pulled away.

As soon as he turned onto the highway, he knew he would not be driving back to his camp to make coffee. His shirt was soaked through, and the humid afternoon showed no sign of cooling off any time soon. Passing the turnoff to Cooper Gap he continued north on the highway, now thinking about Luther's and a frosty mug of something cold. And once he had that cold drink in hand, he considered not thinking about anything for a while.

# Chapter Five

Luther's Liquid Gold was a seductive distraction, Harte knew, even for a man like himself who had never developed a taste for alcohol. The cool air and semidarkness put an arm around him like an old friend ready to buy him a drink and talk to him about any damn thing he wanted. The jukebox filled the room with the lazy twang of a steel guitar and the impassioned voice of a jilted woman who was boarding up the windows of her heart.

The midafternoon watering hole would have been empty but for two men standing at the bar. Harte knew the talker—Brant Sheldon, a former mayor turned real estate agent and subdivision developer. Sheldon wore patriotic suspenders of red, white, and blue over a short-sleeve white shirt. Perched atop his wavy silver hair sat his trademark businessman's straw hat pitched forward over his forehead.

Sheldon alone had probably done more to change the county's landscape than John Deere. The man with him wore khaki cargo pants with big pockets and a short-sleeve nylon shirt with mesh air vents at the back and armpits. Tall lace up boots completed the quintessential Atlanta second-homer in his go-to-the-mountains outfit.

Luther and Julie stood behind the bar. Luther, the owner, had mastered the paradox of being surly and affable at the same time. Julie was as far removed from the stereotypical barmaid as a nun shyly taking bets at a cockfight. She was too frightened to know how pretty she was. Harte remembered her father, who had, when he was alive, kept regular hours in Jim Raburn's lockup for drunks. It was a mystery to Harte that Julie had chosen to work here.

"Hey, Harte," Julie said quietly and immediately lowered her eyes to the tray of mugs she was drying with a towel. "Want the regular?"

"Yes, ma'am."

She took a tall mug from the freezer and dropped in a scant three cubes of ice—her way of giving Harte more for the money. Patiently, she poured from a green bottle to let the fizz settle. It was a Tom Collins, straight—just the mixer. It should have been in a glass, but Julie always made it a mug. Luther allowed it, because Harte was a six-foot-two asset at his establishment. More than once Harte's size and rational demeanor had quelled other customer's propensities for trouble.

"Hey, old man," Harte said to Luther. "Can you remember anything yet from your long and drawn-out past?"

The gray haired bartender bounced once with a silent laugh as he sprinkled peanuts from a jar into a plastic bowl. "Hello, young'n. Have you grown old enough to learn anything of value yet?"

The exchange had become their ritual after Harte and Luther discovered they'd been born in the same month of the same year. Three score and three years ago, Luther had clocked in on the eighteenth to Harte's nineteenth, and, for conflicting reasons, neither wanted the other to forget it.

Harte laid down some bills with the usual generous tip and carried the mug to the front booth farthest from the jukebox. Julie started to follow with the complimentary nuts that had become standard fare, but Luther took them from her and told her to finish drying the beer mugs.

When Harte sat facing the room, Luther swiped his tabletop with a towel, laid down a vinyl coaster, a paper napkin, and the nuts. "Peanuts," he said. "First one's complimentary." It was what he always said, but it was like Luther to make sure that the rules were clear.

Harte set his hat beside him and pointed at the nuts. "Which is the free one?"

Luther made a tired smile and shook his head. "You need to find some new material." He slid into the seat across from Harte and twisted at the waist so he could look around the room. He began squeezing his fingers one by one with the towel.

"You know who'd'a loved this place?" Luther said. "Ernest Hemingway."

Harte surveyed the room to see what he might have missed. "You reading Hemingway?"

"Rereading," Luther corrected. "I'm a coupla years older than he was when he killed himself. Thought I'd see how his writing holds up now to a man of my venerated age."

Harte raised his mug in a silent toast and drank. The tart liquid spread through him like a cool breeze. Maybe a Montana breeze.

Luther jabbed a thumb over his shoulder. "He would'a sat in that back booth . . . done his writing right there, where he could see everything." Luther conjured up a genuine grin. "Could'a wrote a hellava novel here at the Liquid Gold." Then he raised an index finger to make a point. "And I can tell you who he would'a liked on the jukebox. Wanna guess?"

The jukebox had gone silent, but its selection panel was lighted up like a portly, bejeweled, opera diva, awaiting her entrance from the wings. "Patsy Cline?" Harte said, setting down his drink.

Luther shook his head. "Willie. Those two would'a gone huntin' and fishin' together."

Harte worked on his drink and watched the wheels turn in Luther's head.

"But, hell," Luther growled. "What do I know? I'm just an old man sellin' liver poison."

Harte set down his mug and wiped his mouth with the napkin. "I'm just trying to think what Hemingway might have written about here in Lumpkin County."

Luther backhanded the air, as if brushing away such a notion. "Hell, people are the same ever'where . . . and all of 'em got a story."

Harte huffed a quiet laugh through his nose. "Now that sounds just like the kind of thing an old man would say."

Luther shrugged. "Hey, speakin' o' writin', got your Jesse James article over at the bar." He tipped his head toward the counter and then made a deferential bow of his head toward Harte. "Somethin' else Hemingway would'a liked. I show it to some o' the customers. Interestin' story."

Harte ate a peanut—the free one. "The Western magazines keep recycling the same characters. There are only so many famous ones that'll sell a magazine. It was time for a Jesse-story. I just tried for a new slant."

"Hell," Luther said, flopping his forearm on the tabletop and leaning closer. "I could'a been a 'Jesse James' . . . robbin' railroads . . . showin' the sonzabitches with all the money there's enough to go 'round for ever'body else."

Harte smiled and worked on the nuts. "Jesse was a psychopath. I don't think that's you, Luther."

Luther flipped the towel over his shoulder and glowered at the bar. "Well, I wouldn't mind shakin' things up a little in this county." He leaned closer and lowered his voice. "See that peacock at the bar?"

Harte offered a wry smile. "Which one?"

"Mr. High Pockets over there . . . the one talkin' to Sheldon. He's from Atlan'a. Supplies all the high-class restaurants, so he says. Tried to talk me into a *sushi* bar, if you can believe that."

"Hemingway might have liked that," Harte said. "You could change the name of the place. Call it 'The Old Man and the Seafood.' "

With the jukebox still silent, Luther kept his voice at a rough whisper. "You hear about the golf course? Layland Childers bought up all that bottom land around the highway sixty bridge, and he's puttin' in eighteen holes that'll crisscross the river like a sewin' stitch."

Harte had started to take another sip of his drink, but he set down the mug. Staring down at the bubbles rising around the ice cubes, he conjured up a picture of the big hemlock trees on that tract of land.

"Hell," Luther growled. "I been huntin' turkey and fishin' down there since I was eleven." He arched an eyebrow and froze it in place, a fierce whiteness showing in his eye. "They say Layland's got 'im a permit to pump a million gallons o' water a day out o' the river. Got all that grass to water, you know." Luther hissed air through his teeth. "You name me one goddamn person in this county who's got the time to knock a little white ball around in the grass all day."

Harte felt a sudden urge to get up and leave, drive up to the gap and fire up the new kettle. Maybe heat up a can of beans and stretch out like the painting of the cowboy on the kettle box. Or maybe he'd just point his truck toward Montana and be done with Georgia.

"I can talk to Jim Raburn," Harte finally said. "Might be some codes getting bent in all this."

Luther sat back and stared at Harte. "Ain't sure that'll do any good. Jim Raburn's sellin' his granddaddy's old homestead to a developer from Tampa. S'posed to build some kinda resort."

Harte frowned out at the room. "Guess Jim forgot to tell me about that."

Luther stewed a while more and then slapped the table with the flat of his palm. "Well, let me get back to work . . . see if the peacocks need anything." He slid out of the booth, giving the table a last swipe with the towel.

Harte ate a last handful of nuts, scooped up his hat, and left. When he reached his truck under the shade of the trees at the north end of the parking lot, he sat behind the wheel and watched Layland's refurbished red pickup turn into the gravel lot and pull up in front of Luther's blue neon sign. In the hard light of the sun, the truck gleamed like a woman's freshly painted nails.

Layland stepped out of the truck and waited as a black BMW coasted into the lot and stopped next to his Ford. When the driver unlimbered from the car and slipped on his sunglasses, Harte recognized the Latino he had seen with Layland at the hardware store. As they started inside, Layland held the door and the Latino passed through with the balletic walk of a matador.

Harte started his truck and pulled out onto the highway. When his tires settled into a steady hum on the pavement, he began to wonder if the mountains of Montana were getting built up as fast as the Appalachians. And if he did move out West, would he be just like these people moving up here from Atlanta, building a retirement place, and adding to the problem?

*****

At his campsite Harte took the new kettle out of its box and filled it with springwater at the seeping boulders. He built a small fire, arranged three rocks in a tight triangle, and balanced the kettle on top where it could heat over the flame. While he waited for the water, he took out his folding knife and carefully cut out the painting of the cowboy from the box and propped it against his pile of firewood. Standing back to admire his first bit of al fresco camp décor, he tried to empty his mind of everything he didn't want taking up space there: Layland, Callie, school, the barren wasteland of a golf course imposed on the river, and Earl Sandifer and his precious dirt road.

Like the cowboy in the painting, he stretched out by the fire, substituting his briefcase for the saddle. But there was nothing for it. There were just too many irritating notions pinging around inside his head. They were like moths banging against the glass shield of a lantern.

He went to his truck and strapped on the cartridge belt and holster. After loading the Colt, he carried the old burned-out kettle across the dirt road to the steep bank of the road cut. There he secured the leaky pot by driving a stick under the wire handle into the black loam. Stepping back across the road, he faced his target and took a stance as if it had called him out.

At an internal signal, he swept the gun from the holster with a smooth, economical rotation of the wrist and fired five times without using the sights. Like a sustained roar of thunder, the reports echoed off the mountain and tumbled down the valley behind him. He stood frozen in time, the gun still poised, until the sound faded and the quiet of the mountain returned.

Five dark holes were gouged into the metal, the cluster as tight as his fist. The feeling of accomplishment was similar to putting a keen bright edge to his knife and shaving a narrow path through the hairs of his forearm. His returning confidence with the gun had come to him as a surprise, like a long-lost friend who had moved on and presumably died but now had shown up at his backdoor. With spirits lifted, he walked back to the fire and laid out newspapers to clean the gun.

"Born in the wrong century," he said quietly, knowing, this time, that the worth of the words trumped any embarrassment about talking to himself out loud.

It was dark by the time he had reassembled the gun. After feeding the fire, he propped a flashlight in his lap and spent the rest of the evening writing up Friday's exam.

# Chapter Six

On Thursday afternoon the classroom emptied within seconds after three o'clock, leaving Harte and Collette in the post-stampede quiet. Pencil in hand, she waited at her desk as Harte collected the loose leaves of the test into a single stack.

"Would you like a moment for a trip down the hall first? Some water maybe?"

She offered a thin smile and shook her head. "I'm ready."

Harte tapped the edges of the papers on his desktop. "You'll have one hour. I'll be collating the tests for tomorrow. Will the sound of the stapler bother you?"

"No, sir." She came forward, took the papers, returned to her desk, and began reading. Before Harte had lined up the edges of the next batch of papers, she was head-down, writing.

A few minutes into the hour, a movement caught Harte's peripheral attention, and he turned to see Morris Blackadar's puzzled face in the glass window of the door. Harte punched the stapler once more, rose, and walked out into the hall.

"What's this?" the principal said. "Working late?"

"She's taking the test early."

Blackadar frowned through the glass. "Is that the Devereaux girl?"

"Yes."

Blackadar worked up his best principal's scowl. "What's her story?"

"What do you mean?"

"I mean, why is she getting the test a day early?"

Harte hesitated long enough to telegraph his irritation at the question. "She has a conflict."

"Well, I hope it's a good one," Blackadar quipped. He lingered at the window, and when he pulled himself away, he fingered the cuffs of his shirt and tugged them outside the sleeves of his coat. "I had a call from a parent today." With no more sleeves to occupy his time, he frowned at Harte. "Did you bring a firearm to school earlier this week?"

A long two seconds ticked by. "It stays locked in the glove box of my truck."

Blackadar's bald spot seemed to gather light from the fluorescents. "Why, pray tell, do you have a gun in your truck?"

"I have a permit."

Blackadar's soft face tried for granite. "That does not answer my question."

"I have a problem with a neighbor and his shotgun," Harte said dryly.

"Isn't that why we have a sheriff's department, Mr. Canaday?"

"My house is nine miles out from town. I don't think a sheriff's deputy can drive faster than a load of buckshot, do you?"

Blackadar closed his eyes and exhaled. "Wouldn't it be more prudent to carry a cell phone?"

"I have a cell phone, but I don't want to wait fifteen minutes for a deputy to give me permission for a right of way I've already got."

Blackadar crossed his arms over his chest. "I'm sure you know it is against school policy to bring a gun onto the campus. Did you take your class out to the parking lot and show it to them?"

"I loaned three boys a history magazine that was in my glove box. They saw my gun in there, so they asked me about it."

Blackadar tightened his lips into a humorless smile. "I heard you held a little seminar."

Harte shook his head. "That was later . . . at the hardware store."

The principal closed his eyes long enough to convey his shock. "And why did you do that?"

"It was part of a history lesson. Only three students. The gun was unloaded."

" 'A history lesson'," Blackadar repeated. He tried to lock eyes with Harte, but the standoff ended when the principal cleared his throat and thrust his hands into his pants pockets. "Please explain to me how exposing these students to a gun on school property relates to Georgia history."

Harte inhaled deeply, held the breath for a moment, and then let it ease out. "The gun is a period piece. It relates to the post-Civil War days. The students were interested. The questions they asked were best answered with a teaching aid. I had the teaching aid, so I used it."

Blackadar frowned, looked down the length of the hallway and began shaking his head in tiny increments. "It is against the law to bring a gun onto the school property, the parking lot included. That you turned a firearm into the focus of your class, in my view, shows poor judgment."

"Look," Harte said, softening his tone, "I don't have any other place to keep my things right now. I'm going through a transition time."

"Yes, I've heard of your troubles, but—" Blackadar stopped himself and darted his tongue across his lips. "Mr. Canaday, there are many places a person could leave a gun for safe keeping. The school is the one place you cannot bring it."

"It won't happen again," Harte said and reached for his doorknob. "I need to get back. She may have a question about the test."

Blackadar flung a hand toward the room. "And this seems to be another case of poor judgment. What is to keep her from passing along the contents of the test to the others?"

Harte let his hand fall from the doorknob, and soon the silence of the hall gathered around them. "She wouldn't do that, Morris."

"Well, how do you know that? I mean—"

Harte allowed a subtle smile. "Because I trust her."

Blackadar struggled with that. "And you can guarantee that trustworthiness?"

"I can." Harte cocked his head. "I'm surprised this concerns you so much."

Blackadar raised both eyebrows. "And why is that?"

Harte kept his poker face. "Well, say she did pass along the contents of the test. Tomorrow my class would come through with flying colors. You'd have the best scores in the state."

Blackadar's eyes went as dead as the dark muzzles of Earl Sandifer's shotgun. "I resent that, Mr. Canaday."

"I would hope you would resent that. Much as I resented your insinuation that I should assure my students would pass the test. Exactly what did you have in mind for me in pulling that off? Perhaps you hoped that I would go over the test questions with them the day before?"

"I never suggested any such thing!" Blackadar snapped. He tugged at his shirt cuffs again. "You would do well to leave your gun at home." He glanced at Harte. "Or wherever."

"Look, Morris. I'm turning in my retirement request at the end of next week. So, lighten up a little. You won't have to put up with me much longer."

Now Blackadar looked confused. "Retirement! Well . . . what will you do?"

Harte turned to look down the hall where the front windows afforded him a view of the mountains. "There's always Montana," he said and gave Blackadar what Callie called his enigmatic smile. "I've got to get back," he said and was through the door before Blackadar could reply.

Fifty minutes into the hour, Harte was lost in the Hickok book, taking notes on the Deadwood days, where Wild Bill's story would come to its ignominious end. Even though he knew the story well—an assassin's bullet from behind during a card game—the hair on the back of Harte's neck bristled when he read the account of the heinous crime.

"Mr. Canaday?"

Harte closed the book and found Collette standing before him. "Finished?"

"Yes, sir." She laid the papers on his desk.

"How'd you do?"

She looked surprised at the question. "I guess you'll have to tell me." On his desk she placed a fist-sized package wrapped in red tissue and tied off with a length of gold yarn.

"What's this?" He picked it up. It was cylindrical and light.

"Just something we had in the kitchen. I thought you'd like it."

Harte peeled away the paper from a blue metal cup, its white-speckled enamel a match for his new kettle. Turning it in his hand, he examined the constellation of irregular white dots.

"I saw the kettle in your truck," she explained. "I thought you'd like the cup."

Harte smiled. "It's a beauty, Collette. But you needn't bring me presents."

With her books pressed to her body, she shrugged. "We never use it, so—" She looked at the wall clock. "I have to go," she said and turned for the door.

"Thank you," he called out just before the door closed behind her. He listened to the brisk pace of her footsteps as she moved down the hallway. When there was only silence again he packed the cup in his briefcase with the tests, walked outside to his truck, and started for his camp.

As soon as he had made the turn for Cooper Gap, he spotted Collette a hundred yards away walking in the tall grass where the Chester brothers' meadow extended into the right of way. He slowed the truck to match her speed and inched up beside her. Even after several seconds, she hadn't looked at him.

"Can I give you a lift?" he called.

She glanced at him only briefly, took six more steps, and stopped. After biting her lower lip for a time, she walked around the front of his truck, swung open the door, and climbed up to the seat. Once she belted in and got settled, she pressed her books to her stomach again and looked through the windshield glass as though willing him forward.

"Everything all right?" he said.

"I'm late, is all."

Harte put the truck into gear. "Well, why don't you tell me where you live?"

"I'm going to the stables."

Harte nodded. "Cherokee Rose? Do you take riding lessons from Mrs. Haversack?"

She continued to stare at the road ahead. "I used to. I do some grooming and exercising, soaping tack . . . that kind of thing. I live there now."

They rode in silence for three miles. When he pulled into the entrance to the Haversack farm, Harte saw the sheriff's GMC parked on the grass at the side of the house. In the backyard, Wylie Haversack's new forest green Jeep sat in the shade of an oak. Collette took a grip on the door handle beside her.

"This is fine right here." She leaned forward, ready to exit.

"You live in the Haversacks' house?" Harte asked.

She hesitated and nodded beyond the house. "No, sir . . . at the back of the pasture, but I—"

"I'll drive you back there."

Her protest was lost in the truck's acceleration. They moved past the main house, following a set of double tracks pressed into the meadow grass. Beyond the barn the tracks turned left and ran beside the three-rail fence that rode the swells and troughs of the rolling pastureland. Crouching in the shadow of two big tulip trees, a weathered single-wide trailer stood atop stacks of gray cinder blocks and scraps of lumber. Behind the trailer, just inside the woods, a small outhouse had been cobbled together with mismatched boards and slabs of plywood.

The trailer was dirty white with blooms of brown rust stains running from the riveted seams of the aluminum panels. Three wooden crates had been nailed together to serve as front steps at the entrance. The door had once been comprised of louvered windows for most of its length, but some had been replaced by slats of corrugated cardboard. The lone window on the front wall was covered by a screen attached to the paneling by gray duct tape.

Pulling up to the trailer, Harte noticed a man in a folding lawn chair. He sat unmoving at the far end of the rhomboid shadow cast by the trailer. Despite the eighty-something-degree heat, he was wrapped in a flower-print bedspread. It was this and his absolute stillness that had hidden him. He did not look their way as the truck pushed through the grass. Collette was out of the truck even before it rolled to a stop.

"Father?" she called, hurrying to him. When she leaned over him and began loosening the blanket at his throat, she spoke so softly that Harte could not hear the words.

He shut off the engine and stepped out, leaving one boot propped inside the truck's open doorway, one forearm resting on the roof of the cab. The sky was pale blue and nearly cloudless. The heat bore down without mercy on the trailer, and the humidity in the open field was oppressive. Harte removed his hat and fanned at the flies buzzing in his face as he watched daughter and father interact with limited results.

"Everything okay?" he called out.

Collette turned her head long enough to give him a quick nod. Harte responded in kind and looked around the pasture. The idyllic vista aside, the squalor of the trailer was unsettling. There were no electric lines running from the main house. Harte gazed at the single-wide and imagined Collette at night reading her lessons by candle or flashlight.

Closing his door quietly, he approached and noticed for the first time a walking cane hooked to one arm of the man's chair. Collette's hands were busy tending to her father's appearance, combing hair from his eyes with her fingers, wiping a crust of dried food from the corner of his mouth, and unbuttoning the top collar of his shirt. Despite the heat and blanket, his skin was dry. Flies intermittently walked across his face, but he seemed not to notice.

"Father, let's go back inside now," she said, her voice as gentle as a mother's to her newborn.

Harte stopped five yards away. "Can I be of help?" he said.

Helping the man to his feet, Collette did not answer. Harte turned at a sound in the grass and saw three mares—two bays and a chestnut—approaching the fence. They stopped as a flank, their long bony heads hooked over the top rail of the fence, their attention directed toward the girl.

With the bedspread wadded under one arm, Collette guided her father toward the trailer. When they came abreast of Harte, the man stopped and studied him with a bewildered expression.

"Doctor Rhodes?" The words scraped from his throat at a price. A coughing fit filled his eyes with tears. When he quieted, his head tilted back as he tried to take in the whole of Harte.

"No, Father," Collette whispered. "This is my teacher, Mr. Canaday."

The man squinted at Harte. "I'm Kenneth Fallon," he said in his scratchy voice. He offered a palsied hand, and Harte took it, feeling the man's loose skin slide over the flesh and bone beneath.

"Pleasure to meet you, sir," Harte said.

"She'll be coming back before long," Fallon rasped, now a little animated. "She's just gone into town to pick up the car. She'll be coming . . . and our little boy . . . and then maybe we'll have some spaghetti." He turned to Collette. "Are we having spaghetti tonight?"

"Yes, Father, I can make spaghetti."

The confused man turned his excitement on Harte. "You can stay, can't you? You'll like it."

Harte looked into the void of the man's gray eyes and found nothing there to attach to. From a distance, the father had appeared to be about Harte's age, but up close he looked to be eighty.

"Thank you," Harte said. "But I can't stay. I just wanted to give Collette a ride home."

Fallon narrowed his empty eyes to slits and then smiled with such pleasure that Harte could not help feeling some sense of relief for the lost man's delusions. "Collette is in school," he said and turned to his daughter. "You'll have to pick her up. Do you know where the school is?"

"Father, I'm Collette. I'm home from school now. We'll have some spaghetti, okay?"

Kenneth Fallon nodded tentatively at the teenaged girl, who seemed to handle the mistaken identity as though it were her daily fare. She combed more hair from his forehead.

"Come on, Father," she prodded gently. "You can watch me start supper." When Collette pulled him along a trodden path in the grass, Harte picked up the cane and followed closely, in case the man lost his balance. The girl was experienced in managing him, a firm grip on his arm and the bundle of blanket pressed into his back. "We go to the hospital tomorrow," she whispered back to Harte. "That's why he thought you were the doctor."

Harte nodded. "How will you get there?"

"I'll use Mrs. Haversack's truck," she said and assisted her father up the makeshift steps. "Thank you, Mr. Canaday," she said, managing a pained smile before father and daughter disappeared inside.

When the door closed, Harte propped the cane beside the steps and turned to the trio of curious horses. "You ladies act like you haven't seen company down here for a while." He took off his hat and walked to the fence, where the three mares began to nod and nicker. He stroked their foreheads one by one, giving each its due.

"I used to ride," he said, as if he owed some explanation for his approach. "Might even think about doing some more." He looked out over the pasture to the west where the property dipped down behind a rise. "It's not Montana," he muttered, "but it's not bad." He smiled, thinking that riding a horse might be the perfect addition to his life about now.

As he walked back to his truck, he tried to hold the picture of the three horses in his mind—the amber depths of their liquid eyes, the soft blow of warm air from their nostrils—but it was the image of Kenneth Fallon's ashen face that insinuated into his thoughts. It hung there like a high-resolution photograph imprinted on his retina.

He remembered the story of Fallon's wife and child had been one of the worst tragedies in the county's history.

After firing the engine, he turned on the radio, but it was dead. He slapped the top of the dashboard twice to no effect, and then, accepting another loss, he drove for the Haversack house.

# Chapter Seven

When Harte reached the front of the house, Jim Raburn was striding across the yard beneath the pecan tree, signaling with an index finger held high. Wylie Haversack stood on his front porch, both hands slung into the bib of blue overalls. Harte braked and waited with the engine idling.

"What're you doing out this way?" Harte said.

" 'Bout to ask you the same." Jim gestured back toward the house. "Nothin' much to speak of here. Just a little complaint to sort out." He gave Harte an amused look. "Not gettin' back into horses, are you?"

Harte kept his face blank. "Why not?"

Jim leaned on the truck with one arm and propped his other hand on his hip above his gun belt. "At your ripe old arthritic age?"

Harte lifted an eyebrow. "I figure I can still sit a horse without too much complaint from the animal." He nodded at Jim's expanding waistline. "One of us here still weighs less than a horse."

The sheriff laughed and patted his belly. "Hell, don't you know anything 'bout bein' a sher'ff? The gut goes with the job." He gave his cruiser a nod. "I guess I can blame it on that ol' hoss with its AC, cushioned seats, and a high-performance V-eight." Jim laughed again. "At least she don't buck . . . 'xcept maybe on the dirt roads."

Harte shut off his engine, and the quiet of the farm enveloped them. "How about supper Saturday?" Harte suggested. "I'd like to talk to you about a couple of things."

The sheriff made a pained expression. "Can't Saturday. Already got plans."

When Harte nodded, Jim's eyes took on the empathetic slant that had always endeared him to men and women alike. "You doin' okay, pard?

You want to go somewhere and talk now? Hell, I know all about how altering your marital status can mess with your head."

Harte shook his head. "Not about me. It's about the county." He cut his eyes to the house and saw that Wylie had gone inside. "This complaint here . . . anything to do with the trailer in back?"

"Nah. It's a neighbor . . . a Miss Seagrave." Jim looked off toward the west end of the pasture. "Got 'er a little orchard out there. Grows what she claims are the best apples in the county." He made a smacking sound with his lips. "And they *are* damned good. Had some o' her apple butter, and it flat turned a damned biscuit into a first-class dessert. Even gave me a jar."

"So what's the problem?"

Jim produced a wan smile that suggested he had seen every manner of discord between neighbors. "The fence is down over there, and Wylie's horses are gettin' into her apples. Wylie's prostate is actin' up, and he says he ain't got around to repairin' the fence yet. Bella says—"

"Bella?" Harte interrupted.

"That's the Seagrave woman," Jim explained, keeping his eyes on the pasture. "She says she wants the fence mended." He snorted a laugh and shook his head. " 'Course, she never even approached Wylie 'bout it. Just went straight to us." He shook his head. "I ain't even sure we all know each other out here anymore."

"This Seagrave woman," Harte probed, "she from around here?"

"Nope. From up north. Came down here to get away from all the crime, she says." He feigned a look of concern. "And now, wouldn' you know it, she's mixed up with a larcenous gang of equines eatin' her prize apples." He raised his chin to Harte. "So, what're you doin' out here?"

"Gave one of my students a lift home. Collette Devereaux." Harte watched the sheriff process that with a weary shake of the head.

"Now *there's* a story to tie your heart in a knot," Jim said, his voice somber now. "I guess you remember Kenneth Fallon?"

Harte nodded. "I didn't realize Collette was part of all that."

Jim nodded. "Took her mother's name—Devereaux—tryin' to distance herself from all the publicity, I guess. Didn't like all the attention. 'Course, who would under those circumstances?"

Harte felt his body sag as fragments of the story came flying back at him. "All that happened the summer Callie and I went out West to that conference."

Jim smiled and pointed at Harte's hat. "When you bought your Montana hat . . . in Arizona." As usual, he raised an eyebrow at the irony. "That was a good summer to be gone from here." He squatted beside the truck and picked up a stick fallen from the pecan tree. Using the stick, he began a casual probe into a tuft of grass, as if he were searching for something. "It was a drug bust gone bad in the worst kind o' way . . . down at Denbow's Body Shop." Jim's face set hard with the memory. "Damn place turned out to be the outlet mall for narcotics. Meth, coke, crack, heroine, prescriptions . . . you name it." He looked up quickly. "And it was all local boys. People you and I grew up with."

It was Jim who had told Harte the tragic news all those years ago, when Harte had returned from Arizona. Now he seemed to need to tell it again, and so Harte settled in for the story.

"Six people died that day. One o' those was my chief deputy. Danny Culp. You 'member him? Big black boy with that deep voice? That was Cody's big brother. Cody's my right arm now." Jim tightened his mouth to a false smile and shook his head. "Danny was a damned good man. Left behind a wife and a little boy." He turned his head and spat. "Goddamn Denbows . . . they were a vicious bunch. Weren't goin' to jail, by God. Every one of 'em was hell-bent on dyin', you ask me."

Harte waited while Jim's resentment ran its course. The sheriff dropped the stick, stood, and brushed his hands together, the sound as dry as paper.

"So the Fallon woman and child," Harte said, "that was Collette's mother and little brother?"

Jim kept his eyes on the horizon as he nodded. "She was a customer. Gone down there to pick up her car. Took her little boy, 'bout two years old. They'd been in the bathroom."

Throughout the telling, Jim's face colored as if he were radiating a surplus of heat, yet his words came from a cold vault of memory where, as a law officer, he had learned to lock away the unspeakable facets of his job. He took in a lot of air and calmed himself.

"Tell you what," Jim said, "I didn' expect to be voted back into office after that. We just didn' know they were in there. The deputies stakin' out the place never saw 'em go in." Jim shook his head. "Anyway, we went in and about the time the woman and the boy came out of that bathroom, all hell broke loose. Danny yelled for everybody to cease fire. It was the Denbows cut 'em down. And that's when they got Danny."

Sunlight streamed down through the pecan tree and across the rolling meadow, but the nightmare of Collette's mother and brother seemed to expose the pastoral scene as a facade of life. Harte visualized the mother and child caught in a crossfire, both of them bursting with blood-red designs on their clean laundered clothing, their faces frozen in primal fear.

The mental picture took a sudden leap to the school parking lot, and now Harte was watching himself show off his magazine article to his students, Collette standing by the school building watching. He thanked God he had not brought out the weapon there and delivered an impromptu exposition on a relic of history to be admired. He took off his hat, set it in the passenger seat, and ran his fingers through his hair. Then he let his head ease back against the headrest.

"Damn," Harte whispered.

"Yeah," Jim agreed. He leaned away, spat again, and looked off in the direction of the trailer. "They used to live up on Brandy Mountain. Nice home. Fallon was some kind o' consultant. Real smart. Married this beautiful French lady. Good income. Kind o' job where you study a company, figure out how to make it more efficient, and then provide a plan on how to make that happen. Did that for a lotta big businesses in Atlan'a, so I heard." The sheriff shook his head. "He had a stroke just a week later. On a good day, he might be able to brush his teeth. The girl . . . she tries to take care of him, but—" He curled his mouth into disappointment and shook his head again.

For a time they didn't speak. The sheriff leaned against the truck as he gazed at the mountains. Harte wondered if this might be the ultimate purpose of mountains: to give people something to look at that was bigger and grander than the tragedies in their own lives.

"Listen, pard," Jim said, "I'm pretty tied up this weekend. Sa'urday I promised Lauren I'd drive her out to Amicalola Falls. And Sunday I got to head up a funeral that's bound to run late. After that I got a honest-to-God date." Jim smiled but only for a moment. "Mondays are never good. What say we get together on Tuesday? We'll get somethin' to eat and talk over supper."

Harte nodded. "Sounds good."

Jim stood and patted the roof of the truck twice. "Six at The Rusty Bucket?"

Harte nodded again. As he gripped the key in the ignition, he felt the sheriff staring at him.

"Is this about Earl Sandifer?" Jim asked.

That turned Harte's head. "How'd you know about that?"

Jim shrugged. "I'm the sheriff. It's my job to know about things."

"You get this from Earl?"

When Jim nodded, Harte propped his arm on the windowsill. "Bet he forgot to mention the part about pulling a shotgun on me."

Jim Raburn's eyebrows pushed low over his eyes, and the blue color of his irises turned to steel. "Yeah," Jim drawled. "I reckon he did forget about that part."

"I've got ingress and egress on that road. It's in my deed just like it's in his."

Jim spread his feet and crossed his arms over his chest. "Was this a real threat?"

Harte gave him a look. "I'd say a loaded shotgun pointed your way is a real threat."

"I'll have a talk with Earl," Jim promised.

"I already did that," Harte explained. "I don't expect any more trouble."

Jim stared across the meadow for a time, and finally he unfolded his arms. "All right then, I'll see you on Tuesday."

After Jim's GMC pulled out onto the paved road, Harte jerked open the door, stepped out of his truck, and walked the spaced fieldstones to the Haversacks' front door. He clapped the horseshoe door knocker against its metal plate, and then he waited. The exterior of the house radiated a quaint charm, but he remembered its disheveled interior from decades ago when he had sold to Jan Haversack his hand-tooled saddle after his quarter horse had died.

When the door opened Wylie stood in the entrance holding a can of beer and wearing a jaded smile. The overalls had been replaced by baggy sweatpants, and a Grateful Dead tee-shirt that snagged on the swell of his beach-ball stomach. Up close he looked pale and soft, his skin the color of biscuit dough. Though Wylie was only a year younger than

Harte, the bags under his eyes formed tiers of fleshy hammocks that aged him a decade.

"Well, hey, Harte." He raised the can. "How 'bout a cold one?" He took a long swallow, closed his puffy eyes, and released a breathy, "Aaahhh." Then he flashed an impish smile. "Oh, I forgot. You don't pickle your liver, do you? Come on in anyway."

Harte removed his hat and followed the shuffle of Wylie's sheep-skin-trimmed slippers across the shiny pinewood floor. The air conditioning gave the house the chill of a walk-in freezer. In the main room, most every part of the décor was linked to horses—a lamp stem of welded horseshoes, a saddle built into a stool, and an oval rug bordered by primitive drawings of mounted Native Americans bearing lances. The mantle was topped by trophies looped with ribbons of blue and red. Only the big-screen TV and a depression in the sofa hinted of Wylie's claim on the room. That and the scent of alcohol and cigarette smoke tainting the air. The room was lighted only by the TV screen, where a jewelry auction was in progress with the sound turned down. The bib overalls lay in a pile on the floor next to Wylie's work boots. Dirty dishes and newspapers lay strewn across the floor. The dark room was like a cave with its multicolored fire hanging flat against the wall.

Wylie plucked the front of his tee-shirt from his round belly, settled into his niche on the sofa, and perched his feet on a coffee table. Atop the table equestrian-related magazines lay fanned out next to a laptop. When Wylie opened the computer, the screen displayed a floating hand of playing cards. With a flop of his hand, Wylie motioned Harte to a seat.

Harte lowered himself into a caned chair, and right away a sharp chemical smell assaulted his nose. He laid his hat in his lap and watched Wylie screw down the cap on a small glass bottle and set it back on the table. Gradually, the unpleasant odor faded.

"How's your health these days, Wylie?"

Wylie dredged up a resentful laugh. "Hell, don't even ask." He exhaled with a flutter of his lips, the sound so horse-like that Harte almost laughed. "I get up at night nine times to empty my bladder. Might as well sleep in the bathroom. Doctor says my prostate is the size of a billiard ball."

"No cancer, I hope," Harte said.

Wylie's smile slanted. "Well, that'll prob'ly be next on the agenda." He let his head drop back on the sofa, and he checked the bids scrolled across the bottom of the TV screen. "Seems like this cancer is just a mad dog out there prowling around, stalking every damned one of us." He snorted. "Hell, we all just wait around to see who's next to git bit in the ass by the sonovabitch."

Leaning to the laptop, he used the index finger of each hand to drag a card from the poker hand to a discard pile. Another card popped up in its place, and Wylie hissed his irritation.

"I hear your fence needs a little work," Harte said. "I wanted to talk to you about that."

Wylie sat back and shrugged. "Talk away."

"Well, I was thinking about trading off some manual work for some time in a saddle."

Wylie cut his eyes to Harte as if he had heard a suspicious sound. "At your age?" he laughed. "Hell, your prostate must not have turned on you yet." He looked Harte over as he might appraise a horse at auction. "I guess you didn't let yourself go like most of us do." He patted his belly.

"I'm holding together all right," Harte said. "Just got the urge to ride again."

Wylie sipped his beer and nodded. "So, what'd you have in mind, Harte?"

"Well, I know you've got some fencing down on your west end. I can repair it for you. I'm pretty handy around a farm. Grew up on one, you know."

"You lived just down the road here, didn't you?" Wylie said and pointed.

"Out past the old Blackshear Mill. I ran the farm after my daddy started driving a truck."

Wylie nodded but his eyes remained dedicated to the TV screen. "Twelve hundred?" Wylie laughed, as if the buyer in the auction could hear him. "Dumb sucker!"

Harte waited, but now Wylie was absorbed by the hand of poker that awaited his move.

"After I fix the fence," Harte went on, "I can tackle most anything else that comes up. In return why don't you let me have the use of a horse from time to time? I'll do the grooming and feeding and whatever else you see fit." Harte nodded toward the back of the house. "I know you got the Devereaux girl handling that for you, but seems she's got more on her plate than she can handle. Won't cost you a cent except for the fence materials."

Wylie frowned. "Well, Jan handles all the horse stuff. You'll need to ask her."

Right on cue, Jan Haversack strode into the room. Tall and densely freckled across her sunbaked nose and cheeks, she wore faded denim jeans that looked like they were seldom separated from her long legs. Her tee-shirt was a threadbare top that rippled like water. Its simple logo read: *Cowgirl Up!* across the minimal peaks of her breasts. The skin on her arms was like leather. She was like a scarecrow in motion, a stick-figure whose joints seemed to favor bent angles over curves.

"Harte Canaday! I thought that was your truck I saw back at the trailer." She nodded toward her husband without looking at him. "This slacker offer you some refreshment?"

Harte stood and shook the hand to which every horse she had trained had eventually succumbed. "Don't need a thing, thanks."

Jan sat on the sofa's armrest farthest from Wylie, perching sidesaddle to face Harte. The marital tension in the room was palpable. Harte sat as quietly as a man arriving late to church.

Jan pointed to the small glass vial next to Wiley's crossed ankles. "You're not getting that wretched stuff on the table again, are you? It eats right through the varnish."

Ignoring the question, Wylie swept a flaccid arm toward Harte. "He's wantin' to get in some ridin'. Wants to trade off for repairin' the fence down at the Seagrave woman's apple empire." He snorted again. "That Yankee fuss-bucket prob'ly lost less than a dozen apples off our stock. I'm surprised she didn't put 'em down right there with a sniper rifle. Lucky for us her arsenal consists of a Nikon." Wylie turned his sneer to Harte. "You should'a seen the photos of the arch crime she showed to the sheriff," he said, chuckling. "Horses were feedin' off the fruit that already dropped onto the ground. Hell, all she's gotta do is walk out there and pick up the goddamned fruit."

"Maybe she's got a prostate problem and can't get out," Jan said, pouring on the sarcasm.

Wylie didn't challenge it. He sat back deeper in the sofa and checked his poker hand.

"Have you ever strung wire, Harte?" Jan asked.

"You bet."

"Income is off," Jan said. "We're not gonna be buying any new fence rail right now. There's a roll of barbed wire in the tool shed. And come-along, cutters, brads, and a posthole digger."

Harte sat forward. "Far as the rest goes, I know my way around horses. I'll groom before saddling, ride easy, and put up my mount dry, brushed, watered, and fed. How's that sound?"

"Sounds good to me," Jan said, not bothering to get her husband's input. "If you've got the time from your teaching, we've got the horses that need the attention. That'll take some of the load off the Fallon girl. She could use the break looking after her daddy like she does."

"She goes by 'Devereaux,' " Harte said.

Jan shrugged. "Well . . . whatever."

"How long have they been back there in your trailer?"

"Since before last Christmas."

Harte picked up his hat and turned it in his hands. "They've got no electricity out there."

Jan shrugged again. "Well, I put in a small propane tank for them."

"What about running water?" Harte asked.

"Collette fills up jugs at the barn. I let her use my truck to haul it out to the trailer."

Harte frowned down at the stilled hat in his hands. "So, how do they bathe?"

Jan's face went stony. "Look, I know it's not much, but it's a roof and they needed something. We never had plans to hook that trailer up to power and water. And now we just can't tackle something like that with our income down." Jan's expression softened. "That's a sweet girl. Was one of my best riding students . . . one you could depend on."

Wylie mumbled something and hissed through his teeth. He punched a key and then frowned at what must have been a misplayed strategy in his card game.

Harte put some gratitude in his voice. "I understand you're loaning her your truck to get her father to the doctor tomorrow."

Jan shrugged with a tilt of her head. "Well, Wylie's not going anywhere in the Jeep until we install a urinal in it, and I don't think that's going to happen anytime soon."

Wylie scowled at her. "You know what? I wish you had a goddamned prostate."

Jan stood and hitched up her jeans around her rail-thin waist. "Tell you what, dear husband. You lay aside your hunting trips, cancel your Tuesday night poker games with *the boys*, bear a child, tackle menopause head on and feel your body flip-flop from a cold storage freezer to an oven in a matter of seconds, cook every meal for this household, go back in time and raise the daughter you sometimes bumped into each morning before skipping out to ride your damn tractor around the property, then be sure to get a lump cut out your breast and by all means butt your head up against the all-male county commission about the land taxes you thought I'd be better at negotiating . . . then come back here and talk to me about a goddamned prostate, okay?"

Harte felt invisible in the room. Wylie focused on his laptop and angrily tapped a key, the sound a weak response to the diatribe still hanging in the air. Jan just shook her head.

Harte stood and put on his hat. "Can I just show up or do I need to call first?"

"Just come on," Jan said. "The horses I'm using for lessons are always in the front stalls. I leave saddle blankets hung over their gates. My students will groom them. It's the others you'll need to ride. Get with Collette. No need for y'all to exercise the same horses." Her face brightened. "Oh, your old saddle is still out there. That oughta feel like a reunion to your backside."

She walked to a desk and opened a drawer. "You all right with signing a waiver, Harte? I learned a long time ago that friendships can sink under the weight a legal matter."

Harte nodded. "Got no problem with that."

"That big paint," she continued, "the one called 'Pied Piper,' she can't tolerate a thunderstorm. Get out in the lightning with her and you'll likely be limping back to the barn with a knot on your head." She eyed him with the pragmatism of that prophecy.

"I had a paint once," he said. "We got along real fine."

"Well, when do you want to start?"

"I'll start with the fence first. How about Saturday?"

Jan stepped forward, handed Harte the waiver, and shook his hand. He liked her directness. It left less to wonder about how the relationship would work. Wylie, immersed in his electronic card game, ignored the proceedings.

Jan pointed at the paper. "There's a clause in there about wearing a helmet. I may not have one large enough for you."

Harte adjusted his hat and grinned. "I wouldn't know how to ride without this. I'll write up an amendment that releases you from all liability. How's that sound?"

Jan's crooked smile widened. "Well, since I've never seen you without that hat, I guess I figured you'd say that." She pushed at the air between them. "Just write it up."

# Chapter Eight

Harte sat in his truck in the only shade available in the parking lot of Callie's office building. Her burgundy Mini Cooper crouched at the front door like a perky chipmunk. He was content to wait outside, away from her professional territory and the timbre of her voice that went with it.

In ten minutes she emerged from the building in deep conversation with a thin angular woman in a yellow pants suit. The dark-haired woman appeared Callie's opposite in every way, lacking the bouncy blonde hair, the smooth agile walk, and the comely lines of Callie's eye-catching profile. As soon as they parted ways, Harte stepped out onto the pavement and stood by his truck.

When Callie noticed him, she seemed to go limp. Her keys dangled from her hand, and her head sagged toward the pavement as though she were deciding whether or not to drive away. When she started toward him, her walk was measured and thoughtful. Her pleated skirt eddied around her strong legs in fluid swirls that changed direction with each pace. In another time and place, she could have led armies of Amazons into battle.

Her hair was gathered in back into some kind of twist he had never seen her wear. The change made it seem as though she had already gained some distance from him and their common history. He might still consider her a beautiful woman were it not for the icy core that lay at her center. They faced one another for a moment like strangers with nothing to say.

"Did you need something, Harte?"

For a time he said nothing, hoping the harshness in her voice might boomerang and register on her ears. But the silence only served to fortify her impatience. She shifted her briefcase to both hands and let it come to rest on her knees like the first brick in a wall going up between them.

She took two steps toward his truck, set the briefcase on the hood, and rifled through papers. "Well, you've saved me the trouble of stopping by the school or trying to find you."

"I'm up on the mountain where we used to go for the meteor showers. You remember?"

She tried to remain uninterested, but he could see the memory turn on a pale blue light in her eyes. It flickered for a moment like a dying candle flame and then disappeared.

"Here," she said, thrusting a sheaf of papers at him. "You need to sign these."

He took the papers and glanced at them long enough to check which lawyer she had chosen. "So . . . we're at the point of no return?" he asked.

His face was an open scrapbook of the last twenty-one years. She jerked the briefcase off the hood and hugged it to her torso.

"Harte," she began with a pleading in her voice. "When you leave home and cut off all communication, you pretty well define 'the point of no return.' "

"The communication ended before I left home, Callie. It's *why* I left." He was careful to filter out any trace of bitterness from his voice. "I've always favored the quiet," he said. "You know that. But the kind of quiet you seem to practice is like an ulcer eating at us both from the inside."

Her knee-jerk anger chiseled her face, and once again he knew he had said things wrong.

"Well, thank you, Harte. What a nice image. Just what a woman wants to hear. An ulcer, for God's sake." She coughed up a laugh, but he could see that she was hurt. "And may I say that bearing up under your stone-age sensitivities has been like serving time in a dungeon. You live in a dark place, Harte, and you need help." There was spite in her words, and when she seemed to hear herself, she made an effort to sound upbeat. "I'm ready for some light in my life."

"You're sure this darkness is mine, Callie?" he said quietly.

Her face flushed, and her head began to shake like a palsy. "What is *that* supposed to mean?" she demanded, letting her voice carry out into the lot.

"I just mean that—."

"You're like a time bomb, Harte!" she interrupted. "Ticking! One day when you go off—" She seemed not to know how to finish her thought, so she glared at the side of his truck.

"When have you ever seen me 'go off'?" he asked simply. Then, he put as much gentleness into his voice as he could muster. "It's not me with the anger, Callie."

Her eyes took on a fierce light. "Harte, you're so—" Again she began to shake her head in tiny increments. "We haven't made love in . . . I don't know how long it's been."

He watched her fume as he debated between the needs for truth or diplomacy. "Callie," he finally said, conjuring up the tenderness they had once shared when their disembodied voices had woven together in the dark of their bedroom. "I have to like the person I'm making love to."

He watched the shock of that wash over her, and for the briefest moment she was as vulnerable as the first time he had told her that he loved her. Now the angles of her face sharpened to the mask of ice that was impervious to anything he could say.

"The truth is, Callie, I do love you . . . still. But I haven't liked you for some time."

Callie's widened eyes blinked, and two large tears rolled down her cheeks. She looked away toward the alleyway that separated her building from the neighboring business.

"You shit!" she hissed and wiped at her cheekbones with the back of one hand. Her mascara ran, and when she saw the black smear on her knuckles, she finally broke down and sobbed. Turning, Harte rummaged in the truck and came up with a tissue. He was surprised when she took it.

"I'm thinking about leaving, Callie."

"You already left," she said, her voice small and defeated.

"I mean I'm leaving town."

"To where?" she said, looking at him now through her tears.

"I don't know . . . Montana, maybe." He hefted the papers in his hand. "I'll sign these for you. I hope by doing that you'll find a way to be happy. I mean that."

She sniffed, set down the briefcase, and blotted her eyes with the tissue. "Montana," she said quietly, as if she had only now heard him. "Why there?"

"I've always wanted to see what it's like there."

She looked hurt in some new way. "You never told me that."

"Sure I have. Lots of times."

She looked away again and forgot about tending to her face. "You did?"

He nodded, and she must have seen the movement because she looked at him quickly, as if his answer surprised her. "I don't think you've really been able to level with me, Callie . . . about what's wrong with us. Have we just gotten into a complaisance . . . with our routines? Is that it? Because this thing about my anger . . . it just doesn't ring true. I'm not the one with anger here."

"Oh, so it's back on me, is it?" she snapped.

"I'm just trying to talk this out. I'm telling you how I see it."

She closed her eyes and pushed out a dry, humorless laugh as she shook her head. Then, surprising him, she reached to his face and gently cupped her hand to his cheek.

"You're a good man, Harte, but you can be such an asshole." She lowered her hand and tried for a smile of pity. "I know you think that saying everything in complete honesty makes everything work out right, Harte. But the truth is . . . it doesn't. Heaven forbid you should ever bend the truth."

He felt more confused now than when she had yelled at him. "I always told you I would never lie to you."

For several seconds she watched the traffic on the highway. When she faced him again, he could see that she had steadied her emotions.

"Maybe that's just not what I need now, Harte."

He tried to keep his voice nonjudgmental. "And Layland Childers is? He ought to be just about right in the department of bending the truth."

Her teary eyes looked away, and she sniffed again. "We have fun."

"Is that what you need? Some fun?"

"That's part of it."

The quiet stretched out between them until a semi roared by and sucked up a swirl of air behind it. A cloud of dust drifted over them, but neither made a move to get out of its path. Callie turned her head away from the grit in the air and dabbed at her eyes with the tissue. Harte reached up and brushed at some cat hairs on her jacket. The touch surprised her, and she made an involuntary jerk that had the effect of breaking the spell of tenderness that might have fallen over them.

Harte looked down at the papers in his hand. "You're sure you want me to sign this?"

She nodded twice. Harte tossed the papers into his truck, opened the door, and sat. He looked out the open window and waited for her to meet his eyes.

"Be careful with Layland, Callie. I wouldn't want to see you get hurt."

She stiffened and raised her chin. He knew that look. It said that Callie had had enough.

"Just sign the damn papers, will you, Harte? And stop trying to tell me how to run my life."

The harshness in her voice seemed to upset her, and the hostile look on her face relaxed. "I'm gonna be all right, and I wish the same for you, okay?" She picked up her briefcase and walked away at a brisk pace. Halfway to her car she stopped and spun around. "Montana," she called out and managed a smile. "Maybe that's just the place for an old cowboy like you."

\*\*\*\*\*

On Saturday at sunrise Harte was alone in the west pasture of Cherokee Rose, wrestling half-rotted fence posts out of the ground and hammering what was left of the rails off the posts. He stacked the wood in the bed of his truck and laid out the cured locust posts he had found in one of the outbuildings. Then he began widening the holes for the concrete that the new posts would need to withstand the tension of strung wire.

He got into a rhythm with the posthole digger, slicing, expanding the helves, prying the dirt up into a pile. It was good clean work, and the steadiness of it felt satisfying. Very Montanan.

The Seagrave woman's orchard was only a stone's throw away. It was a modest stand—two rows of six trees each—and appeared healthy and well cared for. Behind the trees he could see part of her house through a tunnel in the leaves. The structure was small and cottage-like with forest green wood siding and white working shutters that framed the windows. It lay in the broad shadow of a spreading post oak, beyond which stood a grape trellis and what might have been fencing for a garden. A bird feeder hung at the one window that he could see, and as he watched a yellow swirl of goldfinches scattered from it like sparks flying from a fire.

As the day warmed, so came the flies. Harte had come prepared for it and sprayed himself with a repellent he had found in his truck. After twenty minutes and two more sprayings, he read the expiration date on the can and tossed the useless mixture into the bed of the truck.

He planted the posts, leveled them, mixed the concrete in a wheelbarrow and shoveled in adequate portions. As he straightened from the last post, a movement in the meadow caught his eye. A chestnut mare cantered over the rise carrying a helmeted rider astride a Western saddle. The horse slowed to a walk, and the rider watched him for a while before reining the animal around to approach. Collette was hardly recognizable with her long hair tucked inside her headgear.

"Mr. Canaday?"

He knew he was equally out of character without his dress shirt and tie. Sweat ran down his face and dripped off the tip of his nose. His stained jeans and work boots were ancient.

"Good morning," he said, removing his hat and fanning away flies. He bent forward and swiped his face with the lower half of his tee-shirt. When he straightened, he returned the hat to his head and leaned on the shovel. "How'd it go with the doctor yesterday?"

She appeared surprised by the question. "We got new medication, but—" Her head dipped to one side. "Father's asleep now." She looked down and combed the horse's mane with her fingers.

Harte removed his hat again, and for a moment they both looked off toward the forest. A breeze whipped the grass into a brief frenzy and cooled his scalp. He pulled off his gloves and dropped them into the crown of the hat and let the hat fall to the grass.

"It's not my business, I know," Harte said. "But is there some medical insurance in all this?"

She nodded. "There's some. From Father's old job." She looked toward the Haversack house, and Harte understood that the barter arrangement that Collette had negotiated was probably what kept her father and her afloat.

"So, you've got a good doctor?" Harte asked offhandedly as he stepped closer to the chestnut. The horse stretched toward him, blowing softly, and he carefully raised a hand to scratch the tight skin at the base of the animal's ears.

Collette shrugged. "I think so. He's nice to Father."

Harte nodded and stroked the backs of his finger along the velvet beneath the horse's nostrils. Collette watched and seemed interested in how the animal tolerated the touch.

"This is Roxie," she said.

"Well, you and Roxie go have a good ride in the woods. Get away from all these flies."

Before she reined the mare around, the backdoor to the cottage slammed, and a lean woman with short fawn-colored hair came through the trees carrying an oval basket made of varnished grapevine. She was dressed for the practical considerations of work on a farm, but the loose fit of work clothes enjoyed a stylish look on her lithe body. She appeared to be about Harte's age and carried herself with quiet dignity. Her face was handsome and honest. When she emerged from the trees into the sunlight, her hazel eyes illuminated from within as if by a soft emerald light.

"Good morning, Collette," she said and then nodded to Harte. "And good morning to you, sir." She offered up the basket. "I know it's hot to be working. I thought you two might like some cold cider." When she saw the roll of wire in the grass, the light in her eyes dulled.

"Name's Canaday, ma'am," Harte said. He lifted a mug to Collette and then took one for himself, raising it toward the woman in a silent toast. Tilting his head back, he cooled his parched throat with the cider. Placing the empty back in the basket, he said, "I teach over at the high school, but right now I'm repairing this fence so we can keep your apples safe from hoofed outlaws." He smiled, but the joke fell flat. He nodded toward the prickly roll of wire. "This would not be my choice either, but it's what the Haversacks want."

She eyed the wire's gnarled spikes. "Well, I suppose it has its advantages."

Harte nodded. "Horses have an affinity for apples but a dedicated aversion to barbed wire."

The woman smiled. "I'm not so worried about the fruit as I am about them stripping my bark in the winter. That will kill my trees, you know."

"Yes, ma'am, I know," Harte said and nodded toward the basket. "Mighty good cider."

"And how is your father, Collette? Would he enjoy some more apple butter?"

"Thank you, Miss Seagrave, but we're still using what you gave us."

Collette upended her mug and handed the empty vessel back to Harte, who relayed it to the woman. "I'd better get this girl moving," Collette said. "I've got four others to get to today."

When she lifted the reins the mare shook its head, making the bridle and bit rattle.

"Save me a couple?" Harte said. The girl stared at him with a question in her eyes.

"I'll be taking out a couple," he explained, "in the late afternoon when it starts to cool off."

"All right," she said, still confused. "I'll take the two Arabs. You take the other two."

"Will do," Harte said.

When Collette had crossed the open ground, negotiated the gate, and disappeared into the dark of the trees, Harte and the woman remained standing on their respective sides of the barren fence posts. The wind had died. In the growing heat the pasture radiated a late summer silence.

"What is it you teach, Mr. Canaday?"

"It's Harte, ma'am. I teach American history. This summer it's Georgia history."

She tilted her head. "Are today's young people interested in anything that happened more than a week ago? I hope you can say 'yes' to that. I'd like not to be so cynical."

Harte smiled down at the grass and looked up. "I'm afraid you'll have to hold on to that cynicism, Miss Seagrave. It's like teaching snakes to juggle."

She laughed. "Poor you." She stepped forward and offered her hand.

"Poor all of us," he returned and shook her hand.

She canted her head. "Who was it that said, 'Those who cannot remember the past are condemned to repeat it?' "

"George Santayana."

She looked surprised. "Well, dear me. I don't even know who that gentleman was. I suppose I shouldn't be so quick to judge."

Harte laughed quietly. "Well, he had something to say about *that*, too. 'A man is morally free when, in full possession of his living humanity, he judges the world, and judges other men, with uncompromising sincerity.' "

She hugged the basket to her and seemed to consider this new quote. "And what about a sixty-something man who still likes to do an honest day's work on a fence?" she said, raising her chin to Harte. "Are you all-cynicism or are there any dreams left in a high school teacher?"

Harte couldn't decide whether to frown because he looked his age or smile because she didn't mind naming it. "Probably a little of both," he admitted.

"And why is an erudite teacher like yourself putting up a fence for the Haversacks?"

Harte waved at the flies bothering his face. "I'm bartering. Thought I might enjoy a little riding again, if my joints can stay glued together." He eyed the neat row of vertical posts. "Besides, I like work where you can see things take shape . . . something that can be measured."

She narrowed her eyes. "And what about those dreams, Mr. Canaday? Will *they* take shape?"

Harte fanned at the flies again. "Well, there's always Montana."

"Pardon?"

He smiled and focused on the mountains. "It's an idea I've been holding on to for a while."

"Montana," she said a little intrigued. "And what would be different there, do you think?"

"Well, for one thing, might not be all these merciless flies."

This woman had an uncommon way about her . . . of drawing him out. Less than five minutes had passed and already he had unloaded his dream of Montana on her. He felt as comfortable in her presence as he did with the horses.

She hitched up the basket in both hands and, without a word, returned to her house. After she had gone inside, Harte huffed a private laugh at the woman's brusqueness. But before he had picked up his tools again, she came marching back through the orchard trees. She handed Harte a small blue bottle with a corked mouth.

"Dab some of this around your face and neck. It's an herbal mixture. It doesn't take much."

He took the bottle and raised it to his nose. "What's in it?"

Her eyes clicked from side to side as she recited the list. "Penny royal . . . beautyberry . . . perilla . . . all in a base of citronella oil."

"You made this?"

She nodded. "I grow herbs."

He noticed for the first time that there were no flies circling her face. "Well," he said, studying the bottle. "I'll give it a try." He uncorked the bottle.

"You may need to apply it more than once today. Just hang onto the bottle."

"Thank you, Miss Seagrave."

"I suppose if you're going to be slathering my homemade concoctions on you, you'd better call me 'Bella.' " She started backing away. "It was nice to meet you, Harte," she said. "Thank you for fixing the fence." She hesitated. "I hope you make it to Montana, if that's your dream. But I also hope you know there are blackflies in that country. When *they* bite . . . you *bleed*."

Harte had started to uncork the bottle, but he stopped. "You've been there?"

She shook her head. "Only by way of The Discovery Channel."

Harte studied the little bottle in his hand. "Does this work on blackflies?"

Bella pursed her lips. "It should. Before you go to Montana, stop by. I'll give you a bigger bottle." And with that she walked back into the shadows of her tiny orchard and disappeared around the side of her house.

*****

In the semi-dark of the barn, a gauntlet of nostalgic smells hit him, and along with these scents came a flood of childhood memories. The aroma of cured alfalfa hay gave the stalls a clean and nurturing atmosphere. The mix of dry grain in the feed troughs was rich and molasses-sweet. The oil-scent of soaped leather wafted from the tack room. Beneath it all, the sweat and manure of horses permeated the air, and the dry dirt floor boasted the alchemy of all barns: a soft, friable substrate underfoot.

Harte stepped into the last stall, where a paint mare took a step backward and cautiously eyed him. He took his time unfolding a saddle blanket, talking to the animal in the same tone he used with a student who was new to the county.

"I'm running about a hundred and eighty pounds, girl. When you divide it up, that's forty-five for each of your legs. Reckon you can handle that?" He stroked the mare's long neck muscles and eased the blanket onto the sway of the back behind the withers. From his shoulder he hooked the bridle with his thumb and slipped it over the paint's muzzle, gently pushing the bit into her mouth. The metal clicked across the molars with a hollow rattle.

When he threw his old saddle over the blanket, the paint stood for it. "So you're Pied Piper," Harte said, simply to let the horse hear the steadiness in his voice. "I hear you've got a little problem with thunder." He stroked the horse as he leaned to gather the cinch and thread it through the rings. Watching the rhythm of the horse's breathing, he gave the strap a firm tug. "Well, it's clear today, girl. What do you say let's you and I go out and strike up a new friendship?"

Outside the barn, Harte mounted and felt the old saddle fit him like a lost piece of a puzzle snapping into place. The horse tested him with a few sidesteps, but Harte jounced along with it, returning the patience that the paint had afforded him in the stall. When they settled into a mutual give and take, he rode north toward the mountains and was surprised to feel the first pangs of freedom and excitement that he had experienced in years.

Going up and over the ridge, they followed a logging road that circled back by the old Moss family graveyard. There he reined up and read the rough inscriptions that he had not seen in decades.

"This is what it all comes to, girl" he said. The paint's ears pricked up and turned as if awaiting more. "We live . . . we die . . . and then someone sums us up with a few words and dates."

The mare turned her head to show one bland eye, and then she softly blew. The paint faced ahead, shifted her weight on her front legs, and snorted.

"Yeah, I know," Harte said. "I tend to wax philosophic. Just bear with me." He leaned as he reined the paint around to the trail. "And feel free to join in anytime. I'm a good listener."

After returning to the barn, he brushed down the paint until she was dry. Then he brushed and saddled a swaybacked roan that balked at his weight. Within an hour, the two settled on a partnership and by the end of the session, the roan responded to his commands with an unexpected enthusiasm for performance. He groomed the roan, fed and watered both animals, and watched while they ate their fill, so that they would connect his presence to their pleasure.

When he drove away from the barn, he could already feel some soreness in his upper hamstrings and crotch, but his spirit had been anointed, like leather brightly polished and loosened up by saddle soap. The wind came through his window like Holy Water. As the farmlands gave way to the darker stands of national forest, he smiled and spoke not even once to his truck.

At his camp, he got a fire going and buried a potato in the coals. As it cooked, he rounded out a good day by mounting the old kettle on the road bank and practicing with the Colt Peacemaker. From ten yards he pulled and fired, hitting five for five. At fifteen yards he repeated the perfect score. And then again at twenty.

After the meal, he crawled into his tent and found his state of mind to be healthier than when he had awakened here that morning. He attributed this to the physical labor, exploring the mountains from a saddle, and revisiting the intimate bond he had once enjoyed with horses.

And there was Bella Seagrave. He liked the way she had talked with him—straightforward yet courteous, which made it hard to understand why she had not approached the Haversacks directly about the horse problem. It seemed out of character for her to call the sheriff.

Harte smiled at the thought of Jim Raburn looking into her problem. He was betting Jim didn't mind making the trip out to Cherokee Rose one bit. Jim never passed up a chance to talk to a woman he had not yet met, especially one so easy to look at . . . like the Seagrave woman. But there was more to Bella than looks. She spoke well and handled herself with dignity. Already, he considered her someone he could believe. She must have had a reason to call Jim.

As he undressed, he found the small bottle of repellent that Bella had supplied him. Now that he thought about it, he'd not been bothered by a fly all afternoon. He set the vial aside, but its scent had already filled the tent. To his surprise, he didn't mind the smell at all.

# Chapter Nine

Very early Sunday morning, Harte pulled down the dirt road that led to his former home. He'd been thinking about his pointed-toe boots, which were better suited for stirrups. Unless Callie had gone through a wild purging of his belongings, they would be in the laundry room closet.

The first thing he saw was Earl Sandifer jamming a crowbar behind the hasp on the jimmied door of his storage shed. The hinges, Harte could see, had been pried off by the thieves, leaving the door cracked and splintered in several places. Against the shed leaned a new door, as flimsy as the original. Next to the door leaned his shotgun.

Harte felt his blood run hot when he saw two bronze-red metal gateposts sunk into concrete, one on each side of the dirt driveway. Driving past them to where Earl was working, Harte shut down the truck and propped his left arm in the window.

Sandifer turned, stood stock-still, and then picked up the shotgun. "That gate is going up soon's I can git it d'livered!" He walked to the fence. "If you wanna try an' snatch my gun away again, I'll shoot out your goddamn tires."

Harte pinched the bridge of his nose and then stared at Earl. "You're threatening me now?"

Sandifer licked his lips. "Well, I'm threat'nin' your tires, anyway."

"Sounds like to me you've convinced yourself that I stole your tractor parts. Is that about right, Earl? Because if it is, I don't take kindly to the accusation."

Sandifer raised the point of his chin to Harte. "It don't matter to me what you think about it. I'm closin' off this goddamn road."

Harte leaned to the glove box, set his cell phone aside, removed the .45, and laid the gun in his lap. Then he beckoned Earl by curling a finger. Sandifer's bird-like neck stretched upward, but otherwise he did not move.

"I can hear you from here," Earl mewled.

Harte curled the finger again and waited. Sandifer tightened his grip on the shotgun and walked through the swinging section of limp fence wire that served as his gate into the meadow. At the edge of the road he stopped and shifted his gun to aim at the lower half of the truck door.

"I'm getting tired of you pointing a gun my way, Earl. That's how bad things get started. I'm going to ask you to put that shotgun down one last time. Then I want to talk to you."

"You ain't in no position to make the rules here," Sandifer said. "I got—"

The farmer stopped talking when Harte laid the revolver casually on the elbow he had propped on the windowsill, the barrel of the gun pointing back at the road, the hammer uncocked.

"How's that feel, Earl?" Harte said.

A mockingbird sang from high in the tulip tree that stood in the pasture. The song was as inappropriate to the moment as a calliope playing at a funeral. When the farmer swallowed, the lump in his throat moved like a frog trying to crawl up his gullet. Harte stepped out of the truck, the pistol by his leg pointing at the ground beside him.

"When you point a gun at a man, Earl, you cross a line. A man can feel justified in shooting you." He walked up to Sandifer and took the shotgun from him.

Earl Sandifer swallowed again. "Well, I didn' 'xactly point—"

"Is anyone in there, Earl?" Harte said, pointing to the broken door.

Earl made a quick glance at the shed. "What? Whatta ya mean?"

"Some people need vivid lessons. Is anybody in there? Any animals?"

"No, but—"

"I'm going to help you dismantle that hasp," Harte interrupted. "Any objections?"

When Sandifer said nothing, Harte sidestepped and faced the shed. His arm swept up, and the gun thundered five times. With the echoes coming off the front of the building, the extended roar rolled down the valley behind him and floated off into the distance. Earl came out of his shock enough to turn and look at the five dark holes that circled the hasp.

The hardware still clung fast to the splintered door. Harte stuffed the gun behind his waistband, walked to the shed, leaned the shotgun against the wall, picked up the crowbar, and swung it once, knocking the locked hasp through the door. Now a saucer-sized hole gaped in the door.

Sandifer opened his mouth but closed it and seemed content to pout.

"An expensive lock on a cheap door doesn't help your problem, Earl. Get a better door." Harte returned to his truck, turned, and pointed to the metal posts. "And there won't be a gate there." After hearing no rebuttal, he started the engine and drove up the road to his house.

The boots stood upright on the front porch, along with several other items Callie had left out. He took only the boots and an ammo box filled with maps, cruised through the Sandifer war zone, and reached the paved road without incident.

By mid-morning Harte had the wire strung as taut as harp strings to the posts he had sunk, and in the time that he had been working, he had not seen anyone—not Collette, not the Haversacks, nor Bella Seagrave. He tested each strand of wire with a final pluck of his thumb and was satisfied that Bella's apple trees were safe and that he had earned some more time in the saddle.

After gathering his tools, he drove across the meadow and parked behind the barn. Humming softly, he saddled up the roan, who appeared a little colicky. He led her out into the pasture to let her move around on a long tether as he pulled on his riding boots, but the horse planted her hooves in the grass, transfixed on nothing, moving only to swish a tail or to flutter a muscle to shoo the flies away.

He rode the horse toward the woods trails, but with the bloated belly stiffening its gait, she was slow to find her natural rhythm. Harte gave her time, letting her warm up at her own pace.

After an hour on the trail, the mare dropped a load of steaming manure, perked up, and greedily watered at one of the branches. On the return, Harte let her graze in the sweet fescue by the creek, and then rider and horse returned to the stall to begin the grooming.

Sometime after one o'clock, Collette appeared and, not seeing Harte in the dark, led a black Arab from its stall. Next to the girl the stallion was massive with tufts of hair that feathered from the fetlocks like the winged feet of Mercury.

"Afternoon, Collette," Harte said.

The girl started as if she had backed into an electric fence, her eyes big as silver coins. "Oh, Mr. Canaday," she breathed with relief. "What are you doing here?"

Harte fitted a bridle over the head of a bay mare and began buckling the cheek strap. "I'm going to limber up this old girl a bit." He tied off the reins to a post and threw a new blanket over the bay's back. "I took the roan out earlier."

She kept staring as if she were still unsure of what might happen next. "Are you alone?"

Harte rocked the saddle into place on the blanket, threaded the cinch, and buckled it. "Not unless this old girl decides to buck and leave me in a ditch somewhere." He smiled, but she continued to look around the barn as if expecting someone else. He rested his forearms in the bow of the saddle and looked at her over the horse's back. "Everything okay?" he asked.

When her face flushed with color, she turned back to the Arab and busied herself with the saddle. Harte led the bay past Collette out of the barn, where the mare began to balk at the idea of exercise. He walked her in circles, stroking her neck and talking to her each time she responded to his lead. By the time he gained the saddle, Collette emerged, leading the Arabian behind her.

"You've got to go easy on her bit," the girl advised. "She's sensitive around the mouth."

"I thought so," Harte said and stroked the horse's neck. "I'll be gentle."

With hardly a tug on the pommel, Collette rose into the saddle and sat her horse so lightly that Harte began to feel some guilt about his weight on the bay. "Mr. Canaday?" she said, her eyes fixed on her horse's ears, "I feel kind of odd asking."

Harte grinned and adjusted his hat. "You made an 'A.' "

Her troubled expression did not change. "Not that," she said, glancing at him briefly. "Do you really like riding? I mean . . . this is not about me, is it?"

He studied the profile of her face for a time and then spoke out into the openness of the pasture. "You're worried that I'm here to take some of the load off your job. Is that it?"

She still would not look at him. Her posture on the horse seemed stiff and guarded.

"This is a good barter for me," he explained. "I miss the bond that comes from knowing a horse well."

Collette's eyes fixed on the trees. "Are you a friend of Mr. Haversack?"

Harte pursed his lips and thought about his answer. "We were in school at the same time."

She kept her attention on the meadow. "So, you're not . . . like . . . close friends?"

Harte shook his head. "Can't say we are. Why?"

Collette looked down at the reins in her hands. "I just wondered."

Boot to boot they sat their horses as they faced the rolling grassland. Harte swept off his hat, wiped his forehead with the sleeve of his shirt, and replaced the hat.

"Everything working out okay with you and the Haversacks, Collette?"

Only when he looked at her did she answer. "Mrs. Haversack lets me use her truck when I need it. She's been great."

"And the trailer?" Harte asked. "That working out? Without plumbing or power?"

She shrugged. "I know it's not much, but—" She frowned. "What's that smell?"

"Fly repellent. Miss Seagrave gave it to me."

They eased across the grass at a walk, their saddle leather creaking in syncopated rhythms. Up on the mountain, crows scolded like a mob of malcontents, and Harte knew that perched somewhere up there was a hawk that had triggered the cacophony. When they reached the edge of the meadow, the cool of the woods came to them as a balm. Collette leaned to open the gate, prodded her horse, and splashed across the creek. Harte had to rein in the bay from following.

"I'm going to work this one in the meadow," he called to her back. Unsure that she had heard him, he watched her coax her mount up and over the far bank until she disappeared into the forest.

After an hour of exercise, he returned along the fence line near the orchard. Just as he reached the triple-strand of barbed wire, Bella approached from the side of the house. Dressed in her Sunday clothes, she carried the same vine basket, but this time it was full of greenery.

"Hello," she said, walking toward him at an easy pace.

"Afternoon," Harte replied, tipping the brim of his hat.

She nodded toward the fence. "Admiring your handiwork?"

He had to grin. "So to speak."

She raised her face and narrowed her eyes. "Still using my herb blend, I see."

"You make one hell of a repellent, ma'am. I'm obliged."

She looked mildly surprised. " 'Obliged' and 'ma'am' all in one sentence? Goodness. Maybe you *do* belong in Montana."

He studied the assortment of herbs in the basket. "What are you making now?"

She smiled down at the leaves. "Oh . . . female stuff. Nothing for you here."

"Been to church?" he said, admiring her long print dress.

She nodded and fixed her gaze on his hat. "You, too, I see . . . so to speak."

He didn't catch her meaning until he remembered the grouse feather he had stuck into his hatband on his first ride up the mountain. Looking off toward the forest he thought of where he and the roan had walked the aisles of their own cathedral.

"You look nice," he said, surprising both her and himself.

She waved that off. "It's just the contrast of clean clothes to my usual fare." She squinted and looked toward the barn. "Have you seen Collette today?"

"She's riding. Probably be back before too long."

"Were you two riding together?"

"No, ma'am. But she's fine. She seems to know what she's doing."

She narrowed one eye at him. "I know it's very un-Montana-like, but do you think you could drop the 'ma'am' and call me 'Bella?' We are about the same age, after all."

Harte smiled down at his pommel and nodded. "I can do that."

She handed the basket across the fence. "Would you drop these off at Collette's door? She knows what to do with them."

"Sure." He raised the basket and smelled the greenery. The aroma was like fresh celery.

"Don't give them to her father. Leave them under the front steps. That's our secret spot."

For a time they did not talk. In the apple trees a wren started up a chatter of raspy notes.

"Did you meet Kenneth? Collette's father?" she asked.

"I did," Harte said.

Bella stared at the rise that hid the trailer. "Collette is quite a girl, isn't she? And in spite of all she does here, I'll bet she's a good student."

"You'd win that bet. She's quiet. I guess no one in the class really knows her. But I figure she's about five years ahead of everybody else in the room."

Bella allowed a knowing smile, as if this was something she already knew. "Do you have any children, Harte?"

"No, ma'—" He smiled, catching himself. "No, I don't. What about you, Bella?"

"I have a daughter in Seattle. She's a writer. Novels and a little poetry."

"Any I would have heard of?"

She shook her head. "It's all rather dark. I'm afraid I might not have been a very good mother." There was no self-pity in the admission, only honesty. "I was so busy saving the world."

Harte wondered about the way this woman was willing to open a curtain on her life for a stranger. It seemed neither cathartic nor self-serving—more a simple acceptance of the way things were.

"Well," he said, "you took your shot." He turned to face the mountains. "I'd like to think my shot has been working with the kids who have come through my classes." His head bounced once with a private laugh. "But, hell . . . I can't remember but a handful of them now."

Her face radiated a quiet generosity. "They'll remember you."

Harte fingered the reins in his hands and hoped she was right. "What's your daughter's name . . . in case I get an urge to read some dark poetry?"

"Lane Seagrave. I have her books, of course, so—" She left the invitation open-ended.

"Where's her father?"

"I don't know. He left before she was born."

Harte looked away. There was a lot he could have said about that, but he saw no reason to clutter her history with his words. When he turned to say goodbye, Bella wore a sad but noble smile.

"Some things in this world are never going to make sense, are they?" she said.

Harte looked down into the basket and pursed his lips. "Nope." In his mind he saw Callie's back, striding away in the parking lot after she had given him the divorce papers. "One thing we can be sure of. Every now and then . . . our worlds are going to turn upside down."

With a finger she plucked one of the strands of fence wire. "Does that explain all the concrete?" Seeing the question on his face, she pointed down the fence line. "For next time the world turns upside down." She smiled at him. "Keep all these posts from falling into the sky."

Harte chuckled. "I'd hate to go down in history as the one who started littering the sky."

She laughed, the sound both pleasing and melancholic—like the liquid notes of a wood thrush in early evening.

"Well, I guess we just remember who we are and do the best we can," he said.

"Yes," she said. " 'Remember who we are.' That's always the starting point, isn't it?"

The certainty in her eyes made him feel that he had said the right thing. Behind him, Harte heard the rhythm of hooves, and he twisted in the saddle to see Collette returning to the barn at a slow gallop. Clods of dirt flew up behind the horse's hindquarters, and its mane rippled like water. The Arabian ran smoothly, and the girl moved with it in natural harmony.

"Can I ask you a question, Bella?" He plucked off his hat by the crown and pointed the brim at her apple trees. "Why didn't you approach the Haversacks about the problem with the horses?"

Bella's hazel eyes turned frosty, and her smile disappeared. "I can't talk to Wylie Haversack. And if I have to talk to his wife, I'm afraid of what I might say to her about him."

"You have a run-in with him?"

She cast an icy gaze toward the Haversacks' home. "Maybe all this barbed wire belongs over there," she said, "around *his* house."

"Well, I guess Wylie can be a little hard to be around sometimes. Kind of cynical."

She gave Harte a look that suggested he knew nothing of Wylie Haversack. "Has he told you about his prostate problem? How he says it's the size of a baseball?"

Harte perched his hat back on his head. "Well, yeah, I think he said 'a billiard ball' to me."

Bella kept staring across the meadow. "Frankly, I wish it was the size of a watermelon."

Harte waited for her to explain, but she only fussed with the tie-cord that circled her dress.

"I'm sorry," she said quietly. "This is far too beautiful a day to talk about Wylie Haversack."

From her cottage came the muted sound of a telephone ringing. "Let me get that," she said. "I'm expecting a call from Lane." She began backing away. "See you another time?"

Harte waved. The first drops of rain began tapping in the apple trees. He spoke to the horse, reined around, and headed for the barn. There would be plenty of time to get to know Bella Seagrave. And he would much rather talk to her when the subject matter was not Wylie's prostate.

# Chapter Ten

Harte handed out the graded test papers and spent the day straightening out his students' misconceptions about Georgia history. One student had the Civil War in the wrong century and another had confused the Trail of Tears with a Civil Rights demonstration in Atlanta. As Harte prompted discussions on these subjects, Collette sat quietly at her desk with her hands discreetly covering her grade. Despite the new connection she and Harte had established around the horses, she remained aloof in the crowded setting of the classroom.

Ten minutes before the clock would emancipate the class, Blackadar made his surprise face-in-the-window appearance. Harte ignored him, handed out copies of the State Constitution to the students, and then stacked the extras on his desk, taking his time to tap their edges to align them. Only after stowing the papers in a drawer did he get up, cross the room, and open the door.

"Come to my office after class," the principal said without preamble. "We need to talk."

"I've got to be somewhere at four sharp," Harte explained, thinking of the horses.

"This won't take long," Blackadar quipped and turned on his heel.

Harte closed the door, returned to his class, and leaned back against the front of his desk. "To those of you who made a "D" or an "F," you have a chance to redeem yourselves. Offer me a paper on something original—something that shows me you have some savvy about the formation of Georgia as a state. Eight-thousand words minimum. It's due by Wednesday."

A groan rose from Lamar Dowdy's part of the room.

"This paper," Harte continued, "might save you from repeating the course in the fall. If I smell one phrase of plagiarism—anything off the Internet—I'll file your paper in the waste basket. Write about something that early Georgians did that in some way determines who we are today. I don't want an invoice of exports and imports or a list of battles and dates. I want you thinking."

Harte walked around the desk to his chair, but instead of sitting, he leaned over his desktop on his fists. "Empty your hands and look at me. I want you to hear this." He waited, making eye contact with every student. "For some of you, your habit is to be rescued. A parent comes in at the pivotal moment and saves the day." He straightened and extended his arm to point out the window. "Out there . . . accountability is waiting. It's going to hit you right between the eyes. There is no rescue except self-rescue . . . and that's not always going to work out."

The students sat so still that Harte could hear the hum of the electric clock on the wall behind him. When he dismissed the class, the students were slow to react. For once, he was first to walk out.

Blackadar's secretary was already gone for the day. Harte set his briefcase in a chair, leaned on the doorjamb of the principal's inner sanctum, and let his head trespass into the room. Blackadar wrote at his desk, but when he saw Harte he laid down his pen and beckoned.

Harte took the chair across from the desk and watched the man punch numbers on the desk phone. "This is Morris Blackadar. Is he there?" Without looking at Harte, Blackadar straightened things on his desk that didn't need straightening. "Yes, I'm here," he said into the receiver. "All right, then tell him we'll meet him in the parking lot." He hung up.

"What's up?" Harte asked.

The principal threaded his fingers together on his desktop and crimped his mouth into a perfunctory smile. "They say you are one of our best teachers . . . that you relate to the students."

Harte propped an elbow on the chair's armrest and lowered his chin into the cup of his palm. "That sounded a little like a compliment, Morris."

"Can we step outside together, Mr. Canaday?"

Harte followed and scooped up his briefcase. When they reached the lot, Blackadar kept up a brisk pace toward Harte's Chevy pickup. Just about the time they reached it, Jim Raburn pulled into the lot and parked his cruiser at an obtuse angle. Jim put on his stiff-brimmed hat and heaved himself out of the car. Not looking at Harte, he wore the expression of a man about to deliver a eulogy.

"Sheriff, shall I just leave this to you?"

The sheriff stood looking at the truck but did not answer. Finally he nodded to Harte.

"Jim," Harte greeted.

"Mind if we have a look inside your truck, Harte?" Jim asked. Mandatory duty was etched into his jawline. In contrast, his eyes were dull with embarrassment. "Open it up for me?"

Harte stared at his friend for several seconds. "You need a warrant for that, don't you?"

Jim took no offense at the question. "Not here. Got a standing warrant from the county magistrate to search any car on school property any time." He nodded. "It's legal."

When Harte turned to Blackadar, the principal looked away and began tumbling coins in his pants pocket. Harte tossed his keys to the sheriff, who caught them reflexively.

"Rather have you do it, Harte," Jim said, and walked the keys back to him. Now there was police business in the tone of his voice. He dangled the keys and waited until Harte took them. "What I'm going to do," Jim said, "is sit down inside and just have a look around. I need you to stand over by my cruiser. Will you do that for me? Mr. Blackadar, I need you to stand there and witness."

A deputy's cruiser pulled into the lot and parked beside Jim's car. Cody Culp stepped out of his car and approached. Cody had been a student of Harte's and one of the first black students fully appreciated in the county. He had broken all the school's track records from the sixty meter dash to the four-forty. But those records were barely noticed. It was the State AA Football Championship that people remembered.

"How're you doin', Mr. C?" Cody said, and then he nodded to Blackadar. Harte walked to the sheriff's GMC, turned, leaned back against the side panel, and crossed his arms over his chest. Mostly he watched Blackadar, but he was aware of the discomfiture in Jim Raburn's movements inside the cab of his truck. Deputy Culp observed the sheriff's procedure as if mentally recording it for a report he would write up later. Jim pushed on the glove box button. Nothing happened.

"Small key on the ring," Harte said.

When the box door swung open, Jim stared for a while as if he was not sure he was going to take things any farther. Finally, he pulled out the holstered gun wrapped in its cartridge belt.

"Loaded?" Jim called out from the cab.

Harte waited for Jim to look his way before shaking his head.

The sheriff loosed the hammer thong and slid the weapon from the worn leather pocket. The old Colt looked unnatural in his hand. He set the hammer at half-cock, opened the loading gate, and slowly clicked the cylinder through a full revolution. He snapped the gate shut, holstered the gun, and set the thong back in place. He tried to wrap the rig back into the tight coil in which he had found it but did not succeed. Managing to stuff it back into the glove box, he locked the button and pushed his way out of the cab. He looked at Harte, then at Blackadar, and then back at Harte.

"Can't keep a gun anywhere on school property, Harte. Generally, your truck is an extension of your home. Here at the school, that's the exception. No guns. Period."

"I know a teacher in Corpus Christi who does. Says it's legal if it's locked up."

Raburn nodded deeply. "It goes state by state. Doesn't go in ours."

Harte set his mouth in a hard line and stared at the school. "You arresting me?"

The sheriff inhaled deeply and turned to Blackadar. "You pressing charges?"

Blackadar frowned. "This is not me cooking up a complaint, Sheriff. This is the law."

"You sure you wanna do this . . . lose one o' your best teachers?" Jim narrowed his eyes. "Morris, I'm going to make a suggestion I hope both of you will take very seriously. I propose a warning and a condition. If it happens again—" He gestured toward the glove box. ". . . You formally press charges. But today we go a better route and get a promise from Mr. Canaday that, starting tomorrow, his truck comes to school free of all weapons. How does that sound?"

Blackadar cleared his throat. "May I have a private word with him, Sheriff?"

Jim stuffed his hands into his pockets, spread his feet on the asphalt, and settled in to wait. Stepping before Harte, Blackadar propped his hands on his ample hips.

"You know this can affect your pension, don't you?"

Harte had been staring off to the east at nothing, but his head came around at that. He saw Montana breaking off at its borders and sinking into the magma of the earth.

"Thirty-six years, Morris. When I started teaching here, you had acne."

Blackadar's hands slipped into his pockets again, and the coins resumed their jangling. "What if I decided not to pursue this?" he said quietly. "Provided, of course, you follow the sheriff's condition . . . and say you stayed on for another year?"

Harte's eyes half-closed, and he made an airy snort. "I know what you're doing, Morris."

"I'm trying to help you get the retirement money you've earned."

"No, you're trying to blackmail me."

"You can call it what you want," Blackadar shot back. "I think it's a fair trade."

Harte walked past Blackadar and stepped in front of Jim. "Better lock me up quick, Sheriff. This old desperado is about to snap."

Jim looked past Harte to Blackadar. The principal appeared confused.

"I've made him an offer," Blackadar said stiffly. "He would do well to consider it. Now I have work to do. I'll leave this to you, Sheriff Raburn."

Jim and Harte watched the school bureaucrat walk to the building. His feet splayed outward, giving his gait the side-to-side waddle of a determined penguin. Throughout all of this, Cody Culp stood with the patience of a fence post.

"Jackass," Harte mumbled.

Jim turned to Harte. "There's a pair of 'em out here, if you ask me." When Harte turned to him, the sheriff held eye contact but spoke up to his deputy. "Cody, drive out to the Walmart and write up some tickets for those campers and boat trailers that aren't supposed to be parked out there. I believe they've been squattin' for three days."

"Yes, sir." Already moving, the deputy caught Harte's eye and let his eyebrows rise. He buckled into his car, fired up the engine, and drove off as if both banks were being robbed.

Side by side the two friends leaned back into Harte's truck and watched Cody's cruiser pull out onto the highway. "Remember when we used to jump that high for Coach Tollerson?" Jim said.

Harte huffed a laugh through his nose. "I'll bet you couldn't jump over his big toe now."

Raburn frowned at Harte. "Tollerson's been dead for ten years."

Harte shrugged. "I'm sticking with my original assessment."

They were quiet for a time, listening to the sound of someone hammering something metallic across the street in the repair yard at the hardware store.

"Any more trouble with Earl Sandifer?" Jim said. "Anything that might involve me?"

Harte shook his head. "I'm thinking it's going to settle down."

Jim nodded toward the door where Blackadar had disappeared. "But *this* ain't likely goin' away," he said. "Tell me I'm wrong."

"He knows I'm ready to retire. He's threatening my pension."

The sheriff smiled. "You're that good, are you? Blackmailin' you to stay on?" When Harte said nothing, Jim lost his smile. "Reckon you can consider leavin' your gun at home a while?"

Harte gave him a look. "What home?"

"You know it ain't my call, Harte. Blackadar calls me out here, I gotta come." The sheriff folded his arms across his chest and crossed his legs at the ankles. He let his chin drop down so that it almost rested on his chest. "Well, like you say, if Sandifer's easin' up, maybe you can, too. Maybe you don't need that gun all the time."

"Hell, I don't even live on that road anymore, Jim."

Jim pursed his lips and began nodding. "I know where you're stayin'. And I know you can't leave your gun out there for some jasper to carry it off." He softened his voice. "You know the Forest Service will make you move on from there, don't you? You can't set up a permanent camp."

Harte frowned at the horizon. "You boys are not ganging up on me, are you?"

Jim exhaled a long sigh. "Look, I know you got a lot on your plate right now . . . with Callie, Earl Sandifer, and now Morris Blackadar. Why don't you take up my offer and come stay with me?"

Harte felt his resentments begin to subside, but he made no reply.

"At least you could keep your gun at my place. What about that?"

A parade of vehicles passed by on the highway, but the sound of traffic only magnified the silence between them. The sky showed indigo in the east. From the west a great tide of imbricate clouds rolled in—a fish-scale pattern that predicted more rain. The afternoon was cooler today. Harte took it all in, noting that the daylight hours were starting to get shorter. The radio in the cruiser crackled, and a tinny female voice ran on in monotonic sentences from the speaker.

"You need to get that?" Harte said.

Jim shrugged. The radio finally quieted, and the afternoon traffic dropped to a sudden lull.

"Don't take my gun, Jim," Harte said.

Jim Raburn pushed away from the truck and stretched, pushing his fists into his lower back.

"Harte," he said, "you better think on this hard. I might not have a choice next time. You ask me, you're playin' into Blackadar's hands." He nodded across the street. "Wyman's got a safe over at the hardware store. I bet he wouldn' care a lick if you wanted to lock up your gun during school hours."

That was all they said on the matter. The two lifelong friends continued to watch the change of color in the eastern sky until the stratum above the horizon turned a dingy gray. Finally, Harte opened his door and got in behind the wheel.

"I've got some horses waiting on me," Harte said. "We still on for tomorrow?"

Jim patted his gun. "Target practice and tortillas. Wouldn' miss it."

Harte inserted the key but hesitated. "How was your date last night?"

Jim pushed his hat back and showed a doubtful expression. "Got changed to tonight," he said and faced Harte as though he were open for suggestions.

Harte started his truck. "Behave yourself."

Jim Raburn made a two-fingered salute from under the brim of his hat, and Harte drove out the school driveway.

# Chapter Eleven

He saddled up the paint and joined the myriad greens of the late summer forest, where a sudden emergence of mushrooms had invaded the valley after last night's rain. Staying on the low trail, he followed the creek along its winding incision through dark stands of hemlocks and white pine, where the sky was all but shut out. Even in deep shadow the creek boiled with white luminescence. The tumbling water seemed to conjure bright light out of nothing. Like patches of snow in moonlight.

Two pileated woodpeckers leap-frogged ahead of him through the trees, retreating in their swooping arcs and making a racket with their nasal cackling. Squirrels barked and flicked their tails before scurrying across tree limbs and climbing ever upward. It was like a chain of telegraphs dispatched before him to announce his arrival. Harte pulled up on the reins and waited for the creatures to calm.

After a few minutes of quiet, he reined around to exit the way he had come in, and the paint, sensing an end to the outing, picked up her pace. When they reached the meadow the paint broke into a full gallop and tore across the grass making a beeline for the barn. The wind almost took his hat, but he tugged down on the brim and allowed the animal to enjoy its speed and freedom.

Next, he saddled the roan and took it through a regimen of spirited, wide figure-eights in the open grassland. Then he ran the mare in tight circles, alternating directions as though training it for cattle work. At the end of an hour, he returned to the barn and groomed the horses through the twilight until their coats were as smooth and dry as a finely brushed felt hat.

When the horses were fed and watered, a light rain fell from out of the dark and grew to a gentle drum roll on the metal roof. Standing in the doorway, he looked through the rain at the faint pink halo of light that hovered over town three miles distant. With the rain coming down harder, a sit-down dinner in a restaurant appealed to him. Then he could drive to the gap and slip into his tent without a fire and fall asleep to the sound of the rain.

He chose The Brassy Ring, a new addition to the town square. Pulling into a space at the front window, he shut off the engine and stared through the glass at lighted candles illuminating white tablecloths. His riding clothes smelled of horse, leather, and sweat, and his jeans were dotted with seeds of beggar's lice. His appearance was reason enough not to get out of the truck, but with the summer session almost over and retirement looking like the right direction, he thought of this meal as a "last supper." A fitting farewell memory to hold onto once he got to Montana.

He got out and strode into the restaurant with a little bounce in his step. Just minutes after he had ordered, Harte watched the hostess lead Jim Raburn and Bella Seagrave into the dining area. Bella wore her Sunday print dress and appeared essentially the same as Harte had remembered her. But Jim was transformed in his dark blue suit. Seeing him in something other than his sheriff's uniform, Harte could see just how much his friend had aged in the last few years. The silver in his hair contrasted sharply against the dark suit, and the lines in his face were etched deep by the candlelight.

Jim walked behind Bella to a table cattycornered across the room. They moved carefully among the tables, Jim touching one of Bella's elbows and talking to each diner who greeted him. Bella pulled out her own chair, but Jim took over to seat her snugly against the table. While still standing, Jim spotted Harte and stared, showing a little surprise. When Harte raised his chin as a greeting, Jim smiled, fingered the knot in his necktie, and bobbed his eyebrows once.

Harte set down his water glass. "Well, hell," he breathed. He told himself not to look up, but in seconds he was watching the couple study their menus. Jim leaned forward and pointed out something on the page. Bella nodded, seemingly attentive to his suggestions.

The waitress brought Harte's salad and stood awkwardly in her white uniform and gold vest.

"I'm sorry, sir, the kitchen has run out of duck. I didn't know till now." She offered a rueful smile.

"Run out of duck," he mumbled. "I think I know the feeling."

"Sorry?" she said. When he waved away the question, she tried to return his menu.

"Just let me have the check," Harte said. "The salad will be plenty."

"I'm so sorry, sir," she said, her voice whiny but sincere.

"Don't be. The salad looks good, and you served it with panache."

She frowned. "Was *that* not supposed to be on the salad?" She opened the menu and peered intently at the bottom of a page.

Harte moved his hand through the air as if erasing a chalkboard. "It's all right. I'll just take the check." He smiled as best he could for a duck-deprived schoolteacher on his way to Montana without a pension.

She left his bill on the table beside his hat and apologized again before retreating to the kitchen. It was a twelve-dollar salad. He left a ten and a five. Then he rose and weaved his way through the tables, making for the exit as quickly as possible without drawing attention. He had made it halfway across the room when someone called out his name so loudly that everyone within three tables in every direction turned a head. Which included Bella.

Sheldon, the real estate man, sat right in Harte's path, and, with a big smile showing most of his teeth, he flattened his hands on either side of his dinner plate and waited until Harte was within reach. Sheldon clasped Harte's hand with the fierceness of a C-clamp.

"Meet some friends of mine, Harte. They're going to be a part of our little community before too long." The realtor swept a hand out and introductions went around the table—two couples in their thirties, plus Sheldon's wife. The men half-stood to shake Harte's hand, and the women smiled.

"You're the school teacher I've heard about," one of the women remarked.

"According to our daughter," Sheldon said, "he's the best we've got." He opened his hand toward his guests. "Between these two families, we're talkin' three daughters and two sons. Prob'ly be comin' through your history classes one day." Sheldon, who had put the town in debt as mayor and then gotten rich off selling land, leaned to confide in Harte. "They're both building down on the new golf course, and they're going with the same theme—logs and cedar shakes. Kind of an old homestead look." Sheldon winked at Harte. "Right down your historic alley, so to speak. Decks reaching out over the river." Sheldon smiled at his clients, and they smiled back. Harte could see they were bursting to add something to Sheldon's description, but he did not encourage them. Harte started to leave, but Sheldon quickly stood, blocking his way.

"Layland!" the realtor called out. "Come over here and meet these folks."

Harte turned to see Callie standing so close to him they could have been partners on a crowded dance floor. Sheldon was busy shaking hands with Layland and guiding him around the table. Harte could not keep his eyes from taking in the length of his wife. She wore a saffron dress he had never seen, and it did for her body what a good oiling did for a gun. Her hair was still arranged with an intricate weave at one side of her head.

"This is the man I was tellin' you about," Sheldon announced. "Layland Childers is the one building our new golf course."

Layland received the appropriate praise from the group and practiced his engaging version of hometown modesty. He wore an open-collared white shirt beneath a thin and supple leather jacket. As Sheldon championed the cultural enhancement of a world-class golf course, Layland grinned and looked around the room to see who was looking at him. When he met Harte's dour expression, the muscles of his face relaxed as if they had been snipped by a surgeon.

"So, who's designing your course for you?" one man said. "Tiger?" He laughed.

Layland reignited his smile for the table. "We're still in negotiations with several people. So you folks are moving from—?"

"Atlanta," the two women replied in unison. Then one took over. "Escaping really. It's just too much. The traffic, the noise, the pace. God, it's a nightmare." When she talked, her head shook in quick jerks that made her hair bounce around her ears.

"Well, you've made it to the promised land," Layland crooned. "You're gonna love it here."

Harte looked for an exit route, but a waiter had set up a stand full of platters in his path. One of the servings looked like duck.

"Well," one of the men said, "we won't be up here all the time. We do have to work, you know." He laughed. "This will be our little getaway. Eventually, we might expand the place and think about retiring up here."

"Well, remember," his wife said, "I'll want a swimming pool when that happens."

"Play golf, Harte?" the man asked, giving Harte a keen look of masculine camaraderie.

Harte shook his head. The walls of the room were suddenly too close for him. Too many people. Too much money. He found himself studying one of the wives' mascara.

"You want a swimming pool next to the river?" Harte said.

She showed a row of perfect teeth. "I love sitting by water and reading."

Harte looked at the others. They were all smiling. A hand clamped down on his elbow, but Callie's familiar censure held no power over him now.

"Are you a swimmer?" Harte asked the woman needing a pool.

She made a face and curled a lock of hair between scissored fingers. "Do you know what chlorine does to your hair?"

"You could sit by the river," Harte said, and Callie's fingernails dug into his arm.

The woman smiled, but her eyes worried. "Well, the children will want to swim."

Harte stared at her and wondered if he needed to explain that rivers had swimming holes.

Sheldon chuckled to defuse the moment. "Right now, we just want you folks to have that mountain retreat. The roaring fireplace. Deer out the window. You're gonna love it."

The image seemed to mesmerize the newcomers as they smiled at their realtor.

"Nice to meet all you folks," Layland said. "Y'all excuse us so we can—"

"Aren't you going to introduce your date, Layland?" Harte said. Callie's grip slackened, and her fingers slipped off his arm.

Layland's smile was frozen in place. "Of course. This is—"

"My wife," Harte finished for him.

The group at the table was like a nest of fledgling birds, openmouthed and hungry for a punch line—not knowing that they had just received it. Layland pushed an easy laugh into the void, and then Harte's elbow was in the grip of Jim Raburn's large hand.

"Evening, everybody," Jim said and eased beside Harte. "I'm the sheriff. Y'all 'xcuse my interruption." He turned to Harte. "How we doin' tonight, pard? Wonder if I could have a private word?" His grip tightened and led Harte toward the foyer, where the hostess wished them a good night. Neither man responded.

Outside on the sidewalk Harte disengaged and headed for his truck. Jim had to call him to a halt with some iron in his voice. Harte stopped but did not turn around. Jim walked around him and stood face to face, so close that Harte could smell the scent of his aftershave.

"Didn' start drinkin' tonight, did you, pard?" Jim said.

Harte studied the tourist shops that lined the square. "We're losing what we got up here, Jim. And nobody's doing a damned thing about it." He looked directly into the sheriff's eyes. "Hell, Sheldon is a county commissioner. If that's not a conflict of interests—" Harte gritted his teeth and looked back at the town. "We need a golf course like we need a case of skin cancer."

Raburn's face compressed into a web of wrinkles. "What the hell's gotten into you? This is growth for the county. This is good for us. This is a good class of people moving up here." Raburn flung an arm south toward the river. "And what the hell is so God-awful bad about a game o' golf? Is it because it's Layland's baby?"

Harte looked deep into his friend's eyes. "We've been fishin' the river since we were boys."

The change of subject lowered the sheriff's brow. "Yeah? And?"

Harte raised his arms from his sides and let them fall back with a slap. "When the trees are gone, the shade is gone; the water temperature rises. You know what happens to the trout then?"

Raburn smiled and looked around him as if searching for the answer. "Well, I guess they hole up under logs and such. I don't know. But I do know this. I got a lot o' other things to think about before I start worryin' 'bout fish. I got a daughter hooked on cocaine, Harte." Jim's jaws flexed beneath his flaccid jowls. "The daughter of the goddamned sheriff!" he hissed angrily.

They both turned to lean back into Harte's truck, where they stood shoulder to shoulder staring down the street where the traffic light changed with no vehicles there to take its cue.

"I know what you're thinkin'," Jim said. "How is it I got time to take someone out to eat when my daughter is in such trouble?"

Harte shook his head. "I wasn't thinking that."

Jim took in a lot of air and exhaled a long sigh. "Hell, I can't even *see* her now."

Harte recalled that Lauren had been absent from class today. "Is she in rehab?"

Jim shook his head. "Doin' it on her own . . . at home. She wouldn' check into a facility on account o' me. Didn' want to embarrass me." Jim shook his head, and the worse kind of hurt showed in his face. "Part o' why Emily won't talk to me. She thinks that was my idea."

An elderly man and woman, led by a small terrier on a leash, walked by on the sidewalk. Jim spoke to them in his friendly way. They returned the greeting and moved out of earshot.

"So," Jim said, "how is Lauren doing in your summer class?"

Harte shook his head. "She's detached . . . from the class . . . from me."

Jim nodded. "Prob'ly looks at you and sees me."

Harte brought up the image of Lauren sitting in the back row of his classroom. "A daughter doesn't stop loving her father that easily, Jim. Give her time."

They stood without speaking as a couple left the restaurant, then Jim pushed away from the truck to stand in front of Harte. "I got to get back in there. I got enough women pissed off at me. Look, we'll burn some powder tomorr' and talk at supper. All right?" He reached out and squeezed Harte's upper arm. "Just cut people a little slack, will you? And stay clear o' Layland, okay?"

Jim walked back into the restaurant, and Harte watched through the window as he returned to his table. Bella's sober expression did not change when Jim smiled and said something to her. In the candlelight, Jim's eyes appeared large and moist, and he wasted no time covering his face with the menu. Bella looked down at her hands folded on the linen as if deep in prayer.

# Chapter Twelve

"Give me something with some kick, Luther," Harte said over the blare of the jukebox.

Luther was rubbing at a wet spot on the bar, but now he stopped the motion and gave Harte the look he reserved for shiftless patrons looking for a handout. "Come again?" he said.

Harte raised his chin toward the shelves of bottles. "You know more about this than I do. Pour me something that can burn up a memory or two."

Luther stacked his forearms on the bar and smirked. "And what might *that* be?"

"You decide," Harte instructed and looked toward the sink where Julie stared back at him, her hands idle in the soapy water. Turning away and frowning, she went back to her washing.

"Just to be clear," Luther said, "are we talking 'alcohol' here?"

Harte glared at Luther. "This *is* a bar, *right*?"

Luther straightened and flipped the rag over his shoulder. "I'll come up with somethin'."

Harte pointed to the last booth—the only one not occupied. "I'll be back there . . . with Mr. Hemingway. And how about a bowl of nuts? I didn't eat tonight."

Luther leaned into the bar on stiffened arms. "Maybe you oughta have some food on your stomach b'fore you go exper'mentin' with the hard stuff."

Harte took off his hat and ran his fingers back through his hair. "The nuts will do," he said.

Luther shrugged and pulled down a bottle from the shelf.

The room was noisy, mostly male but for a mixed group of college kids at the front tables. A pool game had drawn an audience in back. Harte walked the most direct line he could fashion through tables bristling with chair legs, bent knees, and work boots. He slid into the booth, set down his hat, and, to keep his mind off his behavior, watched the pool game in progress.

A lean Hispanic boy in his early twenties concentrated on the table. Wearing jeans, T-shirt, and tan work boots, he leaned over the cue ball and took his shot, sinking a solid blue ball that brought instant congratulations from spectators. The boy's lower pant legs were flecked with dried concrete. His moustache curled down around his mouth, and his dark eyes turned thoughtful as he chalked his stick. When he studied the lie of the balls this time, his face hardened. Nearby, a short stocky friend kept touting him as the "*Señor* Ball-Cracker from Sonora."

The "ball-cracker's" opponent was Grady Dillard, an auto mechanic, whom Harte knew from the Shell station in town. Grady was a good natured boy, a diehard who never gave up on an engine problem. He had a local reputation as a skilled player on the green felt.

The Mexican played with a quiet, economical rhythm, sinking four balls in a row before Julie arrived at Harte's booth with a tray. She set down a coaster, mug, napkin, and a full bowl of peanuts. Last, she laid down a saucer with an egg that rolled to a stop.

"It's boiled," she said through a shy smile, "left over from my lunch." She frowned as though trying to recall something she'd memorized. "Luther said there's no charge for the extra nuts."

Harte pointed at the pink drink. "Just so I know, what's in it?"

She shook her head. "Luther made it." She frowned again. "Harte, are you all right?"

The balls clicked on the table, and from the crowd rose a groan with a decidedly Hispanic timbre. Harte looked idly toward the game. The mechanic took three warm-up strokes with the stick sliding over his grease-stained fingers before the white ball rocketed across the felt and dropped one of the striped balls into a corner pocket. This time the approval was local.

Harte mustered a smile. "Just an off night, Julie. Don't pay me any mind."

Masked by the sound of the cheer, the door opened, and Harte watched the Bulloch brothers file into the room—Bobby Lee, Varley, and the big one called "Breed." Harte could not help thinking that they looked like the cast of a B-movie about three prisoners who had escaped from a chain-gang. He had seen them in the bar only once before, but once was plenty. The three of them—especially Bobby Lee—were born trouble-makers. Harte thought of them as a three-headed monster, because he could not imagine any one of them operating on his own.

The Bullochs hailed from Union County, where, Jim Raburn had told Harte, the brothers had spent more time at county lockup than some of the guards who worked there. Their reputations were made from petty offenses—fighting, reckless driving, and disturbing the peace. Jim, himself, had twice arrested the trio when they were in their teens. The charges had been auto theft and assault, but on both occasions the accusers had backed away unscathed by the legal process. Jim held a solemn contempt for the family. Now the Bulloch boys were in their late twenties and early thirties, and their defiance of the law had grown along with their greasy hair.

Julie followed Harte's gaze to the front of the room. "Oh, shit," she whispered and hurried back behind the bar and began drying mugs with her back to the room.

From a distance Bobby Lee carried a resemblance to James Dean—small sharp nose, small eyes, a narrow chin, all of it crowded together on his small face. He could never seem to talk enough, either bragging about himself or ridiculing someone in his presence.

As a kind of balance to Bobby Lee's size and overactive mouth, Breed was a loutish giant. His eyes were as baleful as the stare of a mad dog. One of his hands could have covered a dinner plate. The one time Harte had seen him here, Breed had sat at a table for an hour without speaking or moving, save the emptying of a dozen bottles of beer.

Varley was a rat-faced misfit, dark and jittery like an animal gone feral and filthy. His surly smile was a permanent fixture, as if he constantly dredged up in his mind the same vulgar joke. When the song on the jukebox ended, the Bullochs' presence dominated the room. Men from every table made furtive glances toward them. Only the pool players were oblivious.

"Let's play a *real* game, boys!" Bobby Lee announced as he strutted toward the table, his razor-edged voice trespassing on the game in progress. He threw down a wad of bills on the green felt, sending a striped ball into motion until it tapped another ball. Harte checked the face of Grady Dillard, who glared at Bobby Lee and worked the tendon in his jaw like a heartbeat. The Mexican boy stared at the roll of money.

Breed stepped around Bobby Lee, leaned on the pool table, and rolled one of the balls with a backhanded flick of his thick fingers. From the bar, Varley cackled.

"Who wants to put up some *real* money?" Bobby Lee crowed, ". . . and lose it to a Bulloch?" He looked around the table, but other than Grady Dillard's disapproving glare, no one responded. "Any o' you assholes named 'McAllister?' " he asked offhandedly.

Grady slapped his stick down on the table, his face flushed now, the veins in his neck swollen like blue cords inserted under his skin. "We *had* us a game goin', asshole." Dillard was big and strong and, from the tone of his voice, not accustomed to brooking insults. Harte had never seen the boy with his dander up, but he knew it did not bode well for him—not with the Bullochs.

Smiling, Varley sauntered from the bar. "Uh, oh! Looks like we riled up the grease monkey."

Grady turned to Varley, but Breed stepped between them so as to be the sole object of Grady's attention. While these two faced one another, Bobby Lee sidled to the wall, chose a pool stick from the rack, and eased around to the mechanic's blind side. There he turned the stick around to grasp the tapered end and, before anyone could voice a warning, swung it in a vicious arc that caught Grady just behind the ear. The visceral sound of impact tightened Harte's stomach. The mechanic dropped to the floor like so much deadweight.

Varley laughed the loudest, but it was the glow of pleasure on Bobby Lee's face that Harte would remember. Scratching the whiskers on his face, Breed stared down at the unconscious boy and cocked his head to one side as if he were analyzing a work of art.

"I guess you all saw that," Bobby Lee announced to the stunned room. He pointed to the Dillard boy. "This big'n here started to take a swing at my brother." He smiled. "I's just defendin' 'im, same as you would for your brother." His smile widened as he checked the faces in the crowd. "Right?"

When Harte started to get up, Luther appeared next to him, set down a tray, and forced his way into the seat, pushing Harte closer to the wall. "Better sit this one out," Luther whispered out of the side of his mouth. "Bobby Lee's got a gun under his shirt. Breed, too."

Performing for the patrons, Bobby Lee held the stick at an upward angle and rotated it as he sighted down its length, checking its alignment. Then he pointed the cue at the Mexican player.

"Money on the table, Mex. It's you an' me." Bobby Lee's eyes danced with the challenge.

Mark Warren

Harte leaned to Luther. "Call the sheriff's department, Luther."

Luther took in a deep breath, looked at the Dillard boy sprawled on the floor, and nodded. When Bobby Lee scooped up his money and began racking the balls on the table, Luther stood and picked up the tray.

"Just wait," he whispered to Harte. "Let the sheriff handle it."

When Harte made no reply, Luther returned to the bar. After rattling a few bottles, Luther blindly fumbled for the telephone, and Bobby Lee's sharp eyes fixed on the motion. His smile was enough to make Luther straighten and show both hands on the bar. Laying down the cue stick, Bobby Lee started for the front of the room, his walk slow and menacing. Then, cat-like, he hopped up and sat on the countertop and twisted around to face Luther.

"Who we callin', old man?"

"Nobody," Luther said. "My hand bumped the phone."

Bobby Lee laughed and called to the back of the room. "Varl, git some music goin'!"

Varley dug into his pockets and began pushing coins into the jukebox. When the rhythmic strum of a guitar introduced the wail of a country song, the patrons pretended to retreat to their drinks and former conversations, but their eyes darted covertly to the boy lying on the floor.

Amid all the noise, Bobby Lee casually leaned behind the bar and make a loop of the phone cord. Harte watched him produce a large folding knife from his jeans pocket, flip it open with his thumb, and sever the wire. Luther, arms limp by his sides, watched Bobby Lee close the knife and gesture for Breed to approach.

When Breed lumbered to the bar, Bobby Lee leaned to his ear and talked behind a cupped hand pressed into his brother's straggly hair. Breed straightened and marched like the walking dead into the dark hallway that led to the bathrooms. Soon returning, he laid the pay

130

phone's hand-piece on the bar, its cord dangling like the tail of a creature he had snatched from its den.

Bobby Lee made a high-pitched laugh that could barely be heard over the jukebox. Harte watched him switch his attention from Luther to Julie, who had squeezed herself far back into the corner by the sink. As Bobby Lee spoke, she stared at him like a doe caught in a car's head-lights.

Leaving his hat beside his drink, Harte stood and walked to the pool table, where the crowd had backed away from the Dillard boy's inert body. Kneeling, he gently cradled the mechanic's head as he turned him by a shoulder. The Mexican pool player appeared beside him and helped by rotating the legs. Probing the Dillard boy's hair, Harte found a lump the size of a hickory nut.

"You ain't McAllister, are you?" said a whispery voice.

Harte turned to Varley Bulloch's rat-like face. His dark beady eyes seemed to vibrate in their sockets, as though he could not decide where to look from one millisecond to the next.

"This boy needs medical help," Harte said.

Varley coughed up a laugh. "He got what was comin' to 'im. Leave 'im alone."

Harte stood, his eyes scanning the room and settling on a front booth, where a heavy-set, balding man sat. Harte walked to his table, leaned to the man's ear and spoke over the music.

"Aren't you a doctor?"

The man's eyes widened. "I'm a veterinarian," he whispered, trying for anonymity.

"We're going to need your help, Doc," Harte said, and lifted the star-tled man to his feet.

"I only work with animals," the man protested in a rush.

Harte pulled the vet toward the back of the room. "We're doing what we can for this boy."

The Bullochs watched but said nothing as both men knelt to the unconscious mechanic.

"Luther's phones have been disabled," Harte whispered. "I'm going out to my truck for my phone." He started for the door but was stopped when Breed blocked his way. The jukebox song faded, and the room seemed to come up for air.

"Move," Harte said in a quiet and even undertone. "I'm going to call in an ambulance."

Breed's face remained as unanimated as a tree stump. A shiny coat of sweat covered his dirty face, and though his eyes were fixed on Harte's, he seemed somehow remote and uninterested.

A new song started up on the jukebox, its driving beat filling the room, a steel guitar bending its notes over a throbbing bass and pounding drums. When Harte reached past Breed to take the door handle, the giant did not budge. His body odor was as much an impediment as his bulk. Harte stepped back to face him, and the big man just stared with a dead-eyed emptiness.

"Hey, old man," Bobby Lee called out over the music. He slid from the bar top and practiced his swagger as he approached. "You ain't McAllister, are you?"

Turning to Bobby Lee, Harte ignored the question and jerked his thumb toward the pool table. "If that boy dies, you up the ante from barroom fight to manslaughter . . . maybe murder." Harte pointed to the bar. "You cutting that phone cord ramps it up another notch. A good prosecutor could turn that into conspiracy to murder."

Bobby Lee pushed his chin forward to the beat of the song. Now that the alpha Bulloch was up close, it was evident to Harte that all three brothers were more than deranged. They were high on drugs. Bobby Lee was jittery, like an over-wound toy, whose spring was about to snap.

"That big sonovabitch grease monkey started it. Hell, I was just defending my brother. That's what happens in a goddamn bar fight. If you can't handle gittin' hit, you oughtn't go to a bar. So what if he's got a damn knot on his head? What's it to you anyway?"

Harte gritted his teeth and, against his better judgment, began throwing out an argument of logic. "You don't seem to get it, Bulloch. Everybody in here saw you—"

"Hold on, hold on!" Luther interrupted. He sidled nervously into the conversation. "This man is a doctor!" he announced, laying a hand on Harte's shoulder. Then he looked Harte squarely in the eye. "Dr. Canaday, go out and get your medical bag. We need to help the Dillard boy."

Bobby Lee was frowning, looking from face to face. Shifting his weight repeatedly from one leg to the other, he looked around the room with quick jerks of his head. Then all the concern dropped from his face as he began thrusting his head in time with the music again.

Luther leaned to Harte's ear. "We gotta do somethin'. Julie's scared outta her wits."

When Harte looked over the bar, he saw her cowering against the wall. The whites of her eyes were piercing as she returned his stare. Turning back to Breed, Harte widened his stance.

"Move aside," he said, his voice flat as the drone of tractor.

Breed's big hand disappeared behind his dirty shirt and closed around the handle of a large revolver stuffed into his waistband. Placing his left hand on Harte's chest, he raised the gun high enough to expose its chrome finish. It was a .44 magnum.

Luther gripped Harte's arm and turned him away from Breed. "Let's don't make this any worse than it already is," Luther whispered. "Would you go talk to Julie? She's askin' for you."

Bobby Lee slipped into the place where Harte had been standing, shielding the patrons in the room from Breed's gun. "Put that away till I tell you!" he said in a rush. Then the urgency in his voice disappeared, and he made his maniacal smile. "Hell," he laughed, "we might have to kill ever'body in this damned place before we're done here." Then he laughed.

In the back of the room, several men were helping the veterinarian with the Dillard boy. They knelt like medics on a battlefield, their heads bowed, their hands reassuring. The jukebox rambled on, its upbeat song perversely indifferent to the situation. Harte walked to the bar and beckoned Julie with a curl of his fingers. She approached like a wild animal, fearful and cautious.

"Harte," she pleaded, her whisper like a dying breath, "don't let them hurt me."

"Nobody's going to hurt you, Julie."

Her eyes filled with tears. "I know Bobby Lee. I mean, I know what he can do. He hurt a friend of mine and told her, if she talked, his brothers would kill her mama and daddy and sister . . . and her dog." She widened her eyes as she leaned in. "He raped her, Harte."

Seeing her lips begin to quiver, Harte gripped her arm. "That's not going to happen, Julie."

The jukebox song reached a climactic moment, shutting down the drums and backup instruments to give center stage to the female singer's lyrics: *"You'll never fill me up if all you have are empty promises . . ."* Before Harte could say more, the vet and the Mexican pool player carried the Dillard boy to the bar. Harte lowered the boy's head onto a rolled up towel that Julie provided.

"He probably has a concussion," the vet said. "He needs to be in a hospital."

Harte examined the back of Grady's skull. The swelling had grown to the size of half an eight ball. Across the bar Julie stared at the wound as though she were in a trance. Reaching over the boy's inert body, Harte touched her shoulder, snapping her out of the spell.

"Can you wrap up some ice in a towel?" he asked.

Glad for something to do, she flattened a rag on the bar, and scooped ice. As she and Harte gathered the corners of the rag together, he kept his eyes on his hands and spoke under his breath.

"Wait ten seconds, go to the bathroom, and make a call on your cell phone. Get an ambulance and some deputies out here . . . and tell them to be quick."

She seemed paralyzed, staring at Harte as if he had asked her to recite a poem to the room. "Cell phones don't work here at the bottom of the mountain," she said in a rushed whisper.

"Try it," Harte encouraged and squeezed her slender wrist.

Julie swallowed and then looked at the room with haunted eyes.

"It's all right to be scared," he said. "But I need you to make that call."

Bobby Lee strutted to the bar and beat a quick drumroll on the countertop with his hands. "Well, hey, girlie!" He made a fiendish smile. "I b'lieve you and me're gonna be sweethearts."

Julie's shoulders began to shake. "I got to pee," she said. "When I get scared, I got to pee."

"Well, go drop your panties then. But hurry! You'n me got things to talk about."

Julie's eyes fixed on Harte, her tears now coursing down her cheeks. When he gave her a nod, she wiped at her tears and walked mechanically into the dark hallway to the bathroom.

Bobby Lee delivered a cascading falsetto laugh, spun around, and walked back to the pool table, where he chalked a stick and called out to the Mexican at the bar. "Let's see what you got, Chico!" He dug into his pocket and flashed the wad of bills again. " 'Course," Bobby Lee announced to whoever would listen, "I don' really think a Mex can beat a white man at anythin'."

As the Hispanic player walked to the back of the room, the muted sound of a toilet flushing came from the hallway. Then Julie reappeared, her eyebrows knitted with worry.

"There's no signal," she whispered to Harte.

Harte moved down the bar to the vet. "Do you have a cell phone?"

The balding man shook his head. "In my car . . . it never works in here."

Harte waved that away. "I need you to get in your car and drive until you can get a signal. We need an ambulance, and we need the law here."

The vet gave Harte a doubtful look. "You think these cretins will let me leave?"

"If I make a big enough fuss," Harte said. "Get ready."

Without giving the man time to respond, Harte crossed the room to the pool table, where Bobby Lee was lining up for a shot at the racked balls. Picking up one of the solid balls, Harte rolled it at the cue ball for a direct hit, and Bobby Lee straightened like a jack-in-the-box, his taut face reddening like heated metal.

"You goddamned sonovabitch!" Bobby Lee snapped.

"Ooh-whee!" Varley squealed. "Another asshole wantin' his head busted."

With the jukebox silent, a new quiet carved out the space around the pool table like a lighted stage. Harte put a hand on a pool stick in the rack and settled his gaze on Bobby Lee.

"You like to run your mouth and come at a man from behind," Harte said, his voice filled with challenge. "What happens when a man faces you?"

Bobby Lee's stiff body seemed to ramp up with a current of electricity. He ran his tongue across the front of his teeth as he studied Harte.

"Hey, Breed," Bobby Lee called to the front of the room. "You wanna in'erduce this old fart to the fear o' God?"

Harte heard a light footfall behind him and was surprised when the young Mexican stepped beside him. Turning to the boy, Harte saw in his profile the deliberate calm of a man who had reached some decision and would stick to it.

"We make the odds a little better, *señor*," the Mexican said.

Breed ambled from the front of the room. All the customers turned in their seats to watch him. Harte cut his eyes to the veterinarian just long enough to prompt the man to action.

"Hey, Chico," Bobby Lee laughed. "How the hell am I gonna whip your ass at the pool table if you're lyin' on the floor bleedin'? How much money you got on you, anyway?"

"Enough," the boy said and raised his chin to Bobby Lee. "You put down your money and we go at it either way you want . . . on the table . . . or right here."

Bobby Lee extended an arm and flattened his hand as a signal to his brother. Breed stopped as if he had come to the end of a tether.

"I wanna see if Chico's cahones are as big as he says. We'll save him for later. But while I crack this young'n's balls, you can tear a new asshole for the old fart."

Harte snorted a whispery laugh through his nose. "So," he said, "no face to face for you."

Bobby Lee checked the faces around him. Once again the color of his cheeks darkened. Luther eased past Breed, gripped Harte by the upper arm, and began to tug him toward the bar, his momentum so set that Breed pivoted to let them pass.

"Dr. Canaday," Luther said loudly, "I think the Dillard boy is dying."

Letting himself be pulled along, Harte noted the faces near the door. The veterinarian was gone. At the bar Grady Dillard's blinking eyes struggled to focus on Julie.

"I cain't be payin' for no ambulance," Grady was saying, trying to sit up.

Harte eased the boy back to a prone position. "Rest easy, son. Don't you worry about that."

As Harte held a towel to Grady's forehead, he heard the balls being racked at the table. Then came Bobby Lee's litany of boasts about his prowess with a cue stick. Harte caught Luther's eye and nodded a thank-you. Luther nodded back.

Then Breed appeared in the mirror, looming behind Harte, but the hulking giant only moved away to the door to take up his post. No sooner had Breed faced the room than the door opened and banged against his boot heels. With the music going full-tilt again and the pool game shaping up at the back of the room, only Harte saw the man who squeezed through the opening to speak to Breed.

He was a robust, middle-aged man with a boxy jaw and close-cropped silver hair. Over a white tee-shirt he wore a burgundy windbreaker. Khaki work pants fell over his brown lace-up boots. Stopping abruptly, he frowned at Breed and said something that could not be heard. But one word Harte deciphered by reading the man's lips: "McAllister."

# Chapter Thirteen

The silver-haired man made his way to the bar, where he ignored Harte and the body laid out on the counter. "Gimme a cold beer," he said, and Julie went into motion filling a mug.

Within seconds Bobby Lee stood at the newcomer's back. "Are you McAllister?"

The man kept his eyes on the mirror across the bar as he raised his mug and sipped. Bobby Lee extended the pool stick and tapped the countertop at the man's elbow.

The man set down his mug. "Yeah, I'm McAllister." He tilted his head toward the boy stretched out next to him. "This was supposed to be a quiet meeting. Not a goddamned circus."

Ignoring the man's anger, Bobby Lee leaned on the bar. "You bring the stuff?"

McAllister drank from his beer as he watched Harte tend to the semi-conscious boy. "It's ten minutes away," McAllister mumbled, keeping his eyes on Harte.

" 'Ten minutes away!' " Bobby Lee huffed.

"This is the way we do it," McAllister explained quietly. "Make sure the site is secure."

Bobby Lee rattled off one of his high-pitched laughs and jerked his head toward the room. "There ain't nobody here stupid enough to testify against a Bulloch in court."

McAllister turned to show his smirk. "You'd be surprised what people do in court."

Bobby Lee pointed his finger, almost touching the man's nose. "They might just wake up one night to find their house all lit up and their family lookin' like burnt toast." Straightening suddenly, Bobby Lee shifted his weight from leg to leg like a human metronome. "So, go git the stuff!"

"Let's do this outside," McAllister urged quietly. "You bring the money?"

Bobby Lee kept up his nervous tottering. "We came to do bus'ness, dumb ass!"

McAllister remained calm, checked his cell phone for messages, and then set the phone on the counter. "Take it easy. This is the way it's done. You never know what you might be walking into. It'll only take twenty minutes for me to get it here."

Bobby Lee stood stock-still and glared at the man. "You said 'ten minutes.' "

McAllister stared. "Ten minutes each way, imbecile."

Bobby Lee sniffed and resumed his rocking. "Aw-right, I'll go with you."

McAllister shook his head. "Doesn't work that way." He pulled out his wallet and slapped four one-dollar bills on the bar. "Meet me in the parking lot, north end, in twenty minutes." He checked his wristwatch and then turned cold blue eyes on Bobby Lee.

"Tell you what," Bobby Lee snarled. He snatched up McAllister's wallet and phone with one hand and grabbed his windbreaker in the other. When the material bunched, a gun showed in McAllister's waistband. Pocketing the wallet and phone, Bobby Lee smiled. "Let us know when you're ready for bus'ness. I'm gonna play some pool." Quick as a snake, he snatched the man's gun and stepped back, waggling a blue-finished revolver like a tease. "I'll hang on to these." He stuffed the gun in his own waistband and then swung the pool stick to his shoulder. "Now go an' git it!"

McAllister straightened his jacket. "I'll be back," he said and walked out.

Bobby Lee scuffed toward the back of the room. "Let's play some eight ball, Chico," he crowed. Halfway to the table, he stopped and looked back at Julie. "Hey, girlie, you wanna come watch me crack some balls?" When Julie lowered her eyes and shook her head, Bobby Lee laughed. "Well, what *do* you like to do?"

Julie's face came up, an equal mix of surprise and fear. "What do you mean?"

"I mean what do you *like*?"

She made a pained expression and licked her lips. "I like to cook," she said. "I've been putting up peaches all weekend."

Bobby Lee laughed. "Well, then . . . we'll see what we can cook up together later. Maybe you can put up my peaches." With that he paraded to the pool table, where the Mexican leaned on his stick, waiting. Bobby Lee pointed a finger at him and then tapped the butt end of his stick on the floor. "A hun'rd dollars says I whip your ass, Chico. You got that kinda money?"

The Mexican watched as Bobby Lee peeled off five bills from his roll. "*Si*, I got it, *Gringo*."

Bobby Lee counted off five more bills and fanned them like a hand of cards to wave in front of the boy. "Hell, then . . . let's make it two hun'rd." His mouth stretched into a vicious smile when he added, ". . . Greaser!" Then he cackled. "I'll break!"

The boy ignored the insult and laid down twenty ten dollar bills. "We tap for break," he said, "after you put money down."

Bobby Lee feigned surprise. "What, you don't trust me? Hell, son, my money is good!"

The Mexican offered a thin smile. "Then lay it down with mine. We get someone to hold it, and then we don't need no trust."

Scoffing, Bobby Lee threw his money on the table. "Varley, you're the bank!"

Varley started to reach for the money, but the Mexican slapped his cue stick on the bills and shook his head. "Someone else," he said.

Bobby Lee sneered. "Let the girl hold it," he said and turned to yell to the front of the room. "Hey, girlie . . . come here an' hold this money till I can win it back from this smart-mouth greaser."

Julie looked at Harte, who gave her a go-ahead nod. She seemed weightless as she walked to the back of the room. After she picked up the cash off the green felt, the Mexican grabbed a spare cue ball from the wall rack and joined Bobby Lee at the end of the table. Simultaneously, they tapped gentle shots, the two balls rolling on opposite sides of the triangle of racked balls, the sound on the felt undetectable even in the absolute quiet of the room. Bobby Lee's ball bounced off the bumper and rolled back half a foot, while the Mexican's ball barely touched the bumper and stalled within a finger's breadth of the edge.

Bobby Lee cursed. "Okay, Chico, you break. Enjoy it while you can."

The Mexican set the cue ball and punched it with authority, breaking the tight cluster of multicolored balls with an explosive *crack*. The balls scattered to every corner of the rectangle of green, tapping out random *clicks* as they slowed. When a ball dropped, Bobby Lee banged his stick on the floor and cursed again.

The Mexican sank three more balls in quick order. Just as the fifth striped ball dropped, the door opened and Breed caught it and filled the gap. Turning, he gave Bobby Lee a nod.

"Hang on!" Bobby Lee announced to the crowd. He dropped his stick onto the green felt, knocking balls out of place. "We'll start over when I finish my bus'ness. How's that sound?"

The Hispanic's dark eyes fixed on Bobby Lee's back. "Sound like bull-sheet," he said.

Bobby Lee stopped and turned, his eyes narrowed. "What'd you say, Mex?"

"Finish the game or forfeit. Either way I take your money."

Bobby Lee took a step toward him and smiled. "I thought all you Mex was a bunch o' limp dicks. Are you gittin' a hard-on for me, boy?" He tapped his opponent's chest with a stiff finger, but the Mexican paid no attention to it.

"You start a game," the young Mexican said, "you finish it, or else you lose the money. Are you afraid of finish game, *señor*?"

Bobby Lee's face soured. "No, *seen-yore*, I ain't afraid *of finish* nothin' or nob'dy." Then, in an instant, his garish smile returned. "I like you, Chico. Stay right here. But we're gonna double the stakes and see can you stand that kind o' heat."

The Mexican's expression remained unchanged. "I live in the desert for many years."

Bobby Lee frowned, but shrugged away his confusion and pointed at Julie as he passed the bar. "You stick around, too, honey pot. You'n me got some unfinished bus'ness."

Julie pressed her forearms to her stomach, and her shoulders began to shake. "Harte?" she whispered. "Please help me?"

Harte leaned over Grady Dillard and gently drew her closer. "I already sent someone to call."

Her eyes slanted with doubt. "What if they come too late?" she whispered.

Her misery debilitated her so that Harte was forced to face a solemn truth: Without a weapon he could not promise to protect her from armed men. He needed the Colt revolver in his truck.

Moving to the door, Harte turned Bobby Lee by his elbow only to have a big automatic pressed into his gut. "That boy's pulse rate has dropped into the danger zone," Harte lied. "Let me go out to my truck for my bag. Without medicine, he's going to die."

As if seeking brotherly advice, Bobby Lee looked up into Breed's flat face, but the biggest Bulloch merely gazed at Harte just as he would watch a fly groom itself on a windowsill. Bobby Lee held the gun on Harte as he frowned at the body on the bar.

"Varley!" Bobby Lee called out. Varley appeared beside Harte and watched fascinated as his brother pushed the gun into the soft tissue under Harte's chin. "Varley, git your piece out and go with this asshole doctor to his truck. He's gonna git some medicine." He rose on his toes to deliver an ultimatum to Harte's face. "Then *you* git back in here with your damn medicine. You do somethin' I don't like, and this place is goin' to hell on a fast train." Then he nodded to Breed. "Stay here an' keep a eye on things," he whispered.

Bobby Lee prodded Varley and Harte to the door. "Let's go!"

As he stepped into the parking lot, Harte saw a dark Cadillac parked at the north end of the lot. The man named McAllister stood beside the Caddie smoking a cigar, the smoke rising above his head like a cloud of impatience. As Bobby Lee sauntered toward the Cadillac, Harte started toward his truck with Varley following him.

"Hey!" Varley said. "You got 'xactly thirty seconds. You see what I got here?"

Harte turned his head to see a small automatic in Varley's hand.

"Thirty seconds ain't long, you know," Varley said. "Better git that medicine and git inside."

At the passenger side of his truck, Harte sorted through his keys and casually checked on Bobby Lee and McAllister, now talking next to a battered pickup truck closer to the building.

Varley pushed the gun into Harte's back. "Hurry up! Stop horsin' around!"

144

A car slowed on the highway, turned into the lot crunching the gravel, and stopped with its headlights trained through the aisles of vehicles. The high beams blinked up, and Varley squinted into the light with a hand leveled across his forehead like a visor.

"Who the hell is *that*?" Varley hissed, hiding the gun in the shadow of his leg.

Harte leaned into the cab and peered out the back window, half-sure that it was Jim Raburn's GMC idling at the entrance to the lot. Behind him he heard Varley work the slide on the automatic.

"Hurry up! I ain't standin' in this spotlight all night! *Jesus*! Who the hell *is* that!"

Harte turned the key in the glove box, but right away Varley's spindly fingers knotted the material at the back of Harte's shirt and tugged. "I cain't see what the hell you're doin'. You step over here, and I'll git it."

Harte backed away. "It's behind the driver's seat. A black leather bag."

Varley kept his gun leveled on Harte as he backed into the cab. He sat on the passenger seat and craned his neck through the slot between the seats. Harte checked on the two men at the rusted pickup and then watched Varley raise the barrel of the gun vertically as he searched behind the seat.

Ducking into the cab, Harte clamped his left hand on the automatic with his little finger wedged between the hammer and firing pin. He twisted violently, feeling the hammer close on tendon and bone. His right hand clasped Varley's throat, and the little man's eyes widened as he was pushed into the driver's seat. His mouth opened, and a raspy gargling issued from his throat.

When Harte wrenched the weapon free, a wet *snap* of cartilage announced the ruin of one of Varley's fingers. He set the safety on the automatic, pushed it under his belt in the small of his back, and clapped his palm over Varley's mouth. Even as Varley's eyes were clamped shut in pain, Harte kneed him in the groin with such force that the little man's head rammed into the far door. Beneath the wet seal of Harte's hand, Varley's cry was a silent implosion.

When Harte eased his hand away, Varley's now-bloody mouth formed a small circle, and his cheeks began to inflate and empty in a fast puffing rhythm. One hand lightly cupped his crotch; the other lay against his chest, its index finger bent at an unnatural angle.

With Varley absorbed in his misery, Harte slipped the Colt out of the glove box, began freeing rounds from the belt loops, and pushing them into the chambers. Hearing a scuffle at the front of the building, he peered over the dashboard to see Bobby Lee squinting into the head-lights, holding McAllister in front of him like a shield, one arm locked around the man's throat, the other pressing a gun into the side of his head. In the glare of light, McAllister's face was pale as alabaster.

"Turn out those goddamn lights!" Bobby Lee screamed. "I'll blow his brains all over this parking lot." Then he pressed his mouth to McAllister's ear. "You damn narc."

"I'm not a narc!" McAllister croaked through the stranglehold.

Bobby Lee tightened his hold and yelled toward Harte's truck. "Varley! Who the hell is that out there shinin' those damned lights?"

Hart crouched behind his open door. Five seconds stretched out, and nothing happened.

"Varley!" Bobby Lee screamed with a cracking voice. "You hear me?"

Harte jerked Varley closer and spoke in his ear. "You're going to show yourself! Tell your brother you're coming." He pushed the barrel of the gun under Varley's ribs.

Varley was in a separate world, his face stretched with the pain. "You done ruint me!"

Harte lifted Varley to face Bobby Lee from behind the open truck door.

"He's got my damned gun, Bobby Lee!" Varley yelled through his damaged throat.

Bobby Lee, looking wild-eyed, screamed into the lot, his voice as high-pitched as a woman's. "Goddamn you! You better throw out Varley's gun, else I'll blow this fucker's head off."

"We each have a hostage," Harte called out. "But I don't care a damn about yours."

Bobby Lee bared his small foxlike teeth, and the white rims of his eyes shone in the light from Jim's car. "How 'bout inside the bar? Anybody in *there* you care a damn about, old man?"

Harte jammed his Colt into his belt and pressed Varley harder into the door. "All right! You win!" He flung the automatic out into the lot, where it clattered across the gravel.

"Now send my brother out here!" Bobby Lee ordered.

Varley's eyes were closed, and he was breathing in sharp, shallow gasps.

"He can't walk!" Harte answered. "He's hurt!"

"Goddamn you!" Bobby Lee screamed. Over McAllister's wincing body he fired off three rounds. One bullet punched into Harte's door. The other two shots went wide, ricocheting off metal and whining out into the night.

"You almost hit your brother," Harte yelled. Peering through the crack in the door he saw Breed now standing next to Bobby Lee and McAllister. The tall Bulloch seemed only mildly vexed, like a man who had come outside to check on a barking dog. Hanging down by his leg was the big .44, which changed everything. Harte knew that it could shoot through an engine block.

The car's headlights blinked to low beams and then back to high. Harte took this to be a signal from Jim, insisting that he retreat. But it must have served as an insult to Bobby Lee, who cursed and fired at Jim's car.

Breed raised his gun and joined in the target practice. The explosions of the two guns were deafening. Glass shattered and bullets tore into metal. When it ended, Jim's lights were dead. The GMC's engine roared, and the wheels spun backward, spraying gravel into the lot as the car clawed its way in reverse through the entrance and onto the road. When the tires caught on the asphalt, the rubber squealed, and the car lurched forward and sped south on the highway.

Peering out, Harte watched Bobby Lee push a fresh magazine into his gun, as Breed loaded cartridges into his revolver. In this new darkness, Harte slammed the barrel of his gun into the side of his captive's head and pushed him into the cab. Varley slumped over both seats, limp as a corpse.

As McAllister and Bobby Lee screamed at each other, Harte retreated to the rear of his truck. Hunkered down by the tailgate, he thought of Julie and the promise he had made to her over the bar. His top priority became clear: the Bullochs must not go back into the building.

To his left, footsteps grated in the gravel. Harte lowered himself and by the faint light from the neon sign saw someone moving beside a van two cars over. But his attention was drawn to a more immediate threat from the front of the bar. Breed was marching out into the lot, the big magnum outstretched before him. Quietly, Harte backed to the next row of parked cars and watched the tall Bulloch lean and pick up Varley's automatic.

When Breed reached Harte's pickup, he leaned into the window. "Varl? That you?" He opened the door and then straightened to call back to Bobby Lee. "Varl don't look so good!"

"He ain't dead, is he?" Bobby Lee yelled.

Breed shook Varley, eliciting a moan. "No!" he called out. "He ain't dead!"

Bobby Lee pushed McAllister aside. "Fetch Varley and let's git the hell outta here."

As Harte started to move, the dark silhouette of a man rose up from behind his truck, blocking his view of the Bullochs. Jim Raburn's big voice boomed in the lot.

"Drop your guns and raise your hands! This is the sheriff talkin'!"

For five heartbeats, no one spoke or moved. Then Breed bent at the knees and made a heaving adjustment as he backed out of Harte's cab. Holding Varley in his arms, he began walking toward the sheriff.

"This'n here needs some help, Sher'ff," Breed said in his dull monotone.

"Just stop right—"

Jim's words cut off with a deafening explosion. Harte had just stood up to his full height when he saw the muzzle flash of the gun beneath Varley's body. Suddenly Jim was no longer there.

"Breed?" Bobby Lee yelled.

Breed wheezed a laugh from deep in his chest. "I just kilt me a sher'ff," he announced and set Varley back in the cab. Bobby Lee came running. Neither noticed as Harte raised the Colt, stepped into full view between the vehicles, and thumbed back the hammer.

"Drop your guns!" he commanded. "I'll kill you both where you stand!"

The three men stood like statues in the dark lot. Breed stepped away from the truck, and when Harte made the shift to follow him, the barrel of the Colt went into shadow, no longer illuminated by the faint blue neon sign at the building. He was sighting blindly now.

Far down the road came the first wail of a siren. In that moment, Harte could sense the violence yet to come. It was like the rarefied moment when all the life seemed to be sucked from a place just before lightning seared into it, connecting heaven and earth with its unstoppable force.

Breed had just begun raising his gun when headlights spread across the lot from the car parked behind and to one side of Harte. The light caught the metal of the Colt's barrel and highlighted the direction of his aim like a bright line drawn on a graph. He didn't need to look at it. He only needed that shining vector in his peripheral calculations.

When Harte fired, Breed shuddered and stumbled backward, falling onto the gravel, the big .44 clacking on the loose stone. Swinging his arm a few degrees, Harte aimed at Bobby Lee, who was backing toward the bar in stutter-steps, firing wildly, his shots banging into metal and splintering glass somewhere behind Harte. Squeezing off the shot, he saw Bobby Lee's face fill with shock just before his expression went flat and lifeless. With all his quick, nervous energy now gone, Bobby Lee reeled in a slow turn and fell on his face.

Jim Raburn lay unmoving in his good suit. The harsh light of the parked car's beams exposed a garish wound. Harte rushed forward and pressed his fingertips into the hollow of Jim's throat.

"Jim?" he managed to say, but there was no pulse. Lowering his ear to Jim's lips, he prayed for a stir of warm breath, but he could detect no life in the still body.

Out on the highway multiple sirens howled. The first car skidded to a halt on the right of way. An ambulance pulled in behind it, both their headlights shining north on the road. Then the emergency sounds from the vehicles shut down, and the quiet of the night fell around Harte like the interior of a flashing blue tomb.

Jim's white shirt now glistened with wetness in the beam of head-lights, the stain black as oil. Footsteps came on fast from the road and stopped two cars away.

"Sher'ff?" someone called out. It was a full-throated voice that Harte recognized.

"Cody! It's Harte Canaday! Jim's been shot! Get an ambulance in here, now!"

"Soon as we stabilize the situation," Cody replied in a steady voice. "Where is the shooter?"

Harte checked inside his truck and saw Varley was still sprawled across the seats. "Two dead, one out of action!" he called out. "The Bulloch brothers. There's one more somewhere. Short gray hair, about a hundred-eighty pounds. Might be armed. Headed for the north end of the lot."

Emerging from behind a van, Cody's silhouette was etched out by the blue lights of the emergency vehicles on the highway. As the deputy made his way closer, he spoke into a hand radio.

"EMTs, come to the south end of the lot. The sheriff's been shot. Joe-Joe move in on the north end. Suspect has short gray hair, weighs one hundred-eighty pounds. May be armed."

Harte continued to press his hand to the spreading stain on Jim's shirt. He wanted to put his weight on Jim's chest, to pump life back into his friend, but the saturation in the shirt was a swamp.

When Cody reached Harte, the deputy stood transfixed at the array of bodies lying between the cars. He leveled his gun at Harte's truck, where a pair of loafer-clad feet protruded from the cab.

"Who's that?"

Harte shook his head. "One of the Bullochs. Varley. He's out."

Cody knelt to the sheriff. "Is he gone?"

Harte wanted to yell at Cody, to demand that the EMTs arrive. But he could not form the words. All he could do was nod.

"Tell me about the man who ran north," Cody said, his voice all-business.

Harte swallowed and cleared his throat. "Calls himself 'McAllister.' White, well-built, mid-forties, short gray hair, white tee shirt, dull red windbreaker. Looked like a drug deal. McAllister supplying, Bullochs buying. McAllister is driving a dark Cadillac."

Varley moaned from the truck, and Cody turned his attention there. After cuffing Varley's wrists behind him, the deputy searched for a weapon.

"Mr. Bulloch, you do anything more than breathe and I'll make your night a hellava lot worse. Do you understand?"

Varley struggled to turn his head. "I cain't hardly move! My privates is all swole up!"

Cody's radio crackled, and a tinny voice came through. "We got the Caddy guy, Cody. Is the lot secure?"

Cody spoke into the unit. "Ten-four. Get the medics in here quick! The sheriff's been shot. Tell them to look for the car lights near the middle of the lot. We're right in front of 'em."

Within seconds a male-female team dressed in dark uniforms hurried into the space beside Harte's truck. Harte backed away and watched them go through the motions that he knew were in vain. In his peripheral vision he saw Cody transfer Varley to another deputy. As Varley was being hustled away, Cody examined the bodies of Breed and Bobby Lee.

The male medic, his hands now idle, sat back on his heels. "He's done," he said, his assessment clinical and detached. His partner—a tall lean woman with blonde hair banded in a ponytail—stripped off blood-soaked latex gloves and dropped them into a plastic bag. Donning another pair, she stepped to Harte, gently took his left hand in both of hers, and began to examine the finger where the hammer of Varley's automatic had torn the flesh.

"What happened here?" she asked, probing the open wound. "Were you shot?"

Harte shook his head. "I'm all right. There's a boy inside the bar . . . head trauma."

"We've got a team going in there now," she said. Her partner moved from Breed to Bobby Lee, while she seemed to know the exercise was pointless. "Let's find you a place to sit down," she said, trying to turn Harte by his arm. "I'll bandage this for you."

Harte didn't move. "I'll stay with Jim," he said, his voice sounding distant, disembodied.

She narrowed her eyes at Harte, at the old pistol stuffed in his belt. "You're an officer?"

"A friend," Harte said.

"Looks like everybody is dead," her partner reported casually. "Must'a been some fight."

The woman touched Harte's elbow, and the small act of humanity seemed to sink to the center of him. Feeling his throat constrict, he tightened the tendons in his jaw.

"I'm sorry about your friend, sir," she said and gently squeezed his arm.

Harte nodded but said nothing. The young man unfolded a long rectangular sheet of black plastic and covered Jim's body as if he were hastily making up a bed. The woman knelt to help and made a show of slowing the work until her partner looked up at her.

"He kill both these Bulloch boys?" the young man whispered, hitching his head toward Harte. As an answer she just stared at him. "He on the force?" he pressed. When still she did not reply, he shrugged. "Hell, maybe he oughta be."

# Chapter Fourteen

One by one, more deputies arrived and stood quietly around the covered body of their fallen sheriff. Harte sensed their need for some kind of explanation, but he could not bring himself to speak. A light spit of rain blew out of the darkness and fell through the yellow-orange glow of fading headlights that had saved his life. The tiny droplets of mist caught fire in the beams. As he stared at the car, two new paramedics set down a stretcher and unrolled two vinyl body bags.

Cody returned and stood next to Harte, and together they watched the first team of EMTs cocoon the sheriff in a body bag and strap him to the stretcher. When they carried the corpse away, the small group of deputies quietly broke up, leaving Harte and Cody alone.

"What the hell happened here, Mr. C?"

Harte told it all, beginning with the Bullochs blindsiding the Dillard boy. As the story unfolded, Cody made occasional furtive glances at the old Colt revolver stuffed behind Harte's belt. When Harte finished with the tally of shots fired in the parking lot, he gazed through the open door of the bar, where deputies milled with Luther's customers.

"I knew the Bullochs," Cody said. "Sons o' bitches, every one." His voice was hard, but his ebony face softened as he looked directly into Harte's eyes. "The world's better off, and that's the damned truth. Too bad Varley didn't die with them."

Harte continued to watch the goings-on inside the bar. "I was too damned late," he said.

Cody took a firm grip on Harte's upper arm and shook him gently. "Don't do that, Mr. C. This could've gone a hellava lot worse. We were all too late . . . all of us."

The paramedics carried the Dillard boy from the building and transferred him into the back of an ambulance. Julie watched from the doorway until behind her a deputy holding a clipboard said something to her, and she turned to go back inside.

"I got to get in there and question folks," Cody explained. "Can you come inside when you're ready? We'd like to get all the statements we can tonight."

Harte nodded, and Cody offered his hand. Harte looked down at the deputy's hand but could not bring himself to raise his own. The young man clasped Harte's upper arm again and squeezed.

"What you did here tonight, Mr. C . . . it was the right thing. We're all grateful." He gave Harte's shoulder a light pat. "Now let me go do what Sheriff Jim taught me to do."

As Cody walked to the bar, the team of EMTs huddled over Breed and struggled to bag the body. After finally zipping up the bag, they groaned as they lifted the weight onto a stretcher.

"Damn, they grow 'em big in Union County," one man said.

On a verbal count, they raised the stretcher and shuffled toward the same ambulance where the sheriff had been installed. Harte followed and stopped them at the rear of the vehicle.

"Don't put him in there," he said, his voice harder than he had intended.

Their faces turned to Harte, and the two men stood in place under the strain of the weight. Harte looked into the interior of the ambulance, where the young woman was seated beside Jim's body as she wrote in a notebook. She laid down her pen and closed it inside the book.

"You heard him, boys," she said quietly. "Let's get that other ambulance in here."

The medics backed away with their burden, and Harte stepped closer to the door. The woman checked the tightness of the straps that secured the body bag to a bunk bolted to the vehicle's frame. Her movements brought to mind Elmer Dowdy testing the tie-downs on the bales of wheat straw he had stacked in his truck. Feeling suddenly tired, Harte put a hand on the door frame.

"Go easy," he said only a little above a whisper. "This was a good man."

She made a modest smile. "Yes, sir. We'll go easy."

To the south, the glow of the town pushed up a dome-shaped halo of pink against the night. The light drizzle had stopped. From the ambulance radio, monotonic phrases crackled with static.

"Are you all right, sir?" The EMT eased out of the ambulance and stood beside him.

"I was lucky tonight," he said. He nodded toward the Toyota Camry, its faint orange headlights now like two smoldering candle wicks. "If those lights had not come on when they did—"

The woman frowned at the car in question. "Who turned them on?"

Harte closed his eyes and shook his head. "I've got no idea." Then he looked the woman in the eyes. "Thank you for your work, miss."

Walking into Luther's, he negotiated his way through the clusters of customers being questioned by the officers. Those who noticed his arrival kept their eyes on him as he made his way to the back of the room. The cue sticks and balls lay on the pool table just as he had last seen them. Now they seemed still and ominous, like an array of bones, sticks, and feathers dropped by some ancient conjurer who had stopped here unnoticed to foretell the tragedy that would unfold this night.

At the last booth he picked up his hat, fitted it to his head, and walked to the bar, where Luther leaned his forearms on the countertop, staring at the room as if watching a movie on a screen.

"Is Jim Raburn really dead?" Luther asked.

When Harte nodded, Luther exhaled a long stream of air through his nose. "Damned Bobby Lee was higher'n a buzzard in an updraft." He shook his head. "Jim Raburn killed by someone like him. What a waste."

"It was Breed who killed Jim."

Luther's gaze dropped to Harte's gun. "Deputy says you sent 'em all to hell."

"Two of them," Harte said as he surveyed the room. "Varley's alive."

Harte noticed the Mexican pool player leaning against the wall near the silent jukebox, awaiting his turn at questions with a deputy. When their gazes met across the room, Harte nodded once. The Mexican raised his chin, unhooked one thumb from his belt and opened his hand toward Harte as though returning a compliment.

"Where's Julie?" Harte said to Luther.

"Bathroom. She's still pretty shook up."

"Anybody back there with her?"

"Don't think so."

They were quiet for a time, watching the talkative customers who just an hour ago had been so reserved. Now their voices were reeling off yards of run-on sentences.

"EMTs said the ice might'a saved the Dillard boy," Luther said. He reached under the bar and tapped down two clean shot glasses. "Here, I owe you." He unscrewed the cap on a bottle.

Harte covered the glass with his hand. "What was it you put in my drink tonight?"

Luther poured himself a drink, set down the bottle, and threw back the shot with a jerk of his head. Then, to Harte's surprise, the barman smiled.

"It was your usual—a Tom Collins. I added a little maraschino cherry juice for color." Luther shrugged. "Prob'ly a good choice considering how this night turned out, don't you think?"

"I'm going to check on Julie," Harte said.

Luther nodded and poured a second drink for himself.

At the door of the restroom, Harte knocked quietly. "Julie? It's Harte Canaday."

After ten seconds, the lock tripped and the door swung open. Julie held a bar rag in her hand. Her face was raw and tear-streaked. She leaned forward and peered past him down the hall.

"I don't want to go out there," she insisted and backed onto the tiled floor.

"Don't blame you," Harte said. Stepping inside he took the rag from her and walked to the sink to wet it. In the mirror he watched her hold the door open with her back.

"Bobby Lee was going to rape me, wasn't he?"

Harte wrung out the cloth. "He was big on talking. He won't ever hurt anybody again."

Standing before her, he wiped at the dark smears around her big eyes. Her irises were light-brown and her expression childlike with a perpetual sense of being startled by whatever was around her. Her eyes stayed on his while he worked on her.

"Is he really dead . . . Bobby Lee, I mean?"

"He is."

A shadow of fear seemed to pass across her face. "That friend of mine he hurt," she whispered. "She won't leave her home now. She's afraid."

Harte kept dabbing at her face. "We wouldn't have let anything happen to you, Julie."

Her face hardened with certainty. "You mean *you* wouldn't have. All those other people seemed as scared as I was." Her brow lowered. "You killed him, didn't you?"

When he tried not to answer, she leaned to get her face in front of his.

"Didn't you?"

He nodded. "Breed and Bobby Lee are dead. Varley is on his way to jail." He returned to the sink and rinsed out the cloth and when he looked up, he saw that she was watching him in the reflection of the mirror. "You'll never have to worry about the Bullochs," he assured her. He wrung out the rag and handed it to her. "You can talk to the deputies tomorrow. Go home. Is there somebody there to be with you?"

Her little-girl eyes widened. "No, no one. Just my cat, Turnips."

He nodded and narrowed his eyes. "You don't drive a Camry, do you?"

She nodded.

"Well, I guess that's your car that got all shot up out there."

Seemingly unfazed by that news, she filled with hope. "Can you take me home, Harte?"

"I'll ask Luther to do it," he said and pretended not to see the disappointment in her face. "I need to go over to the Raburn place and tell Jim's parents about this. Then over to Lauren's . . . Jim's daughter." He exhaled heavily. "It's going to be a tough night for a lot of people."

She stepped to the mirror and looked at herself. "Sheriff Raburn let my daddy out of jail once . . . for my sixteenth birthday party."

Harte nodded. "That was Jim for you."

Her eyes angled to Harte in the mirror. "He was your friend, wasn't he?"

Harte smiled. "Best I ever had . . . since we were six years old."

Julie turned and faced him, as though trying to memorize his features. "You're a good man, Harte." Then her expression went flat. "But I'm glad you killed them. They were bad men." She stepped forward, rose up on her tiptoes, and kissed him on the cheek. "Thank you," she whispered and backed away, clasping her hands in front of her like an embarrassed school girl. Gesturing toward the stalls, she blushed. "I got to pee again."

Harte tipped his hat. "That'd be my cue. Goodnight, Julie."

When Harte stepped back into the noise of the room, Cody Culp broke away from a small conference of law officers and approached. The other men in the group quietly studied Harte and the gun stuffed behind his belt buckle.

"We found a box-load o' drugs in the Bullochs' truck," Cody reported. "Haven't found any money. McAllister was hidin' in the Caddie at the north end of the lot. Says he was minding his own business out there . . . tryin' to stay away from the Bullochs, who'd been giving him a hard time."

"I saw him hand a box to Bobby Lee in the parking lot," Harte said. "He should have the money on him. Either that or in his car."

Cody nodded. "We'll haul the Caddie and the pickup into our compound tonight. Then, the state boys will pick them up and take them apart."

Harte nodded. "Okay with you if I come down tomorrow and give you my statement? I need to drive out to the Raburn Farm and let Jim Senior and Alma know."

"We got somebody can do that, Mr. C."

Harte shook his head and checked his wristwatch. "It ought to be me. I'll need to go see Lauren, too. I'll check with you tomorrow afternoon." When he started for the door, Cody followed, and together they walked out into the night.

"If it's all the same to you, Mr. C, I'd like to be the one to tell Lauren."

Harte stopped and studied Cody's face, seeing an obvious emotional investment. Harte nodded and looked out over the lot. Only one ambulance remained, but the lights from the police cars kept up a constant flash of blue that reflected off the customers' vehicles. Without a word the two men started walking together through the lot, their footsteps matching stride for stride.

"Why did Jim come in without backup?" Harte asked.

Cody shook his head with regret. "Sheriff Jim . . . he was always on the job. He had the night off, but he was close by, so he answered the call." Cody looked up at the gauzy sky. "I mean, nothin' was beneath him. Hell, if a cat was up a tree, he was first on the scene and first up the damn tree."

"He was with a lady friend tonight. What became of her?"

"Don't know anything about that," Cody said. "None of us knew what to expect down here till that second call came in."

Harte stopped walking, and Cody did the same. "Second call?"

Cody nodded. "Yeah, the first call was from a veterinarian. The second caller didn' leave a name. Said there was a drug deal goin' down and a lotta guns to oversee it. So, we knew we had something bigger than a barroom fight." He shook his head and scanned the parking lot. "But we sure as hell didn' figure on this."

Harte studied the side of the deputy's ebony face and knew that Cody, too, had lost an important friend. "Jim thought very highly of you, Cody. Said you were his right-hand man."

Cody turned his head away, but Harte saw the tendons in his jaws flex like clockwork. "I know he took some flak for that . . . political shit . . . but he stuck with me."

Together they gazed at the distant pink aura that hovered over the town. On this night the glow appeared as a pall of loss ready to smother the people of Lumpkin County.

"I'd better get out to the Raburn place," Harte said.

Cody stopped him with a light touch on the arm. "I need to say somethin' to you, Mr. C." He looked down at the ground for a time, and, when his head came up, his face appeared chiseled out of obsidian. "You were always a good teacher, Mr. C . . . to all us kids. But this here—" he said, pausing to look around the scene of the shootings, ". . . this here is something else altogether. You did damned good here tonight." The lines of his face softened, as if the bones beneath the skin had smoothed their edges. His moist eyes shone with the blue light from the cruisers. "I just wanted to thank you." He offered his hand, and this time Harte took it. "The sheriff'd be proud of you."

Harte made a sheepish smile. "I'll tell you something, Cody. If those headlights hadn't come on behind me, I think you boys would have been carrying me out of here tonight." They both turned to the Camry behind Harte's truck, its headlights now flickering like a dying orange moth.

"Who the hell turned 'em on?" Cody said. When Harte shook his head, Cody patted Harte's shoulder and turned. "I gotta finish up here," he said and walked back into the bar.

When Harte reached his truck and hooked his fingers on the door handle, he heard a faint mewling sound that gave him pause. When he heard it again, he turned toward the Camry. A deep guttural sound of swallowing drew him closer, and a sick feeling spread through his stomach when he saw slumped across both seats a body curled as close to the fetal position as the space allowed.

Harte opened the door, and from the shaft of light spilling from the bar he recognized Bella Seagrave in her light print dress, now sequined with tiny shards of glass. Gripping her shoulders he helped her sit upright.

"Bella?" he said softly. "Are you hurt?"

She sniffed wetly, shook her head, and then wrapped her arms around herself and shivered. Harte surveyed the damage inside the car: bullet holes, pieces of broken metal, chips of plastic, splinters of glass. Debris was scattered everywhere. The passenger side of the floor was filled with Mason jars, their gold lids neatly rowed inside a cardboard box.

He called out to the ambulance parked across the lot, and the female EMT approached at a run with her boxy black kit. "What do we have?"

"Find a blanket, a coat, anything! This woman is cold."

"I need to know if she is hurt," the medic demanded.

Harte leaned into the car. "Bella," he whispered. "Are you sure you don't have an injury?"

Bella dropped her face into her hands and nodded. "Just cold," she said, her voice muffled inside her hands. Harte knelt beside the open door and stayed with her while she cried.

"Is Sheriff Raburn dead?" she managed to ask between sobs.

Harte placed a hand on her back and moved it in slow circles. "Yes, Jim is dead." Tiny slivers of glass loosened from her dress and fell to the seat. More pieces of glass shone in her hair.

She pressed her hands harder against her face, and her shoulders shook in spasms. Harte looked around the interior of the car as if something there might explain her presence in the Camry. The silence inside the car was like the cold stillness at the bottom of a lake. He waited while she composed herself.

"He let me out on the highway," she began to explain. "I was supposed to hide in the trees. But when the gunshots went off and he backed his car onto the road, he picked me up and parked the car farther down the road. He came back here to the lot, and I waited there like he told me to. Then when I heard more gunshots, it scared me. I tried to keep waiting, but finally I couldn't sit in the car any longer." She dropped her hands into her lap and shook her head. "I know it was foolish to run this way, but I was afraid he might be hurt." She turned her raw eyes to Harte. "There was no one else to help him." She started to continue but broke into tears.

"It's all right, Bella. You don't have to talk."

He molded his hand to the back of her skull and gently nestled her head into his neck, her cheek resting against his shoulder. Her breathing moved across his skin like warm water.

"I had just gotten here," she went on, "when that tall, ugly man set down the smaller man there." She pointed through the windshield toward Harte's truck. "I could see Mr. Raburn lying on the ground. I was so scared. My legs were like jelly, so I hid in here."

Harte stared at the spider-web cracks in the windshield. The fracture lines took on a sharp white definition against the light spilling from the bar. It was like looking up at the moon through a lens of broken ice.

"Then I heard you yell at the big man," she said.

"And you turned on these lights," he said, studying the dashboard, wondering how she had found the switch in the dark. "Bella, you probably saved my life."

"I tried to fit down in the floor," she continued, "but I couldn't with that box of jars."

"Sir?" The deferential voice came from just behind Harte, and he turned his head enough to see a young black paramedic. "I was told to bring this." He held out a folded blanket, his eyes taking in the bullet-riddled interior of the car.

Harte opened up the blanket and wrapped it around Bella's shoulders. When she cinched it close to her throat, he turned back to the EMT.

165

"Can you ask one of the deputies to take this lady where she needs to go?" Harte turned to Bella and softened his voice. "Is there someone you can be with tonight? You shouldn't be alone."

She shook her head. "I'll be fine at home."

Harte turned back to the EMT. "Out near Cherokee Rose Stables. You know it?"

"Yes, sir," the young man said. "We'll get her there." He opened the door wider.

Helping her from the car, Harte could better see her misery by the flashing blue lights. She walked away on her own, refusing the arm offered by the EMT. Harte knew that this night would leave its lasting mark on her. In a matter of minutes she had witnessed a nightmare of violence that most people would not experience in a lifetime.

Returning to his truck, he locked up his gun, and turned on the engine. Looking out the window at the place where his best friend had died, he thought of Jim's parents and felt the hollow space that had opened up inside him on this night expand to a crueler dimension.

" 'Miles to go before I sleep,' " he whispered and pulled out of the lot.

# Chapter Fifteen

The pews were filled to capacity. People stood crowded at the back of the church and along the walls under the stained glass windows all the way to the altar. Harte had never seen such a gathering in the building. It was as if the county had sought refuge here from some natural catastrophe.

Harte was seated in the first pew between Jim's second wife, Sarah, on his left, and Lauren and her mother on his right. Lauren's red-rimmed eyes stared straight ahead, and the tears on her gaunt cheeks gave her face an angelic glow. Emily Raburn put an arm around her daughter's shoulders, and Lauren bobbled as if her body had arrived here without a soul. Or, perhaps, shored up on cocaine.

Harte barely heard the solemn words the preacher intoned. Nothing could be said about Jim that Harte did not already know. The flank of deputies lined up against the right wall stood attentive in their starched uniforms, their hats in their hands. Each man appeared uncomfortable and self-conscious—except Cody, who watched Lauren with the eyes of a hawk.

The service went on too long, longer than Jim would have wanted. Harte kept his head down, fingering the bandage on his little finger. The few times he looked around at the congregation, he caught someone staring at him, and, each time, that person quickly found something else to focus on.

\*\*\*\*\*

Under a gray blanket of clouds a smaller cortege of citizens followed the family to the quaint cemetery at Shady Grove, where the casket was lowered into a neatly excavated rectangular hole in the red dirt. Sarah and Emily and Jim's parents sat under a green canvas awning erected on poles. There they received a line of well-wishers. Lauren sat a little apart inside her adolescent misery, staring numbly at the hole where her father's body had been deposited. Not once did she acknowledge the mourners who leaned and tried to speak to her.

Those who came near Harte passed by with hesitant smiles and furtive glances. They nodded and, if they spoke at all, their words either directly or indirectly tried to acknowledge his friendship with the sheriff. But their expressions did not match the content of their words. In their eyes Harte could see they looked at him from some new distance. It was about the killings. What he saw in their faces could have been gratitude or fear, condemnation or pity. He hadn't a clue which.

When the rain began, most of the crowd hurried for their cars and trucks. Harte stood fast under the spreading oak, as did the deputies opposite him beside the tent, where they took the rain without cover, their hats still in their hands. Beside them, with one arm across her chest and the other hand covering her mouth, stood Jim's diminutive dispatcher, Maxie-Rose Cotillion, her tears pouring freely, faster than the rain could wash them away.

When the family approached under a caravan of umbrellas held by the funeral home ushers, Harte watched them pass, their faces like the individual tiles of a mosaic rendering a common loss. Each looked straight ahead through the rain, until Lauren turned her thin face to Harte. She broke ranks and stepped into the sunburst of spreading oak roots to stand before him. Behind her, Emily Raburn stopped and waited, expressionless as she watched her daughter.

Harte gave her what smile he could muster, leaned forward, and kissed her sunken cheek. "I'm always here for you," he said quietly into her ear. When he straightened he was surprised to see the intensity in her face. Her eyes held on his with a fierce will.

"It's only a start," she said in a jaded monotone.

He frowned and leaned forward slightly as he cocked an ear. "Sorry?"

"You stepped on two bugs," she said, her moist eyes unblinking. "There's a nest of them out there." Without breaking eye contact, she bobbed her head vaguely toward the town.

Straightening, Harte looked over Lauren's head, where her mother stood in the sodden grass, waiting. Emily's face looked pale and puffy framed inside her black veil and hat.

Harte placed his hands on Lauren's upper arms and bent slightly at the knees. "Are you getting the help you need?" he said quietly. "If I can help with that—"

Lauren shrugged him off with a show of impatience. "Why bother?" she said. Surprising him, a single dry laugh scraped up from her throat. "I'm damaged goods."

After letting him see the coldness in her stare, she turned and rejoined her mother, and the young usher tried in vain to cover both women with his umbrella as they made their way to the parking lot. Lauren walked ahead briskly, impervious to the rain.

Bringing up the rear of the retreat, Callie huddled under Layland Childers' umbrella. When she spotted Harte, her face pinched with concern. He gave her a nod to let her know that he was all right. Then one of her high-heels caught a root and she stumbled, catching herself on Layland's arm. She did not look back again.

Lyle Ferribee, the chair of the county commissioners, marched deliberately to Harte, turned, and took a place beside him. Together they watched the funeral home director instruct the two workers—one black, one white—who had stood patiently behind the tent. Both wore hooded

169

raincoats, but their blue work pants were soaked and molded to their legs.

"Hell of a thing," Lyle said. "Jim served us for a lot o' years. He deserved better'n this."

Harte was barely listening, paying attention instead to the steady percussion of the rain in the leaves overhead and the sporadic taps becoming more frequent on his head. The workmen shuffled forward without enthusiasm and sank their shovels into the neat pile of dirt beside the open grave. Each time a shovelful of dirt thumped on the casket, Harte thought of the words Lauren Raburn had spoken to him and wondered how much she had shared with her father.

"We can sure use this rain," Lyle said.

Harte watched the last of the mourners move down the grassy hill, weaving through the haphazard pattern of gravestones. All that dark clothing . . . retreating in such abject sorrow . . . it was like a uniformed army disbanding after the final defeat.

"Listen, Harte, I know this is not the time or the place . . . but the commission would like to talk to you . . . and soon. Can you come by in the morning?"

Harte kept his eyes on the cavity in the earth. "I've got school tomorrow, Lyle."

"Well, what about after that? What time do you finish up?"

Harte planned to spend time with the horses, not just today after the funeral but every afternoon after school until he left for Montana. He imagined himself riding the paint into the mountains within an hour, getting lost for a while, enjoying the companionship of a friend who had no interest in talking. And later he had in mind to stop by to check on Bella. He had not seen her here today. As he thought about her now, he imagined her sitting in that Camry, all that glass shining like jewelry in her hair and on her clothes . . . and her watching all that killing.

"Can't come by tomorrow, Lyle." He turned to look at the commissioner. "I just can't."

Lyle slipped his hands into his pants pockets and watched the workmen fill the grave. His fingers began turning coins in his pockets, the sound a discordant accompaniment to the rain.

"Then let me buy you a cup of coffee right now, Harte. It's important."

Harte turned. "Now?"

"Now," Lyle said, punctuating the word with the authority of his position.

Harte checked his watch. "I'm going by the hospital to see the Dillard boy."

"He's already been released. He's doin' fine. The family has tried to get in touch with you to thank you for all you did, but I guess you're not at home anymore. Do you have a cell phone?"

"No service where I'm staying. Why don't you just tell me what's on your mind."

Lyle's coins stopped jangling, and his chest expanded with a deep intake of air. "Harte, what you did out there at Luther's . . . well, it's got all of us on the commission talking. Three men against one . . . and you handled them all." Ferribee arched his eyebrows and looked down at the sprawl of roots at their feet. He began shaking his head in tiny increments. "It almost defies belief, Harte."

The commissioner turned to show the in-charge lift of his chin. "We've got this unspeakable tragedy here, and our county feels like it's been violated. We've lost an important man." He reached out and started to touch Harte's arm at the elbow but changed his mind. "But something happened that helps to balance that out some. You brought us instant justice. The plainest way to say it is that you've given us some hope, Harte. And the county can use that right now."

Harte stared out at the rain-soaked gravestones in the lawn. "I was just trying to stay alive, Lyle." He frowned. "If I'd done things a little sooner . . . or better . . . Jim might still be alive."

Lyle took Harte's arm now and shook with enough force to jostle Harte's shoulders. "Now, don't you be talkin' like that. That was one hellava tough situation out there in that parking lot. You did just fine. *Better* than fine. Better than any other man I know, including the sheriff's deputies. I doubt anyone else could have survived those Bullochs. How the hell'd you learn to shoot like that?"

"It just played out the way it did. Wasn't anything to do but just try and survive it."

"That's what I mean, Harte. You did what you had to do, and it was the goddamn right thing! And you didn't fold! The odds were all against you. Hell, those boys could have killed everybody in the bar. Luther told me how you talked those boys out of there. That was smart. Real smart."

"They were going out anyway . . . for the drug sale. I was just trying to get to my gun."

Lyle licked his lips. "Exactly. That was smart." He released Harte's arm, and his face took on the formality of a business transaction. "Harte, we want you to think about taking over Jim Raburn's position as county sheriff. The whole commission backs you on this. There will be an election in November, but right now we want you to fill that spot by special appointment. Come election time, there'll be a landslide vote in your favor anyway."

Harte suddenly felt like a stranger talking to this man he had known all his life. When the rain had begun earlier, he had let himself believe that the weeping tree above him was shedding surrogate tears for him as he tried to hold himself together. Now the old oak seemed to be bleeding.

"I don't know anything about running a sheriff's office, Lyle. I'm a teacher."

Ferribee smiled. "You have the respect of every man on the force, and there are plenty there who can help you learn the system. You run a classroom of teenagers, which means you are a leader of the most challenging of groups. Our deputies are ready to follow your lead, believe me. I've already talked to a few of them about it."

When the rain let up to a fine mist, the workmen peeled off their hoods and continued their job without talking. For Harte the slice of the shovel blades into the wet dirt evoked the smell of field work and memories of his childhood on the farm.

"I'm a little old for it, Lyle, don't you think?"

Ferribee pushed out his lower lip. "Same age Jim was."

"Jim was coming to the end of his career. I guess I'm doing about the same."

"Harte, the sheriff's job takes the kind of wisdom that comes with years. The young bucks can do the footwork, and they'll work hard for you. They look up to you."

Harte stared at the grave, wondering what Jim might have to say about this. The dirt had ceased making any sound as it fell into the grave. The men worked mechanically. They could have been a crew covering a buried power line or filling a pothole in the highway.

"Can I think on this, Lyle?"

"Well, o' course you can. Let me give you a call tomorrow. Would that be all right?"

Harte lifted one corner of his mouth. "How 'bout I call you?"

"Well," Lyle said, "all right, but I need to hear from you by late morning, okay?"

Harte turned his gaze beyond the iron fence to the wet forest beyond. Inhaling deeply, he wondered what smells he would miss if he went to

Montana. He knew they had the Big Horns and the Bitterroots there, but he knew enough not to expect those mountains to be like the Appalachians.

"I'll call you," he promised.

When Lyle gathered his raincoat collar under his chin and hurried to his car, Harte walked to the grave and stood within an arm's reach of the men with the shovels, waiting to see which of them would notice him first. "Do you mind?" he said, reaching out with an open hand.

The older man straightened, lowered the shovel blade to the ground and laced his fingers over the rounded end of the haft. The other man stopped with a load of dirt and stared at Harte.

"Augustus, isn't it? You're not working for the county anymore?"

The man smiled, his teeth radiant against his dark skin. "Me and Linus wanted to do somethin' for Mistah Jim."

Harte continued to hold out his hand. "My turn," he said. "You two go get a hot drink someplace where it's dry. I'll finish up."

The two men exchanged glances, and then Augustus surrendered the shovel. Linus dropped his load into the pit and then stabbed his shovel into the sod.

"The funeral man say to leave the shovels under the canvas here."

Harte nodded and pushed the shovel blade into the dirt with his shoe. The two men watched for a time as he filled the hole. He wasn't sure when they left, but when he shook out what dirt was left on the underlying tarp, he was the only man left standing in the graveyard.

*****

He took the paint—the one called "Pied Piper"—through a stand of beeches and hemlocks along the creek's floodplain, until the trail began to climb toward Locust Ridge. On the high ground they followed the ridge path that wove through the thick-barked trunks of chestnut oaks, around which a few of their oversized acorns had already fallen. Atop one of the larger rock outcrops, a great slab of lichen-frilled stone lay flat against the slope of the land. From there he could see down to the rich green island of the Haversack's pasture. Off to the west, he made out Bella's apple trees and the roofline of her little house.

Descending by the Three Forks Trail he bottomed out at the creek and spotted the fresh tracks of a horse cutting his trail, and he knew that Collette was taking a creek-side ride toward the old Blackshear mill. Harte eased the paint down the bank and let the mare drink her fill. Listening to the horse suck up the cool water, he envied the simplicity of her needs. It was an uncomplicated life, or so he believed. He dismounted and stood in the shallow creek, the water rippling below the ankles of his boots. Standing beside the mare, he watched her velvet muzzle dip purposefully into a pool where the current was slow.

"A lady oughta have a drink sometime without someone on her back," he said.

At the sound of his voice, the horse rolled her eyes but kept drinking. Finally, her head came up with beads of water dripping from the stainless steel bit like a string of glass beads catching light from the sky. The paint turned her muscular neck to look at Harte.

"What do you think, girl . . . a burned out schoolteacher being sheriff?" Harte stroked the horse's flank. "Here I am in the middle of a stream pondering on changing horses."

The paint lowered her head again and drank. Soon satisfied, she snorted, and Harte led her up the far bank, mounted, and rode out into the muted light of the overcast sky hovering over the meadow. He sidled the paint up to the plank gate and, leaning from the saddle, opened it just enough for the horse to enter. Reining around, he closed it by backing the horse into the grass. The maneuver was an act of perfect harmony between horse and rider, and Harte leaned to stroke her neck.

"We're gettin' there, aren't we, girl?"

He rode the fence line up the hill until he was just shy of the new section of barbed wire. There he dismounted and tied the paint off to one of the older posts, leaving her with enough slack to graze without getting involved with the wire. Harte scissored through the wood rails and walked through the little orchard, admiring the yield of apples now reddening on the branches.

Before he had cleared the trees, Bella's door opened. She stood in the doorway and waited, a white apron wrapped around her flannel shirt and jeans. Her face was unreadable. He wasn't sure what he would say to her, but he felt nothing anxious about their meeting. The words, he knew, would come.

Stopping below the back stoop, he took off his hat, and they looked at one another as she dried her hands on a kitchen towel. She hung the towel on the door knob and stepped into the grass, where they stood side by side facing the orchard.

"I hardly knew him," she said quietly. "I didn't feel that I should go to the funeral. I knew he had two ex-wives and a daughter who would be there, so—"

Though he knew she wasn't looking at him, Harte nodded.

"I'd met him only the once," she said, "when he came out to see about the problem with the horses and my trees. And then later he called. He asked me out to dinner."

When she sat on the bottom step, Harte did the same. Turning his hat on his hand, he spoke softly.

"Jim always had good taste in women. I guess it was just hard to make a marriage work as a sheriff." He stopped turning his hat and tested the tightness of the leather band around the crown. "I guess he was married to his job because people depended on him. He was a good mediator." Harte turned to see how she was receiving his words, but her face showed nothing. "In all his years as a peace officer," Harte went on, "he never had to kill a man."

"Those men," she said in a whisper, ". . . the Bullochs . . . what was wrong with them?"

He shook his head. "Somewhere along the way, I guess they made a choice, Bella. Good versus evil, I guess you'd say. They were all hopped up on drugs."

"You make it sound like they were *all* bad . . . with *nothing* good inside them."

Reinforcing the crease in the crown of his hat, Harte thought about that, and then he propped the hat on his knee. "Well . . . if there was any good in them . . . they never showed it to me or anybody else who was there that night."

A breeze wafted out of the north and lifted their faces. The coolness in the air carried a promise of the coming change of the season. A fine drizzle began to stipple the grass, and the pinto nickered. Harte looked through the trees and saw the spotted head hanging over the top fence rail.

"I just wanted to stop by and see how you were doing," Harte said, putting on his hat.

Bella showed no response that he could see. When she narrowed her eyes, he caught a glimpse of what she might have looked like as a little girl turning a question in her mind.

"Are there really men who are so evil, Harte?" Her eyes turned opaque and hard.

"Some people play with a different deck that most of us can't even imagine, Bella. For whatever reason, the Bullochs were bad men."

Her eyes angled to the ground. "People can change, you know. It happens."

Harte pursed his lips. "Maybe. Or maybe those boys had the bad bred into them so deep there was no losing it."

"But we'll never know," she said. "When you kill a man, you take away the chance to change."

He looked down into his hands for a time, wondering if, in Bella's eyes, a man who killed out of necessity was any better than one who killed for pleasure.

"I'd better get to the barn," he said and stood. "Take care of yourself, Bella."

As he turned to leave, her hand slipped into his, stopping him. She rose and, with her head bowed, lifted his hand in both of hers, studying the bandage on his finger.

"I know there must be a price you paid, too," she said. "Sometimes we have to do things we're not prepared to do . . . just to survive." She brought up her eyes. "I'm glad you're all right."

Pursing his lips, he stared off into the middle distance and thought about what she'd said. "The truth is, I didn't mind killing them. In some strange way, I think I was prepared to do it."

The skin on her brow wrinkled with three lines. "I'm not sure I can understand that, Harte . . . but I suppose I should be glad you were 'prepared.' " She released his hand and stuffed her own hands into the pockets of the apron. "You could have easily died that night . . . just like Jim."

She walked to the nearest tree, picked an early red apple, and dropped it into one pocket as she continued on to the fence. There she carefully raised a hand to the paint's head, testing its tolerance, and stroked the long nasal bone.

Harte followed her, stepped through the fence rails, and unlooped the reins from the post. When he mounted, the wet saddle leather groaned. As if to answer this sound, a distant thunder rolled far off to the west. The paint nickered nervously and sidestepped. He steadied the horse and then looked down at Bella. The rain had flattened her hair, and tiny droplets of water bejeweled the shoulders of her flannel shirt much the way the splinters of glass had clung to her inside the Camry.

"Are you still thinking about Montana?" she said.

He smiled. "I'll probably always be thinking about Montana, but I might stick for a while."

She dug out the apple from her pocket and tossed it to him. "For you and your horse."

After shifting his grip on the fruit, he broke it open between his palms and tossed half back to her. "Offer it to her on the flat of your palm," he said, "and you might make a friend for life."

She did as instructed, and the paint took the offering with enthusiasm. It was the first time Harte had seen Bella really smile since the first day he had met her.

"So," she said and looked directly at Harte. "Friends for life now?"

He frowned down at the half still in his hand. "Wasn't there a scene like this in the Bible?"

"No horses," she said. "I think there was a reptile involved."

As she held a poker face, he took a bite out of the apple and chewed. He smiled just enough to relay his thanks and then reined the paint around to head for the barn. With a *chick-chick* from the side of his mouth, he nudged the horse's flanks with the heels of his boots. The paint lunged into a gallop from a standstill. Horse and rider took off across the grass in a burst of shared freedom, and Harte felt the hollow space that had taken up residence inside his chest the last few days fill with an unexpected ballast. He could sense something pulling at him . . .

like a compass needle sluing to true north. It was in that moment he knew that he would take the offer to become sheriff of Lumpkin County.

# Chapter Sixteen

It was Friday and the last day of the summer session. Before class, Harte had posted the final grades outside his door, and with all the students passing the course, the general mood was festive. They spent the morning going over the most frequently missed questions on the exam, but after lunch they gave up all pretense of doing anything relating to history. Instead, the afternoon hours passed pleasantly enough with relaxed conversations about potential vocations, avocations, and the occasional career planned for some other part of the state or country.

Lauren Raburn was back. Harte had expected her to attend the last day, so he had invoked a mandate on the class: there would be no talk about the shooting incident. He had not allowed it at all in the classroom, but he had overheard students in the hallway and at lunch, as they dramatized the details as if they themselves had been eye witnesses, inflating the story like a summer blockbuster action movie.

Lauren sat in her private world and added nothing to the conversations going on around her. When Harte saw Collette put a card on Lauren's desk, he stood and signaled for quiet.

"We're almost done here," he began. "I just wanted to thank you all for putting in the time for study that made this an unprecedented one hundred percent passing class. Congratulations."

After the students applauded themselves, Streak stood with both hands in his pockets, his shoulders hiked up to his ears. "Mr. C," he began formally, "we heard you were leaving . . . the school, I mean. So we all chipped in and, like, got you something to remember us by. Well, actually, to, I guess, celebrate your career." Streak paused to look at Lamar and then Lonny, as if he expected some ribbing, but they were hanging onto his every word.

Harte sat against the front of his desk and waited. "I guess we're your last students," Streak continued. "So—" He reached into his desk and brought out a small package. "We got you—well, Collette really—she found it on the Internet. But we all chipped in." Streak hesitated and then leaned to Collette's desk and set down the package. "You oughta be the one to do this," he mumbled to her.

Someone started a steady cadence of Collette's name, and the others joined in, until the chant coaxed her to her feet. She approached the front of the room, and the students clapped again. Standing before her teacher, Collette produced a rare smile and offered the gift. When Harte took it, the class applauded again, and Collette returned to her seat.

"Open it, Mr. C!" Lonny prodded.

It was a small box wrapped in plain brown paper and tied with green baling twine that he recognized from the hay storage at Cherokee Rose. He removed the lid and right away recognized the card that Collette had slipped to Lauren a few minutes earlier. The front of the card showed a pre-printed *Thank You*, and inside he found fourteen signatures crowded into the white space. The pleasing smell of new leather rose to him from the box. A belt was tightly coiled inside. It was a rich golden brown mottled by darker blotches, reminding him of aged parchment.

"Take it out, Mr. C!" Streak prompted.

He held the belt high and let gravity unroll the coil, until a gold and silver buckle swung at the bottom. The metalwork ambushed him like a bucket of ice water. On a beveled brass plate was attached an antique badge, once silver, he knew, but now discolored and pockmarked by time. The shield read "Deputy U.S. Marshal," just like the ones worn in the nineteenth century.

"My pop soldered the badge on, Mr. C," Lamar announced.

Running his thumb over the recessed letters, Harte felt a pressure in his throat, like a smooth stone he was trying to swallow . . . but couldn't.

Straightening before his desk, he unbuckled the belt Callie had bought him years ago and whipped it off. Streak and Lonny provided the appropriate catcalls and whistles. Harte tossed the old belt to Lamar.

"That ought to fit you," Harte said. Everyone but Lamar laughed.

Harte threaded the new belt through his pant loops and hooked the handsome buckle. It was a good fit. When he looked up, the students' attention was fixed on his waistline.

"Thank you, everyone. This means a lot to me." He studied the buckle and was surprised to feel a little piece of that magic that he remembered from his childhood on the day he had purchased the antiquated Colt Peacemaker. Harte sat back on the edge of his desk and indulged in a last contemplative appraisal of his students—who they might become, what they might achieve, where they might go. Then he checked the clock and smiled. "Now get out of here. Go enjoy what's left of your summer break."

The students roiled into action. Crosscurrents of conversations shot across the room, and bodies began to stream out the door in an air of celebration. Their voices filled the hallway, and someone whooped a victory cry that shattered the limits of hall protocol. Laughter resonated down the corridor. Collette and Lauren were talking quietly as they gathered their books, and as they started out Harte stepped into Lauren's path. Against school policy, he put his arms around her and gathered her into him. Limp and unresponsive, she felt like a bag of sticks.

"I'll be by to see you and your mother," Harte said. "Meanwhile, if you need anything—" Remembering that he had no telephone on the mountain, he left the sentence unfinished. When he stepped back from her, Lauren stared at the floor, waiting as though it were her duty to hear him out. When he said nothing more, she walked in measured steps to the door and Collette followed.

"Collette?" Harte said, stopping her. "What's next for you?"

She withdrew behind lackluster eyes. "I'll be staying with Father," she said quietly.

Harte nodded and tempered his voice for kindness. "Have you thought about a facility? There is financial assistance for this kind of thing, you know."

The smile that crept onto her mouth made his heart shrink. It was, he supposed, a symbol of pity for the things he did not understand about caring for an invalid parent.

"I'll be staying with Father," she said again. There was no mocking or reprimand in repeating her answer. She spoke the words exactly as she had before.

Harte nodded. "Well, I suppose I'll see you out at the stables."

Collette's eyes angled to the window. "We need to find a new place to live, Mr. Canaday." She put on a brave face and met his eyes. "If you hear of a place where I might be able to trade off for some work, I'd appreciate it if you'd let me know."

As he watched her, a dark cloud seemed to pass across her soul. He wanted to ask more, but her need to leave the room was obvious.

"Thank you for a good course, Mr. Canaday. You're an excellent teacher."

For the briefest moment he imagined a veiled cry for help behind the dullness in her eyes, but the image vanished when she walked out and left him staring at the empty doorway. In her place appeared Morris Blackadar, snapping Harte out of his reverie. The principal clasped his hands into a double fist that he shook once like a sign of victory.

"Well, I see you managed to pass everyone, Mr. Canaday."

Harte sat at his desk, opened a drawer, and began setting the contents on top of his desk. "It was the students who managed to pass, Morris . . . not *me* passing *them*."

Blackadar waved away the mincing of words and watched Harte continue to empty his desk. "So you're really calling it quits?"

Harte opened another drawer. "I am."

Blackadar strolled into the room. "Couple more years and your retirement benefits would improve substantially. Are you really burned out that badly?"

Harte sat back in his chair and gave Blackadar his full attention. "There is that. But there's something else I need to do."

When the principal asked nothing more, Harte opened another drawer.

"Harte," Blackadar said, his tone like a confessor in a booth. "I never told the board about the parking lot incident and your gun. I was trying to get you to stay on."

"I know that, Morris." Harte stuffed his personal things into his briefcase, leaving one paper on the desk, which he handed to Blackadar. "Would you file this retirement form for me?"

Blackadar sighed. "Yes . . . reluctantly." He scanned the paper and came up with a hopeful smile. "If you *did* stay on, I could see about getting you more money for those replacement textbooks you've been wanting."

Harte snapped the briefcase lock. "Too little, too late, Morris." He stood to offer his hand, and Blackadar took it. They shook with a firm grip. When Blackadar loosened his hold and tried to withdraw his hand, Harte held firm.

"Try loosening up a little, Morris. Let your teachers know you appreciate them. Let them work out of teamwork instead of on eggshells. They've got enough problems with their students without having to skirmish with their principal."

Pulling in his lips, Blackadar nodded, taking the lecture with unexpected grace. "You are the best I've had, Harte. We'll miss you." He coughed up an embarrassed laugh. "*I'll* miss you."

Harte gave the man a crooked grin. "Maybe you're not quite the stiff-necked, anal-retentive, bureaucratic bastard you make yourself out to be, Morris."

Blackadar tried to stiffen but didn't quite pull it off. "I'm just trying to do my job and hang on to it . . . just like everybody else." He pumped Harte's hand again. "Good luck to you." The words seemed both heartfelt and hopeful.

After the principal's footsteps grew faint in the hall, Harte set down the briefcase and sat back against the edge of his desk. He looked around the room at the posters he had pinned to the walls, at the large postcolonial flag that was Georgia's first, at the maps and time lines he had framed for reference. He gazed out the windows at the parking lot—the only view of the world afforded him from his classroom for all these years.

When he turned back to the empty desks, a gallery of faces filled his mind, running back to students who would now be well into their careers and rearing children. These faces were the closest thing he had to an extended family, and they were spread out all over the country.

Last, he stared at Collette's desk and considered the courageous life the quiet girl had fashioned for herself. She was the class's unsung hero, who might never be acknowledged for her accomplishments. Harte seldom felt the vacuum of having no child of his own, but, if he did, it would be the memory of students like Collette that he would depend on to fill that void.

A series of taps turned his head to the window. A wren perched on the concrete sill and pecked at the glass. He wondered for a moment if the world were sending him an omen. Maybe the bird was telling him to remain at school and peck away at being a teacher. When the wren kept jabbing at the bottom corner of the pane, Harte got up and walked slowly toward the window. When he stopped three feet away, he could see the wren was dismantling a dirt dauber's nest and gorging on wasp larvae. He laughed quietly. If there was a message here, perhaps it was about cleaning up the county.

# Chapter Seventeen

In a week's time, he wore the badge. It was seven o'clock in the morning. Sitting behind Jim Raburn's desk, he plodded through a manual that had been issued by the state back in the seventies. The dispatcher—a petite fireball in her thirties named Maxie-Rose Cotillion—had brought him coffee, the manual, and the assurance of privacy during his sheriff's tutorial. After an hour of this, he picked up the phone and asked Maxie-Rose to send in Cody Culp.

"Cody's out doing surveillance on a tip we got about a meth lab."

"Where?"

"It's out Pot Leg Road. He's been out there since before dawn."

"Call him in for me, would you, Maxie?"

"Sher'ff, he won't be in his car, and he won't be carryin' his radio, that or it'll be turned off. He's prob'ly up a tree sharin' a nest with a squirrel."

Harte frowned at that image. "Are we talking about the Moody place?"

Five seconds ticked by before she answered. "How in the Sam Hill did you know that?"

Harte shrugged. "Only so many houses out there. Moodys would be my guess."

Five more seconds passed. "Well, I guess that figures."

"Maxie, I want everything having to do with drugs to go through me first, understood?"

"Yes'r. Oh . . . the GBI called. They found nothing in McAllister's Cadillac. No drugs, no gun, no money, nothing of interest." When he made no reply, she added, "Bye!" and hung up.

Ten minutes later, two sharp raps sounded just before Maxie-Rose opened his door. She stood in the doorway in her jeans and white blouse and could have passed for a slight-of-frame high school halfback. Her short-cropped hair made golden brown parentheses around her face.

"Sher'ff, I got me a headache. Permission to take two *Advils*?"

Holding his poker face, Harte leaned back in his chair. "This my initiation into office?"

Maxie-Rose smiled and walked into the room with a sprightly bounce. "I'm sorta the keeper o' the spirits 'round the office, Sher'ff." She leaned one stiff arm on the desk, crossed her legs at the ankles, and propped the other hand on her hip. "This place would be a morgue without me. I appointed myself to the position. Sher'ff Jim called it 'a spree of décor.' " She straightened and her face turned as sober as a banker turning down a loan. "But I want you to know . . . when I'm on that dispatch radio, I'm all business . . . hun'erd percent. You won't hear joke one out o' me. You can hang your hat on that." Her blue eyes darkened when she turned serious.

"It's been awful moody and sad-like 'round here since Sher'ff Jim died. I cain't hardly tell you how it's hit me." Her eyes glazed over like mirrors and reflected the light from the window. "I don't mean no offense to you, but I miss Sher'ff Jim, and I think he saw it as part o' my job to keep up the morale here, and that's what I think he'd want me still to be doin'." She pulled in her lower lip with her teeth and studied the room as if making sure everything was in order.

"Maxie, I'll need some help learning the ropes."

Her brow lowered as she searched his eyes for a meaning. "What ropes?"

Harte cranked circles in the air with his hand. "How things work in the office. Those ropes."

"O-h-h-h," she sang on a long downslide of notes. "I can do that all right. I'm the glue that holds this bunch together. 'Cept for Cody, that is. He's the engine in this bus. The rest of 'em need a instruction booklet on how to git on board, if you ask me." She dipped her head to one side as a concession. "Well . . . there's Joe-Joe . . . he might show some promise." She squinted her eyes and wagged a finger at Harte. "I knew there was somethin'. You're growin' a moustache!"

Harte pointed across the room. "Maxie, I want to move that file cabinet over by the door and set up a bunk for myself by that wall. Any problem with that?"

"*You're* the sher'ff," she chirped. "Plannin' on some naps, are you?"

"I plan on living here."

She pushed out her lower lip and considered the space in the room. "What about a sofa that folds out into a bed? Might look better for a sheriff's office."

"Think you could look into that for me? And maybe a small stand-up closet?"

"Yes'r, I can handle that." She cocked her head to one side. "What about a uniform, Sher'ff."

Harte stared down at the manual. "Is that mandatory?"

Maxie shrugged. "I guess you can wear whatever you want. Like I said, 'you're the sher'ff.' "

He nodded. "If I ever need it, I can use one of Jim's." He pointed to a cardboard box in the corner. "The family passed on some of his things to me."

She poked a thumb over her shoulder. "Let me git back to the dispatch and see can I round up Cody for you, Sher'ff. Then I'll git on the In'ernet and find you a nice chifforobe." She walked her fast-paced gait to the door.

"Maxie?"

She stopped and turned with the same quick energy and then stilled herself like a retriever on point. Harte opened his school briefcase and pulled out the blue enamel coffee pot and cup.

"Is there a hotplate around here I can use?"

Perking up, she clapped her hands. "We got one in storage. Meeks—he's the day-shift jailer—he used to make soup on it, but he cain't eat nothin' hot now on account o' his ulcer. I'll hunt it up and dust it off for you." As she studied the blue kettle, a question showed on her face, but she didn't ask it. She turned to go.

"One more thing," Harte said. She stopped again. "No need to run *Advil* requests by me."

"Yes'r," she said with sober contrition, but she was giggling as she closed the door.

\*\*\*\*\*

Cody Culp came into the office just before the lunch hour. Bits and pieces of bark and grass and seeds clung to the front of his camo sweat suit. Wet mud stains covered his chest, hips, and thighs. By the way he dropped into the chair across from the desk, Harte could see that this was not Cody's first informal parley in the sheriff's office.

"Growing a moustache, Mr. C?" Cody said.

Harte nodded. "Learn anything out there at the Moody place?"

Cody sat up straighter. "They got a pre-fab aluminum shed, forty by twenty, behind the house 'bout thirty yards into the woods. Looks like meth."

"How do you know?"

"Old propane tank outside's got a brass fitting turned green as a traffic light. That means ammonium hydroxide. And *that* means meth.

191

Maybe more. I was set up by two in the morning. Seven cars came in, each one staying five or ten minutes. I got the tags."

"That it?"

"Sun comes up, no more visitors. Moodys come out of the shed about an hour after dawn. Both of 'em got bandanas hanging loose around their necks. Cheapo breathing filters. Garret's jacked up like the guy sells that miracle cleaning chemical on TV, talking a mile a minute. Then they chain a mean-looking pit bull by each door of the shed, and the brothers go into the house."

They were quiet for a time as Harte studied the deputy's face. "Hard being deputy in this county as a black man?"

Cody's muscular body made the merest of bounces as he allowed a single quiet laugh through his nose. "I worked for Atlan'a police for a year. Down there . . . most o' the ones we hauled into jail were black. Makes you feel like part o' the problem. Up here, black is more like bein' from Mars." He patted the Glock in the holster at his side. "But you carry a gun and a badge, black is like a bear showin' up in the back seat of your car while you're drivin' ninety down the freeway. Ain't a whole lot you can do about it."

Harte turned around the manual and pushed it toward Cody. "Ever read this?"

"Never been asked to. Sheriff Jim taught me all I needed to know about policin' this county."

Harte tossed the book into a drawer. "It's like learning Arabic from an Eskimo." He laid his forearms on the desktop. "I'm going to need to get up to speed, and I'll need your help with that. How about having lunch with me right now?"

Cody nodded. "Yeah, I need to talk to you, too. Let me go clean up." He stood.

"I'll ask Maxie to get a warrant for the Moodys," Harte said and put a hand on the phone. "Rainbow Grill okay?"

Cody arched his eyebrows and paused. "Rainbow's run by Jerry Nichols. He won't say so to your face, but he don't much care for blacks comin' in."

Harte knew that this information had been offered for his own image as the new sheriff. He crossed his arms over his chest and leaned back deeper into his chair.

"Then why don't we go as bears with badges."

Cody shrugged. "You pretty pale for a black bear."

"I'll be a polar bear . . . visiting on special assignment."

\*\*\*\*\*

They sat in the back booth, talked about office protocol, and worked on their chicken fried steaks, mashed potatoes, and vegetable medley. Cody wore a freshly ironed uniform. The waitress, who had not been indoctrinated into Jerry Nichol's racist policy, had eyed Cody like he was a fudge sundae.

"You still gettin' hounded by the press, Sheriff?"

Harte shook his head as he chewed. "That should be old news by now." Harte set down his fork and wiped his mouth with his napkin. "Are you still into martial arts?"

"Oh, yeah," Cody purred. "I teach it now. Share a little studio with a friend out on highway nine. Myself, I'm into the competitive end."

Harte nodded. "You find that useful in your work?"

Cody's smile broke across his face like the cover coming off a piano keyboard. "Oh, yeah," he sang again. Then the smile was gone as quickly as it had arrived. "But I'll tell you . . . once the word gets out, it's mostly the potential that works for you."

"You mean . . . a reputation?"

Cody nodded and pointed a finger at Harte. "Same way it's gonna work for you."

Keeping his eyes on his deputy's face, Harte wiped his mouth again to hide his frown.

Cody waggled his fingers in a come-hither gesture. "Listen," he said, leaning forward. "I know . . . that *you* know . . . exactly what I'm talkin' about. I read your Jesse James article. Came a time when all Jesse had to do was introduce himself to a bank teller. The reputation did the rest."

"I'm not so sure that reputation sits too well with everybody in this county," Harte confided.

Cody laughed. "Gonna sit real fine when somebody is thinkin' on goin' up against you."

As they waited for dessert, Harte continued drilling his deputy with a long list of questions. Cody had instant answers to each one, and he provided insights on details about which Harte did not know to ask. It was easy to see why Cody Culp had been Jim Raburn's right hand.

"On the force, who's dependable?" Harte asked. "I mean, when the situation gets gritty?"

Cody looked Harte dead in the eyes. "You," he said in a level voice. "And me."

"Tell me about that," Harte said. "And forget about any idea of ratting out your friends."

Cody steepled his hands and rubbed them together, the sound dry and whispery. "First of all, they ain't all my friends. Everybody in the office hasn't bought into civil rights. I gotta watch out for my own back most o' the time. You know what I mean?"

Harte nodded. "Just tell me about them."

Cody counted off on his fingers. "Okay, you got your jailer, Meeks. We get along. He's steady enough at what he does. We pull him out into the field when we need more numbers, but he ain't much with a gun, and he's slow to move in. Says he's got a bad gut. Think maybe it's more like *no* guts. He'll be the last one through the door every time."

"You got six more deputies," Cody continued. "Three of 'em couldn't get a brawlin' biker out of a bar without a thirty-minute parley. They're whiners. Afraid to represent the law and more afraid about what folks think of 'em. That's Beasley, Fortenberry, and Hooper. Ask me, they're in the wrong line of work. I wouldn' want any of 'em coverin' my ass."

"Burns, he's a hard-ass. He'd throw his grandmother on the ground and cuff her. Sooner or later there'll be a complaint. He's useful, but only in certain situations. He's not useful to me 'cause of my color. Only name he ever uses on me is 'boy.' But he'll be the first man through a door. Thinks he's got Kevlar skin. He's not smart. He's aggressive. Probably get shot one day goin' up against the wrong crowd."

Cody's face lost its hard edge. "Joe-Joe Chester does a good job. Me and him get along. You give him a job, he'll get it done.

"That leaves the blond one," Harte said.

"Ash," Cody said and squinted one eye. "Roland Ash . . . he's a hard one to figure."

"Roland?" Harte said, frowning. "What name does he go by?"

" 'Ash,' " Cody replied without hesitation.

"Okay, tell me about Ash."

Cody shifted in his seat and settled in for the telling. "Talks friendly enough around me, but word gets back that he says he works with a coon who thinks he's a Green Beret. He's smarter than he lets on. And he's got some sand. I've seen 'im stand up while bullets are flying all over hell, and he returns fire as cool as a preacher baptizin' a baby. Other times I've seen 'im hunker down with his gun jammed. Thing is . . . I've never seen his gun jam at the shootin' range. Even checked it once while he was in the shower. Nothin' wrong with his Glock. And I know guns."

"What about Maxie-Rose?" Harte asked.

Cody sat back and pushed a series of hissing laughs through his teeth. "Give *her* a gun and I think we could clean up the county inside a week." He waved away his joke and sat forward. "She's good. Dependable. Stays cool on the radio when all hell is breakin' loose."

"Are you the chief deputy?"

"Sheriff Jim never made such a rank. But I know he thought of me that way. He said as much. Just couldn't make it official. Said it would put a dent in the morale."

"I'm making such a rank right now," Harte announced. "You are my chief deputy."

The blonde waitress brought their slices of pie, and they were quiet as she poured more coffee. She gave Harte that same glance that the rest of the community was using to inspect their new gunfighter sheriff—part curiosity, part awe, part fear. It was probably the way the folks of Abilene used to look at Hickok, he decided. He would have preferred the look she gave Cody.

Harte dug into the pie with his fork, but Cody propped his elbows on the table, laced his fingers into a tight knot, the fingertips moving up and down like an idle butterfly.

"I'm leavin' the force, Mr. C," he said in an earnest voice.

Harte sipped coffee and quietly set down the cup. "Is it the racism in the department?"

Cody shook his head. "It's Lauren." He picked up his fork, poked at his pie, and laid the fork back down. "She's needin' help." Cody took in a lot of air and made a pained expression. "Long as I wear this uniform," he began, but then he only shook his head again and started from another angle. "She can't be losin' another man to a bullet."

Harte frowned. "I thought you had a family."

"Well, it's Danny's family. You remember my brother. Killed in the line of duty. I try and look after his wife and little girl much as I can." Cody's eyes softened. "I *love* Lauren, Mr. C."

Harte sipped his coffee and wondered about Lauren's mother and her social sensibilities. "That's good," Harte said. "I hope it's reciprocated."

Cody straightened and see-sawed a hand over the table. "She's just messed up right now and don't always know what she's thinkin'. She needs help, and I'm the one who needs to help her."

"Does she want that help?"

Cody forced a grim smile. "Not yet. I got to give her a reason to want it, you know?"

Harte pushed his half-eaten pie aside and stared out the front window. He thought of Lauren's vulnerability during this sinking time of her life. The one thing he knew about addiction was that only the addict could make the choice to quit.

"I hope you can do that, Cody."

The tendons in Cody's jaws knotted like chunks of granite. "Yeah, me, too."

Harte waited until Cody had sampled his pie and chased it with coffee. "Still cocaine?"

Cody stopped chewing and looked up quickly.

"Jim and I were close," Harte reminded him. "Do you know where she gets it?"

The deputy's eyes glazed over, the skin on his face hard and shining like black ice. "If I did, I'm afraid I might cross the line and kill somebody. One more reason I'd best turn in this uniform."

They were quiet for a time, each man looking down into his plate, but neither touching his food. "By the way," Cody said, "autopsy report on the Bullochs came back. Bobby Lee had more uppers than red blood cells runnin' through his system. Breed was loaded up on cocaine."

Harte looked down into his coffee cup, at the stillness of its dark surface. A dishwasher turned on behind the wall in the kitchen and set up a frenetic vibration that put the coffee into delirium tremens.

"Cody, these people bringing these drugs into our mountains . . . they're a disease. I want you to think about staying on to help me cut it out of our community."

Cody leaned forward on his thick forearms and let his face go stone-cold sober. "I've pretty much made up my mind, Sheriff . . . but I guess I can think about it."

# Chapter Eighteen

Harte took off work at three and started for his pickup in the lot. A rail-thin, thirty-ish man in a khaki suit sat on the slab bench in the small grassy area between the office and the parking lot. The crown of his head was bald, showing an oval of pallid skin. At the sound of the door closing, the man turned and came off the seat in one movement. He carried a small notebook in one hand. The other hand dug into a shirt pocket and came out with a business card.

"Sheriff Canaday?"

"Still not interested," Harte said.

"Sir, I understand your need for privacy. I'm not here to challenge that."

Harte stopped and watched the man approach. "What *are* you here for?"

The man held out the card. "Yes, I'm a reporter, but not like you think."

Harte waited with a cold smile. When the reporter did not fill the lull with a salvo of questions, Harte scanned the card.

"What can I do for you, Mr. Saldini?"

"Sheriff," the man began quietly, "it has been my experience that when a man does not want to interview with newspapermen and women, he probably does have something to say . . . just not what the reporters want to hear. I drove up here to give you that chance."

Harte looked at the card again. "I've not heard of your newspaper. *The Boost?*"

Saldini smiled. "We're new. We're an electronic newspaper . . . on the Internet."

" 'Electronic newspaper,' " Harte mumbled and smiled. "Our culture just might be remembered for its oxymorons, Mr. Saldini."

Saldini glanced down at the old pistol strapped to Harte's side. "Indeed, sir."

Harte propped his hands on his hips. "Okay, what can I do for you?"

"We're offering the public the flip side of the news, Sheriff. Nothing dark. Nothing to feed our baser side. We're publishing the good stuff. I thought there might be a way to find something good in this gory tale that you've survived."

Harte narrowed his eyes at the man. "So . . . what are you . . . New Age?"

Saldini smiled patiently. "No, sir. That term is anathema to our credo."

"Do you use words like 'anathema' in your publication?"

Saldini lifted both eyebrows and made a pleasant smile. "Sure do."

Harte bowed his head and nodded slowly. "So you want to know what it is that I want to say to the world . . . something positive."

Saldini nodded. "Yes, sir. In your own words."

Harte looked toward the end of the lot, where a rag-tag quintet of wild-haired boys were skateboarding on the downslope of the asphalt, where Jim Raburn's bullet-riddled GMC had been towed and abandoned. A tall black boy appeared at the top of the slope, set down his board, and took off on it, pushing aggressively at the pavement with one foot. When he dropped out of sight, Harte heard the grind of the wheels go hollow and then the sound disappeared abruptly. After a loud *clack* that must have been a landing, a chorus of cheers rose up like a tribal war cry.

"Mr. Saldini, when I was a boy growing up here, things were hard . . . but it was a good place . . . with good people." Harte slipped the man's card into his shirt pocket. "I'll hold onto this. When I can get this county a little closer to the way I remember it, I'll call you with some good news."

Saldini shrugged off his disappointment and offered his hand. "Fair enough, Sheriff. I wish you the best of luck."

As they shook hands a cruiser pulled into the lot and parked in front of the building. Roland Ash got out and stared across the roof of his car at the boys skating down the paved slope.

"Hey!" he yelled and snapped off his sunglasses to let the boys see his displeasure. "What'd I tell you about that!"

Harte left the reporter and stepped up behind his deputy. "Problem?"

Ash turned, surprised, but quickly exhumed his animus to glare at the boys again. "Aw, those little wise-asses are the ones cluttered up the parking lot at the shopping center. I drove 'em out of there, and now here they are at our front door." Ash's expression hardened. "Arrogant sonzabitches."

Harte studied the group of boys at the end of the lot. Two were black and of the three whites, one was Lamar Dowdy's little brother. They stared back at the two officers as if expecting instructions—all but the tallest one in back. He had jet black hair that hung over half his pallid face. Stepping on one end of his skateboard, he levered it upward in a deft move and propped it under one arm as he assumed a contrapposto stance of defiance. With his head cocked to one side, the sunlight glinted off something metallic on his face.

"Do you plan on using that end of our lot for anything?" Harte asked Ash.

Frowning, Ash turned to Harte. "What?"

"Cut 'em some slack," Harte ordered. "I'd rather have 'em hanging around the sheriff's department than a pool hall or the like, wouldn't you?"

Ash affected an indifferent shrug. "You're the boss," he said and walked to the office.

Harte walked the length of the lot to where the skaters stood. Up close he could see that the tall boy had dyed his hair so black that his face appeared bloodless. A row of small silver rings bordered the rim of one nostril like the spine of a spiral notebook.

Giving the boys a friendly nod, Harte glanced down the slope to the lower lot, where a ramp had been set up—a four-by two-foot rectangle of heavy plywood propped up at one end by a riprap of bricks.

"Well," he said, looking the boys over, "I don't see any blood or broken bones. I guess you know what you're doing."

Lamar's little brother spoke up. "You don't mind us skating here?"

Harte shook his head. "Mind if I watch a little?"

One of the boys ran to the top of the hill, *clacked* his board down on the asphalt, and began gliding down the slope. Crouching, he picked up speed on the asphalt in a high treble whir of grinding wheels that reminded Harte of his first childhood visit to a dentist. When the boy gained the ramp, the sound dropped to a brief resonant roar that cut off as soon as he went airborne. As he sailed, his feet set the board spinning on an invisible axis beneath him. By the time he landed, the board had somehow righted itself, and he was balanced atop the sandpaper surface, arms outstretched like a high-wire walker. A smile of victory stretched across the skater's face.

"Hey, Sheriff," another boy called out as he ran his skateboard up the incline. "Wanna try?"

"Not in this life," Harte said and waved as he started for his truck. "Be safe, fellows."

"Hey, are you the one that shot those dope-heads at that roadhouse?"

Harte stopped and saw that the alpha male—the boy with the hardware in his nose—awaited an answer. Alpha tossed his ink-black hair and raised his chin. "And you weren't even a cop then, right?"

Harte knew the boy was talking to impress his friends, but he also knew that the manner in which he answered could mean a lot to boys who were trying to become men. "I didn't have much of a choice," Harte said, his voice confiding and quiet.

The alpha-boy pointed at the old Colt at Harte's side. "You do it with that?"

Harte nodded. "I did."

"Looks old," Alpha said.

"It is."

With a quick jerk of his neck, Alpha whipped his hair out of his face, but it fell right back. "How old is it?"

Harte looked down at his sidearm. "Made in the decade after the Civil War." He made eye contact with each of the boys. By the common expression on their faces, Harte knew he may as well have dated it to the Iron Age.

"So, you like old stuff?" This from the boy who had demonstrated his skating prowess.

Harte smiled. "Guess I do."

The Dowdy boy cleared his throat. "Hey, Sheriff, my brother said you showed 'im how you get that thing into action. Will you show *us*?"

Harte shook his head. "Last time I did that, I found myself on the receiving end of a lecture from the school principal."

Alpha smirked. "Now that you're sheriff, you should go lecture *him* a little."

Harte had to smile. "Let me go be a sheriff somewhere else," he said. "I can see you outlaws are too busy with this ramp to shoot up the town."

*****

He drove up to Cooper Gap and struck camp. After piling everything into his truck, he took a last look at the site and drove down the mountain back into town. At the department he spent the remainder of the afternoon arranging his belongings in his office. Finding hammer and nails, a section of jail bar, and some scrap two-by-fours in the supply closet downstairs, he jerry-rigged a high bar in one corner of the room. Testing his weight on the apparatus, he pumped out a few pull-ups and dropped to the hardwood floor. Then he laid down blankets for a pallet and unrolled his sleeping bag. At best, the arrangement looked Spartan and ironic, but it was more convenient than Cooper Gap.

Maxie-Rose's shift ended at six, but she stayed late to hunt down a sofa and clothes cabinet on the Internet. Hooper, who usually took over as dispatcher on the night shift, helped Harte move the file cabinet. As they readied to do the same with the desk, Maxie burst into the room with her all-business face on. She stopped abruptly and stared at Harte with fire in her eyes.

"Beasley and Burns are out on Auraria Road. A flatbed loaded with cinder blocks lost some of its load on that curve just north o' the old Castleberry Store. Beasley said there's a mess a drugs stuffed inside the bricks. Burns is out in the woods running down the driver on foot." Her report complete, she frowned at the pull-up bar high up in one corner of the room, but she said nothing.

Harte strapped on his gun belt and lifted his hat from the coat-rack. "Maxie, go home and get some rest. Hooper will take the radio." He rifled the desk drawers, looking for the flashlight he had run across earlier in the day. Maxie-Rose opened the second drawer of the file cabinet and pulled out a two-foot-long flashlight and a small radio unit in its leather carrier.

"Here, Sher'ff, you're gonna always need to have this on when you go out in the field. You never know when you'll have to leave your vehicle, and we'll need to know where you are." She dropped some papers on his desk and tested the switch on the radio. A spurt of static crackled, the sound like a skillet full of bacon cooking in the room.

"Sher'ff," Maxie said, nodding toward the papers, "I found a fold-out sofa and a chifforobe. Have a look when you get back."

Harte gave her a nod of appreciation, "Maxie, just keep doing what you're doing till I figure all this out."

"Heck, Sher'ff Harte," she replied, her smile transforming her face. "This is what I do." Her eyes shone like blue cat's eye marbles catching direct sun. "I keep the sheriff-boat afloat."

*****

He spotted the pylons and blue flashing lights a quarter mile away. When Harte eased his pickup off the road behind the two deputy cruisers, he saw Beasley in the road rummaging through a pile of broken block in the beams of his headlights. Harte got out and noted the lettering on an abandoned truck: *Equip Enterprises.* He shone his light on the tag. It was a rental with a Chatham County plate.

"What's the story?" Harte said.

Beasley straightened, dusted off his hands, and pulled a flashlight from his rear pocket. He trained the beam on a crude pyramid of olive-green plastic bags piled on the right of way. Each bag was firm and plump from unseen contents, but the nearby weeds and dirt bank were dusted white as if a bucket of talcum powder had been thrown from a moving car.

Beasley pointed toward town. "I was coming from the north and spotted the truck pulled over . . . bricks all over the road. Some guy was frantic, stackin' the bricks back on the truck. When I slowed and he saw me, he just took off runnin' into the woods. I called it in. Burns was just a few miles up the road, so he come down and took off like a blood-hound tryin' to run the guy down. I don't think the driver had a flashlight. He didn' have more'n a coupla minutes on Burns."

Harte knelt, fingered the loose powder and smelled it. "Any idea what it is?"

Beasley aimed his light at the spill. "For all I know, could be self-rising flour, 'cept I don't think Pillsbury ships it inside concrete blocks."

Harte walked to the back of the flatbed and examined one of the blocks stacked there. Inside each cavity was a roll of burlap. He pulled one out, unwrapped it, and found a green plastic bag.

"These blocks aren't the norm," Harte said. "Spaces are more round-ed than squared."

Beasley joined him. "Makes 'em stronger," he said in an edifying tone. "S'posed to spread out the stress o' the weight on top better."

Harte gave the deputy a look. "You know something about cinder blocks?"

Beasley shrugged. "I watch the Hist'ry Channel. They got programs on everything."

Harte turned the block around and angled his flashlight beam across one of the flat surfaces. " 'A.B.W.' . . . you know what that stands for?"

Beasley shrugged again. "No idea."

Harte shut off his light. A sliver of first-quarter moon was sinking into the trees. The stars cast a faint glow on the road, but the forest beyond the embankment was black as tar.

"You're sure the runner didn't have a flashlight?"

Beasley frowned into the night. "Not that I could see." He kept thinking about it and began shaking his head. "No, he couldn' have. When I happened up on him, he was working with both hands in the dark. I guess he coulda had one stuffed in his overalls, but I never saw it."

"Can Burns track?"

"Hell, Sheriff, I don't know. He don't hunt, least far as I know. He spends all his time pumping weights in the gym."

"Any shots fired?" Harte asked.

"I didn't see a gun. Not on the man that run off. 'Course Burns had his out."

"Show me where the driver went in." Harte followed Beasley to the road bank, where the deputy moved into the weeds. Harte trained his light on a gouge in the slope.

"Burns ran in here, too, once I showed him." Beasley's light flashed into Harte's face, and the sheriff shielded his eyes with a hand. "You growin' a moustache, Sheriff?"

Another cruiser came in from the north flashing its blue lights. It pulled partially off the road, and Joe-Joe heaved his considerable weight out of the car, his flashlight beam fixed on the pile of bags stacked in the weeds.

"What's all this?" he said, approaching the contraband.

"Cocaine, probably," Harte said. "You got a tarp in your car?"

Joe-Joe glanced back at his vehicle. "Gotta rain poncho in the trunk."

Harte pointed at the drugs. "Cover this up and direct any traffic that might come along. No one is to get out of a car, understood?"

As Joe-Joe jogged heavily for his cruiser, Harte turned back to Beasley and pointed south. "Walk about thirty yards out that way. I'm going in this way. We're going to walk parallel into the woods. Sweep your light back and forth as you go."

Beasley stared at the woods for five seconds. "What're we doin', Sheriff?"

"It's too dark in the trees for a man to run without a light. He'd turn off to one side and find a place to hide. We'll keep abreast by calling out every minute or so. If you see anything that looks like it could hide a man, check it out. Pay attention to tree limbs about this high." Harte leveled a hand at his chest. "If you see any freshly broken branches, call out."

Throughout these instructions, Beasley's frown deepened. "How do I know if it's fresh?"

"You break it again and compare the color."

"To what?" Beasley whined.

"Come here," Harte said and climbed the boot-scarred bank. At the top he held his light on the nearest pine. "You see this dead branch here? The broken end is bright." He snapped the same branch an inch from the break and held the two broken ends side by side. "Look at the wood inside."

Beasley examined the sticks. "Look the same to me," he said, as if he had failed a test.

"That's because they were broken about the same time." Harte fixed his light on a neighboring tree with a dead broken limb.

"That'n's kinda grayish," Beasley said, his face screwing up with questions.

"That's an old break." Harte broke this limb and held the old break next to the new. He waited until Beasley finally caught on.

"I get it!"

They entered the woods thirty yards apart, their flashlight beams roving in broad arcs that brought the forest alive with the pulse of shadows.

Beasley called out within seconds. "You out there, Sheriff?"

"I'm here!" Harte called. "Keep moving."

Harte traveled ten more paces, and his light illuminated the bright edge of a broken pine limb pointed right at him. He shone the light on the ground and spotted the piece that had broken off. The pine needles were bunched and scuffed on a trail perpendicular to his own. Training his beam to the right, he saw the black void of a gully twenty yards away. Approaching it, he found the ditch jammed with storm-felled pines. He lowered his flashlight almost to ground level to bring out the shadows of disturbances in the carpet of needles. The trail led directly over the edge of the gully.

He took out his gun and moved forward, holding the flashlight as far out to his left as he could reach, giving him a better chance of avoiding a bullet if someone took a shot at his light. Six feet from the edge he stopped and let the silence of the night woods congeal around him. Sweeping the light beam across the gully, he saw no signs on the far bank. He cocked the hammer of the Colt, letting the crisp sound announce his intent.

"I want to see two empty hands first. If I don't, this ditch is going to be your grave."

Right away he heard a rustle in the branches below. "Don't shoot me," a rusty voice said. "I'm comin' out. I'm 'bout tied up here in all these limbs and vines."

Two hands and a head rose from the shadows. Harte crouched and leveled the flashlight beam with one hand and his revolver with the other.

"Are you alone?"

"Yes'r, I shorely am alone aw-right. Never been more alone."

Harte waited and listened. "If you're lying to me . . . if someone else pops up . . . I'll shoot you first. You understand that?"

"Yes'r, it's just me, I swear by God Aw-mighty. Just don't shoot me for the Lord's sake!"

Harte stood back and watched a middle-aged man in gray coveralls and a plaid shirt try to climb out with his hands held high. Under his John Deere cap, his unshaven face was rough with gray whiskers, and his eyes were wide with the possibility of dying in a ditch.

"Can I use my hands to git outta this hole? It's sorta slick down here."

"Climb out," Harte said. "Just keep your hands in front of you. If I can't see one of your hands for half a second, I'll shoot you, do you understand?"

"Yes'r, I understand *that* aw-right."

The man was about Harte's size, only plump rather than stoutly built. He looked as if he had spent a life in manual labor but was quickly going to seed. He struggled to reach the top and finally knelt on all fours with his head hanging between his arms as his breath rasped in and out of his heaving chest. His legs and arms shook like he was waiting out an earth tremor.

"I want you to lie flat on your belly with your arms spread wide," Harte ordered.

"Yes'r," the man said between gasps. He eased himself to the pine-needled floor. Harte stepped to the man's side keeping the flashlight beam in his eyes. Turning his head toward Beasley, Harte whistled a shrill note through his teeth.

"Over here!" Harte yelled. Then quietly to the man he said, "What's your name?"

"Stegler. Donnie Earl Stegler."

"Where do you live, Mr. Stegler?"

"Over to Dawsonville. I do some haulin' . . . dirt and gravel and tree stumps and such."

"And who are you hauling this load for?"

He started to rise up as if to engage in earnest conversation, and Harte put the light back in his eyes. "Stay down. I can hear you from there."

"Yes'r. Thing is . . . I don't rightly know who it was hired me."

"That your truck out there?"

210

"Nos'r, I picked it up."

"Where?"

"Where they said I was s'posed to. Down in some big parkin' lot in S'vanner."

"Savannah, Georgia?"

"Yes'r, it was my first time down there. The whole place smells sorta rotten, you ask me."

Harte wondered if the man was trying to be descriptive or philosophical. "Who is 'they?' "

"Well, some feller calls me up on the telephone one night and offers me this job drivin' a load up from S'vanner. He says the flatbed would be a-waitin' in the parkin' lot of a shoppin' center, and all I had to do was to drive it up here. There was good money in it, so I say 'sure, I'll do it.' Part o' the money before and the rest on deliverin'. Next day, a envelope with six-hunert dollars and a airplane ticket is in my mailbox." Stegler craned around his neck. "Are you the sher'ff?"

"I am," Harte said. "Lumpkin County. So, you flew to Savannah and picked up the truck?"

"Yes'r. First time I ever flowed b'fore. I didn' hardly know how to work my way through that mess in the Atlan'a airport. My wife drove me. She had to help me find my way to the airplane."

"And you have no idea who gave you that money?"

"Nos'r, I swear to you on my mama's Bible I don't. It was just a voice on the telephone, but I was made a believer when I found that envelope. Hell, if I never get the rest o' that money, I'll still come out ahead. I spent a little over a hunert and ten on gas, and it only cost me a day's time to drive back. They wanted me arrivin' back up here at dark."

"Where were you supposed to take the load?"

The man raised an arm and pointed north. "Up yonder at the ball fields. In the parkin' lot behind the building with the bathrooms."

Harte knelt, patted the man down, and found a tobacco tin and a cell phone. Then Beasley appeared, his revolver in hand. The deputy stared at the prostrate man at Harte's feet.

"How were you to get home from there?" Harte continued probing.

"I'm to call Birdie. She's my wife. Lord, but she's gonna have a fit about this."

"Who else were you supposed to call?"

"Nobody. I's just s'posed to leave the truck there with the load, and that was it."

Harte studied the man's face. "Mr. Stegler, if I find out that anything you told me is a lie, this is going to go harder against you."

"I ain't a-lyin' to you, Sher'ff. I didn't have no idea what was in those blocks till that deer run out in front o' me. I swerved to miss it and that's when the stack broke loose." Stegler raised his head to see Harte's face, then he flattened his cheek to the earth, closed his eyes, and breathed for a time with considerable labor. "I found that mess o' powder in the broke-up bricks, and I figured I was in the fry pan then. I damn near panicked when I seen that *po*-lice car a-comin'."

Harte kept his eyes on Stegler. "Beasley, cuff his hands behind his back, and we'll walk him out to your car. Any sign of Burns?"

"No, sir . . . no Burns."

As the deputy attached the cuffs, Harte knelt beside Stegler. "What is 'A.B.W.?' "

Stegler frowned. " 'A.B.W.?' That ain't the root beer, is it?"

"It's imprinted on the cinder blocks you were carrying."

Stegler shook his head. "I got no idea, Sher'ff." Then something changed in his face, and he looked up with eyes round as quarters. "You're the one kilt them Bullochs, ain't you?" He closed his eyes. "Lord God. I'm sure glad you could see my hands were empty."

Harte stood. "I'm glad of that, too, Mr. Stegler."

At the road, Beasley stood the prisoner by his cruiser. The man shivered in an abject crouch. Pine needles clung to his sleeves, and his overalls were muddy from the knees down.

"You have a blanket in your trunk?" Harte said to his deputy.

"Yes, sir. I always carry a blanket."

"Take off his overalls and shirt, wrap him in the blanket, and put him in your car."

Beasley's face wrinkled like an old road map. "You want me to strip him?"

From thirty yards deep in the forest, a flicker of light strobed through the maze of black tree trunks. Then came the sounds of limbs snapping and a disgruntled man cursing to himself.

"That'll be Burns," Beasley said.

Harte removed Stegler's hat. "I need to borrow your clothes, Mr. Stegler . . . and the truck."

"Yes'r," he said, sounding eager to help. "Key's in the ignition."

"Where were you supposed to leave the key after you parked?"

"In the tailpipe."

"Were you supposed to call anyone when you got to the ball field?"

Stegler's eyes were wide with relief at unloading the details of his complicity. "Naw-s'r. Like I tol' you . . . just Birdie. I's tol' to leave the truck there, and that was it."

"How were they to know when you arrived?" Harte asked.

Stegler shook his head slowly, as if he had not considered this. "Got no idea, Sher'ff."

Burns burst out of the woods and jumped down the bank. He was breathing like a racehorse.

"You got the sonovabitch?" Burns said, glaring at the prisoner.

"Sheriff and me tracked 'im," Beasley announced, a little pride lifting his voice.

Burns trained his flashlight on the bags. "Y'all figure out what all this is?"

"We're gonna assume it's an opiate," Harte said. When he began unbuttoning his shirt, both deputies watched him, both wearing the same look of confusion.

"What exactly are we doin'?" Beasley said.

"Stegler and I are about the same height and weight," Harte explained. "I'll drive the truck to the ball field. Every deputy we can muster will cover the routes in and out of there and tail whoever picks up the truck *and* whoever shuttles a driver into there."

"How do you know they'll come in tonight?" Burns said.

"They won't leave their merchandise out there in daylight. Somebody's likely watching the place right now. We'll stake it out from a distance."

Harte checked his watch and gazed blindly out into the darkness to work out a plan. When he had it, he raised his radio to his mouth and pushed the transmit button.

"Hooper, it's the sheriff . . . are you there?"

The speaker hissed with static. "Right here, Sher'ff."

"I want you to call Maxie-Rose and patch her through to me."

There was a pause before Hooper replied. "Now? It's after midnight."

"Call her," Harte ordered.

Another pause. "Okay, Sher'ff . . . but she ain't gonna like it."

In less than a minute a garbled buzz came through the radio, followed by a small, tinny voice that was barely recognizable. "Sher'ff Harte?" came a voice softened by sleep. "It's Maxie-Rose."

"Maxie, I want to deputize you for some field work tonight. Are you up for it?"

214

"I'm up for it." Her voice was clear and strong now. "What do you need, Sher'ff?"

"Get dressed, put a scarf over your head, and drive out to the new ball fields to pick me up. I'll be in gray coveralls and a cap, standing in front of the bathrooms. I need you there at exactly eleven-thirty. Do you have a radio you can bring?"

"Yes'r. I keep one in my car. You want me to bring my gun?"

Harte could hear the hope hidden inside the question. "Bring it. And a thermos of coffee. And, Maxie-Rose . . . you're getting overtime for this."

She laughed. "Sher'ff Harte, that's just the icin' on the cake."

"Hooper, are you still there?"

"I'm here, Sher'ff. What's goin' on?"

"Who's on duty tonight?"

"Let's see, Joe-Joe goes off duty at one. His sister is in the hospital with cancer. Ain't expected to live too many more days. That leaves Beasley, Burns, and Ash . . . and o' course me. Meeks is down in the cellblock. Sounds like Maxie-Rose is workin', too," he added.

"I'm with Beasley and Burns now. Get hold of Ash. Tell him to park behind the recycling bins at the top of the hill above the ball fields. I want him out of sight but able to watch the road. We'll be looking for a one-ton International flatbed with a load of cinder blocks. Chatham County plate BQ70I5. It'll be coming from the ball fields. If he sees it, he's to radio me and follow discreetly. Have you got all that?"

"I got it, Sher'ff. I'll call it in to Ash now."

Harte clicked off the radio and walked to Beasley's car where Stegler was in the cage bundled inside a blanket. "Mr. Stegler," Harte said, leaning into the open driver's window, "would you be willing to help us tonight? It might help your case."

Stegler's face went slack with relief. "I shorely would, Sher'ff. I'd do just about anythin'."

"I want you to take my truck down to Trammel's Tire Shop. You know where that is?"

Stegler looked down at the blanket covering him. "You want me to drive down there in my drawers?"

"I want you to pull in back, out of sight, and wait for me. Can you do that?"

Stegler's face took on a steely determination. "Yes'r, I can do that, shore 'nough."

Beasley frowned. "You're letting him take your vehicle? Alone?" Burns and Joe-Joe moved in closer to hear Harte's answer.

"Listen carefully, all of you. There are four ways to exit the ball field road." Harte pointed at Beasley. "I want you on Happy Hollow. Park where you won't be noticed from the street. If you see this truck go by, radio me, and follow it, discreetly." He pointed at Burns. "You do the same at the Quick Mart near the cemetery." Harte pointed at Joe-Joe. "You need to get to your sister." Harte waited to see if there were questions from anyone, but each deputy was nodding. "The only other exit out of the ball field lot is the landfill, but that's a dead end, right?"

"That's right," Beasley said. "No way outta there, except the way you go in."

Harte looked off into the night and began nodding. "Someone will probably drop off a driver at the ball field. One cruiser will need to follow that car. I'll radio you about its identity when we learn it. But, for all we know, this driver could walk to the ball park, ride a bicycle, or drop in by parachute. The point is, we want to be prepared for anything."

"Well, what about all these bags?" Beasley said, dusting white powder from his hands.

216

"Load them into your trunk," Harte instructed. "We'll do the inventory later at the station. We'll leave the bags still on the truck. We don't have time to unload and restack."

Holding open the door to Beasley's cruiser, Harte said, "Let's go, Mr. Stegler. Time to prove to me I can trust you."

And with that, everyone went into motion.

# Chapter Nineteen

At twenty past eleven, Harte pulled the flatbed into the ball field lot, parked behind the bathroom house, and cut the engine. He got out and stretched, a performance paying homage to the long ride from Savannah. At the rear of the truck he carefully set the key inside the hot exhaust pipe. Pulling the John Deere cap low over his brow, he stuck his hands into the overall pockets and walked his best impression of Donnie Earl Stegler out into the center of the lot.

The parking lot was quiet. Far out on the wide expanse of the new ball fields he could see the dark shapes of deer feeding on weeds at the edge of the grass. It was cool here in the valley. The flannel shirt and coveralls were welcome additions.

At precisely eleven-thirty a Chevy El Camino pulled into the lot, and Harte waved as he started walking toward the approaching headlights. The car swung around to put the passenger door in front of him, and he got in. Over her head Maxie-Rose wore a multi-colored scarf with large flower designs. Taking in Harte's costume, she started to speak.

"Don't say anything," Harte whispered. "We're driving down to Trammel Tire."

Maxie kept her eyes straight ahead as she drove out of the ball field entrance. Only when they started down the hill toward Trammel's did she dare to look at him.

"Sher'ff Harte, why am I wearing this scarf?" she whispered out of the side of her mouth.

"You're undercover . . . literally." As he began slipping out of the coveralls, he noticed a dark, well-oiled revolver nestled in Maxie's lap. "Is that loaded?"

"You bet your Sunday grits it's loaded," she chirped. She glanced at him and then watched the road again. "Cain't shoot with an empty gun." She nodded down the hill. "Here's Trammel's."

She pulled behind the garage where the sheriff's truck was waiting. Stegler sat in the driver's seat cinching the blanket to his throat and staring wide-eyed into the Camino's headlights.

"Who in the Sam Hill is that?" Maxie said.

"That's your prisoner. Name is Stegler. I need you to take him into lock-up."

"What'd he do? Is he dangerous?"

"Ran a truckload of drugs into our county," Harte said, keeping his voice professional. "I'll cuff him to your door, but I think you'll find him harmless." Maxie braked and studied the man cowering in the sheriff's driver's seat. "Maxie," Harte whispered and waited for her to meet his eyes. "Easy does it with your weapon. We need him alive, okay?"

Harte got out with the thermos of coffee, helped Stegler into Maxie's Chevy, cuffed him through the armrest, and tied his bootlaces together with a fisherman's knot. Crouching by the befuddled trucker, he spoke sternly as he laid the man's bundle of clothes in his lap.

"Mr. Stegler, this woman is one of my best deputies. And a dead shot with a pistol." Maxie's eyebrows shot up at this announcement. "I want you to sit quiet and do exactly as she says."

When Stegler dared to turn his head to Maxie, she raised the revolver and waggled it in the air. Harte prayed she would not twirl the gun by the trigger guard. She didn't.

"I'm just gone sit here like a scare't mouse, ma'am. You ain't gotta worry none 'bout me."

Maxie glared at Stegler so hard that he lowered his head in submission. Unseen by the man, she winked at Harte and laid the revolver back in her lap.

"Maxie, after you drop Mr. Stegler at the jail, I need you back here with me. I may have to recon the ball park on foot. If so, you'll need to keep watch here and tail the truck if it passes."

Maxie took a double-grip on the steering wheel. "Will do, Sher'ff." She ratcheted the Chevy into gear. When Harte stepped back, the tires of her El Camino clawed at the gravel, and she and Stegler tore out of the lot and began the climb up the hill. Harte moved his truck beside a mountain of bald tires, turned off the engine, and picked up his radio.

"Beasley, where are you?"

"I'm on Happy Hollow, Sheriff. Second house on the left."

"Burns?" Harte said into the radio. "Are you there?"

The speaker popped like a struck match. "Behind the Quick Mart, Sheriff. Eyes open."

Without being summoned, Ash reported in. "I'm at the recycling bins."

"Stay alert!" Harte said. Switching off the interior light, he stood in the open doorway for a good view of the road. The sky was clear, the stars spread thickly across the sky.

Maxie returned in less than an hour and parked her El Camino beside the pile of tires. The only vehicles Harte had seen were a motorcycle and a Volkswagen Beetle with a pizza delivery sign perched on top. Turning on the radio, he checked in with the others. No one had anything to report.

"Stay with it! Don't fall asleep. Radio me as soon as you see something."

Another hour passed. And then another. The thermos Maxie had brought was empty. Harte checked in on the radio every half-hour, but no one had seen the flatbed.

When the eastern sky showed a bloom of light, Harte yelled from his window. "Maxie!" She turned in her seat with her revolver held vertically in both hands. "I'm walking in by the woods. Radio the others." He watched her wave with the barrel of the gun and pick up her radio.

Cruising slowly down the ball field road, he pulled into a weedy lane that cut twenty yards into the woods. From there he hiked through the dark of the forest to the opening of the lot. At the edge of the trees his body went light as air. The flatbed was gone.

Harte walked the hardpan lot, but the parade of tracks was too much to read. The ball field grass was unmarked. The entrance to the landfill was still chained. He clicked on his radio.

"The truck's gone. Everyone get down here with me. We're going to search the landfill."

Inside a minute the Camino and three county cruisers roared into the lot. Harte hand-signaled with a slicing motion across his throat, and all the engines shut down.

"We're going to search the landfill!" he announced. "Get out flash-lights and guns!"

Burns's face squeezed down like an accordion. "But the chain's still up."

Harte gave him a what-else-is-there look. "It's the only other escape route."

Burns frowned at the road blocked by a chain. "There's nowhere to go that way."

Harte started for the entrance. "Who's got a cutting tool?"

"I do," Burns said and got out of his cruiser. The others followed.

"We're going to cover every inch of ground here," Harte said. "Look for fresh tire tracks or an exit. If you find the truck, call it in, but keep yourself behind cover and wait for us."

They split up and searched for the better part of an hour. There were no tire tracks leaving the main yard of the landfill, just as there were no other routes out of the property. By full light everyone had straggled back in, their combined frustration like a stench in the air.

"This makes no sense," Beasley whined. "How's a flatbed just disappear?"

Ash propped his hands on his hips and scoured the surrounding woods with narrowed eyes. Burns kicked a battered paint can across the open yard, and everyone watched it roll to a stop.

"Tell me straight now," Harte said. "No repercussions . . . I just need to know. Did any of you fall asleep on watch?"

"No, sir!" they answered, almost in unison. Harte glared at the mounds of garbage. He cursed quietly and turned back to the entrance.

"What about a helicopter?" Beasley offered. "I'm just sayin' . . . we gotta consider everything, right? Could a copter lift something that big?"

Maxie blew a flutter of air through her lips. "Don't you think we'd a' heard that, genius?"

Beasley shrugged. "Yeah. I guess."

Ash studied an idle backhoe and a tractor sitting behind the weigh station. "Could they bury it?"

"We would have heard that, too," Harte said. He removed his hat, pushed his fingers through his hair, and returned the hat. "I want the lot cordoned off. You men go over this place again . . . all of it!" He beckoned Maxie, and she stood before him like a Girl Scout receiving her first merit badge. "You've been up all night. Are you up for your regular shift today as dispatch?"

"Yes-sir-ree-bob-tail, Sher'ff. Bright-eyed and bushy tailed."

Harte nodded. "All right, go home, clean up, and eat something. I'll ask Hooper to stay on until you get there."

"Sher'ff Harte, we'll figure this out. A flatbed cain't just vanish like that." She patted his upper arm once and started for the parking lot. Harte breathed in the fetid aroma of the landfill and thought about the bags of drugs that had slipped through their net and would spread into the county. This failed project would affect a lot of people, he knew, but, when he closed his eyes, his mind brought up a single image. He saw Lauren Raburn exit his last class in her silent stupor.

*****

Back at the department Harte used his key and went in the backdoor, tapped down the stairs to the bathroom outside the cellblock, and showered. When he came upstairs and entered the front lobby, Hooper had his nose in a Word-Search Puzzle Book and his ear to a cell phone. The dispatch room smelled like fried onions and catsup.

"Yeah . . . yeah," Hooper said. He drew an elongated oval around a series of letters. "Well, I guess that's what you can expect when a schoolteacher takes over the sher'ff's office."

When Harte entered the lobby, Hooper sat up straight, mumbled, "I gotta go," and put his phone away. The deputy pushed the puzzle book into the cubby hole of the desk.

"Any messages?" Harte asked.

"No, sir. But the GBI feller come by and questioned Bulloch and McAllister."

Harte looked around the room. "Do we have coffee?"

Hooper looked surprised. "Maxie always makes it when she comes in."

Harte stopped in his doorway. "Maxie will be late. You make it."

Hooper stared dumbly at the coffee pot. "Ain't that sort o' women's work?"

Harte had started for his office, but he stopped, turned, and leaned against the door frame. "What did you do before dispatch, Hooper?"

Hooper frowned. "Worked for Barlow puttin' in septic tanks. But what has that got to—"

"Did that prepare you for this?" Harte interrupted, nodding at the radio.

"We didn' have a radio at Barlow's. Just used our cell phones."

Harte nodded. "So you had to learn something new, right?"

Grudgingly, Hooper stood and scuffed across the floor to the kitchen area. "I guess I can figure it out." As he filled the pot under the faucet, he kept his eyes on the water and spoke in a tired voice. "This is 'bout me sayin' somethin' 'bout a schoolteacher takin' over as sher'ff, ain't it?"

"Could be," Harte replied. "Or could be I just need some coffee." He took a step back into his office. "Make a cup for Mr. Stegler, too. I want to have a talk with him."

After closing his door, Harte sat at his desk and called Cody who answered after one ring.

"Tough break, Mr. C. Sometimes it goes against us. Burns told me about it."

"We had to have missed something. I need fresh eyes to look it over. Can you go?"

A telling quiet stretched out over the phone, until Cody finally exhaled a long sigh. "All right, but I got to help Lauren first. She's going through her father's things. How's that sound?"

To Harte it sounded like Cody was half gone from the force, but he managed a tone of gratitude. "Just find out how that flatbed disappeared. It's making our department look inept."

In thirty minutes Hooper knocked on the door and announced coffee was ready. Carrying two cups, Harte descended the stairs to the basement, where Meeks looked up from an open magazine.

"Open up Mr. Stegler's cell, Arthur. He and I are going to have a little parley."

As Meeks sorted through keys, Harte looked into Varley Bulloch's cell. Varley appeared small and lost inside his orange county jumpsuit. Seated on his bunk he glared through the bars. The bright bandages on his head and right hand were the only parts of him that appeared dirt-free. Varley's gaze fixed on the antique badge that was part of Harte's belt buckle.

"So they made you the hot-shit sheriff? Is that 'cause you kilt two Bullochs?"

Harte locked eyes with the prisoner. "You've had your phone call and met with your lawyer. Now you get three square meals, water, medical attention, and time in the yard every day. Conversation with me is not part of the equation."

Harte started to walk away, but Varley sprang from the bed and grabbed one of bars with his good hand in a vain attempt to rattle the door. The knuckles on his fist turned white as chips of quartz.

"You think that's all there is to it, don'cha? You kill my brothers, and then you git to be the goddamn sher'ff. Well, whoopty-doo for you."

Still holding the two coffees, Harte stepped toward Bulloch, and the little man backed away from the bars. "If there's anything you think you need," Harte said, "tell it to the jailor."

Varley mumbled something under his breath, returned to the bunk, and sat. When Harte moved away, he heard Varley jump up again.

"Hey!" Varley screeched. "I don't git no coffee?"

Harte ignored him and walked past the cell where McAllister lay on his bunk facing the wall. In the last cell, Stegler stood up from his bunk, his face expectant.

Dressed in his own clothes again, the truck driver looked like he had aged five years overnight. Meeks opened the door, and Harte carried the drinks inside.

"Were you able to get any sleep, Mr. Stegler?"

"Sher'ff, I don' know that I'll ever sleep again." Stegler's voice was tired, his expression childlike. By reflex he took the cup Harte offered, but he held it as though unaware of its presence.

"Did you call your wife?"

He looked down and shook his head. "Oh, yeah. She don' hardly know what to think."

Harte leaned against the wall and sipped coffee. It wasn't good, but it was hot.

Stegler filled his cheeks with air and expelled it. "How much trouble am I in, Sher'ff?"

"I'm not arresting you yet. I just want to ask you some questions. Why don't you sit down."

Stegler sat on the bunk. "I ain't gone lie to you, Sher'ff. I figured there was somethin' a mite odd 'bout the way all this got arranged. The phone call. The money in the mailbox. I just knew we could really use that money. Bus'ness has been off some." He cringed like he had gulped a shot of vinegar. "But cinder blocks. I mean, who'd a thought anything 'bout *cee*-ment bricks? And when I got down there and there they was . . . all stacked up neat and purty and strapped down and settin' in the parkin' lot of the shoppin' center just like they said . . . it all seemed on the up and up."

He still had not tasted the coffee. At Harte's prodding, Stegler raised it to his mouth but began shaking his head and seemed to forget about the coffee again.

"Then, when I dodged that poor ol' deer . . . Lordy, Lordy . . . I liked to a' kilt it." He set the coffee on the floor, propped his elbows on his knees and rested his forehead in his hands. Slowly, he began pushing his fingers back through his graying hair. His eyes filled with tears. "I just didn' know what I was carryin'. That's the God's truth."

Harte did not think a man could be more contrite, but Stegler managed to evoke more pity than forgiveness. "Tell me about the man who called."

Stegler looked up with his eyebrows peaked. "What about 'im?"

"Anything about his voice?" Harte said.

Stegler shook his head. "He was just a voice, Sher'ff. Listen, I'm right sorry 'bout runnin' off in the woods like I done. I know that's gonna look bad in court. I guess I just panicked."

Harte sipped and nodded. "Do you still have the envelope the money came in?"

Stegler frowned. "No. I gave half of it to Birdie to put in the bank. I stuffed the rest in my wallet for expenses. I guess we threw away the envelope."

"If the rest of the payment comes, I want you to pick it up with tweezers and put it in a plastic bag and bring it down here to me. Will you do that?"

"Yes'r, I shorely will, but I kindly doubt it'll come what with spilling the load like I done." Stegler eyed Harte sheepishly. "But if it does come . . . can we keep the money?"

"That's a question for the District Attorney, Mr. Stegler."

Stegler looked Harte dead in the eye. "It's drug money, ain't it?"

Harte nodded. "Probably. We're waiting on a report. I'd say half a million dollars' worth."

Stegler's face blanched. "Lord, God. I was carryin' *that*?"

"I want you to contact me if you ever get another call like this. Will you do that?"

"Yes'r. Does that mean you're lettin' me go?"

"I'm going to talk to the D.A. I'll tell him how you helped us out last night."

A tear standing in Stegler's eye broke free and coursed down his whiskery cheek. "Thank you, Sher'ff. That's mighty kindly o' you." His eyes roved over Harte's face and then narrowed. "Sher'ff, can I tell you somethin'?"

"Go ahead."

"Well . . . since I know it was you shot up those boys from Union County the other night—" Stegler's face tightened with regret. "Well, I just wanna thank you for not openin' up on me in them woods. Birdie would never forgive me for dyin' out on some lonely road with a truck-load o' broke-up bricks and loco weed dusted over half the county."

"You want me to give that coffee to one of my deputies, Mr. Stegler?"

The trucker's face wrinkled with confusion, until he discovered the cup next to his boot. "Might as well drink it," he said, picking it up. "I cain't sleep anyway."

*****

When Harte left the office, he saw the Dowdy boy and his skateboard tribe at the far end of the lot. The alpha male with the ink-black hair made a waist-high half-wave from the wrist. The others stopped what they were doing and watched Harte. Harte tipped the front of his hat brim with his thumb and forefinger, got into his truck, and fired it up. He turned on his radio for some news, but it was dead.

He watched for a moment as the skaters returned to their acrobatics on the asphalt arena, and then he put the truck in gear and drove to where they were gathered. When he pulled up next to them and lowered his window, the boys approached and eyed him obliquely.

"Any of you men know anything about hooking up a car radio?" he said.

The boys exchanged glances. "Why?" said Alpha, showing a little defiance.

Harte pointed to his dash. "Mine is dead." He nodded down to Jim Raburn's car below the ramp. "I'm wondering if the one in that car could be installed in my truck."

"How come you don't get to drive a cruiser, Mr. Canaday?" It was Lamar Dowdy's brother asking as he eyed Harte's old Chevy truck.

Alpha sidestepped enough to block Harte's view of the Dowdy boy. "Yeah, you're the sheriff now. You oughta have your own cruiser, right?"

"It's on order," Harte said. He nodded toward his dashboard. "Meanwhile I'm going through NPR withdrawal." He looked hopefully at each boy. "I can pay you minimum wage."

"To each of us?" said one of the boys in back.

Harte pursed his lips. "Well, I figure it's a half-day job for two men. You can split it up among yourselves however you see fit. How does that sound?"

"I can wire it up for you, Sheriff," Lamar's brother said.

Harte nodded, picked up his hand radio and looked out his front windshield. "Hooper? This is the sheriff. I've got a mechanic who'll be coming in for the keys to Sheriff Raburn's GMC. Name of Dowdy." Harte looked at the boy and raised his eyebrows.

"It's Lester."

"Lester Dowdy," Harte repeated into the radio.

A five-second pause followed. "Lester Dowdy? Ain't he one o' the—"

"He'll come in sometime this morning," Harte interrupted and looked again at Lester, who nodded encouragingly. "When he does, give him the keys, understood?"

The five seconds of static that followed was like a hypnotist's chant to the five boys. In complete stillness they stared at Harte's radio.

"Got it, Sher'ff," Hooper said.

Alpha turned to Lester with a sneer. "You know how to do that shit?"

"Sure," Lester said, like they were talking about how to breathe.

Harte kept his face neutral as he witnessed Lester's sudden ascent inside the hierarchy of the skateboard culture. He nodded to the boys, pulled down the lot, and watched them in his rearview mirror as Lester led them toward the GMC.

Just as Harte reached the exit, a brand new black GMC pulled in from the street, the word "*SHERIFF*" emblazoned in silver across the door and side panel. A Taurus followed and both vehicles parked in front of the office.

Harte backed up and put his window next to the GMC. "That for me?" Harte asked.

The man did a double-take on Harte's truck. "Sheriff Canaday?"

"Yep."

The man stepped out dangling a thin wire ring with two keys. "Here you go. Just need you to sign a few things."

Harte took the keys and pointed at the door to the lobby. "Step inside there and my deputy—Hooper—will sign everything you need."

Harte turned off the engine of his pickup, stepped out, and worked the ignition key off his old key ring. Then, looking over the roof of his cab, he produced a high-pitched whistle through his teeth. Lester's head bobbed up over the rise, and Harte waved him over.

By the time Lester crossed the lot, Harte had transferred his personal things from the truck. "Here," he said, tossing the key to Lester. "Drive the truck down to the GMC. Make it easier."

One of the black boys caught up to Lester. "Ray's gonna help me," Lester said.

Harte inspected Ray and then Lester, studying them from frazzled hair to torn shoes, as if he were sizing them up for deputy work. "Looks like a good team."

"When do you need it, Mr. C?"

Harte looked off toward town. "Oh . . . three days? How's that sound?"

"We'll have it done tomorrow," Lester said proudly.

Harte nodded. "Just leave the key and a bill with my dispatcher."

Lester's face sagged. "A bill? You mean . . . like . . . something official?"

Harte shrugged. "A piece of paper with your hours, that's all."

Lester slipped into the driver's seat, and Ray ran around the back of the truck to the passenger side. When the engine cranked, Lester looked up at Harte with an impish grin.

"I don't really have a license yet." He shrugged with his eyebrows and waited for a verdict.

"I won't tell if you won't," Harte said.

Lester perked up and put the truck in gear. The Chevy lurched once and then puttered across the lot at the innocent pace of a golf cart. Just after the truck tilted and eased down the slope, Harte heard the boy rev the engine twice and then shut it down.

Harte smiled at the drivers. "Thank you, gentlemen." Then he drove off in his new GMC.

He went to the D.A.'s office, where he learned that the powder was a high-grade cocaine. From there he drove to his former home behind Earl

Sandifer's no-drive zone. Callie would be at work, and it was as good a time as any to pick up the anti-freeze he had left in the storage room. When he pulled off the paved road, he saw that Sandifer was securing a heavy new door and lock to his tractor shed. The farmer turned at the sound and watched the sheriff's new car motor up his road. As Harte passed by in the new cruiser, his neighbor stared slack-jawed and stood as still as a scarecrow. Harte nodded, and after he had entered the shade of the woods felt the grin on his face mark the end of difficulties over the road.

On the drive back through town, he passed the storage shed complex that Layland was constructing. Glancing back, he saw four laborers attaching green aluminum siding to the back wall of one of the units. The siding was covering a long wall of cinder blocks. After turning around at the hardware store, he drove back to enter the construction site and parked near a tall stack of siding propped on four-by-fours. He got out and walked to the back of the building where three Hispanics and one local boy were lifting a sheet of aluminum from one of the stacks.

"Castleberry, isn't it?" Harte said.

"Yes, sir. Charlie Castleberry. How's it goin', Mr. C?" Charlie let the three other workers take the siding to one of the stalls. His eyes brightened as he took in the old Colt Peacemaker. Harte knew the boy wanted to ask about the shootout at Luther's, but, to his credit, he offered only a smile of deference. "See you got you a new moustache, Mr. C. How's the new job?"

"Going fine. You in charge here, Charlie?"

Charlie twisted at the waist to watch the three Hispanics nail the siding to the frame. "I don't know . . . I guess. We're all just putting up this siding. We gotta have it done today."

Harte pretended to admire the building. "Lot of cinder blocks." He stepped to the nearest cubicle. The blocks showed square cavities and no identifying marks.

"Tell me about it," Charlie said. "We laid 'em all. Seventy-two stalls."

Harte nodded. "Ever see a block with rounded cavities and initials 'A.B.W.?' "

Charlie frowned at the building. "Don't recall that. Why?"

"How long have you been working for Childers, Charlie?"

"Oh, off and on coupla years. I work for McA, too. They sometimes switch me back and forth."

" 'McA?' As in 'McAllister?' "

Charlie nodded and pointed at the piles of siding, cinder blocks, and roofing showing under a blue tarp. "McA delivered all this."

Returning to the stack of siding the Hispanic workers cut their eyes to Charlie and Harte.

"*Hola*," Harte said.

"*Hola*," the three mumbled in a staggered chorus.

"Better get back to it, Mr. C," Charlie said and broke off to join his coworkers.

Harte walked idly to the pile of supplies under the tarp. Raising a corner of the plastic, he examined the concrete blocks stacked there. All showed square holes. On the asphalt lay a few broken pieces, one of which showed most of a rounded cavity. Harte picked it up, carried it to his cruiser, and stowed it as the boys banged hammers against the aluminum. When he drove out, the three Hispanics were waiting for Charlie to finish nailing his section of the paneling.

*****

Wallace Rainy had been the chemistry teacher at the high school for twelve years and had done the cocaine analysis from the Stegler load, just as he had done almost all freelance lab work for the county for the last decade. When Harte pulled up the Rainy driveway, he found Wallace working his fall garden inside a high rectangle of chicken wire fencing.

"Annie lock you in there, Wallace?" Harte said, stepping from his cruiser.

Wallace leaned on his hoe and watched Harte approach on foot. "Two hours hard labor. Not sure what I did wrong, but what husband is?" Wallace narrowed his eyes. "Stop shaving, Harte?"

Wallace was two years older than Harte, tall and had been a pretty good high jumper in his day. Now he carried a paunch and habitually slumped forward at the shoulders.

Harte eyed the fencing that rose a foot over the brim of his hat. "Keep the deer out?"

"So far. We'll see what they're willing to do for collards and pole beans."

Wallace leaned his hoe on the fence and sidled out the gate. "Any luck on the cocaine?"

Harte shook his head. "I've got another piece of cinder block that didn't come off that truck. Could you test it for me? Off the books?"

Wallace shrugged. "Sure. Let me get a bag and we'll keep the wind off it."

From his side porch Wallace brought out a plastic garbage bag. "Has it been rained on?"

"It was under a tarp," Harte said. "I picked one up that had the cavity side down."

Wallace gave Harte a keen look and tapped the sheriff's sternum. "You know, as good a teacher as you were, you might have found your real calling." He huffed a laugh through his nose. "People are referring to Luther's place now as 'the O.K. Corral.' " He lost his smile and nodded. "Jim Raburn would be proud of what you're doing."

"Well, first let's see if I'm any damn good at it," Harte said.

Wallace narrowed his eyes and pursed his lips. "Tell me this . . . were you ready to quit the school, or does Morris Blackadar figure into this somehow?"

Harte shrugged. "Guess I was burned out. How much longer do you figure you'll teach?"

Wallace laughed quietly. "I wouldn't know what to do with myself if I wasn't teaching."

They stood for a time watching Wallace's old Irish Setter hobble across the yard to the back porch. Harte figured their thoughts were working in the same vicinity—about what a life adds up to in the end. He looked at the sun, already dipping toward the mountains to the west.

"Looks like an early autumn this year," Wallace said and looked around as if he could see the coolness of the early evening.

"This day's getting away from me," Harte said and climbed into the cruiser.

Wallace carried the wrapped block to Harte's window. "I'll give this a look tonight."

Harte thumbed his hat brim. "I appreciate it."

As Harte drove through town, Maxie's voice came alive on his radio. "Sher'ff?"

Harte spoke into the unit. "Go ahead."

"I found 'A.B.W.,' Sher'ff. It's the Altamaha Brick Works just outside Savannah."

"Stegler picked up the truck at a shopping center. Who picked up the load from A.B.W.?"

"Donnie Earl Stegler . . . eight days ago," Maxie said flatly. "But it wasn't *our* Donnie Earl. Our Donnie Earl don't have a Mexican accent and skin the color of a toasted marshmallow."

"What about Equip Enterprises, who leased the truck?"

"That truck sold at auction last year. They sell off their rentals every four years and restock."

"Did they have a record of the sale?"

"Paid in cash, Sher'ff. The signature on the record was a mess. Close as the fleet manager could make out it was 'Sean' something. Last name looked like 'Galdeer.' No address. Said he couldn't remember the face. DMV says that truck has not been registered since insurance ran out on the original owners. They were just runnin' on dumb luck, I guess. If ever the truck got pulled over, it was gonna be the driver left holdin' the bag . . . or in this case . . . bags."

Harte pulled out a pen and found a manual to write on. "Spell that last name for me, Maxie."

She did, and he read it four times before he spewed a breath of air. "Cute," he huffed. "Maxie, put a hyphen in that last name, between the 'L' and the 'D'."

In a moment she said, "All right, I did that. Now what?"

Harte wadded the paper. " 'Sean' is Irish for 'John.' You know what a 'gal-deer' is."

"You mean a doe?" She was quiet for several seconds. "Well, bless this joker's black heart. He's got a sense a humor, don't he?"

# Chapter Twenty

Harte drove to Layland Childers' construction headquarters on the bypass, cruised to the back of the office building, passed through the open gate of the fenced compound and moved slowly through the yard. Making an informal inventory of the heavy equipment, he noted a dump truck, a backhoe, a grader, two dozers with mud-caked treads, and two long tractor-trailer flatbeds. No cinder blocks were evident. He circled in a turnaround, retraced his route, and parked in front of the office.

In the reception room, Lanie Ledford stood in a chair hanging a framed photograph of the new auto parts store on Highway 60 south of town. The picture was the latest in a gallery of the Childers Company's finished constructions, a display of color photos that spanned one wall. On an adjacent wall were more photos—all groups of men wearing dark suits and big smiles.

"Well, hey, Harte. I almost didn't know you with your moustache." Her eyes were drawn to the antique Colt on his hip. "Goodness, that looks right out of a Western."

Harte removed his hat. "Good to see you, Lanie. Layland in?"

She left the picture hanging crooked, stepped down, and rose up on her tiptoes to hug his neck. Lanie had dated Jim Raburn in high school, and Harte had always felt an unspoken vestige of allegiance from her on that account.

"He's with someone, Harte. But I'll let him know you're here." She moved behind her desk and picked up the telephone. Lanie was still an eye-catching woman, and Harte knew that her shapely legs, dye-preserved hair, and ample bust had probably been résumé enough for Layland.

"Mr. Childers, Harte Canaday is out here and would like to—"

"Our new sheriff! Send 'im on in!" Harte could hear Layland's buoyant reply in stereo, over the telephone as well as through the door.

Lanie smiled as if she had won Business Woman of the Year. "He said to go on in." Dropping the smile, she intercepted him at the door. "I heard about you and Callie. Layland told me."

Harte considered Lanie's two divorces, the last of which—it was said—involved Layland in some way. "Well, he ought to know," he said and nodded toward the door. "Who's he with?"

Her eyebrows shot up, a little mischief playing in her eyes. "A real charmer . . . from Cuba or Puerto Rico or someplace like that," she whispered. Then she leaned closer. "Looks like he stepped right out of one of those Mexican soap operas. He'd be the one who jilts the woman."

Harte went inside to see Layland's grand gesture of standing and spreading his arms. "Come on in, buddy! We're just talking a little business."

A lean man in a pale gray suit relaxed on the sofa, his handsome face partially hidden by an open newspaper—the Miami Herald—which seemed to occupy all his attention. Under the fluorescent lighting, his skin was walnut brown and his hair black as a horse's mane. This was the Hispanic from Layland's truck at the hardware store and later at Luther's in the BMW.

Harte waved his hat toward the sofa. "Am I interrupting?"

"No, 'course not," Layland sang. "Sit down." He gestured to a chair and sat behind his desk.

Harte waded across the pile carpet, dropped his hat into the chair, and remained on his feet.

"Harte," Layland said, "this is my associate . . . Mr. Santiago."

The newspaper lowered partway with a starchy crackle, and Santiago nodded pleasantly. Without his dark glasses his eyes were almost black, and his cheeks cratered with scars that might have been from a childhood illness. In front of the man's left armpit the coat material bulged.

Harte nodded. "Harte Canaday. Do you have a first name, Mr. Santiago?"

The man smiled as though patiently indulging an inconvenience. "*Sí*, I do."

Layland came in on cue. "Turon is working with me on a business deal, and—"

"Where do you call home, Mr. Santiago?" Harte interrupted.

Santiago folded the paper once, twice, and then laid it on the cushion next to him. Spreading his hands in a gesture of wondering where to begin, he pursed his lips.

"Originally from Cuba, but I have homes in many places," he said, his accent barely detectable. "Miami, Guadalajara, Aruba . . ." He shrugged. "And in Europe. My business requires that I travel for periods of time. I find owning is a better investment than hotels."

"And what might that business be?" Harte said.

Layland started to butt in, but a dart of Santiago's eyes cut him off. "I assess, *Señor* Sheriff."

Harte allowed several seconds to pass, showing his patience. "And what do you assess?"

Santiago's face brightened with the obvious. "Usually . . . other men's businesses . . . like Mr. Childers here." A self-amused smile tightened his mouth. "Before I invest in a man, I want to know how he runs his business." He glanced at Harte's old pistol, and the smile ramped up a notch.

Harte hitched his head toward Layland, who had now been relegated to the third person in the room. "You're considering investing in Layland?"

The man turned a hand palm up, the movement fluid, like a submerged leaf tumbling in slow current. "I have not yet completed my assessment." His head bounced once with a private laugh. "Perhaps I will learn something by how he deals with you."

"So, you invest in a small town like ours . . . in what? A carwash? A storage facility?"

Outside the window, a dump truck grumbled out of the compound toward the highway. Santiago patiently waited for the sound to fade and then spread his hands again, this time causing the lapel of his coat to open.

"I place a high value upon my privacy. I am, I suppose, what you Americans like to call . . . 'a celebrity.' " His eyes went to the old Colt again . . . and then to the antique badge on Harte's belt buckle. He barely suppressed a smile. "But you are the sheriff, no? And sheriffs want to know things, so let me say this: for now, I observe *Señor* Childers to assess—" He see-sawed a hand in front of him. ". . . His business acumen."

Harte held his gaze on Santiago. "You have a permit to carry that gun?"

Showing no surprise, Santiago closed his eyes and nodded.

"May I see the permit," Harte said, his request sounding nothing like a question.

From the inside pocket of his jacket, Santiago removed a wallet that appeared to be made from the skin of an armadillo. He extracted a laminated card. Harte neither reached for it nor made an effort to read it, beyond recognizing it as a Georgia license.

"Now the gun."

Santiago sat very still, smiling only with his mouth. The whites of his eyes glowed around his dark irises. He pulled open the coat, exposing a black automatic nestled in a nylon holster.

Harte held out his left hand, and Santiago's smile faded like the sudden wilt of a flower.

"Take it out with two fingers of your left hand," Harte said.

Santiago winced and cocked his head. "That would be awkward, would it not?"

Harte nodded once. "It would."

Santiago tried for elegance as he bent his arm and extracted the gun as directed. Harte stood relaxed and unmoving, forcing the Cuban to lean forward to deliver a slender nine-millimeter Beretta.

When Harte racked the slide back enough to check the chamber, he found a live round already mounted to fire. In a fluid continuous motion, he dropped the magazine into his left hand, tossed it to the far end of the sofa, and jacked the slide back. The remaining cartridge jumped from the chamber and thumped onto the carpet. Letting the slide ratchet forward, he set the safety.

"Dangerous way to carry a gun, Mr. Santiago," Harte said. "A round in the chamber, safety off. Are you expecting trouble?" Taking three casual steps backward, he laid the empty gun on Layland's desk. Layland pushed back in his chair as he stared at the weapon.

Santiago smiled. "It is all a matter of perception. It might be dangerous *not* to have it ready. After all, why do we carry guns?" He shrugged. "I believe there is no law about how we carry."

"Harte," Layland chimed in, "Mr. Santiago often carries large amounts of cash in the States for business transactions. You can understand that."

Santiago steepled his fingertips together in front of his chest and cocked his head. "I believe you are the town's new *pistolero* whom everyone talks about, no?" Studying the holstered Colt on Harte's hip, he narrowed his eyes with curiosity—feigned or genuine, Harte could not tell. "Yours is a gun of interest, no? Antiquated . . . iconic. It is the gun of the American cowboy, I believe." He met Harte's eyes with dead calm. "So, *señor*, I showed you mine. Now may I see yours?" When Santiago smiled this time, he showed a flash of very white teeth.

"No," Harte said, giving the Cuban the same flat expression he had once reserved for a student who offered an inane answer to a fair question.

Santiago's smile melted to thespian regret. Closing his eyes, he made the merest bow of his head. He leaned on the sofa and picked up the magazine off the cushion. Then he stood and walked to the desk, his movements feline . . . almost balletic. Deftly, he reassembled the Beretta and returned it to the holster. He did not bother with the bullet on the floor, just as Harte knew he would not. The Cuban sat on the sofa and re-opened the newspaper, his expression as blank as if he were in the room alone.

"You need a bodyguard now, Layland?" Harte said.

Pretending mild surprise, Santiago raised a slender finger and moved it from side to side like a metronome. "Oh, no, *Señor* Sheriff. This is not what I am, I assure you." His voice was silky with patience. "I am here to see that his organizational affairs are in order so that we may do business."

Harte turned back to Layland. "I guess your *affairs* come in some kind of order."

Layland smiled and shrugged with his open hands rising almost to his shoulders. "Look, there's no sense in kicking a dead horse. You're gettin' divorced. It's common knowledge. She's free to do what she wants, Harte." Layland sat forward and spread his fingers flat on the calendar squared on his desktop. "Look, Harte, I do a hellava lotta good for the county. I create jobs, get things built, provide lots of services that help us all prosper." He swept a hand toward Santiago. "Turon is a consultant who can help me improve how I run things."

Harte gave Layland a long appraising look. "Layland . . . one of these days . . . one of these business schemes you cook up is going to fry your bacon."

From behind the newspaper Santiago spoke with the melodic voice of a bad actor. "You did not tell me you were in the food business, *Señor* Childers." He brought down the newspaper and gave Harte a smile of pity. "*Señor* Sheriff, I am in the business of making money. And I help others make money. It is that simple." When he raised the newspaper in front of his face, his voice dropped. "*Cuando tu negocio es mi negocio, tu tocino cocina, cochino palido.*"

Harte picked up his hat, crossed the plush carpet, and opened the door. "Oh, by the way, Layland," he said and turned, "ever do business with Altamaha Brick Works?"

Layland's face wrinkled. "Maybe. I deal with lots of suppliers. Prices fluctuate."

"Maybe you could check your records and let me know."

"I'll get Lanie on that. She'll call you."

Harte hesitated and said, *"Vamos a ver cómo termina esta historia, caballeros."*

This brought the newspaper down and Santiago's head up. Mild surprise showed in his dark eyes, and that alone was reward enough for Harte's visit.

Closing the door Harte almost bumped into Lanie, who stood holding a tray with three mugs of steaming coffee and shortbread cookies in a porcelain bowl. The mugs were all red with black lettering that advertised Childers Construction.

"I thought y'all might want some refreshments."

"No, thank you, Lanie. But I wonder if I could have a piece of paper?"

She walked to her desk, set down the tray, and opened a drawer. After setting pen and paper before him, she stepped back to watch him write.

"Ever heard of Altamaha Brick Works, Lanie?"

She frowned. "Don't think so," she said absently, as she angled her head to read his writing.

"I never knew you spoke Spanish, Harte," she said quietly. "When did you pick that up?"

He finished writing what he could remember from Santiago's lines and then turned the paper around for her to read. "What about you? Do you know what this means?"

Shaking her head, she squinted at his scribbling. "I took French under Mrs. Lourette."

He folded the paper and stowed it in his shirt pocket. "My Spanish teacher was the Cisco Kid . . . from TV," he confessed. "I think I might know about three sentences, tops."

Lanie smiled, but a sadness crept into her face. "Harte, I didn't get a chance to talk to you at the funeral. I wanted to. But with both of Jim's wives there . . . I didn't stay long."

He nodded. "Sad day for everybody, Lanie." He smiled. "Jim always spoke highly of you."

She shrugged that off. "Well, that was a long time ago." Her eyes filmed over with tears. "We didn't know how simple everything was back in high school, did we, Harte?"

He shook his head. When she looked like she might break down, he cupped his hand to her shoulder and squeezed. "Hey," he said, looking past her at the framed photos on the wall. "Who are all those people in those photographs?"

Lanie sniffed and looked distractedly at the wall. "Oh, those are all Layland's friends in the governor's office." She leaned in and lowered her voice. "That's the 'name-dropper' wall."

"I'll let you get back to your work," he said, tipped his hat, and walked out the door.

# Chapter Twenty-One

Harte was seated at his desk reading Cody's papers of resignation, when Maxie backed through the door carrying a double-burner hotplate. She gave Harte a triumphant smile before making a comic scowl at the sleeping bag on the floor.

"Where do you want this?"

He patted the wide windowsill behind him, and Maxie set down the unit, plugged it in, and stepped back to admire her contribution to his décor.

"Maxie, who is our contact with the state bureau?"

She beamed like the bearer of good news. "Captain William Nesmith, a.k.a. Captain Dreamboat of the Staties." Then her face relaxed to the numbness of a corpse. " 'Course, he's married and prob'ly thinks I was born in a pumpkin patch."

"Can you get him on the phone for me?" Harte said.

Maxie marched out and settled at the switchboard. Within a minute his phone rang.

"Sheriff Canaday," Harte answered.

"Billy Nesmith, Sheriff. Welcome to the long arm of the law. I'm glad you called."

Harte swiveled his chair to the window and tried to place the man's accent but couldn't. "Jim Raburn spoke well of you, Captain. That goes a long way with me."

"I'm going to miss him," Nesmith said quietly. "I know you two were close."

"I probably knew him better than anyone," Harte said, "but I started learning about him a lot more when I sat down behind his desk."

"From what I hear, you're a fast learner. Listen, I have something I think you'll find interesting. When your deputies made the arrests and impounded the Bullochs' truck and McAllister's Caddy, as you know, they collected a cardboard box full of product—a high grade cocaine. Thirty sealed packets. It was sitting in the driver's seat of the truck. Turns out, only the top layer held the coke. Six packets. The remaining twenty-four were filled with a mix of talcum, baking flour, and powdered sugar. Looks like the Bulloch boys were getting stiffed by this McAllister character. And considering the history of the Bullochs, he was playing a dangerous game."

Harte considered the idea of one man pulling a switch on the Bulloch brothers. It was a dangerous proposition. More likely, McAllister was the front man of something much larger.

"What about the money?" Harte asked. "How much was in the Cadillac?"

A brief silence over the phone prepared Harte for disappointment.

"We haven't found any, Sheriff, but we've not taken the vehicles apart yet." After another pause, Nesmith's voice took on an upbeat timbre. "But you called me. What can I do for you?"

"I want to run a name by you . . . Turon Santiago, a Cuban."

"Yeah, I know him. He's a slippery bastard. A drug distributor. We've nailed a few of his operations but not him. Works mostly out of Miami, but he's a world traveler."

"Well, now he's shown up in my backyard."

Nesmith said nothing for a time, but Harte could hear him breathing. "Not a good sign, Sheriff. Are you thinking he's involved with this Bulloch-McAllister deal?"

Harte brought up the image of the Cuban walking into Luther's with Layland Childers. "All I know is he's here and holding meetings with a local businessman."

Nesmith's voice turned casual. "Want to give me a name?"

Harte clenched his teeth and closed his eyes long enough settle his voice. "Can I wait on that, Captain, until I know for sure what the connection is?"

"It's 'Billy'," he said. "I can tell you the connection will be drugs. But I can keep the name to myself for a while, so why don't you go ahead and tell me. We're on the same team, you know."

Harte slowly rocked his chair and looked out the windowglass at the town that now fell under his protection. There was a paradox to being sheriff, he mused—feeling at once both closer to and more distant from the people.

"Layland Childers," he said. "He's in construction."

"Does this tie in with the cinder block episode?" Nesmith asked.

"No leads on that yet," Harte said and then listened to Billy Nesmith breathe over the line.

"Sheriff Canaday, I want Santiago. The Feds want him, but I want him more."

"We have a common goal," Harte assured him. "And call me 'Harte.' "

"Contact me for anything you need," Nesmith said. "And be careful. Santiago is a snake with a lot of venom." Harte could hear sirens in the background on the line. "I gotta go, Sheriff. Hey . . . were you really a schoolteacher?"

"High school . . . history."

Nesmith laughed. "If I see that on a résumé, I may have to give it more weight. So long, Harte."

When he turned back to the desk and hung up the phone, Maxie was waiting, wearing a big smile as she leaned against the door frame. "Well," she said, "isn't he a charmer?"

When Harte gave her a questioning look, she laughed.

"Remember Tyrone Power, the actor? He looks a little like him." Snapping out of her reverie, she scanned the room and frowned at the sleeping bag on the floor. "That sofa bed should be here tomorrow."

When he still made no reply, she stepped inside. "Something wrong, Sher'ff Harte?"

He propped his elbow on the desk and lowered his chin into his palm. "You know that feeling when you know you're about to say the wrong thing, but you're going to go ahead and say it anyway . . . because it needs saying?"

Maxie straightened. "I do something wrong, Sher'ff Harte?"

Harte made a weak smile and shook his head. "I've got to make a private call."

Maxie smiled. "Yes'r." She started to leave.

"Maxie, did Stegler's wife come and get him?"

"Yes'r. Turns out she used to clean house for my preacher. They seem like good folks."

Harte nodded, reached to the sill, and turned on the hotplate. When he picked up the blue kettle from his desk, he was surprised at its weight.

"It's fresh, Sher'ff. I filled it up just before you come in from your errands."

He nodded his thanks and set the pot on the plate. Raising his eyebrows as an apology, he put his hand on the phone. Maxie made a small bow and hesitated at the door.

"Sher'ff Harte, I'm sure whatever it is, you'll say it right."

"If I don't, expect to see me with a size eleven boot in my mouth."

Maxie made a pained smile, backed out of the room, and quietly closed the door. Harte punched in the numbers and swiveled his chair to face the window, where he watched the hotplate glow to a soft red under the kettle. When Callie's receptionist answered, he felt the heat of the burner in the pit of his stomach.

"Callie Canaday, please."

There was a delay before the voice came back on the line, this time less cheerful. "That would be Ms. Callie Tasker," the woman explained. "Just a moment, please."

Harte closed his eyes. He hadn't heard that name in decades.

"Callie Tasker," came his wife's familiar voice, altered only by her clipped professional tone and the return to her maiden name.

"Hey," he said simply and watched a gust of wind release a flurry of yellow leaves from the tulip tree outside. Against the steel-gray sky, the leaves caught stark light from somewhere and glowed like big flat sparks tumbling to earth. "I'm concerned about you right now, Callie."

"Harte," she said with a weariness that dragged out his name. "This is not like you to meddle in someone else's life. It's petty. Get your thoughts on other things. If anyone should be concerned, it should be me about you."

"Callie, did you ever know me to lie to you or behave in a petty way?"

"Lie? No. Petty? Harte, think about the other night at the restaurant."

He took a deep breath and exhaled quietly. "You need to distance yourself from Layland."

A drizzle began misting the window. He heard the wet tick of her tongue on the roof of her mouth, a sound that had always served as the prologue to her anger.

"Harte, you need to get on with *your* life. That's what I'm doing. It's no longer your business. If Layland shows me a good time, that's perfect. It's just what I want right now. I'm not going to mope around about being a divorcee."

"Callie, it's not about you seeing other people. It's about Layland."

"What *about* him? Is it that he's successful in business and has lots of fresh ideas?"

"Yeah . . . actually it is. Some of his ideas might be—"

"Harte, this conversation is over! I'm hanging up."

He waited to hear the phone slam down, but it didn't. He knew by her breathing that she was fighting back tears. He clung to the receiver and waited.

"Harte," she said, her voice thinner now, tinged with fear. "You killed two men in the parking lot of a bar."

"They killed Jim Raburn, Callie."

A long quiet followed. He knew where it would lead.

"Harte, you need to see someone professional. You've kept your feelings bottled up, and—"

"Callie, this is not about me. What I'm trying to do—"

"You know what?" she burst in. "I don't want to know what you're trying to do." Her voice was building to the familiar rage that had always led to long periods of silence between them. "I couldn't understand you before all this, and now—" Her voice broke, and in the silence he knew that she was searching for a tissue. When she came back on the line, the gentleness in her words surprised him. "You take care of yourself, Harte. Let me live my life now. I hope you're—" She sniffed and swallowed. "I don't know what I hope. I'm going now." The line went dead.

*****

He drove the cruiser north on nineteen. The early evening was cool enough to run the heater. The soft blow of warm air filled the void left by the conversation with Callie. When he pulled into Luther's parking lot, the glow of the blue neon tried to suck him back into the memory of Jim's death, but Harte would have none of it. He parked, reported his location by radio, grabbed his coat, and walked toward the muted sound of the jukebox wailing behind the door.

When he entered the room, a twangy steel guitar faded to a song's conclusion, and the smoky room quieted. A pool game was in progress at the back of the room, but the four men playing straightened up around the table. He felt the gaze of every patron as he crossed to the bar.

When the next song began, conversations picked up again, and balls clicked on the table. Harte took off his hat and set it on the bar. On the shelf below the countertop, he noticed that the severed telephone cord had been replaced.

"Hey, Harte," Julie said. "I like your moustache."

He laid down three bills. "No nuts, Julie. Just the drink . . . with the cherry juice."

She pushed the money back to him. "Luther's out back, but he won't take your money." Leaning on the bar she lowered her voice. "He thought what happened might hurt business, but look at the place." Her eyes scanned the crowded room. "We're the main attraction in the county." She pushed away from the bar and took a frosty mug from the long freezer and poured his Collins.

Harte took a sip and turned, but he wasn't looking at the numbers. He was looking for a face. He spotted it at the back booth near the pool table. Harte turned to Julie.

"See the fellow in the last booth? Light blue shirt? You know him?"

"The Mexican?" Julie shrugged. "He's been comin' in a lot the last few weeks. He buys one beer and that's it, but he plays pool for hours. Good at it, too. He was here that night, remember?"

"He ever cause any trouble here?"

Julie frowned and looked at the boy. "No, never."

Harte raised the mug like a toast. "Tell Luther 'thank you,' would you?" He grabbed his hat and started to the back of the room.

"Harte?" Julie called out, her voice louder than he had ever heard it.

He turned and tried not to look surprised. Stepping back to the bar, he waited.

"Everything all right, Julie?"

Her eyes angled down to the bar. "I just wanted to thank you again . . . for that night." Her eyes pinched with worry. "I've been thinking . . . a lot . . . about what might have happened."

He watched her screw down the cap on the Collins bottle. "Get Luther, would you? I want to talk to both of you."

Nursing his drink he watched the crowd until Luther spoke up from behind the bar. "What's up, Sheriff?" Julie stood a little behind him, her eyes fixed on Harte.

Harte leaned on his forearms on the bar. "I had an idea you might want to consider." He nodded at the phone behind the counter. "Do you have another phone jack in the building?"

Frowning, Luther looked around the room. "What the hell for? We got the pay phone."

"On the night the Bullochs came in here, your telephone situation was your weak link in the whole affair. With no cell phone service here, you need another phone."

"Where would I put it?" Luther asked, a little annoyed.

"Women's restroom," Harte said. "Lock it in a box in there, and make sure Julie always has a key. And change the lock on the restroom door to a dead bolt. Works only by a key. Same key works both locks. Only time it will ever be used is during an emergency, like the other night. That way, Julie is safe, understand?"

"And who pays for all this?" Luther said.

Harte stared at Luther, but the bartender would not give up his snide grin. "You can't afford *not* to have it. You can write it off as a business expense . . . and you'll be able to keep Julie." Julie's big eyes widened over Luther's shoulder.

Luther made a sly laugh. "Oh, is that right? And where is *she* going?"

"Somewhere she feels safer."

When Luther turned to look at the mortified face of his only employee, Harte reached out and plucked at the strap of Luther's apron. "Somewhere *I* feel she's safer," he corrected. "This is *my* idea, not hers."

As the two men stared at each other, pool balls collided, and one clattered into a pocket. The crowd around the table voiced its approval and applauded. When the patrons quieted and let the jukebox singer take center stage again, Harte hitched his head toward the full room.

"Looks like with your increased business you can afford it." He leaned an elbow on the bar. "You know whose idea this *should* have been, don't you?"

Luther looked down at the bottles neatly arranged before him. He leaned with both arms on the mixing shelf, and his head dropped down between his raised shoulders.

"Yeah, okay," he muttered. He looked up at Harte. "You're right. But won't it be a little weird havin' a phone ring in the bathroom while someone's in there?"

"Keep it on mute. Only Julie and you will know it's there.

Luther bobbed his eyebrows, and his smile turned mischievous. "Like a Hemingway novel."

"How's that?" Harte said.

"She'll be the one for whom the bell tolls."

Harte gave him a look, but Luther only expanded his smile and tried again. "You hear about the soldier who lost both arms to a cannon blast and retreated twenty miles before he cried about it?"

Harte took in a deep breath and waited.

"A far wail to arms," Luther said straight-faced.

Harte exhaled slowly. "You reading a book on puns now?"

254

Luther shook his head. "Just practicing. I'm entering this pun contest in the *Atlantic Monthly*. See if I can win some punny money, you know? My daddy always loved puns."

Harte took a drink from the mug, and pointed to the phone under the counter. "Call the phone company tomorrow, all right?" He turned and carried his mug to the back of the room.

The Mexican sat with an older Hispanic man, listening as the elder explained something with a feeble chopping motion of his wrinkled hand. Harte figured the boy for nineteen or twenty, lean, strong, and probably quick. The old man stuck a hand-rolled cigarette at the center of his mouth and patted the boy's hand. The boy spoke and stood to better see a shot at the pool table.

Harte stepped beside him, knowing that the boy was aware of his presence. "Like to talk to you a moment," Harte said. The boy showed no reaction at first. Then his head came around slowly. "Unless maybe you've got a stake in this game," Harte added.

The boy glanced at Harte's badge and turned back to the game. "Talk about what?"

"Just talk. Can you give me a few minutes?" Harte raised his mug. "I'll buy you a drink."

The boy's face relaxed. "*Si*, we talk. I already had my drink."

The old man had left the booth, so Harte dropped into the Hickok seat, his back to the wall. The boy slid into the facing seat and watched Harte move empty beer bottles to the end of the table.

"My name is Harte Canaday."

The boy raised his chin. "Emmanuél Vega. I remember you."

Harte drank from his mug and studied Emmanuél Vega, who sat a little stiffly as though facing an uncertainty, and at the same time he seemed relaxed of mind.

"I want you to work for me, Emmanuél."

Vega's expression did not change. "I have already a job. I work construction."

"Doing what exactly?"

Vega looked out at the room. "Unload lumber, bricks, sacks of cement. They maybe let me do some framing soon as they see how I use a hammer."

"How much do you make an hour?"

"Six dollar." The boy spoke softly. Harte knew that he was listening to the pool balls crack.

"That's under minimum wage."

Vega shrugged and nodded toward the pool table. "I make my real money there."

"I can pay better," Harte said. "And maybe the job I'm offering will be more satisfying."

The boy made a little sidewise tilt of his head. "I like construction . . . to see things build."

Harte nodded. "This job I'm offering you . . . it will help put drug dealers in jail." Harte caught Julie's attention, raised his mug with one hand and with the other extended one finger.

Emmanuél turned his head and looked long and hard at Harte. "Why you ask me this?"

Harte nodded toward the door. "That night those three brothers came in here like they owned the place . . . you were the only one with enough spine to stand up to them."

Emmanuél kept his eyes fixed on Harte's. "Not the only one, *señor*."

Harte downed the last of his drink. Because of their one shared night of violence, he already felt some kind of bond with the young Mexican. Vega remained relaxed, his dark hair framing his face and neck like the cowl of medieval monk.

"Are you a U.S. citizen, Emmanuél?"

Vega nodded. "*Si*. For two years now." He kept nodding. "My friends call me 'Manny.' "

Julie appeared at their booth and set down a fresh mug and a bowl of nuts. She collected the empty bottles, dumped the ash tray, and left. Harte pushed the mug to Manny.

"What is this?"

Harte smiled and shrugged. "A bribe. It's the best I can do."

"I tell you already. I have my drink."

"Try it. There's no alcohol."

The Mexican frowned at the pink concoction for a time. Finally he picked it up and sipped. He pushed out his lower lip, raised his eyebrows, and nodded.

"I need to ask you," Harte said quietly, "and I need a square answer. Do you use drugs?"

Emmanuél carefully set down his drink. His gaze fixed on a pool player feeding coins into the jukebox, but his eyes glazed over as if he were staring off into an untold distance.

"My sister," he began, "she ees buried in Sonora. Fourteen years old." He locked eyes with Harte. "The bastard who hook her on heroin . . . he was like the brothers you shoot here that night." He curled his lip. "I no use the drugs, *señor*. Never."

The jukebox came alive with a piece of country rock, its driving beat inappropriate to the moment. But Emmanuél's story was like a curtain falling around the table. No music could touch it.

"Why you ask for me to work with you, *señor*?"

"There are people I'll need to deal with who speak your language. There's that, and there's also what I saw in you that night." Harte removed a paper from his shirt pocket. "Try this." He unfolded the paper and read aloud his notes on what Santiago had said to him in Spanish.

Manny seemed amused, but he stopped short of smiling. Taking the paper from Harte, he read it for himself. Then he took another drink and made an airy laugh through his nose.

"It mean . . . 'When your business ees my business' . . . then something about 'cooking bacon.' Then it say something about a 'pale-skinned pig.' " Manny frowned. "Someone say this to you?"

Harte nodded and took back the paper. "So, you want to do this? Will you work for me?"

Manny watched one of the players drop a ball. "Maybe. When would you want me for start?"

"Think about it for a while. Then meet me here day after tomorrow at noon. You have a car?"

The young Mexican shook his head. "If I need to, I get here."

Harte started to rise but lowered himself back into the seat and looked deeply into the boy's dark eyes. "What happened to the man who gave heroin to your sister?"

Emmanuél's face made no change, but the skin on his forehead seemed to reflect a harder glow of light. "He ees in hell, *señor* . . . without the benefit of a proper burial."

They locked eyes as a husky-voiced woman sang from the jukebox about a man who was too weak to be gentle and too bent to be true. Harte again started to leave, but this time Emmanuél stopped him with a touch on his forearm.

"I wear the uniform?" he asked, raising his eyebrows.

"Undercover," Harte said so softly that the boy had to watch his lips. "You okay with that?"

Emmanuél pursed his lips and nodded. When he offered his hand on the deal, Harte stood and busied his hands by tucking in his shirt. When he finished, he leaned his fists on the table and spoke quietly.

"In case you come on board with me, we'll start that undercover right now." Harte casually eyed the neighboring booth. "Point your finger at me and say something insulting in your language, then I'll walk away. Understand?"

Emmanuél sipped from his mug and set the mug down quietly, just as Harte had done. Extending his forefinger toward Harte's face, he delivered a spate of heated Spanish that could be heard two booths away. Except for the jukebox singer berating her inadequate lover, the people within earshot stilled and went quiet. The Mexican slid nimbly from the booth and walked to the pool table without looking back.

Harte looked around the room only briefly, long enough to see the mass paralysis that had followed the boy's performance. Julie stared at Harte with a tray poised inches off the bar. Her eyes were fearful, as though she might burst into tears.

Harte shrugged with his eyebrows, fitted his hat to his head, and walked out.

# Chapter Twenty-Two

It was 6 A.M. After two knocks on his office door and Harte not bothering to answer, the door opened and Joe-Joe Chester entered as Harte pumped out push-ups on the rug before his desk. The pinewood floor beneath creaked with each repetition, and that sound mixed with the steady cadence of Harte's breathy count. It was like the sound of a steam-driven machine working in the room. Joe-Joe waited as Harte stopped whispering the numbers and lowered himself to a prone position.

"Sorry to interrupt, Sher'ff."

Harte stood and dusted off the front of his tee-shirt and sweat pants. "How's your sister?"

Joe-Joe lowered his eyes. "She died." When he looked up at Harte, he managed a sad smile. "It was time, and she was ready. She'd been sick a long time, Sher'ff. It was liver cancer."

"I hope she went peacefully," Harte said.

Joe-Joe pushed his lower lip forward and nodded. "Yeah, pretty much, Sher'ff." A tear stood in the corner of each eye. "Tell you the truth, I'm glad it's over. She didn' need to suffer anymore."

He seemed to shake off his sorrow as he took in the four walls of the office, gawking like a tourist inside a museum. "Nice new sofa, Sher'ff. See you got you a new standup closet." He scrunched up his face at the iron pipe spanning one corner near the ceiling. "That for hangin' clothes, too?"

Harte sat on the edge of his desk and wiped his face with a towel. "Pull-up bar."

Joe-Joe crossed his arms over his chest and frowned at the bar. For a man of his size, he was somewhat graceful. He looked like a fifty-five-gallon drum with legs but moved like a dancer.

"Sher'ff, you know we got that new gym down at the shoppin' center. Burns uses it. He's always talkin' 'bout it. Lots o' fancy machines."

Harte nodded and dropped the towel on his desk. "What about the ball park, Joe-Joe?"

The deputy straightened, and his face turned all business. "Well, yesterday Cody'n me took apart the landfill, worked it all mornin'. In the afternoon I covered the perimeter again by myself. Drove it, walked it, and even checked a aer'al photo off o' Google. There just ain't no way out o' there 'cept the one road. I'd stake a day's pay on it. 'Less that flatbed sprouted wings or dug its way out o' there, it just don't make sense."

Harte frowned out the window. Autumn was starting to catch fire in the hills north of town.

"I appreciate you being so thorough."

Joe-Joe waited and watched Harte's face. "You got any idea 'bout it, Sher'ff?"

"I might."

Joe-Joe eyed the freshly oiled parts of the disassembled Colt on the desk. "You know, Sher'ff . . . Sher'ff Raburn's forty-caliber Glock is avail'ble to you. It's out in the gun case."

"I'll stick with what I know," Harte said.

Joe-Joe nodded, made a little parting wave with one hand, and turned to leave.

"Joe-Joe," Harte said, stopping him at the door. "Don't say anything about any of this."

Joe-Joe glanced at the pull-up bar. "About what?"

Harte held his hard look. "Your search, this conversation . . . that's strictly between us."

"Aw right, Sher'ff." Joe-Joe frowned and looked again at the pull-up bar. "How many o' them can you do, Sher'ff?"

"Not as many as I used to. I'm waging a war against the years."

"Hell, Sher'ff, you ain't that old."

Harte nodded to the bar. "Maybe that's why."

Joe-Joe took in that bit of philosophy with a nod of appreciation and patted his belly. "I prob'ly ought'a start goin' to that new gym. I hear some good-looking women go down there."

"You never know," Harte said. "Could be your destiny waiting for you at a stationary bicycle."

Joe-Joe frowned. "Don't sound like that would take me anywhere, Sher'ff."

Harte had to smile. He waved his deputy away and knelt for a last set of push-ups.

After showering in the lock-up facility, Harte dressed, and called Cody's number. Getting no answer, he walked to his cruiser. The skateboard gang was huddled around Jim Raburn's GMC—four of them looking into the interior, where a pair of legs shod in high-top sneakers protruded from the front seat. The alpha male had his arms folded over his chest, watching with the others.

The tall yellow grass at the end of the lot bent to the wind and, for a wistful moment, sent Harte to Montana. It was always good to hold that place in reserve, he knew. One day he was going to see it. When he fired up the cruiser, a Baroque piece of classical music filled the interior of the car. The upbeat bounce of the harpsicord and strings threatened to disassemble the picture of Montana in his mind, so he turned off the radio and drove out of the lot in silence.

When he arrived at the house where Lauren Raburn and her mother lived, he found Cody's silver pickup parked on the street. Cody stood on a ladder prying the gutter from the eave at the side of the house. When Harte got out, Cody hung the crowbar on his tool belt and climbed down.

"How're they doing?" Harte said, nodding toward the house.

Cody shook his head. "Mrs. Raburn's stayin' kind o' mad all the time, and she's 'bout the only person Lauren's talkin' to. Never seen Lauren like this." Cody propped his hands on his hips, looked down at the grass, and shook his head again.

"Lauren getting any help?" Harte said.

Cody blew air from his cheeks. "Got to be drugs in the house, Mr. C. She hardly knows I'm around. When I try to talk to her, she's just not there, you know?"

"You're here every day?"

Cody looked down the street. "Yeah. She knows I'm around, but—" His jaw knotted, and his dark skin stretched tightly over the bones of his face.

"Anybody been by? Somebody who looked like they might carry drugs?"

"Hell, anybody can carry drugs, Mr. C. There's a girl in there now 'bout Lauren's age, but I don' know her. And a couple in a black Jeep a while ago. Didn' know them either."

"The woman thin, freckled, long legs, and worn boots? The man the flip side of all that?"

Cody nodded. "That'd be her. The man stayed in the Jeep."

"Haversacks," Harte said. "Who else?"

"Maxie-Rose, Layland Childers, the Episcopal preacher, women from the church, the mayor." Cody frowned. "I didn't know Childers was a friend of the family. I do know Sheriff Raburn didn't have much use for him."

"We all went to high school together." Harte nodded toward the house. "Can you talk to Mrs. Raburn about Lauren's problem?"

Cody tightened his mouth to a false smile, huffed a quiet laugh, and shook his head.

Harte saw movement in a window just a few feet away. "Step around back with me."

Cody unhooked the tool belt and hung it on the ladder. Walking out into the lawn, they sat at the picnic table near the back of the property.

"The night we waited for the flatbed to be picked up," Harte began, "there were five of us staking out the exit roads." Harte stacked his forearms on the table. "I want you to think objectively about this. Forget about any protocol of loyalty to the force, all right?"

When Cody nodded, Harte leaned and picked up five desiccated leaves from the grass. "Let's say this board is the bypass," he said, tapping a finger on one of the table slats. He placed one leaf a few inches from it. "Here's the flatbed at the ball field." He dealt out the remaining leaves. "I'm at Trammel's. Beasley on Happy Hollow. Burns at the Quick Mart. Ash at the recycle bins."

Harte watched Cody digest the logistics. "Every deputy swears he did not doze off," Harte continued. "I believe them. It would have been the biggest drug bust in the county's history. No deputy worth his salt would want to miss out on that." Harte flattened both hands on the table and straightened his back. "There's only one way that flatbed got out of there."

A wind picked up, and the leaves scudded a few inches across the table. Next door a dog barked incessantly until a strident female voice ended the barrage. Neither man paid it any mind.

Slowly, Cody began to nod. "One of the deputies let it pass," he said.

Harte leaned on his arms and lowered his voice. "Who would it be, Cody?"

Cody clasped his hands behind his head and stared out at the yard. "Ash," he stated, his voice unequivocal. Dropping his forearms to the table, he cupped each hand around the opposite elbow and looked squarely at Harte, his stare as cold as the muzzle of a gun.

The wind surged and swept the leaves from the table. The long night's vigil flickered through Harte's mind like a film strip. He saw the flatbed winding out its gears up the bypass, Ash watching it drive by, his cell phone to his ear, talking the driver through the only safe route.

"This surprise you?" Harte asked.

Cody shook his head and glanced at the Raburn house. "Nothin' surprises me anymore, Mr. C."

Harte looked around at the yard. "You going to stick around here?"

Cody was a man of deliberate decisions, and the lost expression he showed was ill-suited to his face. He propped his elbows on the table and ground the heels of his palms into each eye. When his hands dropped to the table, he looked like a man awakened from a deep sleep.

"Neither one of 'em really wants me here," Cody said, ". . . for different reasons." He cocked his head toward the house. "Lauren's mother never has liked the idea of gray."

"Gray?"

Cody nodded. "She likes black and white separate . . . unmixed." He shrugged.

"How was Jim with that?"

Cody lifted one corner of his mouth in a weak smile. "Sheriff Raburn treated me damn good." His eyes angled toward the house. "I was one of the many things they disagreed on." He let the smile go. "I'm trying to hang on, Mr. C." He looked away. "I just know I care about Lauren, and she needs to get off those damned drugs."

Harte brushed a few maple seeds from the tabletop and tempered his voice so as not to sound pedantic. "You know that's got to come from her, don't you?"

"Hell, I know it." Cody made a fist on the table and wrapped his other hand around the hard knot of knuckles. "Even if I caught her supplier, I'm afraid o' what Lauren would feel about me if I cut off her supply, you know? I mean, there's no guarantee *that* would get her into a program, right? She might just go through a living hell, and I'll look like the one delivered her into it."

A teenaged girl with straight blonde hair came out the back door and walked diagonally across the yard. Harte recognized her face from somewhere, but the ripped jeans and oversized sweat-shirt didn't fit with the memory. He and Cody watched her move swiftly across the grass. When she looked back at Harte, her expression was guarded, but something changed in her eyes when she cut her gaze to Cody. She disappeared through a gap in the hedge of azaleas.

"Name's Jen," Cody said. "Works as a waitress at some new restaurant on the square."

Now Harte remembered her in a white uniform and a gold vest. "The Brassy Ring," he said.

"Yeah, that's it." Cody stared at the hedge where the girl had exited the yard. "Probably the one who supplies Lauren with what she needs." He turned back to Harte and hissed air through his teeth. "What am I supposed to do? Search Lauren's only friend that comes to see her?"

They were quiet for a time. A breeze rustled the leaves in the big maple by the garage, and a squadron of pastel leaves launched from the tree, fluttering diagonally across the yard.

"There's another angle to come at all this," Harte said, lowering his voice. "You might do Lauren more good by working with me, Cody . . . getting to the root of this problem." He waited for Cody's eyes to meet his. "I could use you, Cody . . . to tail Ash. If he's involved in this like I think he is, I want to know everyone he talks to. I want to know everywhere he goes."

"That's a twenty-four-seven stakeout," Cody said. "One man can't do that."

"You and Joe-Joe."

Cody thought for a moment and shook his head once. "Harder to do when the subject knows you, and Ash knows both of us." He made a pained look and shook his head again. "Plus, Joe-Joe's not the easiest guy to make unnoticeable. Like a buffalo tryin' to hide in your kitchen."

"Joe-Joe could take the nightshift," Harte suggested. "Mostly he'd be sitting in a car down a dark street. We'd have to get each of you another vehicle."

Cody narrowed his eyes. "I still got my brother's old car. Ash doesn't know it." He chewed on his lip, and his eyes glazed over in deep thought. "Would I be the one in charge of the stakeout?"

"You would," Harte replied.

Cody looked up at the section of sagging gutter. "Hell, I never should'a even thought about leaving the force. Lose my damned health insurance and walk away from the one thing I love doin'."

Harte sat back and crossed his arms over his chest. "I didn't file your resignation papers."

Cody's head came around quickly, his face hard, eyes focused.

"Far as I'm concerned," Harte said, "you never left."

Cody hitched his head toward the Raburn house. "Well," he sighed, "if I'm shadowing Ash, at least I'll be gettin' *paid* to hang around somebody who doesn't know I'm there."

Harte slapped both hands lightly on the table and stood. "Talk to Joe-Joe about this and plan your shifts. I want you two to start as soon as possible." He stepped out of the bench seat and looked up at the roof of the house. "Do you need some help getting this finished?"

Cody frowned at the eave on the backside of the house. "I got this," he said. When he stood before Harte, his face was like chiseled stone. "Thank you, Mr. C."

"Don't thank me yet," Harte countered. "You're about to get so steeped in the intimate details of Ash's life, you'll probably have fantasy dreams about replacing gutters."

Cody laughed out of courtesy. "Well, it'll be good to get back in the uniform."

"No uniform," Harte said. "Nobody else will know about this but Joe-Joe and Maxie-Rose."

"Undercover all the way, huh?" Cody said. "All work and no glory." He looked at the house. "Can't say I haven't been trainin' for that."

*****

Harte turned on the hotplate in the office window and spooned instant coffee into his blue cup. When three knocks sounded on the door, he sat behind his desk, satisfied that his knock-before-entering mandate had finally taken effect, even when he called in Maxie-Rose by phone as he had done now.

"Come!"

Holding an open catalogue Maxie entered and crossed the floor. "Sher'ff, Wallace Rainy called and said to tell you there was no trace o' anything unusual on the cinder block."

"Close that, would you?" Harte said, nodding toward the door.

She returned to the door, shut it, and then planted herself directly across the desk from him, studying the room as if she had arrived to audit the sheriff's office. "Sher'ff Harte, we got to spruce up this room a bit." Again she scanned the room with critical eyes. "If you're gonna be livin' here, the least we can do is lift it out of this theme o' depression."

Harte frowned at the walls. "What's depressing about it?"

She offered a kind smile. "It looks like an office that can't make up its mind what it is. We can do better than this." She walked to the window, where Harte had propped the painting of the cowboy from the kettle box. "Case in point," she said, lifting the cardboard like a piece of evidence.

"I *like* that," he said.

She studied it briefly and then raised an eyebrow. "We can do better," she repeated. "How 'bout we put something up on the wall in a frame."

Without hesitation, he pointed to the wall opposite his desk. "Poster of Montana framed in old barn oak . . . right there."

Maxie frowned at the wall. "Montana," she said. "You mean . . . like a map?"

Harte shook his head. "A scene . . . something that would make you want to head west, put on a sheep-skin-lined coat, and live off of elk meat for a while."

Maxie raked a tooth across her upper lip. "Like mountains with snow on top. They got mountains there, right? Prob'ly why they call it 'Montana.' "

Harte kept staring at the wall. "And a horse," he added. "Got to have a horse in it."

"One horse," Maxie repeated, like a short-order cook. "How 'bout a rider on that horse?"

"Optional," he said. "But he'd have to look a little like me."

She smiled and scribbled a note on the catalogue. "Maxie's got a new project," she mumbled.

"Sit down," Harte said. "We need to talk."

Her face sobered, and she moved to the sofa like a demure visitor in a stranger's house.

"What we say here, Maxie, doesn't leave this room, understood?"

Perched on the edge of the cushion, Maxie sat as stiff as angle iron. "Yes-sir-ree-bob-tail!"

"You did a good job for me as an undercover deputy. I'm going to need you again."

"You want me to start packin' my gun, Sher'ff?"

Harte pretended to consider it. "This is mostly going to be done from the switchboard. There are things you need to know. Some of it might require some acting. You think you can do that?"

She nodded like a woodpecker going full-throttle at larvae-laden tree trunk. "I was in all my high school plays, Sher'ff."

Harte waited to see her contain her energy. "You know about Cody leaving the force, right?"

"Yes'r."

"Well, he's not leaving. He's undercover, and he's going to be coordinating with Joe-Joe, keeping an eye on someone for me." Harte leaned forward. "That someone is on the force."

Maxie's expression darkened. "It's Ash, ain't it?"

Harte studied her for a time. "That was quick. Anything you know that I should know?"

"Intuition mostly," she said. "That and attitude."

"Whose attitude?" Harte asked.

"Ash's. He don't enjoy bein' clever, 'less he knows that others know he's clever. A fella like that don't always keep his secrets all that good."

"I want you to find out what cell phone service he uses and get a copy of his calls for the last few months. How do we go about getting a warrant for that?"

"Sher'ff Jim used to call Judge Somerfield. Or you can ask the D.A. and let him go to whatever judge he's friendly with at the moment. Then I can send it electronically to the phone company, and after their legal boys look it over they'll send us what we need."

"Well," Harte said, "I flunked Judge Somerfield's daughter about ten years ago. I don't expect any favors there."

Maxie winced. "Lordy . . . you're already sloggin' through the swamp o' politics."

"My boots have been muddy for a while, Maxie. High school is not all grading papers and football games." He opened a drawer, withdrew a silver deputy's shield, and quietly placed it on the desktop. "Here's your new calling card when you go over to the D.A."

Maxie slowly stood and approached, her eyes glued to the badge.

"The badge stays in your pocket except for special occasions, like picking up warrants."

"Yes'r," she said, her voice filled with gratitude. She lifted the silver shield from his desk and slipped it into her jeans pocket. "So, I'm undercover, too?"

He nodded. "Cody and I will be your only contacts."

"Just tell me what you'd like me to do, Sher'ff."

"For now, get those phone records."

When the blue kettle rattled on the hotplate, he stood, folded his bandana for a hot pad, and poured water over the coffee crystals in his cup. "That's it for now, Maxie."

She stayed put, dug the badge from her pocket, and held it balanced on her palm. "Sher'ff, I want you to know this means a lot to me. And you'll be able to count on me for anything."

"I know that, Maxie. That's why I chose you."

"And you just let me know if I should start carryin' my gun."

He nodded, but she was studying the badge and did not see him. The shield in her hand could have been a hypnotist's pendulant swinging before her eyes. The office was so quiet, Harte could hear the grind of skateboard wheels at the far end of the parking lot. When Maxie looked up at him he could see tears forming in her eyes. Harte sipped his coffee and waited.

"My daddy was a deputy for a while. Back when it was Sher'ff Berry runnin' the show here." When she smiled at him, a tear made its way down her cheek. "I won't disappoint you, Sher'ff."

"I know that too, Maxie."

She pocketed the badge, walked to the door, and turned. "Oh, there's some teenage kids out in the lot who're askin' 'bout some tools. Said you authorized them to work on Sher'ff Jim's car."

"Accommodate them, Maxie. They're on our side."

Maxie's forehead creased with three lines. "They're not undercover too, are they?"

Harte shook his head. "Underage."

When she closed the door behind her, Harte began reading the office file on Roland Ash.

# Chapter Twenty-Three

The late afternoon cool-off of the forest put its spurs into the paint. The mare leaped the small creeks with surges of energy, snorted, and bobbed her head like an equine rite of emancipation. In the thick lush ferns of the flood plain she lifted her hooves high as a show horse, and yet Harte was able to neck-rein her with a light pressure, to which she eagerly responded.

They took the trail upstream to the old Blackshear Mill site and then climbed the slopes through a patchwork of laurels and deerberry. By the time they reached the ridge the sun had fallen within a single hand span above the undulating backdrop of mountains to the west. The sky reddened to a sea of fire that spread across the horizon like molten lava.

Harte tugged down his hat against the high country wind and rode north, sharing with the paint the solitude of wilderness as if they had risen above the world and ventured into a new territory entire. The clop of hooves on dirt and stone was both efficient and euphonious, and he knew that, along with the soft flap of nostrils from the horse's gentle snorting, there was no better music.

At sundown they descended to the creek and broke from the melting shadows of the forest into the fading light of the open meadow. The mare snorted and pressed for speed. When Harte slackened the reins, the paint lunged forward as if a race gate had opened. The exhilarating run for the barn coaxed Harte to imagine the first time that an adventurous horse-capturer dared to leap upon the back of one of his captives and soar out over the landscape with a speed that would forever transform a human's notion of travel and time.

A light was on in the barn, and Harte spotted the dark silhouette of someone hurrying up the road toward the Haversack house. He figured the light as a courtesy from either Jan or Collette—a beacon for his return. Forty yards from the barn, Harte reined up to walk the paint for the last leg.

Inside the barn he rubbed the paint down from the neck, chest, and flanks back to her hindquarters. When he knelt to run the towel down a rear leg, he heard a whimpering sound that stilled his hand. After several seconds, the paint gave an impatient stamp of her hoof, but Harte remained quiet and unmoving. He stood and walked to the tack room door and listened again.

"Anybody in here?" His voice sounded unnatural after the silence of the long ride. He flipped the light switch, and the room filled with stark contrasts. Hanging on the walls the saddles, bridles, halters, and lead ropes gleamed brightly under the bare bulb overhead. Beneath each piece of equipment a deep-black shadow painted a distorted two-dimensional version of its true shape. The wall was like a montage of ink-blot tests.

To his right on the workbench counter sat a *Coor's* beer can. It looked out of place among the tools spread there. Beneath it the old mattress that was usually corded into a tight cylinder was loosely coiled and collapsed against a feed sack. Its green tie-cord lay loose on the floor.

He backed out of the room and finished rubbing down the paint. After leading her into the stall, he grabbed a bucket off its nail and returned to the tack room. There he measured three scoops of grain into the bucket and looked again at the beer can. Beads of water stood on its surface. He touched the wet aluminum. It was cooler than the night air.

Returning to the stall, he dumped the grain in the paint's feed trough and forked hay from the loose pile outside the stall. With the chore complete, he crossed his arms over the gate and watched the horse nose into the trough with single-minded purpose. When Harte reached inside the tack room and turned out the lights, he heard a sound again—a faint scrape on the rough floorboards. Standing very still, he listened in the dark. Outside the night breeze stirred the distant trees. Against this steady sound he heard a wet sniff.

Stepping back into the tack room, he tripped the light switch and waited. When his gaze dropped to the shadow under the workbench he saw a pair of boots and dark blue jeans. She sat far back against the wall, her arms wrapped around her shins, her head bent forward to her knees so that her dark hair spilled over her legs like a shadow itself.

"Collette?"

She sniffed but did not move. Harte approached, pulled out his bandana, and knelt.

"Are you all right?"

Her hair bobbed around her legs as she made the barest of nods.

"Collette . . . what are you doing down here under the table?"

As he stared at the top of her head, her silent crying broke into a sob. He reached out and gently cupped her shoulder with his hand. Her only response was to tighten her hold on her legs.

"Why don't you come out from there," he whispered and patted her back with his fingers. When she didn't move, he released her and waited. On the workbench, just above his eye level, the beer can caught his eye again. "Are you out here having yourself a beer, honey?"

Her tear-streaked face came up quickly. "Yes," she said in a raspy voice. In the shadow of the table her eyes appeared like the sunken cavities of a skull.

"Everything okay with your father?"

Lowering her face, she nodded again.

"Collette, this is nothing to worry about . . . one beer." When her shoulders began to tremble, he started to reach for her again but stayed the motion. "Are you cold?" Still shivering, she shook her head. Helpless, Harte stared at her misery. "Do you have a flashlight? Want me to walk you home?"

When she spoke, her voice was muffled in the crook of her arm. "I don't need one."

She wanted to be left alone. But leaving her here crying was against all his instincts.

"Have you had any luck finding a new place to live?"

When her head came up again, her eyes were almost as red as an animal's caught by a flashbulb. "I need to find one soon." Burying her face in her arm again, she became absolutely still.

"Do you want to be by yourself?"

Collette nodded. Harte stood and hesitated, but it seemed pointless to stand there looking at her veil of dark hair. He walked softly to the doorway and let his hand hover at the light switch long enough to decide to leave the light burning.

"Goodnight," he said and walked out of the barn for the Haversack house.

Jan Haversack opened the front door. With a yellow kitchen towel draped over one shoulder, she held a paring knife in one hand. Otherwise, she was dressed as Harte had always seen her—jeans, tee-shirt, and boots that looked like relics.

"Well, hey there, Mr. Sheriff. Come on in."

Harte stepped inside and took off his hat. Jan gestured to a hat rack on the wall, where an array of brown, black, dove gray and pearl white Western hats hung. Harte kept his in his hand.

"I was wondering if you'd mind if I took the paint on an overnight one weekend . . . maybe use your bay as a pack horse for gear. I thought I might pack into Three Forks area and look around my granddaddy's old place."

An insistent rattling sound turned Jan to look back down the hallway. "Hang on, Harte. I've got something cooking in the kitchen." She started away in her long, deliberate stride but pointed back toward the den. "Wylie's at his shrine . . . praying to the TV. Go rouse him from his trance and I'll be right back."

He wandered into the dark den, where the glow of the big flat television screen etched out Wylie's slumped body on the sofa. His feet were crossed at the ankles on the coffee table, and he balanced a beer with both hands on his belly. The television blared with a lively musical motif as a game show host asked a question, spacing his words for a dramatic delivery. A woman stood behind a podium with two other contestants.

"It's 'John Glenn,' you idiot," Wylie snarled at the screen.

When Harte spoke a greeting, Wylie half sat up and, stabilizing the beer, stared at him intently. Just as quickly, he relaxed. Raising the beer can as a greeting, he turned back to the TV.

"That moron just blew a quarter million," Wylie said.

Harte approached and saw that Wylie was dressed in the same gray sweatpants and tee shirt. There was a scent in the air that reminded Harte of the chem lab at school. A gas fire flickered on ceramic logs in the fireplace. Wylie took a sip of beer. It was a *Coor's*.

"You been ridin'? I didn't see your truck."

"In my cruiser. Parked around back by Bella's orchard. Figured I'd say hello to her."

Wylie sniggered. "Well, I hope you didn't park too close to her sacred trees and maybe crush an apple." When the game show went into its closing music, he picked up the remote and muted the TV. "Hey, how's the new job?"

Harte nodded. "I'm settling in." He watched Wylie turn back to the screen. "Thought I saw somebody walking from the barn just a while ago. Thought you might be looking for me."

Wylie looked beside him and raised a cell phone from the sofa. "Left my phone out there."

Jan appeared, drying her hands on a towel. "So you wanna trek out to the old homestead?"

Harte turned. "Don't have a date in mind yet. Sometime before it gets too cold."

She nodded. "Sure. You and Pied Piper getting along?"

"She likes this weather. She's settling down to the saddle real fine."

Jan laughed. "You just wait till it thunders. When it does, hold on to your hat."

She jerked her thumb back toward the hallway. "I've got to get back to the kitchen. Good to see you, Harte. You keep coming over to ride all you can. The horses need it."

"Will do," he said. "I appreciate it."

Wylie punched the remote, and the sound of the TV filled the room again. It was an ad for a miracle spot remover. Leaning to the table he replaced the cap on a small bottle of clear liquid.

"Hey," Wylie said, turning to smile, "you're getting a lot of press about the O.K. Corral up at Luther's. The Atlanta papers did a big spread on it. Did you see it?"

"No," Harte said. He had thought the sour smell in the room might be Wylie's clothes, but now he suspected some kind of medicine. Wylie caught him frowning at the vial.

"Stinks to high heaven, don't it?" Wylie chortled and held up the of-fending solution. "It's for a skin condition." His smile was impish, like a young kid who had pulled off a prank.

Harte fingered the crease in the crown of his hat. "I'd best be getting back."

When Wylie saluted and settled into the sofa, Harte let himself out and made for the barn.

He knew before he turned on the light that the tack room would be empty. The *Coor's* can still sat on the workbench. As he stood looking at the empty space beneath the counter, he could feel Collette's misery lingering there. He turned off the light and walked out into the grass under the stars until he could make out the dark silhouette of the trailer. Without electricity out there, he didn't know what he had expected to see. He guessed the faint glow from the window to be candlelight.

He did not want to approach Bella's house from the orchard in the dark, so he fired up the cruiser and drove out of Cherokee Rose to the highway and turned on the first dirt drive, taking the long way around simply to let her see his lights approach. When he pulled into her yard next to her little yellow Volkswagen, he saw the front of her house for the first time. The laurel railing around the porch curved and twisted, giving the house a fairy tale charm. Yellow light spilled through the windows out onto the front porch, illuminating a rocking chair next to a small table. The chair rocked back and forth with the wind, and the fringe of the table cloth fluttered like a flag.

When he shut down the cruiser, the front door opened, and Bella's silhouette showed against the soft interior light. The porch light came on, and he watched her carry a tray to the table.

"I probably should have phoned," he called out from her flagstone walkway.

"I saw your car in the meadow. I've got some hot hazelnut coffee. Want to sit?"

As he climbed the steps, she struck a match and, shielding it from the wind, lighted a candle. Harte took off his hat and stood watching as the wick took the flame. Bella stepped back to the door, turned off the porch light, and paused as she looked back at the table.

"Oh, dear," she mumbled and then laughed quietly into her hand. "This looks like an ambush, doesn't it?" She turned the light back on.

"I liked it," Harte said. "Kill the light."

Bella flipped the switch back to darkness, and, in the faint glow of the candle, she laughed again. "I didn't intend for this to look so romantic. It's one of those insect repellent candles."

"Romantic is fine, Bella. You got another chair?"

She pulled out a stool from under the table and started to sit, but he took her shoulders and guided her to the rocker. "I'm pretty sure this one has your name on it," he said.

She obeyed and sat. He took the stool.

"I've not noticed your belt buckle before. That looks like the real thing."

He set his hat on the floor, picked up a steaming mug, and sipped. "A gift from my students. It's an old federal badge." He looked down at it. "It *is* the real deal." He raised the cup like a toast and drank. "*That's* different. What did you add to it?"

She took his mug. "Here, that's mine. I add cocoa. I'm not completely grown up yet."

Harte took the other cup, sampled it, and nodded. He wrapped the mug in both hands and savored the warmth as he looked out at the night. The mountains cut a black scrim of erose horizon against the lighter sky. The stars were like flecks of mica thrown up into the air beyond the hold of gravity.

Bella rocked slowly. "Well, I've been reading about you. How do you like being the sheriff?"

He drank again and thought about his answer. "It's complicated. But I think I'm up for it."

"Does that mean you like it?"

He looked into his coffee. "The job feels right for me."

When her rocking stopped, he looked up at her. A distant beat of drums throbbed from out in the night from the direction of the high school stadium. When the drums stopped, a broad swell of voices carried to them, howling in the darkness like a far off army rushing into battle.

"Must be Friday," he said.

She raised her eyebrows. "So you do *like* it?" she said, pressing the question again.

He studied her face in the candlelight. "I take it you're the kind of woman who expects an honest answer to a simple question."

"I do."

Harte set his mug on the table. "Bella, I was born to do this."

A smile softened her face. "Good . . . I'm glad it's not an obligation you feel."

"You mean because of Jim," he said and turned his attention back to the night sky. After a time he began to nod slowly. "There might be a little of that. But it's not the reason I signed on."

She began rocking again. "I'm betting you're good at it . . . being sheriff, I mean."

"Learning as I go," he said. "I've encountered a bump or two in the road, but I plan to be good at it."

They sat in silence, hearing nothing more from the football game. A star seared across the sky in a shallow arc and disappeared as if it had dropped into a black ocean. With eerie timing a lively wind snuffed out the candle, and Bella became a silhouette. For a time neither spoke.

"Do you think that was a sign?" she finally said.

"If it was," he said, "do you know anyone who can interpret it for us?"

She laughed quietly. "Certainly not me. I don't know anything about that kind of thing."

"I don't even know what you do, Bella, for work, I mean."

"I was a nurse at the hospital in Gainesville. Now I do some private work in people's homes a few days a week. I don't have my license anymore, so officially it's just general home help. I have an elderly client who lives alone."

"What about the other days?"

"She has a daughter who comes in from Flowery Branch."

"I meant, what about *your* other days."

"Oh, I putter around here in the garden . . . in the orchard. I read. And I like to walk the woods." She leaned to the tray. "More coffee?"

"How about a little cocoa in mine this time?"

"Oh, dear, I've corrupted you." She relit the candle, spooned out the powder, and poured water. "A sheriff drinking cocoa." She pursed her lips. "I could blackmail you with this, you know."

It was the most pleasant evening he had spent with another person in a long time. He had wondered if he could be in Bella's presence again without feeling like he was reduced to a man who simply killed people. He knew now that he had underestimated her.

"I like the moustache. Very becoming. With a little time . . . a little Wyatt Earp-ish, I think."

Harte studied her from an angle. "You know what Earp looked like?"

From under the table Bella produced a magazine—the recent issue of *The American West*. Harte stared at it as if she had performed a sleight of hand.

"There's a photo of him in here," she said. "I read your article," she admitted and smiled. "Mr. Raburn told me about it . . . so I bought it." She looked at the magazine again, her expression thoughtful. "It is well written. I liked your character study. I can't say I liked your character though."

He smiled. "If you did, I'd be a little more worried about this ambush you were alluding to."

"Can I ask you something, Harte?" She set down her mug and crossed her legs beneath her on the cushioned seat. "You seem to know something about why some men can kill."

It was too dark to see her face, but her voice carried compassion. "That's your question?"

Bella crossed her arms in her lap. "This Jesse James . . . he's not someone I would have wanted to drink coffee with, but, of course, he endured the Civil War and all that guerilla warfare and that bomb thrown into his house that maimed his mother and killed his little brother. Perhaps one might see how all that might harden him." She eased into a rocking motion that was as relaxing to watch as it was to listen to the rhythm of the chair's curved runners on the floorboards.

"What happened to you, Harte?" she asked with a gentle tone in her voice.

He let the silence gather, knowing that, if he wanted to, he could let that silence drive a wedge between the question and the need to answer.

"Do you mean . . . what is it that allows me to kill another man?"

She took in a deep breath and eased it out. "I suppose so," she whispered.

"Bella, there are things some men can do and others can't. That night at Luther's, I'd just seen my best friend killed. If Jim could have seen what was coming, he'd a done the same thing I did. But Jim was always cautious about shooting a man. Most men don't want to throw down on a sheriff and he knew that. Maybe even counted on it."

"Throw down?" she said.

"That's from the nineteenth century. It means to pull a gun on a man." He cradled the mug in his hands, feeling the warmth. "Those men at Luther's needed killing because they were killers."

She thought about that for a time. "So you made that judgment that quickly?"

He shook his head. "Not consciously. On a deeper gut level, maybe."

Bella stopped rocking and stared out into her yard.

"You believe in the best of people, Bella . . . that there is good waiting inside every man. But some men learn to live with so much evil, they can't go back. They ruin other lives. They end them. I think those Bulloch boys enjoyed the pain they inflicted. They didn't belong on this Earth with people like you and Collette and—" He made a vague gesture out into the night.

"I saw their evil," she said. "I just don't think I could have done what you did." She hugged herself and shivered. "I was helpless in that car. My body went light and weak and useless. I just balled up like I could hide from the world. I was so afraid."

He knew she was struggling with a conversation that had gone to a place she had not anticipated. For Harte, there was no place for the tragedy at Luther's to go but into the past. If there was something to learn from it, he would take that forward. But, so far, he had found nothing edifying from that night. He finished his coffee concoction and set the mug on the table.

"It may be true," he said, "that no one should have the right to end another man's life. Even a cruel man without any moral compass. But the Bullochs held the power to rob me of my right to a life, and I could not let that happen."

Bella began rocking again. A bass drum boomed in the distance, and the football crowd yelled in unison in the time-honored ritual of saluting a game kickoff.

"Is there a personal price to pay, Harte? For you, I mean?"

He looked directly at her. "No," he said, hardening the word with resolve.

"I'm glad of that," she said. "You seem to be one of those men who can remain exactly who he is, even when thrown into trauma. You've gone from being a teacher to—" She hesitated.

"A killer of men?"

She nodded. "But here you are, the same man who fixed my fence, talked to me about my daughter and, according to Collette, has been a teacher that students are not likely to forget."

Harte tightened his mouth into a false smile. "My wife—my ex-wife—thinks I have a problem with anger. About my father. She believes my being sheriff gives it a way out." He gripped the front of the stool seat and rocked forward on stiffened arms just as he did on the pommel of a saddle. "She's wrong. I don't have any anger locked up inside me. I don't even like anger."

"Oh, I agree," she said quickly. "I know anger when I see it. Could she be projecting?"

He was surprised how easily she had picked up on that, but he wanted to change the subject, so he shrugged. "I'm no psychologist."

She picked up the magazine and turned the cover toward him. "But you probably could have been one." Setting down the magazine she said, "May I ask about your father?"

He gathered a little boy's pieces of memory from a night long ago. It was a story he had told only twice, once to Jim and then later to Callie.

"After we sold the farm, we moved into my granddaddy's old homestead." He pointed north. "Way back in the woods about two miles from the Raburn place. Daddy started driving for a trucking company, hauling liquor from Atlanta to Chattanooga. One night on his way home, he'd stopped at a little gas station to get some coffee, when three guys forced him to open the trailer. There wasn't much in there, just a few crates the buyer had refused, but these guys wanted it, and they made Daddy do the loading into their pickup."

"The gas station attendant saw them but thought it was an impromptu sale going on in his lot." Harte shook his head. "That's about all we ever found out. They shot him. Left him for dead."

"Oh, Harte," Bella breathed. She tilted her head to one side and held her eyes on him.

In the distance the high school band broke into a lively tune punctuated by heavy drumbeats and the crash of cymbals. Rather than trespassing on the mood of the moment, the music had the effect of isolating Bella's porch from the rest of the world.

"I was just a kid, but I knew my daddy," Harte added. "He wouldn't have risked his life over a few crates of liquor. Family came first." He nodded as though, from the vantage point of his present age, he was once again agreeing with that assessment.

"Mama got the call, and we drove over there, but we were too late." Harte looked down at his hands. "It's a picture that stays in my head in the finest detail. Daddy was in the emergency room on a gurney. Mama wouldn't let me look at him, though she had to identify him for the deputy." Harte met Bella's eyes with his own. "The picture is of Mama looking under a white sheet. I remember her straightening his collar. That stays with me."

He looked out into the darkness again and wondered why he had told her so much. Her presence just a few feet away seemed a quiet acceptance of whatever he might offer. The band started in on something familiar to his ear, but it faded into a background noise that could not compete with the comfortable silence on the porch.

"It wasn't anger I carried away from that night," he said quietly. "It was the waste."

Bella tried to smile. "And now you've lost your best friend."

Harte filled his chest with air and released it. "Jim had a daughter."

She nodded. "Yes, he told me."

He turned to her and lowered his voice. "Did he tell you she is addicted to drugs?"

Though Bella had not moved, she seemed to go still. "No."

Harte nodded. "Drugs were destroying the one thing in this world that Jim loved. And then it was drugs that got Jim killed." He straightened and rubbed his palms together. "I guess I didn't know until right now that I took the sheriff's job because of that." He stood. "If I can, I'm going to do something about that."

He stepped to the edge of the porch and set his fingertips on the railing. The band was quiet, but every few minutes a roar from the crowd erupted and air horns blared with inane persistency.

"Do you know how Collette describes you?" Bella said. "She says you are 'noble.' I don't think I've ever heard another contemporary teenager use that word to describe anyone or anything."

Harte said nothing to that. He turned to see her rocking in a steady rhythm.

"I need to ask you a question, Bella. When you had trouble with the horses in your orchard, you called Jim first thing. Why didn't you approach Wylie and Jan about it first?"

Her chair stopped rocking, and her face lost all its warmth. "I'd rather not talk about the Haversacks," she replied in a tight-lipped monotone.

"I need to know, Bella."

She looked away and raked her upper incisors across her lower lip. "Let's just say, I like the idea of that barbed wire back there." She rubbed her face with her hands and let her head settle back on the chair. "He came over here one night . . . to my back door . . . half-drunk. He had a beer in his hand and this God-awful smile that—" She shook her head quickly, as if a fly were worrying her. "He opened the door before I could latch it. I had that kettle on the stove. I picked it up, ready to burn him where it counted."

Harte waited to see if there was more, but Bella stood and began to gather up the tray.

"When was this, Bella?"

She paused upright, the tray in her hands. "Just after I moved in."

"Would that be before the Devereauxs moved in?"

Bella frowned, but then the uncertainty dropped from her face. "Yes, because right after that I remember thinking: *I wonder what he uses that empty trailer for?*"

Harte tapped his hat in a steady rhythm against his leg. "So, what happened?"

Bella continued to stand with the tray. "Nothing happened. He left with his tail between his legs. He's not been back."

Harte exhumed the image of the water-beaded beer can in the tack room. And the mattress thrown against the wall. He took the tray from Bella and set it back on the table.

"Sit down for a minute more, will you?"

She settled into the chair again. Harte slid the stool closer to her and straddled it.

"I want you to do me a favor and talk to Collette."

Bella's eyes slanted to a pained look. "About what?"

Harte held up a palm as a gesture not to jump to a conclusion. "I'm asking you because she's embarrassed to talk to me. I'm her teacher . . . or I *was*. And I'm probably the wrong gender." He looked down in his hat for the proper words. "I'm just wondering how the rent on that trailer gets paid."

He waited as the implied meaning of his question sank in.

"Oh, dear Lord," she breathed. "What's happened?"

Harte shook his head. "I just want to ask the question. Do you think you can do that without upsetting her?"

Bella slumped back in the chair and closed her eyes. "Yes," she breathed. "I can try."

# Chapter Twenty-Four

A brisk knock sounded at his door, and Harte finished stirring his coffee, lipped the spoon dry, and set it on the windowsill. "Come!" he called.

Maxie-Rose shouldered the door open, her morning coffee in one hand and a sheaf of papers in the other. She carefully closed the door with her backside, marched across the room, and dropped a transcript on the desk. She was smiling like a cat who had recently dined on canary.

"Ash's phone records," she reported and sipped her coffee, her eyes shining over the mug.

Harte ran his finger down the page to the night of the cinder block fiasco. "Three calls to the same number. Eleven-eighteen P.M., twelve-fifty A.M., and two-ten A.M." He looked up at Maxie.

"Layland Childers's number," she said.

Looking back at the number, Harte felt the skin along his spine tingle. "Layland," he mumbled. Scanning the page, he found scores of calls to the same number scattered throughout the month. He looked back at the cinder block calls. "First call to let Layland know about the brick spill. Ash would have picked it up on his radio. The second to lay out the plan. Ash knew where he'd be staked out by then. Last call to confirm the escape up the bypass." Harte raised his eyebrows at Maxie-Rose. "Sound about right to you?"

Maxie scowled. "And the son of a bitch has the gall to wear our uniform."

Harte had begun raising his blue coffee cup to his lips, but he hesitated, peering wide-eyed at her over the rim of the cup.

"What?!" Maxie shot back, her face stiff and defensive. She waved away her profanity. "Sher'ff Harte, that's more a insult to the mama dog than to Ash."

Harte dropped the transcript on the desk. "We need to keep this quiet for now, Maxie . . . and act like we don't know. Do you think you can do that?"

Maxie sneered at the transcript and huffed a laugh. "Well, you told me this would involve some actin', Sher'ff. I ought to be pretty good at playin' dumb. I've been watching Burns long enough to know how." She turned to leave.

"Maxie?"

When she stopped at the door and turned, her eyebrows arched like a double sunrise.

"What was Jim's opinion of Ash? Did they get along?"

She pursed her lips and shook her head. "He didn' have the first clue 'bout 'im, Sher'ff. Ash came here two years ago with a résumé from somewhere in North Carolina. Charlotte, I think."

Harte picked up his telephone. "You want to dig into that a little?"

Maxie-Rose's eyes lit up. "With a back-hoe, Sher'ff."

"Rather you do it with a trowel and an archeologist's brush."

"Oh, Sher'ff Harte, I almost forgot. Your mechanic said he was all done." When Harte frowned she added, "Lester Dowdy?"

When he nodded and punched in numbers on the phone, Maxie slipped from the office and closed the door with barely a sound. Cody answered on the third ring.

"What time do you take your shift?" Harte asked.

"Joe-Joe is on until noon. Then it's me."

"I thought he was taking night and you day."

"We got it worked out, Sheriff." Behind Cody's voice an acoustic roar of voices swelled.

"Where are you?" Harte said.

"Martial arts studio," Cody said. "I'm teaching a class here."

"I'll call Joe-Joe, and ask him to stay for a while. I need you behind Luther's place at noon."

"What's up, Sheriff?"

"I want you to drive my truck out to Luther's," Harte explained. "I'll leave it for you outside the Mexican restaurant just down the street from your studio. The key will be in the ash tray."

"What are we doin' out there at Luther's, Sheriff?"

"You're going to meet Emmanuél Vega, a new member of our little cabal."

In the quiet that followed, Harte heard something thud heavily into a mat just before a crowd groaned. "Okay, see you at noon, Sheriff."

When Cody hung up, Harte punched in the numbers for Callie's office.

*****

She was waiting for him under the narrow awning behind her office. She wore her suede coat with the fleece lining that billowed out at the seams in a white on tan design of rectangles. Her boots were a perfect match. Her arms were tightly folded across her breasts, and her hosed legs beneath her skirt were clamped together against the morning chill. Harte waved her to the cruiser.

She walked stiffly through the drizzle to the passenger side, got in, and slammed the door against the weather. She refolded her arms and sat back against the door to glare at Harte. The engine purred, and the heater poured out a warm breath at their feet. He propped his arm on the backrest of her seat.

"Whether you want to believe this or not," he began, "I'm doing you a favor. But I need to ask you not to talk to anyone about what I'm going to tell you. Can you do that for me?"

"Harte, why do you still insist on insinuating yourself into my life? I don't need your favors."

He tried to see her as he once had—engaging, smart. "You need this one, Callie."

She blew out a sharp breath. "Just spit it out. I've got a lot of work to do today."

"You're going to have to loosen up a bit to hear this. Right now you're dead set on bucking whatever I have to say. I'm telling you this for your own good. I care about your reputation. So tell me you won't pass along this information to *anyone*. I need to hear that from you."

She glared at him but then made a dramatic sigh. "Okay, I won't tell a soul. All right?"

He watched her anger settle into a pout, and he decided this was the best he was going to get from her. "I'm pretty sure that Layland is bringing drugs into the county. I think he's working with a Cuban who supplies him. I also believe this man is dangerous."

Callie rolled her eyes. "Is this about Turon Santiago?" Her laugh was derisive and disbelieving. "Harte, he's a charming man. He's in construction. He's working with Layland on—"

"He's an actor, Callie," Harte interrupted. "Builders don't carry guns. I know what I'm talking about. He and Layland are poisoning our county . . . people like Lauren Raburn."

Callie's face wrinkled. "Jim's Lauren? Oh, for God's sake, Harte!" She wore her look of doubt like a criticism of hearsay. "Do you really think Jim would have allowed that?"

"He knew. He found out too late."

She turned her frown to the rain-stippled windshield. "You're trying to make me think this isn't really about Layland and me." Closing her eyes she tried to laugh but didn't quite pull it off. She turned quickly, looking at him through a lens of tears. "You need to turn *my* pleasure into something taboo. Isn't that right?" She shook her head. "Turon is not dangerous, Harte. *You* are."

When she turned back to the windshield, he stared at the profile of her face. "The GBI has been trying to nail him for a while, Callie. This is not about me getting into your private affairs."

She swallowed dryly. "Isn't it? Are *you* seeing anyone?"

He hesitated just long enough to put an arch in Callie's eyebrow. "No, not really."

Her eyes bored into him. "Anyone I know?"

He shook his head. After a few seconds of listening to the light patter of rain on the roof, he reached behind his seat and brought out the divorce papers that he had signed. When he handed them to her, she looked surprised and then looked away. The tears in her eyes threatened to spill over.

"Thank you," she whispered.

She fumbled through the pockets of her coat but found nothing. He pulled his bandana from his shirt pocket and offered it. Taking it, she dabbed at her eyes, trying to keep her eyeliner intact. When she handed it back, her other hand went to the door handle.

"I've got to get back," she said, opened the door, and got out.

He readied himself for the slam of the door, but she remained standing in the open doorway in the light mist of rain. Finally, she leaned back in; but, before she could speak, the radio crackled and Maxie called to remind Beasley to pick up his dry cleaning. Harte turned off the speaker.

"You take care of yourself, Callie."

She lingered a while more. "I do like your moustache."

Harte gave her a doubtful look. "You never liked one on me before."

"Well," she said and shrugged. "Maybe it's not the first time I've been wrong."

She shut the door and started walking at a determined pace. Surprising him, she stopped a few yards from the cruiser and turned back. He rolled down his window.

"Stay out of my life, Harte! It's not your business anymore!" She spun and ran to the building with the papers held above her hair. He watched her until she disappeared through the door.

"I hope you're right," he said in the emptiness of the car. He started the engine and pulled out of the lot, imagining a skein of threads—like spider's silk—snapping in his wake.

*****

Wearing a gray plastic poncho, Emmanuél Vega stood alone beside Luther's Dumpster as Harte pulled the cruiser behind the Liquid Gold. Cody followed in Harte's truck. When both vehicles stopped, Vega still had not moved. Cody got out of the truck, walked to the sheriff's cruiser, opened both right doors, and sat in front.

Emmanuél crossed the lot, slipped out of the poncho, and slid into the cruiser's back seat. He wore a faded turquoise shirt with a Western seam and mother-of-pearl snap buttons and well-worn black jeans that had faded to a near colorless state. On his feet were the tan lace-up work boots that were typical at construction sites. The Mexican set the wet rain gear on the floor and closed the door against the light sprinkle of rain. Cody turned, propped an arm on the top of his seat, and nodded.

"Emmanuél Vega," Harte said, "this is my chief deputy, Cody Culp."

Cody reached through the gap in the seats, and the two young men shook hands. Harte waited as they exchanged greetings, and then he turned to look the Mexican boy in the eye.

"I'm assuming by your presence here, you've decided to work with us."

"*Si*," Emmanuél said. "I work for you."

Harte nodded once and then waited. "Don't you want to know your pay?"

"Sure. How much?"

When Harte told him, Emmanuél looked at Cody. "You make the same?"

"More," Cody replied. "But I'm a chief deputy. I've been at this a while."

"Can you live with that?" Harte asked, watching Vega in the mirror.

"Live with it. Die with it. Long as we stick our finger in the eye of the drug dealers."

Cody smiled at Harte. "I like this guy already."

Harte turned in his seat. "Cody will be your main contact. We're the only ones in my office who will know about you. You're undercover, and you're to tell *no one*, understood?"

Harte waited until the boy acknowledged the mandate by a nod.

"Should something happen to Cody *and* me, you're to tell Maxie-Rose, my dispatcher, to open up my bottom right desk drawer. There'll be a folder there on you. Understand?"

"*Si*," Emmanuél said simply.

"And if something happens to *you*?" Harte asked.

The Mexican shrugged. "Then it does."

Harte glanced at Cody and then leveled his gaze back on the boy. "Until you can fill out the paperwork that I'll get to you, I need a contact . . . in case something happens to you."

Emmanuél shook his head. "There ees no one, *señor*."

"Listen," Cody said. "This is going to be a little different than carrying sacks of concrete. Think you can hold your shit together when a bad man is trying to read your face for lies?"

Emmanuél allowed only the hint of a smile. "Every man knows how to lie, *señor*. He only need a good reason." His eyes flicked to Harte. "I have mine."

The wind howled and rattled the downspout of Luther's gutter. Harte looked to Cody to see if he had more questions.

"Ever do any acting?" Cody said.

Emmanuél looked out the window, but his eyes seemed to look at nothing . . . or everything. "I many times win at poker." He made a little shrug. "Poker sometimes requires the acting."

Cody conceded as much with a nod. "If I was any good at poker, I'd prob'ly agree with you."

"We're going to set up a one-act play," Harte explained. "You and Cody and a Cuban who is probably dangerous. Cody will give you the details." Harte pulled a folded paper from his coat pocket. "Memorize this name and address, then destroy this. You're going to get friendly with him."

Vega took the paper and read aloud. "'Turon Santiago.'" He recited the address and handed back the paper. "I have it."

Harte took the paper and exchanged glances with Cody, who pushed his lower lip forward and arched his eyebrows. "If this goes the way we think it will," Harte said to Emmanuél, "you'll have the man's confidence. You might be able to get on the inside of this."

"This man Santiago . . . he ees part of the drugs?"

"Probably the biggest part. If you don't connect with him, you'll need to follow him. I'll need your eyes and ears. I want to know who he talks to." Harte pointed out the back windshield. "That's my truck. You're going to need transportation."

Cody held out the keys, a cell phone, and charger. Vega took the items and laid them aside.

Harte produced a folded bundle of twenties bound by a rubber band.

"For gas. And oil . . . until I can get a ring job on the pistons. It's burning oil. So be sure to check it often."

Emmanuél slipped the money into his shirt pocket. "I get the time, I fix the rings for you."

"I want you to keep a record of mileage," Harte continued. "Doesn't have to be exact. My odometer is not working, so just make estimates as best you can."

Looking out the window at the old truck, Emmanuél seemed to take it all in stride. "I fix that, too."

Cody smiled at Harte. "Damn, Mr. C, you're getting' a hellava deal out o' this." He turned back to study the Mexican's face. "You play the violin, too, Emmanuél?"

"No, *señor*, only poker and pool," he said without smiling. "You can call me 'Manny.' "

# Chapter Twenty-Five

Four days later, as the sun crept up over the eastern flatlands, Harte drove south on Highway 400, sipping coffee from a thermos and thinking about all the changes coming up this road to his county. He turned west toward the Coal Mountain community where he pulled into Urlene's Country Kitchen on the main drag. There were only two vehicles parked by the restaurant, one being Harte's pickup. It sat in the lot like a long-lost friend, who had already forgotten about him. The other car hunkered at the end of the lot with no tires.

Through the big front window he saw Cody and Emmanuél drinking coffee in a booth. They were the only customers, the two of them looking like laborers who had stopped by to fuel up for a day's work at a construction site.

Emmanuél's eyes had locked on Harte the moment he had entered the lot, while Cody bantered with the heavy-set waitress standing behind the empty counter halfway across the room. When Harte stepped out of the cruiser and walked to the diner, he watched the young Mexican's eyes slide away to a menu. As soon as Harte opened the door, the salt smell of bacon shot a pang of hunger to his stomach.

"You boys ordered yet?" Harte said, standing at their booth.

Cody shook his head, his smile like the closed lid on a jack-in-the-box. "Sit down," he said, his voice charged with energy. "We got some news."

Harte looked at Emmanuél, whose face was unreadable as he sipped his coffee. Cody's jacket and small backpack sat beside him on the seat, so Harte slipped into the booth beside the Mexican. The waitress who had followed Harte to the booth was middle-aged and squat with flaccid mounds of flesh quaking on her arms. Her graying hair was tucked under a net beneath a white cap.

"Y'all ready to order now?" Her eyes darted to Harte's badge. "Well . . . it's a good thing you showed up, Sheriff. These boys've been nothin' but trouble." She winked at Cody.

Harte checked her name tag. "Urlene, I've been hunting these two desperados for over a year now. I'll feed them some breakfast before hauling them off to jail, if that's all right with you."

Urlene bent forward, feigning intense curiosity. "What'd they do, Sheriff?"

"Serial killers, the both of them."

She straightened, put her fists on her ample hips, and raised one eyebrow at Cody. "All right, then . . . no corn flakes for you boys, d'you hear me?"

Harte laughed and pointed at Cody. "He's gonna give you a good tip for that one, Urlene."

When she left with the orders, Cody leaned to Harte. "What the hell was that about corn flakes?"

Harte gave him a deadpan stare. "Serial killer?"

Cody slowly closed his eyes and began shaking his head. Harte took off his hat and propped it on his knee outside the table.

"Is Joe-Joe on Ash?" Harte asked.

Cody nodded. "Like a tick on a hound dog."

Harte settled back in the seat and looked from one deputy to the other. "What's your news?"

Cody pointed at Emmanuél. "Manny is in with Santiago." Cody's smile stretched across his face, and the white of his teeth shone electric against his dark skin. Emmanuél set down his coffee, reached across the table, and sprinkled some black pepper into his cup. As he stirred, Harte and Cody looked at one another, but neither commented.

"Tell me about it," Harte said.

Cody leaned close again and lowered his voice. "Santiago drove into Atlanta last night. Prob'ly misses the Miami night life. We followed him to a club in Buckhead. Wouldn't let the valet park his car for him so he pulled down one o' little side streets. That was our good luck."

Cody pointed to Manny. "This hombre here should'a been a god-damn sniper. Sat like a gravestone in some bushes for about three hours while I walked the sidewalk in a hip-hop hoodie and baggy clothes I took off o' my nephew. About one o'clock, Santiago comes out and walks down this little street toward his car. Street's dead. I'm about ten feet behind him in my running shoes . . . quiet-like . . . 'xcept for the damned clothes. Pants sounded like a flag whippin' in a hurricane. But he doesn't hear me, and by the time he opens his door I've got a knife at his throat and the best midtown jive accent you ever heard."

Harte closed his eyes. "Please tell me you knew he wasn't carrying."

"When you got a blade pressing into your windpipe, it don't matter much what you're carrying. I told him to put his fuckin' hands on top of the car, and he was like a boy scout. I slipped his gun out then and oohed and aahed over my good fortune. Then I took his wallet."

" 'Bout this time, guess who comes strollin' down the sidewalk." Cody nodded to his new partner, who listened as if this were a story he had already heard too many times. "So Manny calls out 'What you doin', nigger?' "

Manny pointed to Cody. "His idea. He make up the words."

"So, Santiago hears Manny's accent and says something in Spanish. Manny answers in the same. I tell Manny to fuck off, and I start backing away from the car, moving down the street where it's darker. Santiago has a few choice words for me in my language. 'Bout then I'm wonder-ing if he's got a gun in his car, but Manny yells out to me and gets between me and Santiago."

Harte turned to Manny. "What'd you say?"

Manny shrugged and nodded to Cody. "His words again. I say something like 'You're on the wrong turf, nigger,' and I pull out my knife."

"Cut to the chase," Cody said. "I duck through an alley between strip malls, and Manny's on my heels like a wildcat let out of its cage. We turn a corner, I give him the gun and wallet. Then I take out my trusty catsup packet from Wendy's, but guess what Manny does? Show 'im, Manny."

Manny raised his shirt. A neat row of stitches ran across one rib.

"This Mexican psycho cuts himself!" Cody laughed.

Harte studied the freshly stitched wound and then checked the boy's eyes for sanity.

Manny shrugged. "I no like the catsup. If Santiago smell it—" He gestured with his hand at the obvious.

Cody circled his hand in the air for Manny to continue the story.

"I need this for to convince him," he said and lowered his shirt. "I go back and Santiago ees coming with another gun. He see me, and I hold up his wallet and gun and he slows. I make sure he sees my cut."

Urlene arrived with a tray of steaming plates. "Sheriff?" she said. "You feeling all right?" Harte lifted his forehead from the cradle of his hand. "Here you go," she said. "This oughta make you feel better." She set down his order before him and then clacked down the other two plates.

When she left, Harte turned a sober eye on his deputies. "You could have been shot, and there's nothing I could do for you down there." He frowned at Cody. "Did he get a look at you?"

Cody shook his head. "Wore a ski mask under the hood. Tell 'im the rest, Manny."

Manny had started on his eggs. "Santiago," he said through a mouthful, "he give me his card and say he has work if I want. I ask him what

302

kind. He say, 'Like tonight.' I say, 'I think about it.' " Manny dug the card from his shirt pocket, and Harte wrote the cell phone number on a paper napkin.

"Have you called him?"

"No, *señor*. We let time go by, *si*?" Manny looked thoughtfully at his plate as he idly pushed food with his fork. "We come back up here for me to see doctor, and I meet your friend at the hospital." His voice was casual, but his eyes angled to Harte with a flash of intensity.

"What friend?"

"Collette," he said. "She ees there with her sick father." Manny began nodding, his face as serious as Harte had ever seen it.

"He met her in the waiting room," Cody explained. "Her father had some kind of meltdown."

Harte looked back and forth from his chief deputy to his newest recruit. "Why did you wait and travel back up here to get yourself sewn up?"

Cody answered for them. "Neither of us had much money on us. I know most of the docs in emergency up here. Thought we might need a familiar face."

Harte shook his head. "You boys've got some wild hairs, you know that?"

"*Si*," Cody said and smiled. "We're the minorities from hell, right, *amigo*?"

Cody backhanded Manny's shoulder, but the boy remained unfazed, forking up hash browns with singular intensity, as if he might not eat for the rest of the day. Cody followed suit, digging into his waffle. Harte sipped coffee and watched the two deputies as they refueled. Picturing the events of their night, he felt grateful that a row of stitches was the only price they had paid.

*****

Back at the department, when Maxie-Rose entered Harte's office, he motioned her to close the door—a semaphore that had come to symbolize Maxie's new status as an undercover officer. She pushed it shut, walked quickly to his desk, and all but saluted.

"Maxie, do all our deputies carry cell phones?"

"Everybody 'xcept Beasley. He lost his. And Meeks, he's too scared o' one."

"I could use you tonight," Harte said. "We're hitting the Moody place. Interested?"

Maxie stood a little straighter. "Yes'r, I'm always ready."

"I want you with Ash from the moment he leaves my office, understand? You'll ride out with him. If he radios out from his car, he might try to get some kind of coded message through to someone. We don't know how many people he's partnered up with out there in the drug networks. I need you sharp, Maxie. If he stops somewhere, go with him."

"So, I should take my gun?"

Harte hesitated for only a moment. "Yes, take your gun."

"Will I be part o' the raid, Sher'ff Harte?"

"You're not cleared for that, Maxie. You'll be in charge of communications and guarding the road. You'll watch for anybody trying to drive out of there. If we're outmanned, you'll need to call the Dawson sheriff. We'll be close enough to the county line out there. You know their frequency?"

"Yes'r. I know every frequency of every county 'round us."

"All right," Harte said. "Radio Ash. Tell him I want to see him now. Then get Cody on his cell phone—private. Since Ash will be with us tonight, Cody and Joe-Joe can take the night off."

"What about Ash's cell phone, Sheriff? He might try to call out on it."

Harte almost smiled. "I'll take care of that."

*****

When Ash walked in, he appeared freshly groomed. His longish blond hair was damp and combed. His rosy-cheeked face held its perpetual neutral expression, as though nothing could surprise him.

"You want me?"

Harte nodded. "Close the door."

Ash shut the door with an indifferent grace, as if he did all things at his own chosen pace.

"We're making a meth bust tonight. I need you to head up one of the flanks."

"Where?" Ash said and followed Harte to the county map pinned to the wall.

"The Moody place, right here at the county line." Harte stabbed his finger to the location.

"How're we goin' in?"

"You go in on foot by this old mining road just east of the property. Do you know it?"

"Yeah, I've seen it."

"I want you and one other car to park on that road. No lights after you turn onto Pot Leg Road. We'll have enough moon tonight for you to see your way. There's a metal shed thirty yards east of the house. Fifty from the old road. Two doors to the building. You boys'll come up from the east. We'll go in from the west."

Ash stared at the map with his hands on his hips. "Moodys are mean sonzabitches."

Harte waited for the deputy to face him. "So are we." Ash widened his eyes. It was the sharpest reaction Harte had seen him show in all the time he'd known him. "You have a cell phone?"

Ash patted his shirt pocket. "Sure, right here."

"I'm going to need one tonight. Mine's not working. Let me use yours."

Ash hesitated but handed it to Harte. "What if *I* need it?" he asked too late.

"You won't. Have a seat." Harte picked up the desk phone. "Maxie, send in Beasley, Burns, and Fortenberry. And get Arthur Meeks from downstairs. Ash is here with me. Then bring in two boxes of shotgun shells for each man."

With all the deputies gathered in his office, Harte leaned back against the front of his desk and held up a folded paper. "We have the warrant for the Moody place, and we're going in tonight. How many of you carry phones?" All hands went up except Beasley, Meeks, and Ash. "Okay, Beasley, you ride with Fortenberry and follow Meeks and me. Maxie-Rose will be with you, Ash. Burns will drive alone." Harte ignored the scowl on Ash's face. "Maxie, you'll stay in a cruiser to handle the radio. Plus, you have a phone. I want all cell phones on vibrate. That'll be our backup . . . in case we have any trouble with the walkie-talkies."

"Sher'ff," Meeks said in his thin, squeaky-wheel voice. "I'm usually just a jailor. Don't ord'nar'ly go out on raids. You sure you want me along?"

Harte studied the man. "If you think you're not up to this, Arthur, I need to know that now."

Meeks's eyes cut briefly to the men around him. "Well, it ain't 'xactly that. It's just that Sher'ff Jim never used me like *this* before."

"I can replace you with Joe-Joe," Harte suggested.

"Hell, Meeks," Burns complained. "You're always talking about how boring your job is. This is your chance to be an honest-to-God officer of the law."

Meeks ran his tongue across his lips. "Well . . . all right. I reckon I'll give it a go."

"Are you up-to-date on firearm qualifications?" Harte asked. "Can you handle a shotgun?"

"Yes'r," he said, sounding a little surprised. "I done my share o' duck huntin'."

"All right, listen up," Harte said. "Beasley and Fortenberry will be behind me. We'll go in on foot from the Winters's Farm and set up outside the west door. Once we're in position, I'll contact you, Ash. You and Burns will be at the east door. At my signal we go in, guns ready, but no shooting unless absolutely necessary. Any questions?"

Harte checked Meeks, who stared out the window with worried eyes. Constantly pushing his left thumb into his right palm in dry circles, he looked as if he were rubbing out a cramp.

"The Moodys aren't likely to go easy, Sher'ff," Burns said. "They'll put up a fight."

"We'll be ready for it," Harte said. He took the time to look each man in the eye. "I want everyone wearing a vest." He pointed to the ammunition Maxie had stacked on the desk. "Each of you pick up two boxes of double-aught and load your shotguns to the max. Pocket the rest." When he nodded and pushed away from the desk, the deputies filed out of the room.

*****

With the dark settled in and the gibbous moon bright above them, the approach went unchallenged—not even a chained-up dog to warn the

Moodys. Inside the corrugated metal building a gas generator purred and fanned its fumes out a vent on the west side. Harte tested the knob of the metal door, turned away, and talked quietly into his walkie-talkie.

"This is the sheriff. The west door is unlocked. What about yours?"

Waiting for a reply, Harte checked on his team. They stood in moonlight that was broken into puzzle pieces by the trees. Fortenberry continuously swallowed. Meeks shivered so badly that his teeth clicked.

"You all right, Meeks?"

"Just c-cold," he said, his voice breaking in and out of a whisper. Beneath the brim of his hat, beads of sweat stood on his face. Harte took off his coat and draped it around Meeks's shoulders.

"Stay at the door, Arthur. We'll go in. Hold that muzzle high unless you need it."

Harte's muted speaker lightly crackled with static, and Ash's low voice came through the radio. "It's unlocked, Sheriff. We'll go in first. Sounds like their backs are to us."

"Negative. We're going in together. Be careful of crossfire. Got that?"

"Copy, Sheriff."

Harte nodded to his men and pressed his mouth to the radio. "On my three-count. One . . . two—" Before Harte could finish, he heard a hard metallic crash from the back of the building. Pulling open the door, he rushed in with Fortenberry and Beasley following. They stood unnoticed as the chugging generator filled the room with sound. The air inside was stifling, tainted by a throat-biting acrid scent. The Moodys stood beside a long counter that looked like it belonged in a high school chemistry lab. Two small gas burners were in use, and above the blue flames of each was a flask suspended as if upon a neon blue mushroom of flame. Both Moody's were looking at the backdoor, red cloths tied in knots at the backs of their heads.

"Sheriff's department!" Harte yelled over the droning motor. "Hands up!"

Garret Moody turned to face Harte, and his hand moved automatically to the edge of the countertop. A large, nickel-plated revolver with a thick-handle lay between the sink and his hand.

"Don't do it!" Harte yelled.

Garret's eyes were pinched and nervous, jumping in small tics above the triangle of red bandana covering his nose and mouth like a nineteenth century bandit. Garret tapped the arm of his brother with the back of his hand, and Grat Moody spun as if he'd been jerked around by a rope. Over his mask, a fierce rage burned in his eyes.

Harte's shotgun was braced against his shoulder, aimed at Garret. Fortenberry's muzzle was leveled beside his. Garret's hands rose, but Grat spun back to face the sounds at the rear door.

"Hands above your heads!" Harte commanded. "Now!"

Two quick explosions rocked the metal backdoor. Grat screamed and doubled over, grabbing his leg as a piece of metal broke from the door and clattered onto the concrete floor. Where the knob had been on the back door, a ragged hole now showed the moving beam of a flashlight. A violent thud buckled the door, and it fell from its frame with a sprawling body tumbling after it. Ash rushed in crouching low, his shotgun extending forward, and then the room filled with the blasts of gunfire.

The air came alive with the sound of thunder unleashing a swarm of bees. Heavy pellets of double-aught slapped into the metal wall behind Harte. He grabbed Fortenberry by the shoulder and pulled him down, and, as he did, he saw Grat disappear behind the lab counter. Beasley tripped over Fortenberry's feet and landed over Harte's legs, and all the while the heavy booms of a shotgun continued to mushroom inside the room. Glass shattered on the counters, and pellets ricocheted with debris flying everywhere.

Harte came up on one knee, bringing up his shotgun and aiming at the place where the Moodys had been standing, but neither brother was in sight.

The flasks were gone. Now tear-shaped blue flames from the burners glowed through the blue-gray smoke hanging in the room. The large, nickel handgun still lay on the countertop. Ash stood stiffly with his shotgun still braced to his shoulder. The smoke began a slow drift, like a gauze curtain slowly rising on the epilog of a play. Harte straightened and saw the two bodies lying on the floor, each with a red rag tied around a neck. He watched Ash probe with his foot and kick something toward him. The deputy bent quickly and then raised something for all to see.

"Sonovabitch tried to kill me," Ash yelled. In his hand he wielded a small, short-barreled revolver by its grips, its muzzle pointed at the roof as though he were about to start a race.

"Check them for pulses," Harte called out, "but be careful and search for more weapons." Activating his walkie-talkie, he cued Maxie and waited. "Somebody turn off that damned generator!" he ordered. Then he looked at Fortenberry, who was lying on his back with his head crammed against the wall so that his chin was on his chest. "You all right?" Harte asked.

"Yeah, I think so," the deputy said.

Beasley pushed himself up from the floor and helped Fortenberry to his feet.

The generator died, and the new quiet was dreamlike, as though the shotgun blasts had evicted all sound from the room. Harte moved across the broken debris to examine the bodies, his boots crunching in glass with every step. As he looked down at the unmoving bodies of the Moodys, a scratchy signal from his radio interposed.

"What happened, Sher'ff?" It was Maxie's voice, sounding authoritative and composed.

"Two men down," Harte said into the mouthpiece. "Call in an ambulance, Maxie."

"Who got shot?" she returned.

"Call it in, Maxie!" Harte ordered. He switched her off and made a count of deputies in the room. "Everybody all right?"

"Nobody hurt over here, Sheriff," Burns called out. "The Moodys are shot all to hell though."

Harte turned back to the west door and saw shock lingering in the blanched faces of Beasley and Fortenberry, as they examined each other for cuts. They appeared unscathed.

"What about Meeks?" Harte said.

When he got no answer, he moved to the door. "Meeks!" he called out into the night.

"Moodys are both dead, Sheriff," Burns announced to his back.

Harte stepped out into the cool of the night air. "Meeks! It's all over!"

A department-issued hat and shotgun lay just outside the doorway. Then Harte saw his own dark coat flung against the wooded slope some thirty feet away. He flicked on his flashlight. Several yards beyond the coat Meeks lay face-down over the roots of an oak.

Harte hurried to him, knelt, and pulled at his shoulder. The body was dead weight. Settled upon his back, Meeks had no face, only torn flesh and fractured bone, all of it glistening wet in the moonlight. Harte felt for a pulse. There was none. He took off his hat and started to lower his ear to listen for breathing, but he knew full-well that Meeks was gone. When he turned off his light, the blood appeared black as tar.

Inside the building the deputies gathered around the bodies looked up at Harte's entrance, all attentive as if awaiting instructions. "What the hell happened?" Harte said, tossing his coat aside.

The four deputies stood like mannequins in the dead quiet. Harte walked over the broken glass to inspect the bodies. Grat's chest was a bright red crater of ruined tissue and loose plates of bone. Garret had taken a similar shot, with blood spreading over his coveralls. Harte turned to Ash and Burns and alternated glaring at each of them.

"Does someone want to tell me what the hell happened?"

Burns lowered his head. "I checked the doorknob," he began in a contrite murmur. "The damned thing turned easy enough. I thought it was unlocked." He hitched a thumb toward Ash. "Ash was goin' in first, so when you started the countdown, he said to go ahead. I turned the knob, but the damned thing wouldn' give. I put my shoulder into it and still got nothin'. Then Ash kicked the hell out of it. Finally, he shot out the lock, and I put my shoulder into it again. This time the door went down and me with it, and then Ash rushed by me and . . . well . . . that's when everything went to hell."

Harte fixed his gaze on Ash and waited as the deputy held up the short-barreled revolver for all to see. "These two boys were crazy," he announced. "Probably wired on uppers. The big one pulled this. Didn' leave me a choice. I had to open up on 'em."

Harte held Ash's eyes with his own. "Both of them? Looks like you emptied your gun."

Ash curled his upper lip and sneered at the Moodys. "Those boys had reputations. They didn't quit easy. I shot to kill." Ash stretched his head in a circle as if he were working a kink out of his neck. "Just tryin' to stay alive, Sheriff. When the shit starts flyin', it's just automatic."

Harte pointed to the small revolver in Ash's hand. "Lay that on the counter."

Ash set down the pistol next to the nickel-plated revolver. Now Harte took time to assess them. A .22 and a .44 magnum. By comparison, it was a pea-shooter sitting beside a cannon.

"Where did that twenty-two come from?" Harte asked.

Ash coughed up a caustic laugh. "All I know is it was pointed at my chest."

Harte raised his walkie-talkie and stared at Ash as he clicked it on. "Maxie? You there?"

The compact radio popped once. "Right here, Sher'ff. You all right?"

"We're going to need two ambulances. We've got three bodies."

"Three?"

Beasley, Fortenberry, and Burns exchanged glances. Ash stood alone and stared at the Moodys on the floor, his face unreadable.

"Sher'ff?" Maxie said through the radio, "there's only two Moodys. Who else got hurt?"

Harte kept his eyes on Ash. "Arthur Meeks is dead."

The other deputies turned their heads in unison toward the west door. Ash's eyes came up slowly and fixed on Harte, his face like a blank sheet of paper.

Harte spoke into the radio. "Maxie, call Nesmith. He'll need to get his people out here. It's a big operation. They're going to need a lot of evidence bags." He clicked off his radio and frowned at his deputies standing amid the rubble left by the firefight. "I want to keep the site undisturbed for the state investigators."

When the deputies filed out the west door, Harte browsed the shelves bracketed to the wall until he found a clean tarp. Picking up his coat, he carried the tarp outside to the knot of deputies gathered around Meeks' body. After covering the corpse, he slipped into the coat and buttoned it to his chin. Meeks was right. This night had turned cold.

*****

Across from the sheriff's desk, Ash stood just as he had before they had left for the raid, feet spread and hands in his pockets, his face neutral. Harte was on the phone with the District Attorney. When Ash pulled a pack of cigarettes from his shirt pocket, Harte shook his head. Ash pocketed the box and resumed his vigil on the window, where the business district around the square was still dormant in the pre-dawn darkness.

"I'll drive out to the Meeks's place," Harte said quietly into the phone. "It'll be light by the time I get out there. Call me later." He hung up the telephone and watched Ash's face for any show of remorse. "You don't strike me as the kind to get so rattled," he said to the deputy. "Eight shotgun blasts, back to back . . . in our direction."

Ash's blue eyes came around. "Didn' have much choice. Not with that gun in my face."

Harte sat still as a rock. "Meeks took a load of buckshot in the face. Can you explain that?"

Ash appeared not to be bothered by the question. "Well, I guess he was in the wrong place at the wrong time. I just saw somebody aiming something at us . . . someone I didn't recognize."

Harte paced his questions. "But you knew we were coming through that door."

"Sure, I knew. But when you, Burns, and Fortenberry went down, for all I knew somebody had opened up on you from behind. I just tried to neutralize him. It didn't look like Meeks, Sheriff."

"He was wearing my coat," Harte said.

"Well, see . . . I guess that coat made him look bigger."

Harte pulled open a drawer and floated a sheaf of papers to his desktop. "You know how this works. There'll be an investigation. Administrative leave is mandatory until the reports are reviewed." He nodded toward the papers. "You need to fill these out. Needs to be typed."

"Well, who reviews the reports?" Ash said.

"G.B.I."

Ash snatched up the papers. "So I'm out of work?"

Harte ignored the indignation. "You'll work in the office." He reached in the drawer again and tossed a ring of keys onto the desk. "Looks like we need a new jailor for the day shift."

Ash stared at the top paper, sucked in his cheeks, and began a slow series of nods.

"And I want you to write up in detail everything that happened tonight, starting from the moment you and Burns reached the Moodys' outbuilding. Have it on my desk before noon."

Ash let out a long breath. "When will I be back on regular duty?"

"I don't know."

Ash let a flash of insolence show. "So, I'm stuck down there in the cellblock?"

Harte sat deeper in his chair and studied Ash. "There is plenty to do there. Meals, mopping the floors, cleaning, overseeing the prisoners during yard time. Maxie will fill you in."

Ash glared out the window. "You think anybody might want to thank me for putting down those two cretins?"

Harte sat expressionless. "I doubt you'll be getting any thanks from the Meeks family."

Ash's eyes finally sent an unfiltered message of contempt. "Seems to me that the only person who got any real police work done at the Moodys tonight is the one getting punished. Wasn't a damn one of you any help to me out there. Burns falls on his ass, and the rest of you dive for cover."

It was the first time that Harte had seen Ash really get his dander up, but he sensed that the performance was an oil and water mix of manufactured outrage and genuine uncertainty. "I wish Arthur Meeks had felt that instinct . . . to dive for cover."

The room went so quiet, they heard the burbling of the coffee urn in the dispatch area.

"That all, Sheriff?" Ash said and picked up the keys. "Can I have my cell phone back now?"

Harte removed the phone from his shirt pocket and pushed it across the desk. Ash picked it up and scuffed across the rug and out the door. The hallway proved to be a better scuffing venue, what with the acoustics and the pinewood floor. Harte listened to see which way he would go. The steps faded down the hall toward the stairs to the cellblock.

Harte stood and removed his black coat from the rack and spread it on the sofa to examine it. There were no holes in the collar or shoulders—nothing. Meeks had taken the full load above the neck. Harte thought about the Kevlar vests they had all worn. The Moodys had been chest-shots, but Arthur Meeks no longer had a face.

At his desk he opened the file on the Moody bust and pulled out the state boys' photos of the .22 pistol. The gun was a cheap Italian model seen in pawn shops. The handle was wrapped in black electrical tape that looked new, judging by the high sheen of its reflective surface. A bright scratch mark shone on the dark metal where the serial number had been.

Standing, he walked to his door and opened it. "Hooper, how long will it take the state to send us fingerprint analysis from the Moody's lab?"

"Prob'ly take a week, Sher'ff." Hooper frowned. "Why? Whatta you expect to find?"

Harte ignored the question. "Just let me know when it comes in."

Hooper's face turned serious. "Will do, Sher'ff."

The front door opened, and Maxie came in and hung up her coat on a wall peg. When she walked directly into the sheriff's office, Harte followed and closed the door. She stood before the window and looked out over the town square, her small hands balled into fists at her sides.

"Why would he kill Meeks?" she said, her voice a forceful whisper echoing off the glass.

Harte stood behind her and kept his voice quiet. "I gave Meeks my coat."

For several seconds she said nothing. Then she turned quickly, her face slack with surprise.

"You think he meant to kill you?"

Harte stepped to the window and settled his gaze on the town. "Maybe I'm getting too close to someone's business." He lifted his coat off the chair. "I'm going out to the Meeks' place."

Maxie's expression softened. "I can go with you if you like."

Harte shook his head and sat on the edge of the desk. "Once we got to the Moodys', I knew Arthur wasn't going to be of much help. He was shaking like a leaf, so I draped my coat over his shoulders and left him outside the building. He must have wanted to help, stepping into the doorway like he did. Got to give him that."

Maxie looked away and nodded. "Just goin' out with you on the raid . . . for him it must'a been like leapin' off a cliff and goin' on faith that there was a soft landing place somewhere."

Harte stood and pushed his arms into the sleeves of his coat. "Not too many soft landing places in this business, Maxie."

# Chapter Twenty-Six

After the trip out to Frogtown to let Carl and Jean Meeks know that their only son—a grown man of forty-seven—had been killed in the line of duty, the day grew tedious with phone calls, paperwork, and crime scene photos. Harte went back and forth between the office and the Moody place three times. By one o'clock, an army of state drug enforcers had descended upon the crime scene and begun the process of probing, labeling, and packing up evidence. It was three o'clock before Harte locked himself in his office and called Cody.

"I guess you heard?"

"Joe-Joe told me," Cody said in a somber tone. "Burns called him. Too bad about Meeks."

"Can you meet me in the lumberyard behind the hardware store? Ten minutes?"

"Ten minutes," Cody agreed. "Back by the railroad ties."

\*\*\*\*\*

They stood behind the stacked ties, where palettes of field stone were bundled up in shrink wrap. Cody wore an immaculate white karate outfit of soft white cotton cinched at the waist by a black sash. On his feet were sandals that appeared to be made of smooth hemp rope.

"How'd the Meeks take it?" Cody asked.

" 'Bout like you'd expect. World turned upside down with all the lights shut off. Arthur was their only child."

Neither man spoke for a time, as a forklift ran the length of the yard somewhere inside the maze of stacked lumber. When the quiet gathered around them again, Harte sat on a stack of rocks and propped his hands on his knees.

"I gave Meeks my coat before we went in. With his uniform hat on, he probably looked like me."

Cody's eyes sharpened. "That sonovabitch Ash. What are you gonna do with him?"

He'll work in the cellblock on a day-shift. He'll only need surveilling after hours."

"You want us to split up the night watch . . . or should I take it all?"

"Split it," Harte said.

"Joe-Joe's gonna like that. He said the nights were gettin' pretty damn long."

Harte stood and walked toward the back of the lot and Cody followed. The view of the Appalachians from there was stunning. The mountains loomed larger, and the blue sky seemed bluer for the myriad colors of the leaves splashed across the slopes. He thought of Sundays from his childhood, when he sat in church and stared at the stained-glass windows as if they were the eyes of God.

"What have you heard from Emmanuél?" Harte asked.

"He's a bodyguard right now, but he's waiting for the Cuban to confide something in him. He's says to be patient."

Harte adjusted his hat on his head, gently rocking the crown forward and back to get the perfect fit. "Keep yourself available for him . . . in case he needs you."

Cody laughed. "I don't think we need to worry 'bout Manny."

Harte grasped Cody's shoulder and bent at the knees to look directly into his eyes. "Don't get complacent. These people we are after . . . they don't give two-cents for our lives."

Cody's smile hardened and his eyes took on a savage light. "I'm still Danny Culp's brother, Sheriff. 'Complacent' is not in my universe."

\*\*\*\*\*

At the department parking lot, Harte stepped out of the cruiser and walked to the far end of the lot, where the skateboarders were taking turns roaring down the sloped asphalt toward the ramp. The lanky alpha male was leaning back against Jim Raburn's car with a smoldering cigarette hanging from his lips. He pushed away from the car to cut off Harte's approach.

"Hey, Chief, what about that money you promised?"

Harte nodded and patted his shirt pocket but kept walking past the boy.

"Hey! Chief!" the boy called to his back.

Harte stopped and turned. " 'Chief' would be city. I'm county."

The boy sauntered forward. "You can pay me. I'll work it out with the others."

Harte smiled pleasantly. "I'll stay with the man I negotiated with." Without looking away from the boy, Harte called out Lester's name.

"We're negotiating now . . . you and me," the boy said.

"You've never introduced yourself," Harte said, surprising the boy by holding out his hand.

The boy whipped his hair with a snap of his neck, but the unnaturally dark hair fell back over half his face where it had been. With the one eye that was visible, he looked suspiciously at Harte.

"Lance," he finally said, as if he expected this name to be challenged. Stuffing his hands into his back pockets, he glared at Harte.

Harte turned to the Dowdy boy standing beside him. "Can I talk to you?" Without waiting for a reply, Harte climbed back to the top of the slope and kept his back to the boys as he pulled an envelope from his pocket. When Lester appeared in front of him, he opened the envelope. "Look about right?"

Lester peered into the envelope and then straightened. "Sure." He glanced briefly at his friends. "His name's not 'Lance,' " he whispered. "It's 'Carter.' But he likes 'Lance,' so—"

Harte closed the envelope. "Did he help with the radio installment?"

Lester splayed his hands on his hips and looked down at the criss-cross of skate tracks on the pavement. When his eyes came up, they were filled with compassion.

"Sheriff, he wouldn't shake your hand because he doesn't trust men." Lester took a half-step forward and lowered his voice. "His father . . . he's made it pretty hard on 'im."

"How so?"

Lester licked his lips and leaned to check his friends again. "I saw his old man whack him with a broke shovel handle about seven times. All for not being home on time one day when we had a project in our math class. Carter's good with math."

"But not with car radios?"

Lester shook his head. "He's good with theories and stuff. You know, the bigger picture?"

Harte turned casually and saw the boys gathered around Carter, listening to the thin boy as he sat on the hood of the scrapped cruiser. "What else have you seen?"

Lester shrugged. "He won't really talk about it, but at P.E. I saw some pretty bad marks on his back. He said they were from falling out of a tree." Lester shook his head. "Carter's not the kind to even climb a tree, you know?" He made a pained look at Carter. "His father is a jerk, Sheriff."

Harte kept his voice low. "What's Carter's last name?"

Lester cleared his throat. "Harliner," he said, barely moving his mouth.

Harte handed the boy the envelope of cash. "I appreciate your work. I might like to use you again. Would that be all right?"

"Yes, sir," Lester said with new enthusiasm, but his smile quickly relaxed and his eyes looked beseechingly into Harte's. "You're not gonna say anything to Carter, are you?"

"If I do, I won't mention your name. Where does he live?"

Lester looked toward the square and nodded. "Over on Sunset Drive."

Harte offered his hand. "Thank you for your work."

The boy made a sheepish smile and shook hands. As Harte headed back across the lot, he glanced back to see Lester counting out bills to the boy named 'Ray,' as most of the others looked on. Carter sat by himself on the hood of the GMC spinning a wheel on his skateboard.

When Harte entered the lobby, Hooper sat up straighter and made fast, deft clicks with his computer mouse. When Harte reached his desk, he saw Hooper's screen filled with the logo of the Lumpkin County Sheriff's Department.

"Where's Maxie?"

Hooper nodded to the south. "Runnin' that gun down to Atlan'a. Called me to take her shift."

Harte ignored the complaint in the deputy's voice. "Our office has a web page?"

"Yes'r," Hooper said. "We post arrests on it. Commissioners think it deters crime."

"What do you think?" Harte said.

Hooper gazed at the screen with a lackluster lift of his eyebrows. "I think it gives me one more thing to do, if you want to know the truth."

"Cuts into your busy day, huh?"

Hooper turned at that, his expression that of a man who'd been tricked into a confession. "Well," he said with a shrug, "I don't think anybody ever really believes he'll get caught once he starts thinkin' about a crime, do you?"

Hooper tapped a key, and a new page came up. Harte saw his faculty picture smiling at him from the screen. Below it was the newspaper article that told the story of the shoot-out at Luther's.

"You manage this site?"

"Me and Maxie," the deputy replied.

Harte leaned and tapped the screen. "I want you to get that off there."

Hooper stared at the screen. "Just the picture or the article?"

"All of it. And see what you can find out about a man named Harliner who lives on Sunset."

Hooper pulled a notepad closer and grabbed a pencil. "How d'you spell that, Sheriff?"

"Probably just like it sounds."

Hooper stared at a blank page for a time and then scratched something on the paper.

"He's supposedly a big fellow and has a son named Carter, probably in the eighth grade. Now you know everything I know. Write up a report for me before you leave."

Hooper sagged, and his basset-hound eyes filled with misery. "Yes'r. Anythin' else?"

"I'd like to see the nine-one-one records for the night that Sheriff Raburn was killed."

Hooper rose, rummaged through a file cabinet, and came up with a disk.

Back at his desk, Harte inserted the disk into Jim Raburn's laptop. After a series of clicks, the screen filled with a list of telephone numbers and dates. After each number was a caller's name, or the word "unknown." He clicked on an 8:20 P.M. call from Rafer C. Gooch. Within seconds the speakers came alive with the white noise of an audio message.

*"I got a bawlin' cow outside my window,"* said a scratchy female voice, *"and you never heard such carryin' on. I called the Grindles, but there ain't nobody answerin' over there. Might be they're out lookin' for it, I don' know. All I do know is a dead person couldn' sleep through this."*

He skipped to a call listed at 10:10 P.M. from J.P. McGarrity, who turned out to be the veterinarian who had tended to the Dillard boy at Luther's. He listened to the nervous voice report the situation at the bar, going into professional detail about the injury.

The next call was at 10:14 P.M. from Calvin Edmonston, who lived at the south end of the county. Skipping ahead Harte clicked on an 10:16 P.M. call from "unknown." A local telephone number was listed but with the additional tag of "ATT 451."

*"Some boys are down at Luther's sellin' drugs. Y'all need to bust that up right now."* The man's voice was blurred and his words drawn out as if trying to affect a drawling dialect. Harte imagined the caller making a tunnel of his hands over the mouthpiece of the phone.

Then Hooper's voice came in: "Is this Luther's Liquid Gold you're talkin' about?"

Before the caller answered, an airy whoosh rose and fell in the background, complete with Doppler effect. "Yeah!" the voice said, and then the connection broke.

Harte punched in the number on his phone and listened to it ring a dozen times before a voice finally yelled "Hello!" into the line. Harte heard the airy passage of a car in the background. The sound of the traveling vehicle was just like the one in the recording.

"This is the sheriff," Harte said. "Who am I talking to?"

"Well hey, Harte. This is Harold Boggs."

"Harold, where are you?"

"I'm out here at Melvin's place on nineteen waitin' on Lula to pick me up. My alt'nator went and died on me. Melvin is gonna order me one. Says he can have it in by Friday. I don' know what I'm gonna do about tomorr'. Lula's goin' to her sister's tomorr'. She's over in Dacula. And I got to get over to the hospital in Gainesville for some tests." Another car passed in the background. "How in the world did you know to find me here, Harte?"

"Are you talking on a pay phone, Harold?"

"Sure am. Didn' cost me nothin' to pick up though. I didn' know who it would be a-callin'. I just picked it up. Might could'a been Lula. You never know."

"Is this Mel Saine's garage about three miles down from Luther's place?"

"Sure is . . . use to be a Standard station. Now it's a auto repair."

"Thank you, Harold. I'll let you go now."

"Well," Harold said, "Lula ain't here yet. Is there anything else you need, Harte?"

"No. Maybe Mel can let you have a car for just tomorrow."

Another car passed by and Harte waited. "Well, I didn' even think o' that," Harold said.

"Okay, Harold, I've got some work to do now. Good luck with your car . . . and your tests."

Harte hung up and listened again to the nameless voice on the 911 disk. The next call was the widow Gooch again. He turned off the laptop, grabbed his coat, and gun and left.

*****

When Harte pulled into Melvin's, he noted the pay phone standing alone in its open Plexiglas cubicle at the north end of the lot. Eight feet away stood an unlighted security lamp perched twenty feet up on a metal pole. Rolling across the gravel lot to the open bay of the garage, he could see Mel Saine's legs sticking out from under a battered blue Dodge that had once been a stylish family car back in the fifties. The car's hood was propped open. He knew it was Mel because the mechanic always wore rolled-up overalls that were too long for his bantam legs.

As Harte stepped out of his vehicle, Melvin wormed his way out from under the car and frowned as he wiped grease-blackened hands on the front of his stained overalls. Squinting his eyes to slits, he poked a dirty finger in the air at Harte.

"I just now called down to your office," Mel started in, his head tilted to one side, and one eye now closed. "Your deputy said you're on your way down here to my place."

"Looks like he was right. How are you Mel?"

Mel was in no mood for amenities. "Why the hell'd you tell Harold Boggs that I'm s'posed to loan him a vehicle for nothin'?"

Harte leaned one hand on the roof of the Dodge and grinned. "I didn't."

"Well, *he* says you did."

Harte looked around the empty lot. There were no cars in the stalls where the hydraulic lifts lay idle. The shelves were sparsely stocked, and the few jugs of motor oil scattered there were covered in a patina of gray dust. Mel's old Model T Ford—the one he drove in parades at the square—hibernated under a low shed roof attached to the side of the building.

"I had to go and loan 'im my own damn truck," Melvin carped.

Harte walked to the front of the Dodge and looked down into the engine well at the disassembled parts lying on a dirty towel. "This is Harold's old dinosaur, isn't it?"

Melvin glared at the gunked-up motor as if the car had just snapped some insult his way. "Hell yeah, it's his. I had to order all the way to Michigan to find that damn alt'nator."

Harte pursed his lips and studied the empty lot again. "Didn't do you much of a favor when they put in the bypass, did they, Mel?"

Melvin blew a sputtering stream of air through his lips. "You're damn right they didn't. And didn' nobody ask me 'bout it neither. They just slapped that road down without talkin' to none 'o us out here that runs a business, and—" He blew through his lips again but this time it was a quick whispery sound, like a blade cutting the air. ". . . There went the traffic . . . and the business with it. It's like a ghost town out here on this section of highway. Ever'thang just dried up here."

Mel watched as Harte walked back to his cruiser, leaned through the window, and stretched the cord of the radio hand-piece. "Hooper, who does the servicing for our department vehicles?"

"Depends, Sher'ff. For tires we send 'em down to the Wal-Mart tire center. That there's the best price in town. I know, because I'm the one who priced 'em. For engine repair and regular servicing, we started usin' that Mr. Turbo franchise on the bypass. They gave us a flat fee for regular oil changes and such. For body work, it's Skipper Dean's shop down below Auraria."

As the deputy's voice droned through the radio, Melvin leaned a hip into the Dodge, crossed his arms over his chest, and peered intently at Harte. Periodically he leaned and spat a brown stream of tobacco and then re-assumed his alert pose of openly eavesdropping.

"Why Skipper's?" Harte asked. "Isn't his body shop over the county line into Dawson?"

"Well, yeah, it is. But Skipper is married to the cousin of somebody on the county commission. Seems like maybe it was Lyle Ferribee's wife."

While the static crackled from the radio, Harte and Melvin stared at one another—Melvin with a self-righteous question gathering in his eyes.

"Sher'ff?" Hooper said. "You havin' car trouble? You ain't broke down, are you?"

Harte pressed the hand-piece into the front of his coat over his stomach. "Mel, think you can handle servicing the sheriff's fleet of cruisers on a regular basis?"

Melvin's eyebrows knitted together as if Harte had asked him to take over the Governor's job. "Hell, yeah," he finally said, his voice defensive, as if someone had made contrary claims.

"What about tires?" Harte said.

Melvin straightened from the Dodge. "I can get any kind o' tires you want. I do a damn good recap, too. Got a mileage guarantee. Ain't had one fail yet." And then before Harte could ask, the mechanic bumped the meaty part of his fist against the side panel of the Dodge. "And I do body work, too, Sher'ff . . . a hellava lot better'n Skipper Dean."

Harte nodded. "I've seen your work. You fixed my wi—. . . my ex-wife's car. By the time you got finished with it, it looked brand new." Harte lifted the radio mic to his mouth again.

"Hooper, we're going to start sending our cars to Mel Saine up on business-nineteen north of town. Whom do we need to talk to about that?"

Hooper delayed coming back on the air for so long that Harte started to lean into the cruiser to check on the radio. "I guess we just do it, Sher'ff," the dispatcher said weakly. "I just need to call Mr. Turbo and cancel that flat-fee deal."

"Anybody's cousin working there?" Harte asked, sharing a grin with Mel.

Another span of silence followed before Hooper chimed in. "Hell, Sher'ff, ever'body's somebody's cousin, ain't they?"

When Harte returned the mic to his cruiser, Mel leaned over the Dodge's engine, his hands propped on the radiator. "Harold ain't much on keepin' his belongin's too clean, is he?"

Harte looked down at the filth on Mel's overalls, but he said nothing.

Mel straightened. "You reckon he'll bring my truck back in one piece?"

Harte studied the way Melvin had meticulously lined up all the disconnected parts for an efficient reassembly after the alternator went in. "Harold seems like a careful driver."

Both men studied the internal workings of the car for a time, and as they did a car pulling a U-Haul trailer drove past on the highway. It was the first sign of traffic since Harte had pulled in.

Mel picked up a small bolt, turned the nut on it as if checking its fit, and then set it back on the towel. "Harold ain't a bad feller," he admitted. "Hell, he's just a little headstrong sometimes." He lowered the hood on the Dodge and let it fall the last inch by its own weight. "Got to wait on that alternator now," he said. "Feller said it might could take up to a week."

"Mel," Harte said and nodded up the road toward Luther's, "do you remember the Saturday night Jim Raburn got killed?"

Melvin looked north up the highway, and his face grew thoughtful. "Yeah, I remember," his voice somber now. "Most flashin' lights I seen since Christmas."

"Before all that, did you see anyone come into your lot that night and use the pay phone?"

Melvin's eyes cut to the phone across the lot. He squinted for a time, as if trying to conjure up an image from memory. Then his jaw dropped enough to part his lips.

"Yeah, there was a guy pulled in. 'Bout a half hour or so before I heard the guns poppin'."

Harte pointed to the utility pole. "Was that light working that night?"

Melvin's face compressed, making crease marks at the corners of his eyes. "Oh, hell yeah. That light has got no mercy. Shines into my curtains like the full moon." He pointed to the extension on the north side of the building. "I sleep right in there. I pretty much check on ever'body who pulls in here at night. I'm a pretty light sleeper these days." He pointed to the closer garage bay. "Coupla years ago I had a three-hun'rd-dollar roll-around jack lifted right off the lot." His jaws hardened like angle-iron. "That ain't gonna happen again, I can gar'ntee you that."

"What do you remember about this caller? What was he driving?"

Mel smiled. "That's a easy one. Dark 'sixty-one Caddie, with the big fins."

"Dark, as in black?" Harte asked.

"Either that or a real dark blue."

"What about the driver?"

Mel stared at the pay phone and pushed his tongue around the inside of his cheek. "Sort o' stocky guy, narrow hips. Maybe a few years younger'n me judgin' by the way he moved . . . but his hair was either white or silver, cut kinda short . . . military-like."

As Melvin talked, Harte kept his eyes on the phone cubicle and watched the scene play out as clearly as if he were watching a film strip. "You know a man in construction, name of McAllister?"

Mel shook his head. "Heard the name. Works with that smilin' jack-ass Childers, don't he?"

"I believe he does, Mel." Harte offered his hand. "You've been a big help. I appreciate it."

Melvin wiped his hand on the front of his dirty coveralls and clamped Harte's hand with a steely grip. "Sure thing."

"I'll have Maxie call you to set up a schedule for taking our cruisers in. How's that sound?"

"Sounds good, Harte." Then a wide smile broke out on his face. "How is ol' Maxie?"

Harte returned the smile. "She's a good deputy." Then he let his face go serious. "You want me to call Harold Boggs and let him know he misunderstood me about the loaner?"

Mel made a face that lifted his upper lip to his nostrils. "Aw, nah!" With the exacting eye of an appraiser he looked back at the old Dodge. When he turned back he was wearing a grin. "I'll just charge 'im more for the alt'nator. It'll all come out in the wash."

*****

Back at the office, Harte found Maxie at the dispatch desk with her headphones clipped over the crown of her head. She was obviously listening to someone rant over the line, and her eyes locked on Harte as if needing to relay some dire message.

"Yes, sir, I know that, but I'm just tellin' you what the sher'ff said, Lyle. I reckon you'll have to talk to him about that." She paused to listen, her face looking more miserable by the second. "No, sir, I don't 'xactly know. Like I said you'll have to—"

Crossing the lobby, Harte shook his head and held both hands palms-out, shielding himself from the exchange. He made it to his office before Maxie could disconnect. He closed the door and heard Maxie yell through the wall.

"Sher'ff, call Lyle Ferribee when you git in. And just so you know, Lyle's son-in-law is the manager over at Mr. Turbo."

As soon as Harte had hung hat, coat, and gun on the coat rack, a knock sounded quietly on the door. The door swung open, and Maxie leaned a shoulder against the doorframe, raised an arm, and clamped a hand around the back of her neck.

"Sher'ff, I think I'm coming down with something." Harte looked at her and narrowed his eyes. "A bad case o' politic-itis. 'Parently, Mel Saine called down to Mr. Turbo to get records on our vehicle maintenance. Elvin Travers runs that place, and he called me wantin' to know why we're takin' our business to Mel. Elvin is married to Lyle's oldest daughter."

Harte sat at his desk. "Mel Saine will be doing all our auto work from now on." Harte swiveled his chair around, checked the Montana kettle for water, and clicked on the hotplate. He spooned coffee crystals into his metal cup, sealed the coffee jar, and stared at its label for a time. "Maxie, do we have any cocoa around here?"

Maxie's eyebrows shot up. "You mean like hot chocolate? Nos'r, we don't. But I can pick some up next time I'm out." She came inside and closed the door behind her.

He nodded. "How long before we'll know about prints on the Moody gun?"

"Maybe two days," Maxie said. She laid a folder on the desk. "Sher'ff, I've been doin' a little researchin' on the In'ernet. Ash was on the police force in Charlotte for two years. Before that, two years in Chattanooga. I called the chief in Charlotte and asked about Ash's record. Did the same in Chattanooga. Neither one could talk about it." She paused for a moment. "There's some kind o' lock on his records. Some kind o' arrangement to let him go quietly. That happened once here, when Sher'ff Jim had somethin' on one o' the deputies but couldn't make it stand up in court."

They locked eyes. "That's interesting," he said and pointed to the visitor's chair. When she sat, he settled back in his chair and crossed his arms over his chest. "The night Jim was killed, it was McAllister who made the anonymous nine-one-one call. "He drove away from Luther's about a half-hour before the shooting started, telling the Bullochs he had to pick up his product. That's when he called it in."

"Why would he do that, Sher'ff Harte?"

He shook his head. With the water roiling, Harte picked up the kettle and poured.

"Maxie, I want to wire McAllister's cell. Do we have the equipment for that?"

She nodded. "Joe-Joe can handle that for you, Sher'ff."

"Let's do that ASAP," Harte said and stirred his coffee. "Next time Ash takes the prisoners into the yard, tell Joe-Joe to get to work down there."

After tasting his coffee, he opened the folder and read her notes on Ash. Closing it he pushed the folder to her.

"See what you can add to this." He stood with his cup in hand. "Meanwhile, I think I'll go downstairs and get things stirred up a bit . . . give McAllister something to talk about later." He left his cup on the desk, walked to the door, and turned. "Maxie, see if you can find some dark chocolate cocoa, will you?"

"Now? What about the front desk? Who's gonna handle that?"

"I'll put Ash there," Harte said. "I need him out of the cellblock for a while."

Harte entered the anteroom of the cellblock, where Ash looked up from a magazine. A cigarette dangled from his lips, and a blue haze of smoke hung in the air around him.

"You have a tobacco addiction problem, Ash?"

Ash dropped the cigarette and ground it with his shoe. "Didn't think it mattered down here."

Harte nodded to the *No Smoking* sign above the door. Then he turned to see a lazy stream of smoke drifting through the bars from McAllister's cell.

"I need you upstairs on dispatch for a while. I'll be down here."

Ash's face pinched with a scowl. "I've never run the switchboard."

"You'll probably be doing a lot of new things for a while. Maxie can take you through it."

Ash gathered up his plastic coffee mug, hat, and magazine and started up the stairs.

"Ash?" Harte said. When the deputy turned, Harte toed the crushed cigarette butt on the floor. Ash scuffed back down the steps, picked up the cigarette, and shuffled up the stairs, each footfall on the treads sounding like a profane challenge.

Harte walked past a sleeping Varley Bulloch to McAllister's cell. The gray-haired prisoner sat slumped on his bunk, feet on the floor, squinting one eye as he took a long draw on a cigarette. When he saw Harte, his bland expression tightened with surprise, and he sat up straighter.

Harte curled his index finger back toward himself. McAllister hesitated, then slapped his hands to his knees and pushed himself up but stood in place. Harte waited. After a few seconds the man ambled to the bars. Two flattened cigarette butts lay on the floor where he had been sitting.

"You can't keep holdin' me here. I want out o' this hole. You got nothin' on me 'xcept I was talkin' to the wrong assholes." He raised the cigarette to his mouth, but Harte reached through the bars and plucked it from his lips.

"No smoking in the building." Harte dropped the half-smoked cigarette and stepped on it. "The state will be taking you off my hands soon enough. Then you can complain to them."

"Why am I still in here," McAllister demanded.

Harte gave him a long look. "You're really going to play this game?"

"You got nothing on me. You say this was about drugs, but you never found anything connecting me to any drugs."

"Witnesses heard your transaction with Bobby Lee. He held on to your gun while you left to pick up your product . . . or so you said to him. But you didn't pick up anything, did you?"

"I don't want to talk to you without my lawyer here." McAllister started to turn.

"You're in construction . . . work for yourself?"

McAllister glared at Harte. "That's right. So what?"

"Who hires you?"

McAllister's eyes sharpened to wariness. "Lotta people. Sutton Brothers, Jay Builders . . . and I put up the ironwork for the gym at the middle school. Did that for Castle Construction."

"That it?"

McAllister laughed. "What . . . you want the whole history?"

"How about Layland Childers? Ever do anything for him?"

McAllister pretended to think about it. "Yeah, the carwash next to the fire station."

"When's the last time you talked to Layland?"

The man went into his thoughtful pose again. "Prob'ly said 'hello' in town some time."

"What about the last time you called him on a telephone?"

McAllister sneered at Harte before shaking his head. "Don't recall."

Harte could see the man's defenses go up. "What about the night you were arrested?"

"What about it?"

"You call him that evening?"

McAllister kept his gaze on Harte. "Can't say as I did."

Harte pursed his lips. "Bobby Lee held on to your cell phone, but you didn't care. You didn't plan on using it anyway. You drove three miles to use a pay phone. *That* was your plan."

The prisoner stared at Harte with the tendons flexing in his jaws. "I got no idea what you're talking about."

"Really?" Harte said pleasantly. "You were right outside Mel Saine's repair shop. There's a clear view right out of his front window to that telephone. Did you know that Mel lives there?"

McAllister sniffed and tried to put a hand into the orange coveralls he'd been issued, but there was no pocket. Harte pulled a notebook from his shirt pocket and clicked open a ballpoint pen.

"I'm making a note here that you've told me you did not make a call from the pay phone at Mel Saine's garage on highway nineteen on the night of October four." He scribbled on the page and then looked up at McAllister. "You going to stick with that story?"

McAllister glared at the little notebook and said nothing.

"Old Mel's a light sleeper," Harte went on. "Goes to his window at all times of the night to check out any car that pulls into his lot." He shook his head and smiled. "With that bright security light out by the phone, he's got a pretty good view of what goes on out there." Harte paused and waited for McAllister to meet his eyes. "I wonder how many people there are in the county with short silver hair and a dark 'sixty-one Cadillac?"

Against his will, McAllister swallowed.

"Let me know when you want to talk," Harte said. "Always goes in your favor when you cooperate." He started to leave but hesitated. "Toss those cigarette butts out here so the guard can clean up without going into your cell. Meanwhile, try and keep it neater in there. You'll be with us until the state agents decide to take you off our hands."

McAllister gripped the bars. "Look, I didn't go anywhere and pick up any drugs that night. I swear it!"

Harte pursed his lips and nodded. "I believe you. But that was your plan from the beginning, wasn't it?" Harte allowed a tight smile. "You went to make an anonymous phone call instead."

The prisoner's face appeared to set with an expression that included both surprise and loathing. Without waiting for a reply, Harte walked out and closed the door to the cellblock.

# Chapter Twenty-Seven

With less than an hour of good light left in the day, Harte gave up any hope of taking the paint for a ride on the ridge. He picked up the phone and called Bella Seagrave, but there was no answer. He decided he was hungry, but when he stepped out of the building, he put restaurants out of his mind.

He drove north, then west, past Cherokee Rose and turned into Bella's drive and parked in front. When she didn't answer his knock on the door, he walked to the back and saw her pruning one of the apple trees. She was straining with a branch as thick as a garden hose. When she saw him, she lowered the shears and narrowed her eyes.

"You look tired," she said.

He took the shears from her and made a clean slice through the branch. "Long day," he said. He dragged the branch to a pile she had started near the fence. Bella picked up a few small limbs and followed. "I tried calling," he said. "Guess I'm making a habit of showing up unannounced."

Bella smiled. "Not a bad habit, not with me."

"Isn't this a little early for pruning?"

She nodded and took the shears from him. "I'm experimenting. Come on, I'll make coffee."

He followed her to the house, where at the back porch she turned with lines of worry showing on her summer-browned face. "I talked to Collette," she said, and together they sat on the back step. Finger by finger she pulled off her gloves. "There's something wrong in all this, Harte."

He set his hat aside and propped his forearms on his knees. "Tell me," he said quietly.

Bella looked off through the apple trees toward the trailer. "I waited until I saw her at the barn. I wanted to ease into it. I walked over on the pretense of asking about a cat I'd seen around the place. Then I asked about her father. I mentioned that I'd heard she was looking for a new place to live. She was polite but reserved."

Bella took a deep breath and spoke as she exhaled. "So . . . I said I had a friend who was looking for a simple place and asked if the rental arrangement with the Haversack trailer was a reasonable one." She turned to Harte, and her hazel eyes were dull as nail heads. "You know what she said?"

He waited, both embarrassed and appreciative for the white lies she had used on his behalf.

"She said 'male or female?' " Bella was so still, she appeared not to be breathing. "When I said 'female,' Collette looked away and was quiet for a while. Then she said, 'Don't do it.' From that point on, the connection between us was broken." Bella's face hardened. "So I just got right to it. I told her what Wylie had tried with me, and I asked if she'd had any trouble." Bella's eyes grew moist. "Harte, she just broke down and sobbed. She never said another word. She got on her horse and rode off toward the creek, and that was that."

Harte's chest felt like a hollow tree cavity buzzing with a nest of bees. He wanted to drive through the barbed wire fence, charge the Haversack house, and drag Wylie outside to unleash the fury building inside him. When Bella placed a hand lightly on his arm, he began to cool.

"Have you had supper, Harte?"

"No. Can't say that I'm hungry now."

Bella picked up her gloves. "Come inside. You need to eat something."

In the kitchen he stood with his hat in his hand studying the room. Bunches of dried herbs and flowers hung from an exposed beam overhead. Baskets of apples lined the floor along two walls. Flanked neatly on a shelf was a row of Mason jars filled with varying shades of brown. The interior of the cottage was much as he had imagined it—a warm extension of Bella's down-to-earth manner.

As she rummaged through a cupboard, Harte felt the forgotten pangs of home life stir somewhere between his heart and stomach. They were not the remnants of his life with Callie but from his childhood at his grandfather's farm. He remembered the smells of the kitchen at the end of a day's work, the warm amber colors in the pine paneling on the walls, and the nurturing sensation of being cared for by people who wasted no time on pretensions.

"How about scrambled eggs and biscuits?" she said. "You won't believe how fast I can whip up biscuits." From the refrigerator she pulled out a cardboard cylinder with aluminum caps and a carton of eggs. She lifted the package of biscuits beside her face, like a housewife in a commercial. Her lips broke into a meager smile of confession.

He took the eggs from her. "I'll work on this. Looks like you'll have your hands full with the biscuits. Do you have an onion?"

They worked together, finding a natural rhythm to the preparations, speaking only when Harte needed to locate something he couldn't find. The aromas mixing in the kitchen put a sharp edge on his hunger, and so the timing was perfect when she handed him a mug of hot coffee.

He looked hopefully into the mug. "Any cocoa in this?"

She smiled and took the cup back to the counter. He watched how much she added as he pushed the congealing eggs with a spatula.

When they sat before their steaming plates, Harte started for his fork but laid his hands flat on the table when he saw Bella smiling at him. "This is nice," she said. "I'm glad you're here."

Harte nodded. "Thank you, Bella." When she lowered her head and closed her eyes, he felt as if he were peering out at her through a secret hole in a wall.

"We give thanks for this nourishment and for the friendship bridged across this table." When she opened her eyes, he could see gratitude on her face. "Hungry now?" she said.

"Yes, ma'am." He forked up some eggs and watched her do the same. "You look different every time I see you, Bella." She tilted her head, and her smile turned curious. "I've always found it interesting," he went on, "how what's inside a person—in their soul, I guess you'd say—works its way out to the surface." He nodded, knowing he'd gotten the words right. "It takes time for that."

"Yes, it does." She laughed to herself as she chewed. "I had a teacher once—this was in college—and I thought he was the best looking man I'd ever seen. Then I found out he had preyed on some of the girls who were having trouble in his course. All those good looks took on the semblance of evil to me. Whenever I imagine the devil, I still see his face."

"It's better when it works the other way," Harte said.

She broke open a biscuit, inserted a pat of butter, and closed it to melt. "So, I'm starting to look better to you? Is this like the joke about the skunk and the warthog stranded on an island?"

Harte shook his head. "More like a seed pushed down into dirt," he said quietly.

She gave him a look. "Are you sure you're the sheriff around these parts, mister?" It was a pretty good rendition of John Wayne. Harte had to laugh.

"Can't sheriffs wax poetic a little, now and then?"

She arched her eyebrows and nodded enthusiastically. "Can in my house."

"Tell me about growing up, Bella. Did you have brothers or sisters?"

"No. I think I was enough to handle for Mama and Daddy. I may have personally pioneered the rank of tomboy. I could outrun all the boys in my neighborhood."

Harte smiled. "Bet you broke a lot of hearts."

"By outrunning them?"

"So to speak."

She laughed that off. "Skinny kid. But strong. I could shimmy up a tree pretty fast, too."

"Parents gone?"

She nodded with a polite smile then pointed to his badge with her fork. "Your daddy would be proud of that, and your mama would be worried, right?"

He laughed. "Probably the other way around. I wish they were here. They'd like you."

She stopped chewing and looked down at her plate. "That's a very nice thing to say, Harte."

When her head came up, something clicked deep in his stomach. It was as if he had known her all his life.

"Harte, I don't presume to judge you . . . about what you have to do in your job."

He nodded. "I know that. But I don't presume you have to like it either."

She tilted her head to one side. "Maybe I just haven't seen what you've seen."

Harte wiped his moustache with his napkin. "What's brought this on, Bella?"

She looked down into her lap for a moment, and, when her head came up, her eyes looked as hard as jade. "What do we do about Collette, Harte?"

He took a bite of biscuit and watched her as he chewed. "After to-night," he said around a mouthful, "Wylie will never go near her again."

Bella studied his face for a time. "I would not want to be an adversarial project of yours."

He shrugged that off. "How about we try some of that famous apple butter?"

✶✶✶✶✶

When Harte pulled up to the trailer, his lights carved out the lone figure of Collette sitting in the lawn chair. She was slumped low, her hips near the front edge of the seat, her neck bent almost perpendicular to her spine by the backrest. Her hands were buried inside the pockets of a puffy oversized coat. The wind blew her hair like a black flame that whipped about her head. She didn't turn her head to him. Her eyes stayed fixed on the meadow.

He cut the engine and his lights. The trailer was dark. He got out and walked to her beneath the broad sea of stars arching over the meadow. The fine points of light held steady in the sky, bright and clear as if cleansed by the rush of the wind. Standing beside her in the grass, he spoke quietly.

"I can help you if you'll let me."

She pushed herself straighter in the chair, pressed her palms together, and sandwiched them between her thighs. Staring down at her knees she said nothing.

"I need to know if Wylie Haversack has mistreated you."

He was surprised when she answered so quickly. "He's gross," she said, her voice whispery like a part of the wind. "He even smells gross."

Harte turned to a soft flapping sound at the nearby fence, where three dark shapes stood in absolute stillness. The trio of horses was like a

343

permanent fixture she had arranged in the meadow. The wind picked up and lifted their manes into a dark frenzy about their necks.

Harte knelt beside her chair. "Tell me about Wylie."

She waited while the wind made a thrumming sound against the front of the trailer. A loose piece of aluminum banged with the beat of a crazed drummer, and one of the remaining glass panes in the louvered door rattled like the dull ring of a telephone.

"Collette, I'm asking you as the sheriff. I need to know this."

She was like a corpse. He started to put a hand on her back but thought better of it.

"I'm asking as your friend, too, Collette?"

She sniffed and looked away. He thought he saw her nod, but the movement could have been part of her sobbing. He checked his pockets for his bandana or a tissue, but he found neither.

"Just tell me what you can. You can trust me."

She swiped at her wet cheeks with the flats of her hands and whipped her hair out of her face with a quick jerk of her head. Finally, she looked at him with eyes both fierce and frightful.

"Is he taking advantage of you, Collette?"

She looked back at the trailer, as if ensuring their privacy. Then she swallowed, and the sound was like a stone being forced down her throat.

"It's hard to talk, Mr. Canaday." She met his eyes squarely. "You're my teacher. I know you. You've been good to me. I don't want to ruin that."

He laid a hand gently on her arm. "Let me tell you something," he began gently. "I respect you, Collette. I like who you are. Nothing is going to change that."

She coughed up a sarcastic laugh and angled her eyes to him. "You don't know that."

"When I have a friend, I stick. You and I are friends." When her face turned to stone again, he added, "We're horse people. There's a bond in that, too."

"Not all people around horses are like that," she muttered.

Harte nodded. "True. But Wylie is not a horse person. He's the horse's ass."

She snorted. "More like something else on the horse."

She sat forward, buried her face in her hands, and burst into tears. The wind swept her hair over her like a veil of mourning. Harte squeezed her arm, and she did not flinch or try to move away.

"I'm going up to the house, Collette. Give me some firm footing for this. Please."

Still covering her face, she shook her head stiffly, as though she was trying to fling thoughts out of her mind. He waited until her racking eased up.

"It's all right, honey. Just tell me this. Do I have a reason to go up there?"

Her breathing slowly settled, sounding hollow inside the bowl of her hands. Then she inhaled deeply, placed her hands together in a prayer position, and tapped her fingertips against her lips. Finally she ran both her hands back over her scalp, pulling the hair tight against her skull. She looked up at the horses and stared for a time, and Harte removed his hand from her arm.

"I just can't talk about it, Mr. Canaday." She turned to show him her regret.

Harte stood and slipped his hands into the pockets of his coat. "I'm going up to the house and put the fear of God into Wylie Haversack. If I'm making a mistake, just shake your head."

She fought the misery swimming in her eyes. "What are you going to do?"

"Give you some assurance and balance things out a little bit . . . unless you shake your head."

She sat and stared at him, only her hair moving as the gusts of cleansing wind lifted dark streamers around her head. Leaving her to the annealing stars, he turned, walked to his cruiser, and drove away. Inside his chest, a furnace was roaring like a backdraft from hell.

Standing on the Haversack's front porch, he wanted to kick down the door with the heel of his boot, but he settled for an authoritative *clack* on the horseshoe doorknocker. Within seconds the latch tripped. In her stockinged feet, Jan Haversack peered out with a surprised expression.

"Harte? Everything okay?"

"Need to have a talk with Wylie?"

She frowned and checked her wristwatch. "Well, let me go find him." She started down the hallway of hats and spoke over her shoulder. "Go on in the den where you can talk."

"I'd like both of you to be there."

She stopped and turned to face him. "All right," she said, her voice subdued, curious.

When she walked to the back of the house, Harte stepped into the den, dropped his hat on the coffee table and noticed the little glass vial that he had seen Wylie handle. He picked it up to read the label, but most of it was torn off. What was left contained printing too small to read, but he refrained from pulling out his glasses so that he would not be wearing them when Wylie walked into the room. Unscrewing the cap, he lifted the bottle to his nose and quickly turned away from the sour stench. He screwed down the cap and set the bottle down and stood with his back to the TV screen.

Within seconds, Jan came into the room and sat on the arm of the sofa just as she had before. She folded one leg under her, and her worn jeans pulled against her stick-legs like a second skin. Wylie shuffled into the room in sweatpants and a white undershirt with a yellowish stain on the loose front where it hung over the swell of his belly. His ragged fleece-lined moccasin slippers looked like throwaway projects from an amateur taxidermist. He carried a *Coor's* beer down by his leg, his palm over the opening, and his fingers hooked around the edges like the talons of a bird.

"Our six-gun sheriff!" Wylie crooned in his lazy slur. "How 'bout it, Harte?" Walking past Harte, he dropped heavily onto the sofa, downed the last of the beer, and set the can on the floor.

Harte forced evenness into his voice. "You keep records of your rental arrangement?"

Wylie frowned, picked up a magazine, and idly studied the cover.

"For boarding horses, you mean?" Jan asked.

Harte shook his head and kept his eyes on Wylie. "The trailer."

Jan looked at her husband. The magazine continued to hold his attention.

"I keep books on the horses," she explained. "Wylie handles everything else."

After a few seconds of enduring Wylie's indifference, Harte kicked the table leg with the toe of his boot, knocking over the small bottle. Wylie looked up and raised his eyebrows.

"The Devereauxs," Harte said. "Records of their monthly payments? I'd like to see them."

Wylie tossed the magazine to the table and folded his arms over his beach ball stomach. He pursed his lips and stared at the blank TV screen.

"Wylie?" Jan's voice was like something flung across the room.

"Well," he said, holding a shrug, "it's more a charity case really." He sniffed and threw an arm over the back of the sofa to better face Harte. His hand tapped the top of the sofa like the fluttering wing a moth.

"Charity!" Jan spat and sat up rigid as a post. "You can't be serious!"

Wylie scowled. "Well, how do you expect that nut-case to cough up money every month?"

"That's not my problem, Wylie!" Jan snapped. "It's yours! Don't you tell me we haven't been getting that rental income. Riding numbers are down. You know that!" Jan straddled the arm of the sofa like she was coming out of the bronc chute at a rodeo.

Wylie flipped his hand palm up. "We've got money. They got problems. It doesn't hurt to extend a helping hand sometimes."

"Maybe it does," Harte said, and they both looked at him. "Maybe it does hurt . . . a hellava lot." He held Wylie's guarded eyes. "She's a minor, Wylie."

Jan's blazing eyes pivoted to her husband, and the skin on her face pulled taut across the bone. "You fat son of a bitch." She breathed the words in a raspy whisper.

Wylie put out his hands in a braking motion, lowered his head, and closed his eyes. "Now wait a minute." He shook his head. "For God's sake, don't be—"

"You worthless little prick," Jan said louder. "You've been fucking her, haven't you?"

Wylie heaved himself forward, trying to appear indignant as his stomach bulged over his thighs. His eyes traveled up and down Harte's tall frame.

"Where the hell do you get off coming in here and—"

Harte stopped him by quickly stepping forward with a finger pointed inches from Wylie's nose. Wylie rocked back into the cushion as if he'd been pushed. Harte pulled back his coat and tapped his badge, his fingernail clicking on the metal.

"If I wasn't wearing this, I'd take you outside right now and beat the living hell out of you . . . show you what it feels like to be taken advantage of."

"Please," Jan snorted, "go right ahead!"

Wylie turned to his wife. "Shut the fuck up! He doesn't know what he's talking about!"

"The hell he doesn't!" Jan shouted. She stood and tightened her hands into bony fists. "It's not like this is the first time. You can't keep that pitiful little thing in your pants, can you?" She turned, took two steps away but stopped and came back. "You little bastard. You don't do a goddamn thing around here! I'm the only one bringing in money and you're out fucking a teenage whore."

"Jan," Harte said, trying to take some of the edge off his voice. "This is not about her. It's about Wylie."

Wylie mustered enough bravado to chance a smirk. "You're real sure about that, are you?"

Harte allowed a false-smile of challenge. "Tell me it was her who came to you about trading sex for rent. Try and tell me that, Wylie."

Wylie grunted and stood. "I don't have to listen to this shit in my own goddamn home." With the table between them, he began poking a finger in the air at Harte. "And I don't care what kind of little toy badge you wear on your shirt." He flung his hand toward Harte's midsection. "Or whatever that thing is on your belt. You can't come in here like this. Where's your goddamn warrant?"

When Harte did not answer, Wylie worked up a vicious smile. "Maybe that little hot-to-trot bitch has got *your* hormones going, now that you're out on your own again. Is that about right?"

He frowned when Harte jerked the badge off his shirt and dropped it on the table. The clatter of the metal shield was harsh and discordant in the room.

"I just went off duty," Harte said through clenched teeth. As he stepped closer, his leg shunted the table forward so that the far edge caught Wylie in the shin. Wylie yelped and bent forward a little, but the

349

sound shut off abruptly when Harte's right fist caught him in the mouth. The sound was like a log popping in a fire. Wylie's head snapped back and his arms flung out, grabbing at the air for something that was not there. When he crashed back against the sofa, it toppled backward and he with it. His head hit the wood floor with a solid *thump*, and for a moment his ratty slippers and bare ankles stood vertically above the bottom of the sofa and its wilderness of cobwebs.

Rolling out of his predicament to his knees, Wylie growled a litany of profanity. When his face rose from behind the sofa, his hand went gingerly to his burst lip, and he cringed at the blood on his fingertips. As he stood, his shirt caught above his belly, revealing half a dozen little tufts of hairs scattered across his stomach, like tiny jungle islands dotting a pale sea. Harte had not seen them since high school in the locker room.

Wylie sputtered, "You cock-sucking sonova—" Harte reached across the toppled sofa and grabbed a fistful of tee-shirt, enough to drag Wylie stumbling back over the furniture.

"It was your mouth that got you that first one," Harte warned. "You'd best shut it!"

"You're the county sheriff," Wylie whined. "You can't come into a man's—"

"Wylie!" Jan yelled. "Just shut your lying mouth and stop bleeding on everything."

When Harte threw him back against the overturned sofa, Wylie cowered like a wounded animal and cupped his hand under his chin. Harte extended his arm, pointed at him, and spoke so quietly that Wylie stopped breathing.

"If you speak to Collette . . . if you walk down there to her trailer—"

"It's my own fuckin' property!" Wylie screamed. "It's not *her* trailer! It's mine! I—"

Harte stepped closer, and Wylie covered his face with his arms. Harte was repulsed by the reek of sweat and fear pouring off the man.

"I wasn't finished," Harte continued. "If you approach her anywhere, I will come back here and make tonight look like a counseling session. That goes for you and Bella Seagrave, too."

"Oh, my God!" Jan rasped. "The Seagrave woman?"

"What!" Wylie spewed air like a horse's flutter. "That old hag?"

Harte looked down at his boots and gritted his teeth. When he looked up, Wylie's arms had lowered cautiously to his chest. Harte hit him again, this time turning his shoulders into the blow to get more weight behind it, catching Wylie squarely on the nose.

Wylie tumbled over the sofa a second time, completing a backward somersault and sprawling on the floor. Rolling to one side he began probing his nose with his fingertips.

"What the hell was that for?" he cried out like a petulant child.

"For Ms. Seagrave," Harte said simply.

Wylie mumbled something that Harte could not hear, and then he scrambled up to his feet and stalked out of the room. One of his slippers was missing, giving his exit an asymmetrical limp. Harte watched the empty entranceway for a while, until a door slammed in the back of the house.

"This is not the first time," Jan said, breaking the awkward silence.

Harte picked up his badge and stared at it. "She's seventeen, Jan." He brought his head around and met her eyes. "That makes it a felony. But she's afraid to talk."

Jan just shook her head and glared at the upset sofa. "You can stick him in a jail and let him rot, for all I care. He doesn't do a damn thing around here."

"Well," Harte said and put on his hat and squared it, "he's doing *something*."

# Chapter Twenty-Eight

In the morning, when Ash took Varley Bulloch and McAllister out into the yard for some sun and fresh air, Harte and Joe-Joe entered the cellblock, where Harte took up vigil at the backdoor. Joe-Joe set up a folding ladder and went to work on the light fixture centered on the ceiling of McAllister's cell. When the cordless drill began to whir, Harte watched Ash and McAllister stand side by side and look off toward the town square.

It took less than a minute. When Joe-Joe strolled from the cell with the collapsed ladder, the two officers climbed the stairs together, Joe-Joe humming a low tune that echoed in the stairwell.

Inside the sheriff's office Joe-Joe plugged in a receiver, connected its cable to a laptop, and pushed the power button. Harte stepped back to his door and leaned into the dispatch room.

"Maxie, you'd better come in and be part of this."

The three of them huddled around the laptop, but there was nothing to hear. "It's sound activated," Joe-Joe explained. "The mic sends a wireless signal here, and the laptop records it digitally." Then the screen lit up with a graph and sliding bar. Harte stared at the control icons and tried not to let the smug little screen of symbols intimidate him.

"Just go through it slowly for me."

After a few minutes of patient council, Joe-Joe walked to Harte's window to let the sheriff look over the instruments at his own speed. Periodically, the deputy leaned close to the glass to look into the fenced-in yard behind the building, and, within a minute, he hurried back to the table.

"They're coming back in," he announced and knelt before the computer. "Now watch this."

A green light began to flash on the receiver box, and, somewhere inside its internal workings, a switch tripped with a tiny *tick*. On the computer screen a barred line pulsed into motion as muffled voices echoed in a hallway and the scuffling of feet on concrete grew louder. Soon the footsteps resonated like the crunch of sand ground with a mortar and pestle. An iron door slid shut with a loud *clang* . . . and then another.

"Don't worry about it," a voice said. It was a low and whispery message but recognizable by its familiar condescending slur. "Just sit tight for a while. You'll be out before you know it."

Joe-Joe snorted softly. "Ash," he whispered, identifying the speaker.

"Sound like old buddies, don't they?" Maxie said. She started to say more, but Joe-Joe, still staring at the screen, held up an index finger to quiet her.

"Can't you make that cretin next to me take a shower?" It was McAllister talking in a low angry voice. "I can smell him from here."

They heard a series of hisses, and Harte pictured Ash laughing through his teeth. "You can lead a Bulloch to water, but you can't make him wash. I sure as hell ain't gonna bathe the bastard."

Footsteps echoed in the hall and faded until the small green light blinked out. With all sound cut off, the bar on the screen was motionless.

Frowning, Harte looked at Joe-Joe. "I don't hear anything."

Keeping his eyes on the screen, Joe-Joe raised his thick index finger again, his expression intent as though he were parsing the individual instruments of a symphony. "Remember, it's sound- activated." The big deputy waited another fifteen seconds and still nothing happened. "Okay," he said and punched two buttons on the keyboard. "Right here, that's your 'rewind.' Then you just tap right here." He thumped his thick index fingertip to the rectangular pad built into the computer. Immediately the playback *popped* and came to life with the seashell acoustics of shuffling footsteps and the garble of muted voices. Then Ash's voice whispered to McAllister again, exactly as it had before, and they listened to the brief conversation again.

When it was done, Joe-Joe dragged the little arrow to the top of the screen and clicked on "activate." "Now it's ready to go again."

"I think I've got it," Harte said. "If I don't, I'll call one of you back in."

Joe-Joe looked down at Harte's antique belt buckle and then at the old leather holster slung over the coat rack, where the Colt Peacemaker perched like a museum piece. "World's changin' fast, Sheriff," Joe-Joe said. "We gotta keep up or get left behind." He made a sweeping gesture with his meaty hand toward the window. "All the bad guys use high-tech stuff." Joe-Joe snorted again. "Hell, all those nerdy guys we kidded in school back when . . . they're the future of law enforcement. They say most of the crimes in America are done on line."

Maxie puffed up a little and propped her fists on her hips. "And how do you think those 'nerdy guys' would'a done goin' up against the Bullochs or the Moodys? It takes a lot more than—"

Maxie cut herself off when the green light shone and the receiver made its little *tick* sound once again. The three officers turned as one to the screen, where the volume bars began bobbing across the bottom of the graph again as a *clackety-clack* rhythm repeated in the speakers. Something was being raked across the bars of a cell.

"Hey, I'm hungry!"

It was Varley Bulloch's surly voice coming through the speakers. No one answered him. Footsteps shuffled on the floor, and a door banged shut, all of it sounding distant from the hidden microphone.

"Hey," Varley yelled, "d'you hear me? I'm starvin' down here!"

"Hey, Bulloch! Shut the fuck up!" This loud and clear from McAllister. "I'm sick o' your whinin'."

After a few exchanges of choice profanities, the light died and the laptop went silent.

"She's workin' fine," Joe-Joe said. "Anything else, Sheriff?"

"Can you make copies of each day's recordings, so that the three of us can alternate taking home a recording and listening for something."

Joe-Joe nodded toward the laptop. "The computer will save it for as long as we need. And if we want to, we can burn a CD every evening." He looked back at Harte and narrowed his friendly eyes. "Exactly what are we listenin' for anyway?"

Staring at the computer, Harte shook his head. "We won't know till we hear it." He patted Joe-Joe's shoulder. "Good job, Joe." Then looking at Maxie, he said, "Can I talk to you?"

When the big deputy lumbered out of the room, Harte moved to the window, turned on the hotplate, and set his blue kettle on the burner. As he stared down into the fenced-in compound, Maxie took her place in front of his desk and waited.

"Do the prisoners ever play basketball out there?" Harte asked and turned to Maxie. "Seems like they always do in the movies."

She fought a smile. "Sher'ff, last time we put balls out there, Clarence Puckett sailed one over the fence all the way to the library. Not to be outdone, the Harding boy heaved one that made it to the square. There was a complaint about hazardous basketballs rolling around town, and Sher'ff Jim said to scrap 'em." Maxie's face turned serious as she pointed at the laptop. "I can be the one to listen to this regular. I can type up a transcript. You and Joe-Joe got your plates full already."

Harte narrowed one eye. "You *want* to do that?"

She lifted her hands from her sides and let them fall back to slap on her jeans. "I got nothin' else to do at home at night. This undercover work has got dispatch beat hands-down."

"But you're doing both."

She smiled. "Sher'ff, when you're hyperactive like I am, you got to feed the beast."

Harte thought about it for the time it took to scan the boxes and wires. "Consider yourself my new administrator of covert interoffice communications." He nodded toward the equipment on his desk. "Let's move all this into the new chifforobe."

Maxie had gone into motion before he had finished his request. "Already on it, Sher'ff."

The kettle rattled and a wisp of steam began to snake from the spout. When Harte reached for the coffee jar, he noticed a small brown paper sack sitting beside his cup. Out of this he pulled a canister labeled *"Mayan Dark Supreme Cacao."* He turned to see that Maxie's smile had stretched into new territory.

"I been readin' about dark chocolate, Sher'ff. They say it's better for you than the reg'lar."

Harte dosed his usual spoonful of coffee into the cup, then added a mound of the chocolate. After pouring and stirring, he sipped, closed his eyes for a moment, and then smiled at Maxie.

"Thank you," he said.

Maxie beamed. "Oh," she said, digging into her shirt pocket. "This was on the dispatch desk this morning. It's from Hooper." She handed him a folded paper with his name printed on the outside. "I'll go see if I can round up some blank CDs for my new assignment."

When he was alone in the office, Harte turned back to the window and added a second spoonful of chocolate to his drink. He sipped, sat, and opened the note.

*Burt Harliner,* it read. *42 years old. Born Odessa, Texas but lived in Mississippi and North Carolina. Three drunk-and-disorderlies in Mississippi, five in Carolina. Now lives at 83 Sunset Drive. A rental. Works for Appalachian Landscaping, which is mostly cutting down trees* *or the parts of trees that need cutting and then hauling them off. He's paid ad valorem taxes on a 2012 Subaru hatchback, license # LI4971. My cousin, Raymond, works for A.L. so I called him and asked about Harliner. Says they call him <u>THE BEAR</u>. Hard-nosed bastard with a chainsaw. People he works with are afraid of him and won't drink with him because he gets mean. Burns knows him. Says the guy comes down to his gym a lot—can bench press 380. Got a son named Carter R. in the middle school. The wife is out of the picture, either divorced or dead. Only record we got on him here is two fights and a complaint from a neighbor. The latter involved some kind of threat or use of force, but the neighbor recanted and it didn't go anywhere.*

Harte dropped the paper on his desk and turned back to the window. "Burt the bear," he said aloud and exhumed the memory of the alpha skater's face when the boy had shied from meeting Harte's handshake. Carter "Lance" Harliner had been like a wild animal staring into an open cage.

When the phone rang, Harte sat and picked up to hear Maxie's voice. "Sher'ff Harte, Captain Nesmith wants to meet with you today to talk about McAllister. He's in town now, over at the courthouse."

"Ask him if he can have lunch with me at the Rainbow Café . . . say, one o'clock?"

"Hang on," Maxie said.

Through the door he heard Maxie make the arrangements, her voice stilted and mechanical. When she came back over the line with Harte, she was her down-home self.

"It's all set, Sher'ff. One o'clock."

Harte hesitated a beat but then went ahead and asked. "Maxie, I thought you liked Nesmith. Why so formal on the phone?"

"Sher'ff," she laughed, "he's a handsome devil, but I learned a long time ago to let the Atlan'a agencies know we are a well-oiled machine that doesn't need anybody holdin' our hands."

Harte rotated the chair so that he could look out at the mountains. "Okay," he said, the lone word sounding like a question. When she made no reply, he forged ahead. "And why would they suspect we are not a well-oiled machine, Maxie?"

" 'Cause we talk different and got nothin' taller'n a three-story building on our square."

Harte sipped his coffee concoction and watched a Cooper's hawk sail over the big oak trees near the library. It angled downward into the valley where Yahoola Creek met the reservoir.

"Maxie, do *you* think we *are* a well-oiled machine?"

He heard her chair squeak, and her voice came back low over the receiver. "Sher'ff Harte, you ask me, you and me and Cody and Joe-Joe . . . we're like those gears turnin' inside one o' those fancy see-through clocks." She was quiet for a time, until he heard her exhale. "The rest of 'em could all stand a dunkin' in a barrel o' dubya-dee forty every morning."

*****

Nesmith was dark-complexioned, a good-looking man in his thirties. He had prominent jawbones and an easy smile that offset his stillness. He was early, standing in the parking lot of the Rainbow with his feet spread and his hands stuffed into the side pockets of his suit coat as he watched a crow peck at something flattened on the gravel lot near the Dumpster. When Harte walked from his cruiser and took his hand, the GBI man looked directly into his eyes, and the smile vanished.

"Billy Nesmith," he said. "I feel like I already know you from conversations with Sheriff Raburn. I'm sorry for the loss of your friend, Sheriff."

"Thank you," Harte said.

Up close, the state officer looked too young to have reached the rank he had attained. His suit was black, but his hair was like a black hole, absorbing all light around it. His olive skin looked smooth as a woman's, his eyes like large ink drops carefully deposited on egg shells.

"Have you been with the bureau long?" Harte asked.

"Thirteen years," he said and smiled at Harte's reaction.

"Are you Hispanic?"

Nesmith held his friendly smile and shook his head. "Part Comanche."

Harte pushed out his lower lip and nodded. "Quanah's people," he purred, injecting a tone of respect to acknowledge the history of the lords of the southern plains.

Nesmith's smile relaxed. "The few of us who survived the small pox."

Harte felt the weight of that statement and shook his head at the wonder of a people's resilience. "And now you're working for the white devil's bureaucracy. How's that working out?"

Nesmith shrugged. "There are assholes of every color in every camp. People are people, wherever you go." He looked appraisingly at the old Colt on Harte's hip. "So, it really *was* a single-action you used on the Bullochs." He nodded his approval. "That's an old one. It got a story?"

Harte looked down at the high sheen of the walnut handles that had absorbed the oils of untold hands. "Must have been one of the first batch of Peacemakers. Probably went to the army. After that it's anybody's guess."

"Lots of desertions in those days," the captain said. "Could've ended up about anywhere."

Harte waited for the question: why a twenty-first century sheriff used an antique piece when there were other options with deadlier firepower? But Nesmith stared at the weapon with admiration.

"Sends a hellava message," the younger man said. "I like it."

Harte liked this man. As if by tacit agreement they turned together and started for the restaurant entrance.

"If you like fish, they cook up a fine rainbow trout here," Harte suggested.

"Only if you promise not to tell," Nesmith said, straight-faced. "My staff thinks I eat only buffalo tongue and the hearts of my enemies."

"Well," Harte said, "they don't serve bison, and I hope to God not the other."

Inside the restaurant the booths were taken, so they walked to a table near the back, where an albino buck was mounted on the wall. The antlers were the color of rose-amethyst and appeared to glow from within. Nesmith stood before it, gazing into the animal's empty glass eyes.

"Wouldn't it be wonderful to know that *that* big fellow was still roaming these mountains?" Nesmith remarked.

They sat and Harte eyed the mute creature overlooking the room. "Some of us seem to have this notion that something like that doesn't really count for anything unless you hang it on a wall."

The captain opened his napkin and laid it in his lap. "You know about the white buffalo?"

Harte nodded. "I do."

Nesmith smoothed the napkin over his thighs. "No warrior would ever take its life."

Harte nodded again, saying nothing. A blonde waitress arrived—the same one who had served him and Cody. She set down two ice waters and took their drink orders. When she left, the two lawmen opened their menus and were quiet for a time.

Nesmith spoke in the thoughtful tone of a man reminding himself of an immutable truth. "We don't get to choose our time, do we, Sheriff?"

Harte knew the GBI man was referring to a century when a colorless bison was held sacred by an entire culture. "Unless we're planning an ambush," Harte said.

Nesmith looked up at that. "Speaking of ambushes . . . we found only your deputy's fingerprints on that gun at the Moody bust. His prints must have smeared over any that belonged to the Moodys. The barrel and frame were wiped clean." He closed his menu, leaned forward, and crossed his forearms on the table. "Which might make sense . . . but I have a little problem with the way things went down out there, Sheriff."

Harte made a smile of regret. "You'll have to get in line behind me for that."

The waitress returned with two ice teas, setting down Harte's without ceremony, but then she held the other as she inspected Nesmith. "Unsweetened, right?"

"Yes, ma'am," he said, though the girl could not have been much more than twenty.

"That how you stay so trim?" she said, presenting the drink with a crooked smile.

Nesmith pointed to the sugar packets. "I add my own. My staff says I'm a control freak."

She raised her eyebrows as she pulled out her pad and pen. "Do you gentlemen know what you want?" She said this looking directly at Nesmith, and it seemed to Harte that her question extended beyond the possibilities of the menu.

Breaking the spell, Harte cleared his throat. "Trout, creamed corn, spinach, rolls."

"Exactly the same for me," Nesmith said.

"Oh," she said, drawing out the word as if she had solved a riddle. "You must be trouble, following the sheriff's lead like that. Trying to get on his good side?" She slipped her pencil over her ear, where it disappeared into her blonde tresses.

Nesmith smiled. "The sheriff has good taste. It's his turf. I'd be a fool not to pay attention."

Her eyes brightened, as if she had decoded some cryptic message meant for her ears alone, and then she turned away. Nesmith watched her walk to the kitchen.

"My wife would eat her for lunch," he said.

"All of her . . . or just her heart? Your wife Comanche, too?"

Nesmith chuckled. "Irish."

"One of the hard things about getting older," Harte said, "is becoming invisible to women."

"But not the smart ones, I'll bet," Nesmith corrected.

Harte thought of Bella Seagrave, raised his glass, and drank a toast to a kind remark. Nesmith began rearranging items on the table: the catsup and tabasco bottles and the salt and pepper shakers.

"Here's my point about the Moodys," he said and tapped the catsup. "Say this is the west door of the meth lab, the one you and three deputies entered." He touched the tabasco. "Here's the east door." Between the two he laid down a knife crosswise. "This is the counter where the Moodys were cooking up their product." He picked up the salt and pepper shakers and offered them to Harte. "Now show me where the Moodys were standing when you went in."

Harte set down the salt. "Garret," he said. Then next to it, he positioned the pepper. "Grat."

"Yeah," Nesmith said. "Exactly where we found the bodies . . . what was left of them." Stiffening his left hand he defined a line from catsup to tabasco. "This angle here . . . from door to door," he said, staring intently into Harte's eyes. "It makes no sense. How does Ash shoot the Moodys here—" Now he propped his right hand on the table, forming an open vee with the left. "And then he swings left thirty or forty degrees and kills your deputy, the jailor."

"There's something else, too," Harte said and pointed at the salt shaker. "Garret had a forty-four mag sitting in front of him on the countertop. But—according to Ash—he pulls out a twenty-two to shoot at the deputies at the east door."

Before Nesmith could comment, the waitress arrived with plates of steaming food and stood poised with her tray, her wide eyes looking down at the new arrangement of condiments. "I think his knight has endangered your queen, Sheriff." Both men looked up at her. "Could you gentlemen finish your game later so I can put down these plates?"

They cleared their places, and the plates went down, each with a sautéed trout laid out among the side dishes. The waitress propped a hand on one hip and stared unabashedly at Nesmith.

"Anything else for you, gentlemen?"

Nesmith looked up at Harte. "Sheriff?"

"No, I think we're set," Harte said to the girl, but her radar remained fixed on his companion.

"Well," she said, "if you need anything, my name is Lorraine."

As soon as she had left, Nesmith's face was all business. "Tell me about Ash, Sheriff."

"He's on suspension from outside duties pending investigation. He's taking over jailor duties."

Showing nothing in his face, Nesmith chewed as he locked eyes with Harte. "I can understand you wanting to hold your cards close to your chest, Sheriff, but I suspect you've put a lot of thought into this. I don't want to seem like I'm telling you how to run your office . . . but, with Santiago in the mix, I just need to know that you're looking out for yourself."

"Is this why we're here today?" Harte said. "To warn me?"

Nesmith picked up his knife, sliced into a roll, and buttered it. "Partly."

"Well," Harte said, "I'll heed that warning."

Billy Nesmith took a bite of roll. "Now that I've met you, I think maybe you didn't need an upstart captain from the state bureau looking you up to offer an unsolicited warning."

Harte smiled. "I don't think you get to be the 'upstart.' Not with thirteen years of service. I've only been on the job a couple of months." He poked at the trout with his fork. "You want to tell me the other part?"

"Parts," Nesmith said, raising two fingers. "Unless we can find something better on McAllister, you'll have to cut him loose."

Harte wiped his mouth with his napkin. "I heard their negotiations about the drug deal."

Nesmith shook his head. "Won't hold up. Pressure came down the bureaucratic ladder from somewhere, and suddenly everything that was heard coming out of McAllister's mouth is circumstantial. We're going to need more."

Harte leaned forward and lowered his voice. "We just might get it. I've bugged his cell."

Nesmith made a lackluster smile. "We're going to need something physical, Harte."

Harte tried the fish and chewed. "You mean like finding the money."

The intensity in Nesmith's eyes was answer enough. He sat back and exhaled his frustration.

"We've taken the Caddy apart," he said, "down to the bare bones. The Bulloch truck, too. We searched the woods all around the parking lot at the bar . . . including the Dumpster. We scoured the ground a good fifty yards deep into the forest. No money." The disappointment on his face summed up his efforts.

The waitress, Lorraine, started to approach until Harte shook his head at her.

"What if I told you it was McAllister who made the nine-one-one call?" Harte said.

Billy Nesmith narrowed his eyes. "I'm listening."

"This is just a theory," Harte said and leaned on the table to confide his idea. "The Bullochs were known to distribute drugs over three counties, right? Maybe McAllister and the people he works for want the Bulloch brothers out of the picture . . . for the sake of a monopoly."

Nesmith frowned. "But you say the Bullochs were buying. Why would they do that when they make the product themselves?"

"Maybe McAllister offered something they didn't have," Harte suggested. "I don't know."

The state captain looked out the front window. "When dealers and buyers meet at a public place, it's to make things run smoothly for both parties. That means the dealer brings his goods and the buyer brings the money. So where's the money?"

Harte shrugged. "All hell broke loose that night. A lot of things could have happened to it."

Nesmith set down his fork. "Okay, here's what you think you know: The deal is a planned double-cross. McAllister delivers a box of worthless powder, except for just enough cocaine to disguise his package. The Bullochs *must* produce the money *then*. The so-called "drugs" go into the pickup. McAllister has called nine-one-one. He knows a bust will go down. Where does he hide the money?"

Harte nodded. "Unless he used an accomplice, it has to be some-where at Luther's."

Nesmith washed down the food with a gulp of tea. "But it's not."

Harte shook his head and spread his hands on the table. "Maybe."

Nesmith's face took on a conflicting mix of regret and anger. "Harte, I can't put any more time into it. The higher ups won't let me." He set down his glass. "They're calling you a 'one-night wonder at the O.K. Corral.' You impressed the hell out of everybody with your performance at Luther's." He flipped over one hand. "But then—"

"The Moody bust," Harte finished for him.

Billy Nesmith nodded. "That and the cinder block incident. Some-body on the other side of this has got some pull with the bureaucracy. Maybe the Governor's office. They're saying you've got no business in this line of work, and they're just wanting this problem up here to go away."

Harte looked out the front window and said nothing.

Nesmith sat forward. "Sheriff Raburn told me once *you* should have been sheriff . . . and *he* the schoolteacher. There are no 'one-night wonders' in a gunfight, Harte. You've either got the nerves for it or you don't. It doesn't come and go like a good day at the golf course." He pointed at Harte's badge. "*I* know what you did out in that parking lot. And I know what it took to do it."

The captain mopped his plate with a piece of dinner roll and popped the bread into his mouth. Probably, Harte thought, exactly as Quanah Parker would have polished off a morsel of bison.

Nesmith wiped his hands on his napkin and propped his elbows on the table. "I also know that something's not right about the Moody bust." He pointed at Harte again. "You did right out there. Probably saved a life or two. Meeks' death was not your fault."

Harte turned to the window. "He was supposed to stay outside."

"I know," Nesmith said. "I've read all the reports."

When Harte looked back at the captain, Nesmith spread his hands with the uncertainty of it all, yet his face was set with conviction. "So, don't expect any help from the state on this. But you're going to need some help at some point. We all do. When that time comes, you're going to call *me*."

Harte looked down at his unfinished lunch. "I might need to pick up this tab today."

Nesmith nodded once. "I'll let you." Then he smiled. "Right after some peach pie."

# Chapter Twenty-Nine

On Saturday morning, Harte—dressed in a fresh shirt and jeans and with a towel draped over his shoulder—stepped back into the dispatch room after a trip downstairs to the showers. Holding a full kettle of water he watched Maxie go through the mundane ritual of straightening her desk after taking over from Hooper's shift.

"Morning," he said.

She smiled like a gambler laying down a royal flush on a poker table. "Mornin', sher'ff."

"What was all that hammering?" he asked, but she only watched him back through his door.

After setting the kettle on the hotplate, he rubbed the towel vigorously into his wet hair and then crossed the room to snap the towel over the pull-up bar. He sat at the desk, slapped down the McAllister file before him and began reviewing all the papers as he ran a comb through his hair.

When the kettle boiled, he spun the chair to the windowsill and prepared his coffee-cocoa mix. Turning back to the desk, he raised his metal cup to his mouth and paused, catching a reflection of light that made him think for an instant that a new window had been cut into the opposing wall. Lowering the cup to the desk, he stared straight ahead.

He could see right away that it was a print of Montana. Contrasting sharply to the institutional green of the stucco wall, the picture hung like an unexpected portal into sanity. Inside the borders of a heavily grained, gray oak frame, a man sat his horse, its legs all but lost in a low stratum of fog that lifted from a grassy flat of winter-yellow blades and ghostly outcrops of blue-gray rock. The horseman looked off into the painting's distance where jagged mountaintops rose up against a gold-burnished sky. The peaks were snow-capped and sharp, like giant predatory teeth.

Harte rose with his cup, stepped around his desk, and perched his glasses on his nose as he stood before the picture. Leaning in close, he admired the detailed work of the painter. Taking a step back, he sipped coffee and took in the whole of the scene again. Only then did he feel Maxie's presence in the doorway. Smiling, she leaned a shoulder into the jamb, her arms folded across her slight torso.

"It's perfect," he said.

"It's Montana," she said, barely able to contain her excitement.

"So I see," he said and raised his cup to her just as the switchboard phone started ringing.

When she took the call, he sat again and alternated reading through the state reports on McAllister and studying his new view of Montana's Bitterroot Range. When he found the file on the contents of the Cadillac, he shuffled through several typewritten pages and a dozen glossy photographs. Starting over at page one of the list, he slowed the process and considered every item, pushing any sense of complaisance from his examination. He would accept none of the sundry items until he could pinpoint some practical application for a life as a construction foreman.

There were the usual accessories and accouterments of any car's trunk: a spare tire, lug wrench, jack, a Castrol box with two quarts of oil, and a plastic gas can holding less than a gallon of fuel. A folded umbrella and paint-stained rain coat were wrapped inside an old wool military blanket. Various pieces of trash littered the thin carpet of the trunk: scraps of torn maps and yellowed blueprints of former worksites, fast food wrappers, greasy cartons that had once held salty fries, and seven empty cans of Dr. Pepper, each of which had been buckled in the middle.

Among these inconsequential items was a semi-rusted, red, metal toolbox with a snap-lock lid. The list of enclosed tools and carpenter's aids covered a page and a half, detailing the contents by size, starting with a three-bubble level, a crowbar, and a hammer. From there the list ran down to the smallest finishing nail, brad, and loose nut and washer. Nothing on the list seemed suspect.

The backseat was relatively empty. The only items counted there were found on the floor: a steel plumb-bob with yellow nylon string tied to its eyelet. The string was an unruly mass wadded into a tangle that would test the patience of any man faced with the task of unraveling it. There was nothing amiss with these articles, except that they probably belonged in the tool chest.

In the front passenger seat was a McDonald's bag with crumpled paper wrapping inside. A cardboard cup sat in the cup holder on the dash. The glove box held maps, vehicle registration, pencils, air pressure gauge, and a pair of well-worn work gloves. In the console were a number of coins—all itemized—a bottle of eye drops, and the charge-cord for a cell phone. A host of tiny objects were retrieved from under the seats: a bottle top, several stale French fries, gas receipts.

In the file he found Cody's arrest report from the night of Jim's death. Detailed there was everything taken from McAllister's pockets: a Verizon cell phone, a pack of Marlboro cigarettes, a cheap lighter, three quarters, a well-worn leather wallet containing seventy-eight dollars, license and other cards, a four-inch-long cardboard spool, and a key ring holding nine keys.

Harte sipped coffee and picked up his phone. "Maxie, do we have McAllister's personal belongings here, or are they with the state people?"

"They sent 'em back, Sher'ff. We got 'em in a locker. Want me to bring 'em in?"

"Please."

When Maxie entered with a large clear Zip-lock bag, her eyes fixed on the new print in the oak frame and remained there as she crossed the room. "You think those mountains are all that different from ours, Sher'ff?" She set down the bag. "I mean, except for the pointy tops?" Then her puzzled eyes came around to Harte. "How come they *do* have those pointy tops, I wonder?"

Harte gazed at the picture. "Appalachians are a lot older. Our mountains used to be like that."

Maxie looked back at the print. "So they start off sharp . . . and then get rounded?"

"Erosion," Harte explained. "It's all about time."

"So, Montana mountains," she said, studying the picture, "they're the young whippersnappers." She turned to look out the window. "And ours are the wise old hills o' the world?"

"Pretty much," Harte said.

As she left the room, she looked again at the print, and, though Harte could only see her face in quarter profile, he thought he detected a haughtiness in her stare.

After emptying the contents of the bag onto his desk, he slipped on his glasses, picked up the lighter and thumbed its striker-wheel. A flame appeared and held steadily, until he let off on the fuel plunger.

Sorting through the keys, he found nothing unusual: Cadillac, padlock, and door keys.

The cardboard cylinder was clean and sturdy, the walls about a quarter inch thick, the hollow core maybe half an inch wide. It was a spool of some kind. He raised it to his moustache and sniffed, detecting only the smell of cardboard.

He emptied the Marlboro package, but only four cigarettes and a few grains of loose tobacco fell out. He stuffed the smokes back into the box and swiped the desk clean with his hand.

After rifling through the wallet and learning which insurance companies looked after McAllister's health and auto needs, he packaged everything back into the bag. When three knocks sounded at his door, Harte called out to enter. Maxie came in and closed the door.

"I typed up yesterday's recordin' of McAllister's cell," she said and handed over a folder. "Nothin' much there, Sher'ff," she admitted. "Mostly snorin'. That McAllister must'a run a sawmill in another life. Sounds like he swallowed the blade and a lotta bark to boot."

Harte scanned the papers. "We have to be patient . . . wait for the results to come to us."

"Yes'r, I know that. Eventually, that silver-haired jasper is gonna get bored outta his skull down there. He'll slip up sooner or later." Maxie narrowed her eyes. "Sher'ff Harte, how'd you catch on to ever'thin' here so fast?" She waved an arm vaguely at the room. "I mean . . . you stepped into all this in a heartbeat, but you seem to know a lot about how it works. Is it from bein' such close friends with Sher'ff Jim?"

"That's part of it. You can't hang around a sheriff without picking up some things. But I was a history teacher first, you know, and I've read an awful lot about early law enforcement."

He watched Maxie's eyes cut to the old Colt hanging in its holster on the coatrack.

"Plus," he continued, "my wife used to watch a TV show about cops and courts." He shrugged. "I was usually in the next room grading papers, but I think it seeped into me by osmosis."

Maxie laughed. "My Aunt Flora used to watch all those shows. She'd go down to the courthouse and nine times outta ten she'd predict the outcomes of the criminal trials."

Harte sat back in his chair and drank the last of his special brew. "Well, if they ever kick me out of here, maybe your Aunt Flora will come down here and take over." He handed the bugged-cell transcript back to Maxie. "We'll keep these locked in the cabinet."

She took the papers. "That ain't all I got, Sher'ff." Maxie laid down a page of newsprint torn from the *Union County Messenger*. "I been doin' more than writing up McAllister's snorin'." She tapped her finger to an article outlined in pink highlighter. "Read that."

Harte adjusted his glasses, and squinted at the top of the page. "This is from four months ago," he said and checked Maxie's face. When she nodded, he began reading aloud.

*"Around two a.m. on Tuesday night, a fire broke out in a metal warehouse on Walnut Street adjacent to the fairgrounds and north of the Holtzclaw Field Stone lot. The blaze spread through both of the building's two large rooms. Most of the contents appears to have been chemicals and laboratory paraphernalia. Firefighters were able to contain the conflagration without damage to neighboring property, although fire volunteer, Jonas Cutchens, Jr., sustained a fractured kneecap and burn when a steel girder sprang at him from the tension of a partially collapsed wall."*

"Ouch," Harte said. He looked at Maxie, but her intent face sent him back to the article.

*"When arson inspector, Brant McNelly, declared the inferno a work of foul play, the Union County Sheriff's Department investigated the scene early Wednesday morning and found traces of illegal drugs. McNelly said, 'We found residue that proves the use of an accelerant. The warehouse may have lost as much as half a million dollars of saleable product and half again that much in chemicals and equipment.'*

*"Investigators contacted the owner of the warehouse, Winton Darcy, a Winter Park, Florida resident, who, in his absence, claims to have no*

*knowledge of who might have been using his facility. The warehouse has been on the market for sale since last February, but the local realtors at Blue Ridge Properties say that no inquiries have been proffered during this sluggish market."*

Harte frowned at Maxie. "What am I not getting here?"

She grinned and bobbed her eyebrows. "I looked up that name 'Winton Darcy.' He's a Florida man with a cabin up on Lake Hiwassee. His wife was found dead in the cabin. Looked like suicide, but the coroner suspected otherwise. Turns out Darcy had gone on an overnight fishing trip to the Chattooga River with a friend. Had a solid alibi, and so the case against him was dropped."

"And?" Harte said.

Maxie hesitated for effect. "And . . . the friend was Bobby Lee Bulloch."

Harte gazed at the lone horseman sitting his mount below the Bitterroots. "So Darcy owed the Bullochs. Maybe they cashed in by making use of his warehouse."

Maxie arched an eyebrow. "It's a workin' theory, Sher'ff."

"So with their lab gone, the Bullochs come down to our county for some product."

Maxie was already nodding. "They don't wanna lose their customers to somebody else before they can get a lab up and running again."

Harte stood and faced the window. Outside, near the leaf-dappled sidewalk, two farmers in blue overalls talked over the roof of a pickup loaded with heavy burlap sacks of feed. These men looked a long way from a world of illicit drugs.

"Could be that McAllister's people set the fire and then offered their product to the Bullochs?" Harte said into the window pane. He turned and leaned back against the edge of the sill. "Then the brothers come down here to Lumpkin, and McAllister sets them up for a fall."

"But why would he let himself get involved like that, Sher'ff? I mean, he's in jail, too."

Harte shook his head. "He knows we have nothing on him but some conversation. All we know is that he talked with the Bullochs and met with Bobby Lee in the parking lot. And no matter how insinuating the conversation, I'm told none of it will hold up in court."

"Sounds like we need to find that money, Sher'ff," Maxie said.

Harte turned and stared out the window toward the square. "Maybe McAllister thinks he's a lot smarter than the Lumpkin County Sheriff's Department and the GBI." Harte walked to the rack for his hat. "I'm going to take a ride out to Luther's."

*****

The parking lot was empty out front, with only Luther's Lincoln Town Car sitting out back by the Dumpster. Harte parked his cruiser in the spot at the north end where he remembered seeing McAllister's Cadillac just before the shooting had started. The woods beyond the lot looked naked and violated, as if a flashflood had swept through the trees. Only a scattering of leaves lay on the ground, where the scrape marks of rake tines still showed in the disturbed dirt among the tree trunks. Shrubs and vines had been cut and cleared, and Harte wondered what had become of all the foliage that had been removed. The state boys had meticulously covered this ground.

Stepping onto the cleared ground, he began walking aimlessly through the altered forest, the bulk of which was comprised of pines and sweetgums, all as thick as his arm. Fifty yards back into the woods he met a wall of discarded brush piled up like a crude corral. Harte remembered from the state report that no flashlight had been found among McAllister's belongings. They had to draw the search limit somewhere, and this looked reasonable enough to Harte. It was doubtful that McAllister would have groped farther from the lot without a light. It had been warm that night, still snake season.

Harte wandered through the trees a while longer and returned to the lot, where he stared at the Dumpster and began double-guessing what the state investigators would or would not do to be thorough in their search. It would do no good to presume anything, so he walked with a deliberate gait toward the Dumpster.

The Dumpster's flat bottom made a tight seal with the gravel lot. After circling it twice, he pushed aside the sliding door with a resonating *bang* and checked the interior of the bin. All he got for his efforts was the rude olfactory awakening that lurked in all Dumpsters. Other than the stench, it was empty, save the grime that saturated the floor.

The backdoor of the building opened, and Luther stood in the doorway, his expression a mix of annoyance and curiosity. In one hand he held a bucket, in the other he gripped a revolver that was stuffed into the waistband at the front of his pants. His hand relaxed on the gun.

"Didn't know you kept a gun, Luther," Harte said, sauntering toward him.

Luther looked down at the gun and patted the handle lightly with his fingers. "Bought *this* the day after those inbred reprobates invaded us. What're you doin' back here, Harte?"

Harte gestured toward the Lincoln. "Did the state police come out and search your car?"

"Oh, hell, yeah . . . even when I told 'em there was no need. I keep it locked out here."

"Did they tell you what they were looking for?"

Luther cocked his head to one side. "No, but I ain't stupid."

Harte approached, leaned on the wall, and tried for a smile of apology. "It's important that I find that money. Is there anything you can tell me about it, Luther?"

The barman set down the bucket, and his brown eyes went as dull as a pair of old pennies. "I ain't gonna pretend I couldn' use it, but I'll tell you flat out, Harte, if I found that damn money, I wouldn' want nothin' to do with it. Jim Raburn was a friend o' mine, too."

Harte pushed back his hat and let out a long slow breath. "Didn't mean to insult you, Luther. Guess I'm feeling a little desperate. I need to find some evidence against that McAllister character; else, he might squeeze right out of this. I don't want that to happen." He gestured toward the woods. "Ever see anybody out here looking around besides the state people?"

"No," Luther said, "but I don't spend much time out here either."

A light scuffling in the forest turned Harte, and he peered around the Dumpster, where a squirrel was digging a hole in the ground amid the busy rake marks. The animal's shining gray and brown coat appeared luxuriant as it caught a lone spear of light through the trees. The squirrel made quick little jerks as it dug, shifting its body position as a safety precaution, to be on guard from all directions. A whole acorn dropped from its mouth into the shallow excavation, and then its little paws began tamping the cache in the same jerky motions.

"Uh-oh, watch this," Luther said. He was looking down at a scruffy gray cat as it crept outside between Luther's feet. The cat was fully focused, on the prowl, and behaved as if Harte and Luther were merely elements of cover in its strategy to close in on its quarry. As the hunter crept out onto the lot, its feline eyes were locked on the squirrel with an intensity both fierce and contained. It was the concentration of the consummate hunter.

"That there is Mosby, my rat killer."

"Mosby?" Harte said.

"Remember the rebel general? They called him 'the gray ghost'?"

The gray cat moved like smoke on a near-windless day as it rounded the corner of the Dumpster. But the squirrel started to chirr and bark as its body trembled in stiff spasms. The cat froze, and the one-sided tirade stretched out to a long, raspy complaint.

Finally, like a thread snapping under too much tension, the squirrel broke for the nearest tree and scaled it in a glissando of chips and snaps as flakes of bark fell to the forest floor.

"You *better* run!" Luther called out. "This cat takes no prisoners."

From its new perch high in the tree, the prey became the teaser, chattering about a victory over the hunter. Aloof and unresponsive, the cat walked away in a leisurely stroll into the lot.

Harte looked for the scolding squirrel but could not make out the creature hidden in the bristly, evergreen foliage. It occurred to him now that the canopy of the forest provided the thickest cover.

"Up in the pines," Harte mumbled aloud.

Luther turned and frowned at him. "What?"

"When the state police searched the woods . . . did they look up in the trees?"

Luther's face squeezed into a question. "I got no idea." He looked at the upper stratum of forest and pushed his lower lip forward. "Be a good place to hide somethin', wouldn' it?"

Harte felt something pop free in his mind, like a bubble that had been trying to rise to the surface. He thought of the plumb-bob and tangle of yellow cord in the Cadillac.

"The spool was in his coat pocket," Harte whispered.

Luther picked up the bucket to sling water into the lot, but he paused. "The *what*?"

"You ever do any logging?" Harte said.

Luther tossed the dirty water in a spreading arc over the gravel. "Can't say as I have."

"When I was boy," Harte said, "I worked for the saw mill after school. Sometimes, on a Saturday, if a crew was a man short, they sent me out with the loggers. Those boys were very demanding about where a tree fell . . . to make the limbing easy . . . and the drag-out more direct. So we had to get a rope high up on the trunk to pull it over in the right direction."

Luther crossed his arms over his chest, and leaned against the door frame. "So?"

"Do you know how we used to get a rope that high?" Harte continued.

Luther made an elaborate shrug. "Climb the tree, I guess."

"You remember Scooter Martingale?"

Luther squinted off toward the Dumpster. "Wasn't he a pitcher on our baseball team?"

Harte nodded. "He had this chrome trailer hitch he tied to a light nylon string. He could swing that thing underhanded and send it a hundred feet up into a tree and it would thread the needle over a limb and then the heavy ball would fall back to earth. Using the string, we'd pulley up a heavier rope and then we'd pull the tree exactly where we wanted it. Saved a lot of time and energy. Saved us any scars on the wood from the climbing cleats."

Luther squinted at the trees. "You think this McAllister feller did somethin' like that?"

Harte turned to Luther. "Guess what was in the floor of McAllister's Cadillac?"

Luther thought about it for a moment. "Scooter Martingale?"

Harte ignored the humor. "A steel plumb-bob and a wad of tangled nylon cord."

Luther's eyebrows floated up as Harte started for his cruiser. "Hey! Where're *you* goin'?"

Without slowing Harte called over his shoulder. "To round up a posse."

# Chapter Thirty

Harte parked in front of the department and walked to the end of the lot, but the skateboarders and their makeshift ramp were nowhere to be seen. When he entered the dispatch office, Maxie looked up from her desk with a cryptic smile and cut her eyes to Ash by the coffee maker. The blond deputy had his back to the room as he stirred a spoon inside a ceramic mug.

"Where's our skateboarding crew?" Harte asked.

Without turning, Ash cleared his throat. "I told 'em to move on." When he faced Harte, he raised his mug and drank, his dead eyes staring over the rim of the cup.

"I told you to give them some slack," Harte said in a level voice.

Ash lowered the mug. "They finished the job you gave them. I thought we'd look a little more professional without a longhaired circus performance in our front yard."

The two men locked eyes. Maxie sat quietly staring at her switchboard.

"Find them," Harte said. "I need to talk to them."

Ash's face clouded. "Now?"

"Get me their location," Harte ordered, "in the next fifteen minutes."

The room was like a mortuary as Ash glared at Harte. "What about my jailor duties?"

"What about them?" Harte replied, his hard face a mirror to Ash's.

Ash set down his mug and took his coat from the rack. Without a word or his coffee, he left.

Harte walked into his office. After setting a full kettle on the hotplate, he began measuring out his newfound ratio of coffee to cocoa. By the time he had settled at his desk with the hot drink, a knock sounded on his door.

"Come!" he said.

Maxie stepped just inside the door. "Wilma Cavender called. Says she's got a raccoon up in her attic. She's askin' us to send somebody out there. Her husband was a commissioner back when." When Harte still did not answer, she looked down at her feet and came up with her lips pressed into a tight line. " 'Course he's dead now."

Harte looked up at her. "The raccoon?"

"Nos'r, the husband."

Harte sipped his coffee. "Do we have a warrant for said raccoon?"

Maxie pursed her lips. "I've not seen one, Sher'ff."

Harte swiveled his chair toward the window and gazed out at the top of the courthouse beyond the tall chestnut oaks that surrounded the building. "Send Ash."

Maxie's face wrinkled. "To the raccoon?"

Harte continued to look out the windowglass. "For a warrant." He stood, put on his coat, and grabbed his hat. "I'll be outside in the compound. Let me know about the skaters."

Blocking his exit, Maxie stood firm in the doorway and stared up at him. "Sher'ff, I guess we've stopped pretendin' we don't know Ash is a skunk o' the first order?"

Harte shrugged. "I never could act worth a damn," he said and walked around her.

"You really want me to tell Ash to get that warrant, Sher'ff?" she called to his back.

Harte stopped and exhaled heavily. "Just send him out to Wilma's. Remind him he can't use a gun."

"Will do, Sher'ff."

Inside the fenced-in compound behind the department, he lashed an extension ladder to the cruiser's roof. As soon as he sat behind the wheel, Maxie's voice came alive on the radio.

"The skateboard gang is at the laundry, Sher'ff. Good asphalt there and a speed bump."

Two minutes later he pulled into the sloped parking lot behind the laundry. Lester Dowdy turned to watch his approach, and then the four other boys followed his lead. They stood quietly as he parked. Noticeably absent was Carter Harliner, a.k.a. "Lance."

"The radio is working fine," Harte said, getting out of his car. "How is high school?"

Lester presented the face of the condemned. "I got Mr. Tolliver for math."

Harte waited. "And that's bad?"

Lester's face compressed with the obvious. "Be like skateboardin' down Blood Mountain." Harte beckoned the boy closer. "I've got a paying job for you men, if you're interested. Probably take a few hours."

The other boys approached and stood behind Lester. "We gotta work with that blond guy?" Lester asked. "The one that run us off?"

Harte shook his head. "You'll be working for me on a crime site. Are you interested?"

"Doin' what?" asked the black boy named Ray.

Harte offered an old man's embarrassed smile. "Something I'm not as good at as I used to be. I want you to climb some trees. I'm looking for a piece of key evidence."

Lester pointed at the smallest boy. "J.J. can climb a tree like a 'rang-a-tang, Sheriff."

Harte nodded. "Exactly what I need. How about it? You men want the job?"

A palpable energy passed through the group as they conferred. "Sure," Lester said.

When Harte offered his hand out the window, Lester shook. The others began to crowd in, and a hand-shaking-fest was underway.

When Ray took his turn, he raised his chin. "So, does this mean we're deputies?"

Harte thought about it. "How about 'arboreal specialists . . . on temporary assignment'?"

Ray cracked a smile. "Cool!" he said. "When do we start?"

Harte bobbed his head toward the back seat. "Climb in. We'll call your parents on the way."

\*\*\*\*\*

"Evergreens first," Harte suggested, laying out a strategy. "If we come up short, we'll start again with the hardwoods."

They stood at the north limit of the Liquid Gold parking lot looking into the clean-swept forest. Sunlight slanted in at an angle giving the bare ground between the trees a mottled appearance, like a swamp reflecting light from scattered pools of water.

"Let's start at the east end and work toward the Dumpster. If you find something, call me over before you touch it."

"Whataya think it'll look like?" Lester asked.

Harte studied the boughs of the pines. "I'm guessing a waterproof bag or a duffel."

The boys started into the woods, and Harte called to their backs, "If you need the ladder—"

The boys stopped and turned as one, as if this were some choreography that they regularly practiced. "Don't need a ladder, Sheriff," Ray informed him and then smiled with what might have been a show of pity for Harte's generation. "If we need help, we help each other."

Harte gave a little nod, leaned back against the side panel of the cruiser, and decided to be quiet. Soon every sneaker had left the ground, and the pines had begun to tremble from the efforts of climbing. Luther appeared beside Harte. Easing back against the car, he looked at the activity in the trees and crossed his arms over his chest.

"This your posse?"

"Yep," Harte said, keeping his eyes on the lively search up in the trees.

Luther let a quiet laugh wheeze from his chest. "This has gotta be a first: a sheriff bringing a carload of teenagers to a bar."

"Just don't ask them any questions," Harte suggested.

Luther turned at that. "I wasn't going to ask anybody anything. Why would I?"

"I'm just trying to spare you the embarrassment. It's bound to be the wrong question."

Luther's brow wrinkled. "Why would I ask the wrong question?"

Harte shook his head. "Not you in particular, Luther. I'm talking about all of us old enough to remember the Cold War and Ipana toothpaste."

Harte was saved from further explanation when someone called out from one of the trees. "Think I found something, Sheriff!"

Harte and Luther exchanged glances, pushed away from the cruiser, and walked side by side.

"Looks like a dark green stuff sack." It was Ray calling down from the thickest pine. The other boys were already shimmying down from surrounding trees. "It's tangled in the limbs."

"Don't touch it!" Harte yelled and turned to Luther. "Mind if I cut down that tree?"

Luther arched his eyebrows. "It's not my tree. That's national forest."

Harte looked around at the groomed floor of the forest and wondered if Billy Nesmith had received permission from the Forest Service to carry out the search. He pulled out his cell phone.

Flakes of bark sprinkled down through the branches. "Heads up!" Ray called.

A compact, army-green pouch shaped like a deflated football came crashing through the limbs until it snagged and hung up on a branch ten feet overhead. Ray was not far behind, working his way down the trunk with the smooth muscular moves of a gymnast. When he reached the level of the bag, he broke a piece of dead branch from the tree and poked the bag until it tumbled to the ground.

Harte crouched over it and spread his hands in a protective gesture. "Nobody touch it!"

Ray dropped lightly to the ground and joined the circle of onlookers. "Got a coupla big fish hooks sewn onto it," he said. "That's what was holdin' it up there."

Harte straightened and turned to Lester. "There are some plastic bags in the back of the cruiser. Would you get us one? And the tool kit near the tire well."

Using a stick, Harte lifted the canvas pouch by one of its straps. The two heavy-duty fish hooks were an obvious makeshift addition, sewn on by hand.

When Lester returned, Harte used two pairs of pliers to open the bag and fold back its cover flap. A clear plastic bag filled the interior, full of neatly banded stacks of hundred dollar bills. Harte's posse—and Luther—stared wide-eyed at the money. Harte dug out his wallet.

"Good job, men. You've earned a finder's fee."

Lester pushed both palms toward Harte. "We don't need you to pay us for climbing a tree, Sheriff." Lester checked the faces of his friends, lingering finally on Ray, who made a cryptic nod that Harte would have missed were he not looking right at the boy.

"A deal's a deal," Harte said. "You're working for me. This bag is going to be evidence."

Lester stood his ground and nodded toward the parking lot. "My pop told me what you did out here the night Sheriff Raburn was killed." He nodded, his face open and earnest without guile or affectation. "I'm bettin' you didn't want any pay for that."

Harte studied each boy's face and saw their solidarity. Slowly, he began nodding.

"Well, what do you say to this?" Harte said and put away the wallet. "You fellows call your parents, and we'll have supper at The Rainbow. My treat."

Ray shouldered in front of Lester. "You just made us an offer we can't refuse, Sheriff."

Harte held up an index finger. "One thing though." He pointed at the money. "We keep this between us for a while. You tell no one until I make it public. Agreed?"

Lester made eye contact with each of his friends. "We can keep a secret, Sheriff."

When the skater clan started for the cruiser, Harte called out Lester's name, and the boy stayed back. "Where's the Harliner boy today?"

"Lance?" Lester's face closed down, as if he'd been accused of something. He shrugged. "He hasn't been at school for a couple of days." When Harte nodded, Lester jogged to the cruiser, where the other boys were claiming their preferred seats.

"Damned good posse," Luther said, watching Harte bag the evidence.

Harte watched the boys begin piling into the cruiser. "Gives you hope, doesn't it?"

The cruiser's engine started. Harte turned to see Ray smiling at him from the front seat.

"Maybe you'd better *hope* they don't steal the sheriff's car," Luther said with a crooked smile.

\*\*\*\*\*

The next morning when Maxie-Rose dropped the new McAllister-cell transcript on Harte's desk, her eyes were raw and bleary. "Sher'ff Harte, ninety per cent of the recording was filled with the shuffle of footsteps, the squeak of bed springs, and snoring. What little conversation there was, it was mostly McAllister wantin' Ash to sneak him some smokes."

Harte looked up from the folder. "And did he?"

"Not as I could tell." Maxie's face went grim. "I sure wish we could program that voice-activation to overlook snorin'. Lord but that man can saw down the national forest in a night's time."

"We caught a break, Maxie," he said quietly. "We found the money."

Maxie's tired eyes came alive and brightened. "Well, where in the Sam Hill was it?"

"In a tree . . . about ten yards inside the woods from Luther's parking lot."

She stared at Harte as he sipped his coffee. "Well, can we connect him to it?"

"I sent Fortenberry to Atlanta to check it for prints. Billy Nesmith is giving it top priority."

"Well, what was the money in?"

"Inside an army surplus bag of some sort. Inside that, a plastic bag." Harte set his metal cup on the hotplate and pushed the "on" button. "We're hoping he handled the plastic without gloves."

"And what if he didn'?"

Harte watched the burner show some color. "Then we're right back where we started, except we've got about fifty-five thousand dollars that would have been in the pocket of McAllister's people."

Maxie-Rose narrowed her eyes. "You don't think *he's* runnin' this show?"

Harte stood, turned off the plate, and used his bandana to lift the cup to his mouth. "I do not." He sipped carefully, frowned, and set down the cup on the windowsill.

"What is it, Sher'ff Harte?" Maxie said.

He continued looking out the window. "I'm out of cocoa," he muttered. With a sudden urge to empty the coffee into the grass below, he struggled with the window lock and began banging on it with the heel of his hand. "Does this damned thing open?"

Maxie waited until he stopped hammering at the metal. "Not since the last time we painted. I guess the lock got painted shut." She stood and picked up his cup. "I'll buy some cocoa today."

He looked out at the mountains and exhaled a long sigh. "Jim ever get frustrated and try to kill a window lock?"

"Not that I recall, Sher'ff. But I think he kicked your trashcan to death a few times."

Harte turned to see her standing patiently, his blue cup in her hand. "Dark chocolate, Maxie. As dark as you can find it."

Maxie smiled. "You got it, Sher'ff. Chocolate from the dark side." Her face sobered. "Have you heard anything from Cody?"

He shook his head and then pointed to the transcript on his desk. "The snoring notwithstanding, keep at this. Maybe we'll get another break." When she started to leave he added, "Thank you, Maxie."

She smiled and winked. "Don't be too hard on yourself, Sher'ff Harte. You're doin' just fine. The good guys are always the underdogs, you know. We'll just keep on keepin' on."

As soon as she had left his office, he sat, punched in Cody's number, spun his chair to the window, and waited. When Cody's recorded voice asked for a message, Harte stood and glared through the glass at the exercise yard.

"Cody, I haven't heard from either one of you. We need some communication if this thing is going to work." Hearing his angry voice echo off the glass, he took in a lot of air and expelled it. "Call me, will you?" he said quietly and hung up. As soon as he had put on his coat, his phone rang.

"Sheriff," Cody said, already driving home his point, "what if Santiago or one o' his goons borrows Manny's phone . . . or takes it while he's in the shower? They bring up the calls-made list, call it, and there you are. Next thing we know, we got a missing person and nobody inside their organization. Sheriff, Manny calls me every day, but I got nothin' to report, so I don't bother you."

"How well is he getting connected to Santiago?"

Cody snorted. "Give him another month, and Manny might be the heir apparent."

"I need to stay updated, Cody, even if there's nothing to report, okay?"

Two-beats of silence fell between them. "Having a bad morning, Sheriff?"

Harte closed his eyes. When he opened them he stared at the Montana print on the wall.

"We found McAllister's money in a pine tree out at Luther's," Harte said.

Cody laughed. "How's GBI like it that a small-town sheriff is makin' 'em look half-ass?"

"We're all working together on this, Cody."

"Yeah, that's the rumor. But there's another rumor around town, too. Manny says Santiago expects all charges dropped against McAllister. The Cuban has some kind of inside track on this."

They were quiet over the line. Harte was thinking about Layland Childers.

"Does the money change this, Sheriff? Can we tie McAllister to it?"

"Waiting on prints. The outer bag was canvas, the inner plastic. We're hoping for prints on the latter. Any contact between Santiago and Childers?"

"Not face to face. Santiago will not talk on his phone in anyone's presence. Manny thinks Santiago is using Childers but has no respect for him. What does Layland have that Santiago needs?"

"On Layland's office wall there are photos of him with people in the Governor's office. Might be where all the string-pulling is coming from."

But for his breathing, Cody was quiet on the line.

"Have you seen Lauren?" Harte asked quietly.

Cody snorted. "Only person she'll see is Jen . . . that girl you saw at the Raburn house that day."

Harte waited, but that was all Cody was going to say on the subject. "Call me, will you?"

"Will do, Sheriff."

Twenty minutes later, a knock sounded on Harte's door. Maxie marched in with a cloth tote bag and a smile. She made a production out of setting a canister of chocolate on the windowsill.

"Fire 'er up, Sher'ff Harte. You're back in business."

When the switchboard buzzed, Maxie hurried back to her desk. Harte was opening the new cocoa when she appeared again in the doorway.

"Sher'ff, we got a little problem behind the Mexican restaurant. A crew was bringin' down part of a tree in the Molson's backyard. It took out part o' the restaurant's outdoor eatin' area. Nobody hurt, but they lost some tables and part of a dry-stacked wall. Tempers are flarin'. Effie Molson called it in, and you know she ain't one to exaggerate."

"Who do we have close by?"

"Beasley's not answerin' his radio. He headed out toward the Dollar Store to pick up a new broom for the cellblock. Burns is covering a wreck out on the bypass. Says he won't be able to get outta there for another half-hour at least. Fortenberry is not back from Atlanta." Maxie propped her hands on her hips. "Looks like you, Sher'ff, 'less you wanna man the switchboard."

"I'll go," Harte said. He flipped off the hotplate, grabbed coat and gun, and walked out.

# Chapter Thirty-One

A thirty-foot-long, sixteen-inch-thick limb lay amid a broken jumble of branches, tables, and Tennessee field stone on the back terrace of Casa Grande. Its point of origin was a hundred-year-old white oak that dominated the Molson's small backyard. Hanging from one of the tree's branches by a long yellow rope was a long-barred chainsaw turning slowly like a dead animal caught in a snare. The massive piece of oak that had crashed into the restaurant's patio was curved like a rib from the hull of an old whaling ship that had unexpectedly washed up on an unlikely beach. Pulleys and ropes were still attached to the giant branch, like maritime rigging that had been dragged ashore.

Because of Abel Molson's contentious reputation regarding zoning in the business district, Harte had expected to find hostilities between him and the restaurant owners. Instead, Abel and Effie stood together on their back porch looking down the hill of their backyard at the mishap, each holding a mug in one hand. Three of the restaurant staff stood in their shirtsleeves and aprons on the patio in the one area not covered by debris.

Between these two factions, two men in green uniforms were squared off toe-to-toe in a David and Goliath yelling match. The other workmen leaned against a white pickup truck and trailer bristling with lawn tools as they watched the argument escalate. On the door of the truck a logo of a stylized leaf advertised *"Appalachian Landscaping."* Just uphill of this company truck sat a battered, white, Ford pickup in which the silhouette of a head showed in the passenger seat.

Harte wanted to approach the Molson's first to hear their version of what had happened, but the tension in the middle arena was about to snap, so he walked directly toward the two workmen facing off in the yard. A multi-chambered purple martin house lay broken on the grass and near it stretched a stout metal pole that had been uprooted from the lawn. Harte stopped six feet away.

"Who's in charge here?" he asked, but the question did nothing to defuse the standoff.

"We can do this here," Harte announced, "or down at the station." The threat fell on deaf ears.

The bigger man stood taller than Harte's six-foot-one frame and easily topped two-hundred-fifty pounds. Square-jawed and muscular, this worker was like a wall of animosity, the skin flushed and tight across his contorted face. The other man was wiry and lean-faced, his fists clenched at his sides like two angular stones.

"Davidson! Bear!" someone called from the street. "That's the sheriff talkin' to you."

Seeming emboldened by Harte's presence, the big one roared an obscenity and rammed a flat hand into the smaller man's chest, pushing him back several feet. The stumbling man caught himself and regained the ground he had lost. It was obvious which man was Davidson and which was Bear.

Harte eased a step closer and spoke so low that the two men cut their eyes to him. "I'm Sheriff Canaday. I want you two to back away from each other so we can talk about this."

Davidson deflated by degrees. Finally, he looked at Harte and took a step back.

Bear laughed. "That's right, shit-for-guts, back away now that your daddy is here."

The fire came back into Davidson's eyes. "Fuck you, you big ape. You don't scare me."

Bear made the grotesque smile of a gargoyle. "Sure I scare you, ass-hole. That's why you're standin' there like a limp dick waitin' for your daddy here to stuff you back in your trousers."

"Last chance," Harte said, putting a casual *or-else* melody into the ultimatum.

Davidson checked the sheriff's face and stepped back again, but Bear lunged forward and feinted a left jab that made the smaller man raise his forearms and duck his head. The big man took a wide stance, propped his fists on his hips, and brayed a laugh.

Harte picked up the pole that had supported the birdhouse. When he approached the two men again, he forced Davidson aside and turned to face Bear. With a quick underhand thrust, Harte speared the pole through the triangle made by Bear's thick legs until the end of the pole found purchase in the sod. When Harte lifted upward, Bear's sneering face instantly transformed to surprise, and he grabbed for the bar as it levered upward into his crotch. The hulking man was strong and heavy, but Harte had the mechanical advantage and hinged the pole upward.

Awkwardly straddling the pole, Bear scrambled backward, trying to extricate himself by hopping on one leg as the other cleared the pole. Catching his heel on the martin house, he went down hard on his back, and his breath rushed out in a raspy wheeze.

Harte threw the pole aside, where it made a hollow, whanging sound as it bounced off a burl of the oak's root. He extended his arm stiffly and pointed at the prostrate man.

"Stay down until you cool off." Harte swung to Davidson. "I'd like you to step over to the tree trunk, sir."

As the thin man lowered his head and complied, Harte turned to the group of workers gathered at the truck. "Who's in charge here?"

A balding man raised a hand like a reluctant volunteer. "That's me."

When Harte signaled the man to approach, he recognized Streak Pendergrass standing with the crew. His hair was cut so short that the scalp shone through. Harte waited until the crew foreman was close enough that the name embroidered on his shirt was legible.

"You want to tell me what this is all about, Mr. Travis?"

The foreman's face wrinkled with apology. "Travis is my first name, Sheriff." He pointed up into the oak. "Well, Bear was up there doing the cutting, and the rest of us were working the ropes. Something went wrong with the pulley system 'cause when the limb started coming down, it swung the wrong way, and Bear had to drop his saw, unclip his harness, and jump to another limb. He came down madder'n hell and blamed it on Nick there." He nodded toward Davidson.

"Who's responsible for final word on the system? Who gives the okay?"

The foreman looked forlornly at the ruined patio. "Me, I guess."

"So who's to blame here," Harte said, not really asking a question.

The man drew in air through his nose and purged it. "Me, I guess."

Harte studied the restaurant staff gathered on the damaged terrace. "Travis, why don't you go down there and assure those people that your company will pay for damages."

Travis gazed at the Hispanics for several seconds. "Do they speak American? 'Cause I don't know any Mexican."

"They're from Uruguay," Harte said. "I think you'll find their English is good."

Bear was on his feet now, all his attention on Harte. Harte ignored him and walked to Davidson, who leaned one hand against the oak.

"You two got a history?"

Davidson raised his chin toward Bear. "He's the one with a history. Bullies everybody. *He* made the damned mistake, cuttin' one o' the ropes with his saw. But he won't admit it."

Harte pivoted his head to Bear and summoned him with a jerk of his head. The big man sauntered over and stood defiantly, his broad chest pumped up like a raft.

"This won't do," Harte said. "You're two grown men who are supposed to be professionals. You're in a public place acting like children."

"I'll tell you what won't do, Jack!" Bear began in a deep sonorous voice. He pointed back to the metal bar. "That's pretty damned close to police brutality, you ask me."

Harte read the man's name over his pocket—"Burt"—but he didn't want to use the man's first name. "And you are Mister—?"

"Harliner," Bear said. The name came out like a growl.

With his face expressionless, Harte connected the name to the hair-dyed skateboarder.

"Mr. Harliner, did you cut one of your swing ropes?"

The skin on Harliner's forehead tightened into horizontal crevices separated by rows of rounded flesh. "I know who you are," he said, poking a finger at Harte. "You're that new county law hick who got his job 'cause he plugged a couple of degenerates in a bar fight." He snorted a laugh. "And now you think you know something about working in trees."

Harte waited. "You didn't answer my question," he said in a level tone.

Harliner jerked a thumb at Davidson. "This asshole can barely tie his shoes, much less rope a tree for a controlled fall." He cocked his head, pleased with himself.

"So you're not going to answer my question?" Harte said.

Harliner rolled his shoulders. "There shouldn'a been a rope there."

"So you did cut it," Harte said. "And I'll bet you dropped a running saw. In the timbering business that's the equivalent of a pilot ejecting from his aircraft. Goes against the code."

"Code!" Harliner huffed. "What fuckin' code?"

"Every job has a code," Harte said. "Farming, truck driving, brick-laying . . . even timbering. The code is tacit."

The lumpy lines returned to Harliner's head, and he thrust his finger at Harte's face again. "I don't like the way you came at me with that pole. Wearin' that badge doesn't mean you can—."

"Maybe," Harte said loud enough to interrupt the man's rant, "next time an officer of the law asks you to do something, you'll comply."

Harliner shook out his arms like a man about to lift a great weight. "Or maybe not."

Harte watched the man play up the moment, pleased with himself that he could defy a sheriff in front of his coworkers. "Are you challenging me, Mr. Harliner?"

Like a bad stage actor, the smiling giant tried to look surprised. "Me? I'm just trying to see what you got behind that shiny badge and that old rusted cannon on your hip." His smile stretched enough to show a row of perfect teeth. "You were a schoolteacher, if I remember right? And now you're pretending to be a sheriff. That about it?"

Harte looked from Davidson back to Harliner. "Do you two gentlemen think you can carry on your work without causing a ruckus?"

Harliner propped his hands on his hips. "Have you really got nothin' better to do than stick your nose into somebody else's argument?"

"Arguments sometimes lead to violence, Mr. Harliner, and policing violence is my job. If I can resolve a situation with words, I'll settle for that. If I can't, then I have the option to arrest."

Harliner showed his teeth again. "Whatever."

Harte managed a cordial smile. "You two seem to have calmed down sufficiently." He looked from man to man. "Am I right about that?"

Davidson continued to pout. "Long as he knows it was him made the mistake . . . cuttin' that rope, I mean." He gave Harte a challenging glare.

Harte looked up in the oak and spotted the fraying end of a freshly cut rope. "Oh, I think he knows that," he said. "What he doesn't know is that it takes a man to admit his mistakes."

Harliner's smile snapped off, and he glared at Harte.

Harte touched the brim of his hat. "You gentlemen be safe in your work," he said. "And act your age. I don't want to have to come back down here." Turning, he walked to the Molson's back porch, where the elderly couple stood as silent spectators. "Effie . . . Abel," Harte said as he pulled at his hat brim again. "Don't think you folks will have any problem with this. The landscaping company should be liable for all the damage. Just call me if there are any problems with that."

Abel cleared his throat. "Well, that's exactly why we hired 'em to come out here, Harte. We were afraid that old limb was going to come down right where it did."

Harte looked back at the damaged area. "Good thing nobody was eating outside."

"Well, that's why we had 'em come early in the day," Abel said stiffly.

Harte gave Molson an appraising nod. "Looks like you thought this through pretty well."

"Well," Abel returned, "except for hiring this bunch." He frowned and pushed his chin toward the truck, where the balding man was marshalling his troops for work.

Harte nodded. "Maybe you ought to let the company know how this went here today." He hitched his head back toward the yard. "I don't mean just the limb hitting the eating area . . . but the behavior you witnessed. The office is not likely to get your version of the story from the crew here."

"He's already called them, Harte," Effie said.

Harte nodded again. "Everything else going okay?"

Abel Molson scowled off into the distance. "Yeah, 'less you wanna talk about mutinous prostates and seventy-year-old hip joints."

Effie backhanded Abel's shoulder, but he didn't flinch, as if this were common practice between them. "The sheriff doesn't want to hear you moan about your ailments, Abel."

Harte said his goodbyes and walked down the lawn to the restaurant, where the landscaping crew had begun collecting pieces of shattered limb, bark, broken rock, and shattered tables. Streak struggled with the smaller end of the main limb that had fallen, while Harliner hoisted the heavy end, hooking it with one arm over his hip.

"Juan," Harte said, singling out the manager, who looked unhappily at the scene before him. "Nobody hurt, I hope."

Juan nodded toward the work crew. "These men . . . they can rebuild my wall?"

"They're landscapers," Harte said. "They ought to be able to handle that."

Juan's mouth curled to a crooked smile, but there was doubt in his eyes. "They suppose to know how to drop a limb from a tree, too, *Señor* Harte."

Together they watched Harliner drop his end of the limb into the Molson yard. When it thudded into the sod, the other end tore out of Streak's hands and vibrated like a tuning fork.

"If it doesn't meet your approval," Harte said, "let me know."

Juan nodded, looking a little more comfortable now. "Is good timing, I guess," he said. "It gets too cold for most to eat out here now."

Up in the yard, Harliner yanked the cord on a chainsaw and revved the engine, letting it sputter and growl like an extension of his anger. When he started sectioning the wood, the whine of the saw filled the yard and sawdust flew back onto Harliner's legs like a spray of dull sparks.

"You come by soon," Juan yelled over the scream of the saw. "I make the chalupa you like."

Harte started for his cruiser, giving a little wave to Streak as he passed through the yard. Streak half rose from his work, but Harliner yelled at him over the rattling idle of the saw and the boy knelt to anchor the limb.

When Harte reached the street he saw the silhouetted head in the pickup duck below the seat. The image lingered in Harte's mind until the way the hair had hung off one side of the head tugged at his memory. He walked to the truck and peered inside to see a body swaddled in a down jacket. The boy lay in the fetal position, an open paperback book spread before his face.

When the boy's cautious eyes peered over the book, Harte opened the door a few inches. "Son, why aren't you in school today?"

After several seconds, the boy sat up and held one hand over his eyes as though shading them from the light. The metal rings adorning the rim of his nostril shone with reflected light.

"I'm sick. My dad didn' want to leave me at home." He barely shrugged and went silent.

Harte reached in and gently pulled at the boy's wrist until the hand reluctantly came away from his face. The eye on that side was bloodshot and underscored by a crescent of purple.

"What happened to your eye, Carter?"

When the boy did not answer, Harte lightly cupped his hand under the boy's chin and turned his head. Very carefully, Harte swept aside the dark hair that fell over half the young face, and Carter allowed it. Even in the dim interior of the cab, the other eye fluttered and was ringed with colors ranging from magenta to yellow. Harte eased onto the seat and rested his hand on the boy's shoulder.

"I want you to tell me what happened to your face, Carter. Can you do that?"

Looking straight ahead out the windshield, Carter took on a hurt expression. "I told you, I don't use that name. Everybody calls me 'Lance.' "

Harte let his hand slide off the thin shoulder and gave the boy time to collect himself. "How'd you get those bruises, Lance?"

The boy swallowed with a wet sound. "I fell off my skateboard."

Harte waited, letting the lie spread through the silent cab. "What did you hit?"

The boy almost looked at Harte but caught himself. "The street . . . the curb, I guess."

Harte began nodding slowly. "You hit both your eyes on the street." It wasn't a question.

"Yeah," the boy answered with some attitude. "My wheels hit some gravel and locked up."

The book fell from his lap to the floor, and Harte looked at its title— *The Crystal Sword*. On the cover an elaborate color illustration showed a long-haired, muscular man in medieval garb wielding a glassy transparent broadsword as he battled a two-headed dragon on a barren moonscape.

"Lance?" Harte whispered. "I want you to tell me how you got those black eyes."

A tear beaded at the corner of the eye that Harte could see. Stooped forward, Carter sniffed, but otherwise he remained so still that Harte could not discern the boy's breathing. He placed his hand lightly between the boy's shoulder blades. Even beneath the puffy material of the oversized jacket the bony spine felt like a row of marbles running down his back.

The chainsaw shut down. Harte saw Burt Harliner approaching in long strides across the lawn. Harte stood and watched over the roof of the truck as the man's face twisted with rage.

"You got a warrant to go inside my truck?" His deep voice boomed like a cannon.

Harte waited until the man stepped into the street and marched around the back of the truck to face him. "What happened to your boy?"

Harliner's eyes darted to his son and then back to Harte. "He fell down . . . in the dark."

"Where?" Harte asked.

Harliner tried not to look at his son. "In the laundry room. I think he hit the dryer."

Harte eased the door shut. "On his skateboard?"

Harliner made a backhanded sweep at the air. "How do I know?"

Harte kept his voice steady. "How big is your laundry room?"

The question angered Harliner. "I don't have time to lay out a blueprint of my house. I'm working." He jerked his head toward Carter. "My boy's sick, so I got to bring him with me. I can't afford to hire somebody to look after him every time he gets sick. I got to work! You understand?"

"I do not understand," Harte said. "You and your boy have different stories about this."

Harliner reached past Harte and jerked open the door, but Harte did not move. "Carter!" the man yelled. "Tell Andy Griffith here how you fell in the laundry room!"

Trapped between the father and the truck, Harte said, "Take two steps back, Mr. Harliner."

The hulking man hesitated, unsure what to do, but, as Harte guessed, the man's basic animal ferocity would not allow him to yield ground. Harliner jabbed a thumb over his shoulder.

"Get outta the way and let the boy sleep. I told you . . . he's sick."

Harte felt the same male territorialism that kept Harliner in place. "Step back, sir."

Harliner's neck swelled as he glared at Harte. Then he stepped back.

"Does he miss a lot of school?" Harte asked, pushing the truck door closed until it *clicked*.

The father sneered. "He gets sick sometimes. All kids do. 'Specially the puny ones."

Harte kept his voice low. "How many show up back at school with two black eyes?"

Harliner looked quickly into the cab. "What the hell did the squirt tell you?"

Harte ignored the question. "If I ask his teachers, will they tell me about seeing marks on his face? Or do you usually try to hit him where it doesn't show?"

Harliner tried to bull his way to his son, but Harte stepped in his way, their faces inches apart.

"What'd you tell this nosy sheriff, Carter?" Harliner barked around Harte's shoulder.

"Nothin'!" the boy shouted, his voice breaking. "I lied to 'im just like you'd want me to."

Harte sidestepped to block the man's view of his son. "I'm going to ask you again to take two steps back." When Harliner didn't budge, Harte put some iron in his voice. "Back up!"

Harliner fumed, but his head turned when a cruiser topped the hill and roared toward them. It braked at the curb, and Burns rushed out, pushing a nightstick into his utility belt.

"Everything okay here, Sheriff?"

Harte kept his eyes on Harliner and raised a hand to stop his deputy. "Call in an ambulance. We've got an injured boy here."

"Ambulance!" Harliner spat. "I ain't payin' for a damn ambulance."

"Bear!" the foreman called from the yard. "You taking a break or what?"

While Harliner scowled at his crew boss, Burns stepped up and pressed the nightstick to the big man's chest. "Back up, Burt, and get out of the sheriff's face."

Harliner turned his frown on Burns but took a step back. Harte opened the truck door and took Carter gently by an arm and coaxed him out of the cab.

"I want you to go get into my deputy's cruiser, son. You'll be safe there."

Carter hesitated and looked uncertainly at his father.

"He's not goin' anywhere," Harliner said and grabbed at the boy's loose jacket. By reflex Carter's arms came up and covered his face. Then, quickly, the boy made a deft twist, slipped out of the jacket and ran toward Burns' car. "Carter!" Harliner roared.

Carter pulled open the cruiser door, slid into the seat, and stared at his father through the windshield, his fearful eyes bright against the contrast of the bruising. Burns walked around to the passenger side, eased the door shut, and spread his feet, his baton held before him like a sentry.

Mr. Harliner," Harte said, "we'll save you that ambulance fee, but we're taking him to the hospital. Then I'm going to call Family Services and have someone come out and talk to you. I'll be coming with them."

Harliner laughed. "Is that supposed to make me feel scared?"

"I would hope that you feel something. You're facing the possibility of losing your son."

Harliner's eyes flared. "You goddamn sonovabitch . . . who the hell do you think you are?"

Harte leaned in close. "Who do you think *you* are!" he whispered, his voice seething with contempt. "A man your size beating on a boy like that. He's your son, for God's sake."

"Every parent disciplines! Didn't yours?"

Harte locked eyes with the man as the crew in the yard froze in their work. "That's not being a parent, Mr. Harliner. It's being a bully and a sadist."

Harliner's face glowed like heated metal. "You prob'ly don't have to live with a little smart ass who dips his head in hair dye and sticks metal rings through his nose."

"He's your son," Harte repeated, putting some compassion into his voice.

Harliner looked away. "Yeah, and he's turned out just like his god-damned mother."

"Where is she?" Harte asked.

When Harliner turned back, Harte saw the rage that the boy must have seen when he had received his injuries. "None o' your goddamned business!"

"Burns," Harte called, keeping his eyes on Harliner, "take the boy to the hospital."

Burns remained standing by his cruiser. "If it's all the same, Sheriff, I'll go when you go."

"Bear!" the foreman yelled from the patio. "You wanna get over here and help with this?"

Harliner's body was so tense that the little curl of hair arching over his forehead vibrated as if in a stiff wind. He spun on his heel and walked toward the restaurant patio.

Burns pushed his baton back into his belt. "Ready to go now, Sheriff?"

Harte said nothing. He turned to the boy, who stared back at him through the glass with the same aloof expression he had used during their interview. Then Carter lowered his head, and his unnaturally black hair fell over his face. Harte opened the truck door and picked up the book.

"Give this to him," he said, tossing the book to Burns. "He'll have a wait in the ER."

"You want me to wait with him?"

Harte gave his deputy a look. "Of course, I do."

"Then what?" Burns said. "What do I do with him when they dismiss him?"

Harte stared through the cruiser windshield at the dark blur of hair in the passenger seat. "Bring him to the office. We'll let Family Services come pick him up there."

# Chapter Thirty-Two

It was late afternoon when Maxie leaned through the open door of Harte's office. "Sher'ff, the state lab called. They pulled a solid print from one o' the plastic money bags." Maxie raised her eyebrows. "It's McAllister's." She broke into a grin, clenched a fist in front of her shoulder, and pumped her elbow in a quick jerk behind her.

"Okay," Harte said, "that's the first thread. Now we just keep pulling at it."

Maxie moved to the laptop, where she removed the newest surveillance CD. After loading another disk into the machine, she waved to Harte.

"Are you off?" Harte said, glancing at the wall clock.

She held up the CD. "Friday night with Ash and McAllister." She gave him a lackluster smile and made a snoring sound. "Hooper's got the switchboard, Sher'ff." She paused at the door, her gaze intent on something in the dispatch room. She stepped back in and closed the door. "What about the Harliner boy? He's been out there for almost two hours."

"Family Services couldn't send anybody. What do we usually do in a situation like this?"

She frowned at the floor. "Never had a situation like this, Sher'ff. We could call the youth minister at the Methodist church. He and his wife sometimes take in some o' the battered women when the shelter is full."

"Would you call them before you leave?"

"Will do, Sher'ff." She started for the door.

"Why don't you send him in here while you make the call," Harte said quietly.

When Carter entered the room, the discolored skin around his eyes reflected the ceiling light like a garish mask that had been coated in oil. Harte could not help but stare.

"What in the world did they put on you at the hospital?"

Carter shrugged and flopped down on the couch. "Some kind o' ointment." He held up a blue cold pack in one hand. "I'm supposed to use these things for ten minutes every hour, too."

Harte nodded and gestured toward the windowsill. "How about some hot cocoa?"

Carter eyed the canisters on the sill. "You got coffee?"

Harte stood, turned on the burner under the blue kettle, and spooned instant coffee into the "visitor's cup" that Maxie insisted he keep on hand. As the water heated, Harte stepped around to the front of his desk and sat back against its edge.

"Do you mind if I ask you some questions about your home life?"

Carter shrugged, settled back into the sofa, and raised the cold pack gently over one eye.

Harte allowed a few seconds of silence to pass, to show the boy that his questions were not perfunctory. "Can you share with me why your father punished you?"

The boy removed the cold pack and pointed to his face. "You mean . . . this time?" When Harte nodded, the boy returned the pack to his face. "I guess it was about the driveway. My board made some marks on the concrete." He snorted. "A stupid driveway with oil stains and cracks and a lot of tire marks where he peels rubber when he's mad."

"How did he punish you exactly?"

Carter gave Harte a dumbfounded glare that had "*duh!*" written all over it. "He hit me."

Harte waited for the boy to lose his smirk. "How did he hit you?"

Carter placed the pack against the other eye. "With his hand."

"Open or closed?"

"He slaps me. His fists are like bricks. If he hit me with those I'd probably be dead."

"So he slapped you around your eyes?"

Carter shook his head. "Usually here." He used his free hand to touch the unnaturally dark hair on the side of his head. "But I tripped over the tool box in the garage and fell on the handlebars of his motorcycle." Now he pointed to the more colorful bruise at his left eye. "I guess I caught the end of it here, but the clutch handle got me in the other eye."

Harte winced. "Must have hurt. What did he do then?"

"I was down, so he kicked me."

"Where?"

He shrugged. "In the butt."

Harte pictured the scene in the garage. "He kick you often?"

Another shrug. "When I'm down, he does."

"And all of this was about marks on your driveway?"

Carter's shrug was now a consistent part of his answers. "That . . . and he probably doesn't like what I say when he hits me, so he hits me harder."

"And what is it that you say?"

The boy's face set hard, and his eyes fixed on Harte's with a solid glint of courage. "I say . . . as big as he is, he's a coward and that's why he has to hit people."

"He hits other people?"

Carter traded the shrug for a nod. "Our neighbor, and a delivery man, and a guy from his work named 'Bones.' He used to come to our house and play poker." The boy almost smiled. "And there was a guy giving out some kind o' religious pamphlet. My dad thought he was gay, so he hit him."

When the kettle rattled, Harte moved to the window. "You take cream or sugar?"

"Both."

Harte turned and raised a hopeful eyebrow. "Want to try some cocoa with it?"

The shrug returned.

When Harte settled against the desk again, they both sipped their drinks with little slurping sounds. The warmth traveled to Harte's stomach and with it the memory of his father talking about Peewee Reese and the Brooklyn Dodgers.

"Like the cocoa part?" Harte asked, raising his blue cup.

Carter's battered face brightened as he looked down into his mug. "Yeah," he replied, giving the word the rise-and-fall melody of sincerity.

"Do you think your father loves you?"

Shrug.

"Do you love your father?"

Carter's eyebrows lowered. "Why should I?"

"Because he's your father?" Harte said, posing the answer as a question.

Carter pushed a quiet airy laugh through his nose. "That's so lame. You don't score points just for passing on chromosomes. He doesn't like me, okay? Love doesn't even enter the equation."

Harte had heard such sad testimonials before from problem students over the years, but the assessment never failed to send a cold shiver down his spine. He drank from his cup and watched the boy move the cold pack to the side of his skull.

"Why do you think he doesn't like you?"

Without hesitation Carter said, "Because I'm not a big he-man like he is."

Harte nodded and looked over his cup at the boy's slight frame. Three quick knocks sounded on the door, and Harte called out to enter. Maxie-Rose cracked the door and leaned in.

"Sher'ff, our Methodist friend and his wife are in Haiti working on water systems." She waited to see if he had a reply, but Harte just stared at the Montana picture. "And, Sher'ff, you've got a call from Buffalo Bill. Says it's important."

" 'Buffalo Bill?' "

"Yes'r. William F."

Harte pointed at her to show he understood. "Go home, Maxie. Thank you for everything."

"G'night, Sher'ff Harte." She cut her eyes to the boy. "G'night, Lance."

Harte put his hand on the phone but hesitated as he watched Carter half-recline in the corner of the sofa. "I'll be leaving in a few minutes for an assignment. We're going to have to find a place for you to sleep tonight. Until we do, you can rest here for a while." He nodded toward the dispatcher's office. "My deputy will be right outside the door. You okay with that?"

Carter stretched a leg out on the cushions. "Sure," he said, barely hiding his excitement.

Harte picked up the phone. "This is the sheriff."

"Tonight's the night," Cody said. "Who you got on duty?"

Harte opened the schedule book. "Beasley, Burns, and Joe-Joe. Hooper is on dispatch. Ash is in the cellblock, but I'll ask him to join us."

Two beats of silence stretched out over the line. "You're kidding, right? About Ash?"

"He'll be with me. I'd rather know where he is. Tell me about tonight."

"Okay, first, Manny is carrying a nine-mil in a shoulder rig under a new herringbone jacket Santiago bought for him." Cody laughed. "I'm thinking about working for Santiago myself. Anyway, there's this other guy—some hard-ass Cuban named "Rico." Manny says he's trouble."

"Just a minute," Harte interrupted. Lowering the phone with his hand over the mouthpiece, he looked at Carter, who was leaning forward with his elbows on his knees, the cold pack pressed to his forehead. "Lance, could I ask you to help with a little law work tonight?"

The boy looked up, surprised. "Sure," he said. There was no shrug.

"Go tell the dispatcher I need Ash on duty tonight. Have you got that?"

"Sure," he said and set the mug and cold pack on the desk.

When the door closed behind Carter, Harte raised the phone. "All right, tell me about it."

Cody cleared his throat. "Okay, apparently Santiago has stamped his seal of approval on Layland Childers. He told Manny he came up here either to take Childers on as a new buyer or take him *out*. In which case, he was gonna let Manny do the latter. Sort of an initiation rite, I guess."

"So, the cinder block load wasn't Santiago's deal?" Harte asked.

"It was Childers and some people out of Savannah. Manny's got the names on that. But so does Santiago. I wouldn't want to be the distributor in Savannah as long as Santiago is loose in this world. Anyway, tonight Santiago has a load coming from Miami. Coming in on an eighteen-wheeler. And get this . . . the product is stuffed inside life-sized Santa Clauses for store windows. They're meeting somewhere out near the Copper Mines. It'll be Santiago, this guy Rico, Childers, Manny, and a few illegals Santiago has brought in. Oh . . . and about two hundred Santas."

"What time?"

"Some time after dark is all Manny knows."

"You're sure Santiago and Childers will both be there?"

"Santiago wants to see Childers manage the unloading . . . see how smooth it goes. If the offload isn't tight, Santiago told Manny to keep his nine oiled and handy."

"Layland knows the county," Harte said as much to himself as to Cody. "He'll know a covert place where the semi can get off the road." He paused. "Tell me about the illegals."

"Hispanics. They don't appear to be shooters. Santiago uses cheap labor, usually women, but Manny says don't underestimate this guy Rico."

"Rico," Harte repeated and sat back in his chair. "You sound tired."

"Well," Cody said and let out a long breath. "I've been putting in the hours. But I want *in* tonight, Sheriff. I'm good to go."

"You're sure about that?"

"Hell, yeah. It's fourth quarter and a minute on the clock. I used to play both ways, you know—offense and defense—and at the end of the game I was still ready to cut out the other team's hearts and eat 'em raw."

"Well, maybe we can skip the cannibalism tonight."

Cody settled himself. "For real, Sheriff, I'm good to go."

"We'll spread out along Coppermine Road at one mile intervals. Everybody out of sight. You tail them in your car and keep me posted by phone. I'll let the others know."

Harte opened the drawer where McAllister's file and phone were stored. "Just a minute," he said, "seems like I remember something." He paged through the transcripts that Maxie had turned in, and his eyes fixed on the word "Coppermine" amid the text.

"Cody, McAllister said something to Ash about an equipment yard out at Coppermine. You know anything about that?"

"No," Cody said, disappointment in his voice. Then he seemed to perk up. "You've got McAllister's phone, right? Check it!"

Harte accessed McAllister's address book and scrolled down until he found "copper yard" followed by a phone number. "Got it. I'll call you back in a few minutes."

He found Carter talking to Hooper at the switchboard desk. "Lance, do you have a cell phone?" From his pocket the boy produced his phone like a magician's trick. Harte waved him inside and then fixed his attention on Hooper. "Tell Ash to be in my office in two hours."

"All right, Sheriff."

Harte returned to his office, closed the door, and faced the Harliner boy. "I need to make an anonymous call. Can you help me with that?"

"No problem, Sheriff." He held out the phone.

Harte shook his head. "I want you to make it. This is police work, Lance. Undercover. Do you think you can do that?"

"Yeah," Carter said and Harte saw, for the first time, a smile on the boy's face. "Whatta ya want me to say?"

Harte walked to the window and looked at the quiet charm of the square. In the fading light the new gaslights flickered in a scene that could have passed for a century ago.

"You'll reach a heavy equipment compound," Harte began. "Ask about renting a backhoe."

"Sheriff, they're gonna know I'm not old enough to operate a backhoe."

Harte nodded. "Tell them you're calling for your father. That he wants to come by and talk to them about it. Just get the address. That's the main thing. Are you okay with this?"

"What if they ask my name?"

"Just make one up. Don't mention anything about the sheriff's department."

"And that's it?"

"That's it. When they give you the address, repeat it out loud, so I can hear it." Harte held out McAllister's phone and showed him the number. Carter punched it in on his own phone and pressed it into the dark waterfall of his hair.

"Hey," he said. "You guys rent out backhoes?" Carter listened, and his eyes cut sharply to Harte. "Oh, okay . . .well then can you rent one out with one o' your own operators?" He listened again, and once more he gave Harte a questioning look. "It'd be my dad. He asked me to call around." He listened again. "Well, say he wanted to buy one used. Can you sell 'im one?" This time as he listened, his eyes turned hopeless. Harte made a circling motion with his hand to encourage the boy to keep at it. "Well, what if he wanted to talk to you about what to look for . . . if he was going to buy one . . . could he come by there sometime during business hours?"

Now relief washed over Carter's face. "Okay, great. Where should he come to?" His eyes cut to Harte. "End of Copper Trace? Yes, sir, he knows where that is. He'll call first. Might be a day or two." Carter nodded. "Yes, sir. I'll tell 'im." He pocketed his phone. "You get all that, Sheriff?"

Harte eyed the boy's confident smile. "That was quick thinking," he said and pointed a forefinger at the boy. "If I'm still sheriff when you finish school, look me up. I might have a job for you. Meanwhile I'll have Hooper order you some food. Mexican okay?"

Carter exhumed his shrug. "Rather have a burger and fries and a *Coke*, Sheriff."

Harte pursed his lips, considering the boy's choice. "Going patriotic, are you?" He pointed to the mug on his desk. "Take that and wash it in the sink, and then tell Hooper what you want to eat."

When Carter left the room, Harte picked up the desk phone and dialed Cody. "It's on Copper Trace," he said. "Off Coppermine. You know where that is?"

"Sure do," Cody said. "I'll be waitin' on your call."

He depressed the button and called Bella. When she answered, he felt the sudden demarcation of a line insinuate itself through his life. There was, on one side, everything about being a sheriff. On the other side was everything else. Right now he knew that he was straddling the line.

"It's Harte," he said. "I have a very big favor to ask you."

"Ask away," she said.

"I've got a fifteen-year-old boy here . . . a pretty good kid . . . his face is a mess . . . parental abuse. I've run out of options on where I can put him tonight. Family Services can take him tomorrow, but tonight he needs a bed. I can't leave him here in the jail."

"Well, goodness, Harte, take him to your home. There shouldn't be anything wrong with that."

"The jail *is* my home," he said, trying not to sound embarrassed. He looked at the desiccated winter grass in the Montana print and imagined a cabin there, nestled between the boulders at the edge of the woods.

"I have an extra bed in a guest room," Bella said without hesitation. "Do you think he would tolerate an old doddering woman if she had some fresh-baked apple pie on hand?"

"With that and some of your hazelnut coffee-cocoa, you might never get rid of him. I've already got him hooked on the drink."

"Bring him out, Harte," she said, and he could tell by her tone that she was smiling.

"I'll owe you, Bella." He could hear the wet sound of her smile expanding.

"You'll owe me big time, Sheriff Canaday."

# Chapter Thirty-Three

"I want to make a stop here before they close," Harte said, pulling his cruiser in front of the Buckhorn Gun Shop. "I won't be but a minute." With his hand on the ignition key, he turned to look at Carter's arms folded over his chest. "Are you cold? I can leave the motor on."

The boy shook his head. "I'm all right."

Harte shut down the engine, got out, and took off his coat. "Here, if you need it."

When Harte returned to the cruiser, Carter had the black wool coat draped over the front of him like a blanket. Harte climbed back in behind the wheel and set down a small brown paper bag on the console. The contents rattled briefly with a telltale sound that turned the boy's head.

"Hard to find ammunition for your old gun, Sheriff?"

Harte shook his head and started the engine. "A lot of people still shoot these old models."

"It's weird for a policeman though, isn't it?"

Harte strapped into his seatbelt. "Probably is."

They pulled out onto the highway and rode in silence through the fading crepuscular light. After they made the turn onto Cooper Gap Road, Carter cleared his throat and removed Harte's coat.

"So how come *you* do?" he said, looking at the sheriff.

"How come I 'do' *what*?"

"How come you use that old-fashioned gun?" Then Carter looked at his own hands, and his voice grew less bold. "And, you know, the hat?"

Harte turned to him, but the boy would not meet his eyes. "Do you know Saine's auto repair shop north of town . . . one with the old Model T Ford that sits beside the garage?"

Carter shook his head.

Harte pursed his lips and slowed for Bella's dirt drive. "How about that English teacher at the middle school? The one who talks a lot like Shakespeare writes?"

"Mr. Garnett?"

Harte nodded. "That's the one."

Carter closed his eyes and nodded. "Okay, I get it."

When Harte shut down the cruiser's engine in front of Bella's, a porch light came on and she stepped out of her front door wrapping a shawl around her shoulders. They approached on the flat stones spaced in her lawn, and she smiled down at them as they stopped at the bottom of her stairs.

"Bella, this is Lance," Harte introduced. He swept a hand toward her. "Ms. Seagrave."

"Goodness, Lance. Don't you have a jacket?"

Carter shrugged. "I'm all right." He surprised Harte by climbing the first two steps and offering his hand. Bella took it, and they shook briefly. Then Carter stuffed his hands into his pockets, pitching his shoulders up to his ears. The skin on his arms was stippled with goose bumps.

"You two come in and have some pie. It's only an hour out of the oven."

"Sorry, Bella," Harte said. "I have to go. Looks like a long night ahead of me."

Carter stepped inside, but Bella remained on the porch, a look of concern slanting her eyes.

"Thank you for this," Harte said, nodding toward the boy. "Save me some pie?"

"You be careful," Bella said.

Before he could fire up the cruiser, Bella jogged out through the gate and opened his door. "For the long night," she said, pushing onto him a triangular package wrapped in foil.

Harte took the offering and lifted it to his nose. The warm smell of apples, butter, cinnamon, and cloves washed over him like a memory. As she watched, he unfolded the gift and took a bite.

He began nodding and then rewrapped the piece of pie. "I'll definitely be back."

On the ride back to the department, Harte used his cell phone to call in stakeout instructions to each deputy on duty. "We won't use radios tonight," he explained to Joe-Joe, "only cell phones. We don't know who might be tuning in to our frequency."

"What about Beasley?" Joe-Joe asked. "He still doesn't have a phone."

"I'll get one for him. You'll need to pass along this information to him face to face and in private. We're keeping Ash out of the loop on this, understand?"

Joe-Joe hesitated before answering. "Yeah, I think I do."

"I'll have Ash with me tonight, because I want to know where he is. But he won't be going in with us on the bust. I'll station him where he can't accidentally shoot someone."

Joe-Joe breathed an audible sigh over the phone. "Sounds about right, Sheriff."

"I'm placing deputies all along Coppermine Road," Harte continued, "in case there is a surprise rendezvous site other than Copper Trace. You'll set up at the south end, at the intersection of highway fifty-two, behind the produce stand. Tell Beasley to set up at the north end next to Crowe's cabinet shop. If I'm right about them heading to McAllister's equipment compound, I'll put out a code on the radio. I'll say something about a jackknifed tractor-trailer on the bypass. If I'm wrong, I'll call in the location by cell phone. Understand?"

"Got it, Sheriff."

It was dark when Harte reached the parking lot at his office. Ash's cruiser sat empty at the end of the building. As Harte pulled into a space, Hooper's voice broke through his radio.

"Sheriff, Maxie's on the line. Says she needs to talk to you. Want me to patch 'er through?"

"Tell her to call my cell," he said and turned off his engine.

In fifteen seconds his phone vibrated. "What's up, Maxie?"

"You're gonna wanna hear this, Sher'ff Harte. It's from the surveillance tapes."

"Let's have it." Through the earpiece he heard the shuffle of papers.

"Okay, it's McAllister talkin' to Ash. About nine A.M. this morning. He says: 'Look, I did exactly what he told me to do. They found no money, and there wasn't an ounce of anything in my car. All they got on me is talkin' to a bunch o' brain-fried rednecks. And you did what he told you, except you shot that idiot jailer instead. And now you get busted down to this job and maybe up on murder charges.' Then Ash growls at him, tellin' him to shut up." She hesitated a beat. "Actually," she added in a sheepish tone, "it's 'shut the fuck up,' if you wanna know."

Harte heard Maxie turn another page. "Okay, then Ash says something, but I can't make out a word of it. It's all whispery and mumbly-jumbly. Then McAllister says: 'Well, why doesn't he get me out o' this hole? He said he would. I did my part.' Then Ash says something I can't hear. After that McAllister gets feisty: 'Well, then tell him to send that jackass Layland down here. I got three job sites I gotta get to.'"

" 'Tell *him*?' " Harte said. "Who is he talking about?"

"I got no idea, Sher'ff." After a pause Maxie's voice turned curious. "Does that give us anything we can use against Ash?"

Harte sat in the quiet of his cruiser and imagined a crafty lawyer putting a different spin on the taped conversation. "No. We're going to need more. Maybe I can make that happen tonight."

"Do you need me to come in this evenin', Sher'ff Harte?"

"I'll let you know if I need you, Maxie. Meanwhile, get some rest."

When Harte entered the building, Hooper was manning the switchboard as Ash sat on the visitors' bench reading a magazine and drinking a soda. Both deputies looked up, but Harte ignored them, crossed the room, and closed himself up in his office to change into his uniform.

So dressed, he sat at his desk, opened a drawer, and pulled out Ash's gun and holster. Slowly, he peeled off the Velcro strap, dropped the magazine from the gun, and, one by one, thumbed out the cartridges into his hand. After reloading the magazine with the new rounds from the gun shop, he reassembled the gun and strapped it in the holster. Then he picked up his desk phone.

"Hooper, send in Ash."

Eyeing Harte's uniform, Ash entered the room with a guarded expression. "Hooper says I'm working the night shift?" he said, trying to sound indignant. "How come?"

Ignoring the question, Harte held out his hand. "Let me have your cell phone."

Ash frowned and hesitated. "What for?"

Harte kept his voice hard and flat. "I need it."

Ash sniffed and glared at the floor, defiance building in his face. "Sheriff, you can't—"

"Yes, I can!" Harte said, his voice filling the room. He waggled his fingers "Cell phone!"

Ash reached into his trouser pocket and handed over the phone.

Harte stood. "You'll be with me tonight. Grab your coat and meet me at my cruiser."

"What are we doing?"

"We're on a stakeout. I'll give you the details on the way."

"Stakeout? Where?" When Harte still refused to answer, Ash assumed a defiant stance. "What about my gun?"

Harte shook his head. "You'll probably be transporting illegals to the jail."

"Illegals?" Ash said, unable to mask his surprise. "Where the hell are we going?"

When Harte just stared blankly at him, Ash conjured up some anger. "I'm not going to transport prisoners without my weapon."

The two men faced each other, waiting to see who would blink. "You don't carry a weapon when you're on suspension. Now go get your coat."

Ash would not budge. "You know, if something happens to me, you'd be liable . . . legally."

Harte hesitated, pursed his lips, and pretended to think about the consequences. Then he jerked open his drawer and slapped Ash's gun rig on the desk.

"All right . . . I'm reinstating you for the night." Unstrapping the Glock, he dropped the magazine, checked the load, slid the jack enough to see the empty chamber, reset the magazine, and holstered the gun. When he handed the rig to Ash, he said, "Full clip, chamber's empty, safety's on." Lifting his own coat, hat, and gun from the rack, he strode into the dispatch room. "Hooper, we're going to need a couple of thermoses of coffee."

When Ash entered the room wearing his weapon, Hooper stared at him and then, breaking out of his trance, rose quickly to tend to the coffee.

*****

"So what are we staking out?" Ash finally asked after they pulled out of the lot.

"Drug bust and entry by illegals," Harte said and turned to Ash. "Off Coppermine Road."

Ash's eyes flashed in momentary surprise. "Coppermine?" Looking out the front windshield, he tried for a nonchalant tone of voice. "Where exactly are we going?"

"Don't know yet," Harte admitted. "We'll get a message from Cody about that."

Ash frowned. "Cody! I thought he quit!"

Harte kept his face neutral and shook his head. "Nope."

They were quiet all the way to Coppermine Road. Pulling down a dirt road south of the river, Harte parked out of sight but with a view of the bridge. Ash tapped the fingers of one hand on a knee like a nervous piano player.

After an hour of drinking hot, cocoa-less coffee, Harte stepped out of the cruiser to relieve himself in the dark. The steady roar of the rapids below filled the air like static. Cold, humid air poured through the river valley and crept under his coat.

When he got back in the cruiser, Ash was lighting up a cigarette. "Put that out! That scent could get me killed tonight." Ash licked his fingers and pinched the red coal of tobacco.

The phone in Harte's pocket buzzed. "Yeah," he said.

"Sheriff, they're comin'," Cody reported, his voice carrying an edge. "Just turned off of fifty-two. It's a big semi with a red cab." An ominous pause followed. "They've got Lauren with 'em, Mr. C."

Harte's stomach clenched like a fist. Closing his eyes, he eased back against the headrest. "All right . . . stay focused," he said and pocketed the phone.

Ash scowled at Harte. "I see your phone is working. Why do you need mine?"

Harte gave him a bland smile. "Why? Do you need to make a call?"

Ash huffed a laugh. "No, but I'd like to have my phone in case I do."

Harte nodded. "Let me know when you do. You can use mine."

Ash exhaled heavily and glared out his side window. "Whatever."

After five minutes of strained silence in the car, an eighteen-wheeler cruised across the bridge. Rather than picking up speed for the climb up the far side of the valley, the rig downshifted, slowed, and made the turn onto Copper Trace. A sedan and an old model pickup truck followed, crossing the bridge slowly in a ghostlike silence and then making the turn. As soon as the three vehicles were out of sight, Cody cruised slowly across the bridge in his brother's car and stopped.

"Who's that?" Ash said.

Without a reply, Harte picked up the radio mic. "All units, a tractor-trailer has jackknifed on the bypass just north of the reservoir. We need all available deputies."

After each car responded, Harte started the engine and eased the cruiser toward the paved road.

"How the hell can you know what's happening on the bypass?" Ash challenged with a smirk.

"I can't," Harte replied.

Making the turn onto Copper Trace, he followed Cody less than fifty yards to a rendezvous point. Within minutes Beasley, Burns, and Joe-Joe arrived quietly, their tires muted on the hard-packed dirt road. After a brief reunion with Cody, the group quieted and turned to Harte. Cody was the only one not wearing the county uniform. With his camo clothing and dark skin he could have stepped back five paces and melted into the night.

"We don't know how many men are back there," Harte began. "Or women, for that matter. I'm guessing most will be busy unloading the truck, but anyone could be carrying a weapon. I want no walkie-talkies. We can't afford any static. We'll communicate by cell phone." He handed Ash's phone to Beasley. "Set them on 'vibrate.' " The deputies muted their phones. Pausing for emphasis, Harte looked into each man's eyes. "Jim Raburn's daughter is with them."

"What the hell is the sheriff's daughter doing with 'em?" Beasley whined.

"We don't know," Harte said. "But I want her unharmed. And I have an undercover deputy with them." Peripherally, Harte watched Ash's head turn at this news. "He is Hispanic, five-ten, lean, about a hundred sixty pounds, dark hair. He's wearing a herringbone coat."

Beasley squinted and checked the faces of the other deputies. "A what?"

"It's like a stitch pattern," Joe-Joe offered. "Like the rocks stacked in an old Celtic wall."

Beasley's wrinkled forehead gained another crease line. "A what?"

"Our man is wearing Levi's and a sharp-looking coat," Cody explained. "Santiago—the Cuban—will be in a suit." He stared at Beasley. "That means coat and pants are the same material."

"I know what a suit is, Cody," Beasley snapped.

Cody swung a small pack to one shoulder, stepped before Harte, and gestured down the dirt road. "The equipment yard is about two hundred yards in. They'll have someone on the road near the entrance. I'll neutralize him and call your phone when it's clear."

Cody was gone by the time Harte began instructions to the others. "We have the element of surprise," he explained. "We lose that, and we're in for a bad night." He turned to look up the dirt lane. "We'll go in by foot on the road. Once we're inside the compound, we'll spread out."

"What if Cody has trouble with the lookout?" Burns said.

Harte shook his head. "He won't." Then he lowered both hands twice, palms down. "We'll move in slowly . . . quietly. If we get into a firefight at night, we're gonna wish we were all schoolteachers." Again he met each man's eyes, locking on Ash last. The blond deputy had not said a word since getting out of the cruiser.

The call came, and they walked the road until a low looping whistle floated to them from the dark of the trees. "Over here!" came the softest of whispers. In the woods they found Cody kneeling next to a tall, wiry, Hispanic man, who was gagged by a silk bandana and sitting with his hands cuffed behind him around the trunk of a stout pine sapling. A rope bound his ankles and tethered him to a second tree a few yards away. His eyes were closed, and his chin slumped on his chest.

Beasley bent to look at the prisoner. "What the hell is that in his mouth behind the bandana?"

"My socks," Cody said. "Sonovabitch got a mouth the size of Tallulah Gorge."

Ash looked down at Cody's bare feet. "Great," he mumbled, "now he's an Apache."

Beasley leaned closer to the unconscious man's makeshift gag. "Oh, man! That's gross!"

"Keep it quiet," Harte whispered. "Huddle in here close and listen."

He laid out a strategy, and within minutes they had slipped through the gate and fanned out in the lot, all but Cody, who ran ahead, catlike, toward the dark, north end of the building. As instructed, Ash stayed with Harte. Inside the chain-link fencing sat two idle dump trucks, two dozers, a backhoe, and a flatbed trailer stacked with lumber. Beyond the big machinery, the pre-fab aluminum building stretched across the clearing for forty yards, its long side facing the yard. Five sliding garage doors were spaced across the length of the front, the open one on the far right fully lighted and blocked by the rear of the semi. Next to it, a small office showed light through a slightly opened door.

Near the office, Layland Childers' antique truck sat dwarfed beside the eighteen-wheeler. On the other side of the semi was the BMW, barely visible in the dark, backed in toward the building as if for a fast getaway. The scene inside the lighted stall was ludicrous—men unloading oversized, stuffed Santa Clauses from the trailer and then walking them deeper into the building.

At the south corner of the building a tiny light blinked three times, and Harte knew that Cody was in place.

"What was that flashing light?" Ash whispered.

"Apache," Harte replied and pulled out his own pocket light. Covering the bulb with his bandana, he clicked it on and off three times.

From behind the flatbed they watched Cody peer into the office window and then quickly dodge back into shadow. No sooner had he hidden than Santiago and Emmanuél came out the door and headed into the lighted garage. Soon Harte could hear Santiago talking in Spanish. A female voice answered in kind, as the Santa carriers kept working. Santiago returned to the office, while Emmanuél joined the workers unloading the truck. Then Harte felt a sinking sensation in his stomach as he watched Emmanuél pull out of his jacket.

"Damn it!" Harte hissed and turned to Ash. "Stay here until I call you by name, understood?"

Ash made no attempt to hide his disdain. "I'll be right here twiddling my thumbs, Sheriff."

With the office door now closed, Harte broke from the cover of the flatbed and ran to the front of the semi, his boots touching down lightly on the hardpan. Just as he gained the shadow of the truck, Santiago stepped out of the office and stared in his direction.

"*¿Emmanuél?*" Santiago called. "*¿Eres tú?*"

Harte pressed his back into the cab's warm grillwork and slipped out the old Colt.

"*¿Quien es?*" Santiago called.

As Santiago approached, Harte hooked his thumb over the pistol's hammer and prepared to pivot, but a hand materialized from nowhere and closed over Harte's gun, pressing it gently against his chest. From the other side of the truck, Emmanuél moved past Harte and stepped into Santiago's shadow, stopping the Cuban before he rounded the cab.

"*Jefé,*" Emmanuél said in a relaxed manner, "I can back the truck more into the building and save us time." He climbed up into the rig and slammed the door shut.

"Where is the driver?" Santiago called up to the cab.

"He sleeps," Emmanuél answered. "He has more to drive tonight."

The diesel engine cranked to life, knocking and growling. Harte could hear nothing else. When Santiago's shadow retreated into the office, the air brakes hissed, and Harte shuffled with the truck as it backed up. Someone yelled. The truck stopped, and the engine shut off.

Emmanuél climbed down from the cab and began tying his bootlace with a foot propped on the front wheel hub. "Why you come in alone?" he whispered to Harte.

"To tell you to put that damned coat on . . . to keep you from getting shot if this thing blows up in our faces. I have four deputies in the yard. How many are we up against here?"

"The truck brings in illegals," he said quietly. "Five men and three women. One man ees near the gate. The women are cutting out the drugs from the stuffing and sewing up the holes. Only the one called 'Rico' carries a gun. He wear a silver jacket." Manny switched feet on the hub and tied the other lace. "Somewhere in the building sleeps the driver of the truck—a big Anglo with a red beard."

"Go back inside," Harte ordered. "Be ready to back us up. But first, get that jacket on."

"*¡Oye! Amigo!*" came a voice from just inside the lighted bay. "*¿Nos vas a ayudar?*" Emmanuél straightened and, speaking casually in Spanish, walked into the building.

Harte flipped open his cell phone and called Joe-Joe. "I'm going in," he whispered. "Call Burns and Beasley but not Ash. I want you three to come in at my signal. Do you have all that?"

"What's the signal, Sheriff?" Joe-Joe asked.

"I'll stand in the light of the garage and wave you in."

"Got it, Sheriff."

Harte strained to see Cody at the corner of the building and was rewarded with a quick blink of light. With a flattened hand pushed forward, he silently ordered his deputy to stay put. Then, after pointing to his own eyes with two forked fingers, he pointed a single index at Cody and finally at the office door. The penlight came on briefly and moved up and down. A semaphore for "yes."

Lowering himself to his hands and knees, Harte quietly crawled beneath the cab and worked his way down the shadowed length of the rig to a metal ramp angled off the end.

# Chapter Thirty-Four

A full two minutes had passed. When one of the male workers approached and received a bear-sized Santa from inside the trailer and turned away, Harte rose up, peered inside the trailer, and saw a man walking toward the remaining Santas piled up in front. This man was stout, wearing a silver jacket with an eagle embroidered on the back.

Rico.

With barely a sound, Harte climbed the ramp and moved into the shadow along one wall. Rico lifted two of the oversized dolls, turned, and, blinded by his load, walked past Harte to the offload point, letting them tumble down the ramp. When Rico turned back, he was looking into the muzzle of Harte's Colt.

"*Pistola,*" Harte said quietly and waggled the fingers of his left hand in a give-me gesture. The old man who showed up to tote the next Santa stood wide-eyed as he took in the scene inside the trailer. Without a word, he sidestepped around the truck and walked out into the night.

Rico shrugged. "No gun," he said, trying for a look of indifference.

"*Pistola,*" Harte repeated and then added, "Rico."

Rico was middle-aged with a broad face, wide shoulders, and thick hands. With defiance now burning in his eyes, he showed no interest in handing over a weapon. Harte cocked his pistol, stepped forward quickly, and pressed the muzzle of the Colt firmly into the man's gut. Opening the front of the silver jacket, Harte found a compact automatic stuffed into the waistband of Rico's pants and jerked it free. After slipping the gun into the side pocket of his coat, he spun Rico around and led him to the open end of the trailer. With the other workers now staring at him, Harte pushed Rico down the ramp to the concrete floor, where he landed off balance, slipped, and fell hard onto his side.

Two Hispanic men stood frozen on the concrete floor. In the back of the garage, amid a mountain of Santas, three women had paused in their work with scissors, needle, and thread. Plastic bags filled with white powder were stacked at their feet.

"I'm the sheriff," Harte said quietly. "Raise your hands and don't make a sound."

Emmanuél, now in the herringbone, raised his hands and translated. All hands went up.

Rico slowly rose from the floor with his hands above his head and, smiling, spoke quietly to Emmanuél. "*El Gringo tiene mi arma. Depende de ti.*"

Emmanuél brought out his gun in an easy manner. "But I am with him," he said and tipped his head toward Harte. Rico's smile snapped like a taut thread.

"Everyone get on your knees," Harte ordered in a whisper. "Hands behind your heads."

When Emmanuél relayed the message, everyone complied. Harte sidled down the ramp and stood beside his undercover deputy.

"Cover them while I get some more help in here. Then Cody and I will take the office."

"*Si*," Emmanuél replied, "but be careful of Santiago. He ees the slippery snake, *señor*."

Harte moved to the doorway and signaled to his men. From the yard, Joe-Joe and Burns came at a run. Harte moved out to intercept them, and the two deputies gathered before him, both breathing hard. He walked them to the side of the semi away from the office.

"Where's Beasley?" Harte asked.

Joe-Joe pointed north. "He went after somebody who walked away from the building."

Harte nodded and glanced that way, where the darkness was complete under the pines beyond the fence. "Okay," he said. "I want you two inside the garage to help Manny."

"Help who?" Burns whispered.

"Emmanuél, my undercover man."

Joe-Joe leaned into Burns. "Herringbone jacket."

Harte grabbed Burns's arm before he started away. "There are three men and three women, all Hispanic. Search them all for weapons and keep them quiet, while Cody and I take the others in the office." He started to release Burns but then held fast. "There's another man . . . the driver. A white male with a red beard. Asleep somewhere in the building."

"We'll find him, Sheriff," Joe-Joe said.

Harte flattened his hand and lowered it twice. "Just keep it quiet in there until we can take care of the ones in the office."

"You got it, sheriff," Burns replied and tiptoed into the garage.

Joe-Joe hesitated. "Sheriff . . . thought you'd wanna know this: Ash came inside the fence and asked to borrow my phone."

Harte's blood ran cold for an instant. "Did you let him use it?"

Joe-Joe cracked a smile. "No way, Sheriff."

Harte nodded again. "Good. Where is he now?"

Joe-Joe shook his head. "Last I saw, he headed back through the gate."

Harte jerked his head toward the garage. "Go take charge in there. I'm going in the office."

When Harte reached the south end of the building, Cody was trying to see through a tiny crack in the curtained window. "There's another girl with Lauren, Sheriff. I think it's Jen."

Harte pulled his gun and pointed to the back corner of the building. "Is there a rear entrance?"

Cody shook his head. "Not to the office. There's a locked backdoor to the middle stall."

Harte waved with his gun for Cody to follow, led the way to the front of the office, and waited beside the door. Cody, still in his bare feet, made no sound. They stood for a few moments, listening to the voices of Layland and Santiago. Then Lauren's laugh bubbled up uninhibited and saucy. Harte gently tried the doorknob. It was unlocked.

*Me first*, Harte mouthed, tapping his chest with the side of the gun barrel. *I go right.* He motioned with his gun. *You left.* He motioned the other direction.

Suddenly, Lauren's laughter was right behind the door, and the knob turned. The two lawmen moved as one, slipping around the corner of the building, where they straightened with their backs to the aluminum siding. The door scraped open, and footsteps moved across the threshold.

"You girls want to wait in my truck?" Layland said, his voice casual and friendly.

Lauren laughed a cascade of carefree notes. "Don't forget my free sample," she giggled.

"I don' care where we wait," said a huskier female voice. "As long as I don't have to be with The Toad tonight." The office door slammed shut.

Harte leaned past the corner of the building, took in the scene, and whispered to Cody. "The girls are with Childers heading to the pickup. You take care of them. I'm going in for Santiago."

"Childers is not a threat," Cody whispered. "Let me help you with Santiago."

Already in motion, Harte shook his head. "I don't want Childers driving off!"

When Cody took off at a run, Harte flung open the door and swung his gun in a smooth arc across an empty room. Facing him across the office a half-naked blonde smiled seductively from an open calendar pinned to a closed door. Cigarette smoke hung in the air, and a still-lighted butt smoldered from a glass ashtray on the desk.

From behind the door in the back of the room, a toilet flushed. Harte sidestepped behind a desk and waited, his gun leveled at the bathroom door. For a long minute, nothing happened. After easing across the room, Harte jerked open the door to find a small space, dark and empty, its only sound the quiet streaming of water refilling the commode tank. Flipping on the light switch, he found a closed door on the left wall, a door that must have led out into the first garage stall. He turned off the light, quietly cracked the door, and peered out.

Beyond a stand-up tool chest inside the bay, he could see the pile of Santas. A number of the bags of powder were gone. Walking into the bay, Harte saw Rico and the other two male Hispanics standing beside Layland's truck as Burns cuffed them. Joe-Joe stood back with his gun trained on the prisoners. Listless and subdued, Layland and the two girls sat in the pickup, watching the arrest procedure. Cody knelt beside a prone body—a heavy-set man with a tangle of red hair. Next to him, Emmanuél sat on the hardpan with his back to the pickup's front wheel, his head sagging forward into his hands.

Harte approached quickly. "Where's Santiago?"

Cody looked up with two sharp vertical lines etched above the bridge of his nose. "You tell me! You went in the office!"

Harte pointed back into the stall. "There's another door. He had to have come through here."

Frowning, Cody slowly rose as he stared into the back of the garage. "Where the hell are the women?"

"Most of the drugs are gone, too," Harte said. "Did you already collect some of them?"

Cody's hard expression was answer enough. He drew his gun from its holster and looked into the darkness of the adjoining bays.

"You're telling me Santiago is back there somewhere?"

Harte made a humorless smile. "I doubt it. There is a rear exit to the building, right?"

The tendons flexed in Cody's jaws as he peered into the dark of the warehouse. "Shit!"

Emmanuél looked up at Harte. A thin rivulet of blood streaked down his neck behind his ear.

"You all right?"

"*Si*," Manny replied quietly. He looked briefly at the red-bearded man lying unconscious. "The driver . . . the one who ees supposedly asleep . . . he come up behind me with a tire iron."

Seeing a heavy, cruciform lug wrench lying on the concrete floor, Harte nodded.

"I already called an ambulance, Sheriff," Joe-Joe offered and pointed at the driver. "Ol' Red-Beard here got the worst of it." With a wry smile, he nodded toward Emmanuél. "Our undercover man introduced him to the business end of a steel-toe work boot. Caught him solid in the cahones."

"Have you seen Beasley?" Harte asked.

Joe-Joe shook his head.

"Santiago is loose out there somewhere," Harte said, scanning the equipment-filled yard. "With some of the drugs. Cody and I will search the building. You and Burns get your cars up here and load these people up. Don't forget about the man tied up at the gate."

Gesturing with his gun for Cody to check the front of the bays, Harte started for the back.

In the second bay, beneath a sixteen-ton road grader, he found a sleeping pallet stacked with freighting blankets. The scraper's blade was big as a war canoe. He searched the machine from back to front, bottom to top, but found nothing.

In the third bay he found the open door. Stepping outside into the night, he shone his light and found no fencing at the back of the property. There was no need for it, as the thick pines were enough to prevent any theft of heavy equipment. When Cody came out shaking his head, they stood for a time without talking, each man feeling the weight of losing their prime target.

"We're going to need some tracking hounds," Harte said. "Do we have someone for that?"

"Walter Hicks has got the best dogs in the county," said Cody. "Want me to call him?"

Harte nodded. "I want you in charge of that. Take anybody you need who's on duty and get that search going as soon as you can."

"What are you going to do?" Cody asked.

Harte stared at the dark scrim of trees and thought about Santiago making his way through the forest at night. "He'll need a vehicle. I'll check the nearby houses."

Harte started inside, but Cody clasped a hand to his arm. "What about Lauren, Mr. C?"

Harte turned, propped his hands on his hips, and looked up at the sky. He thought about Jim Raburn and remembered an old Cherokee story that described the stars as the campfires of the dead.

"It looks like she's gotten mixed up pretty deep in this," Harte finally said, "but I'm going to do my damnedest to protect her." He took in a lot of air and exhaled it before looking at Cody. "That goes for Jen, too. But if I'm going to pull that off, they will have to make some dedicated changes in their lives. You think you can explain that to them?"

Cody's eyes shone like white stones lifted from a creek. "Damned right I can," he promised.

Each man stared at the other. The only sound behind the building was the silky whisper of the breeze pushing around the bristly boughs of the pines. Cody was about to speak again when five rapid gunshots erupted from somewhere out in front of the warehouse. After a brief pause, one more shot rang out, this one quieter but somehow more ominous by its contrasting economy.

"What the hell!" Cody mumbled and both lawmen hurried back into the building.

Far off in the valley, a siren wailed, filling the night with its familiar sense of urgency. Harte and Cody ran out of the lighted garage to find two cruisers in the yard, their cages crammed with prisoners. Burns stood between the two cars and stared out toward the gate. The two girls sat wide-eyed and teary in Layland's truck. The red-haired driver of the semi remained on his back on the ground. Standing over him with gun in hand, Emmanuél looked at Harte and pointed toward the northwest corner of the compound.

"Shots come from over there. Joe-Joe . . . he go out to check."

Harte stared out into the dark for several seconds before turning to Cody. "Go get the dog search running." When he saw that Cody was going to argue, Harte thrust a finger at him. "Do it! I'll take care of the girls."

When Cody took off at a run, Harte walked diagonally across the yard. As soon as he had passed the dump trucks, he saw Joe-Joe at the corner of the fencing. On the other side of the chain-link, Beasley was talking non-stop, his fingers clasping the metal lattice before him like talons.

"Who fired those shots?" Harte called out.

"Ash is dead!" Beasley blurted out. "Took a bullet right between the eyes! I saw it happen, Sheriff!" He pointed to the trees behind him. "I've been stumbling around out here looking for whoever it was walked outta the building, and I saw some movement back there. When I got closer I saw somebody with a big load on his back, so I ran over to try an' cut 'im off. Then Ash comes outta nowhere, steps up to the guy, and just about empties his gun from as close as I am to you right now." Shaking his head, Beasley lifted his shoulders in a frozen shrug. "But nothing happens. So the guy just raises an arm calm as you please and pops Ash right in the head. Ash just kinda falls back like he's gone to sleep on his feet."

Harte could just make out Ash's uniform under the pines. "Did you get off a shot?"

"He was gone too quick, Sheriff. It was like *pow* and then he disappears."

Harte thought for a few moments, then stepped closer to Beasley. "Give me your car keys and get back to the building and help Burns transport the prisoners to the jail."

Beasley pushed his keys through the fence but made no move to leave. "How could Ash miss a target like that, Sheriff? I never saw him get rattled before. And he was so close."

"Go!" Harte ordered. As Beasley began making his way down the fence, an ambulance sped into the yard, its red lights flashing, the tires raising a billowing cloud of dust. Harte handed the keys to Joe-Joe. "Take Beasley's cruiser. Follow the ambulance then stay with Red-Beard. We don't want to lose him at the hospital. Make sure that Emmanuél sees a doctor, too. But, first, call Hooper at the station. I need Maxie and Fortenberry on duty to sweep Coppermine Road to pick up any illegals who might have slipped out of here. We know at least one male and several females did. They'll likely be on a road walking for town. Santiago will not use a road. He will be alone, and he'll need transportation. I'm going to check the nearby houses."

Joe-Joe's brow pushed low over worried eyes. "You're going alone?"

"I'm all we've got right now."

The deputy frowned and looked back toward the building. "What about the girls?"

Harte looked away long enough to compose a face of incontestable authority. "I want you to call Lauren's mother to come pick them up. They're to stay home until I can get by to talk to them."

The flesh on Joe-Joe's forehead creased like an old-fashioned washboard. "We're not taking them in?"

"No," Harte said, the word as clipped as an axe head sinking into wood. "They're hostages."

Joe-Joe's eyes locked on Harte's. "Hostages?"

Harte held his deputy's gaze. "Looked that way to me. How did it look to you?"

Joe-Joe gradually began to nod. "Yeah," he said in a flat tone, "Prob'ly were hostages."

"Cody has gone to get Walter Hicks and his dogs. Any questions?"

Joe-Joe splayed his hands on his hips and looked down at his shoes. "Yeah," he said and looked up. "But I'm not gonna ask."

"Good," Harte said.

# Chapter Thirty-Five

The nearby, opulent homes of the Copper Estates subdivision, Harte knew, would draw Santiago like a magnet. There the Cuban could find a dependable vehicle. And, possibly, hostages. Perhaps even victims who would need silencing. Turning at the Copper Estates sign, he passed a hive of mailboxes nailed into multiple rows on a common trellis, where someone maintained a sprawling rose bush.

Harte shut off his headlights and crept forward. Fifty yards up the hill, the black asphalt drive spoked into four different directions. In a dirt turnout he parked the cruiser, called in his position to Hooper, and continued on foot down the driveway on the right—the first residence that Santiago would likely encounter after groping his way through the dark woods.

The house was lit up from within, a three-storied mansion of dark square-cut logs and tinted glass, topped by a shake roof that glowed cinnamon-red under a security lamp. The yard was landscaped with tiered beds of azalea, rhododendron, and laurel held in place by a fortress of railroad ties. The black asphalt lane curved down around the side of the house, where Harte spotted a silver SUV, a yellow Jeep, and something sporty that, from a distance, might have been a Titan missile under a tarpaulin. At the front door a trail bike leaned on its kick-stand. A four-wheeler ATV was perched on the bank above the drive. If Santiago showed up here, Harte thought, he would have a field day of vehicular options.

Harte checked his watch. One-sixteen A.M. Stepping under the high-beamed front foyer, he clanked the heavy door-knocker on an oak door that would have fit into castle decor. Within seconds an overhead light illuminated the porch, latches clicked, and the door swung open.

A teenaged girl with purple highlights scattered throughout her curly red hair stood looking at him with a mixed expression of surprise, curiosity, and annoyance. She held a half-eaten ice cream bar beside her elfin face as if it were a candle that had guided her to the door. Behind her from deeper in the house, a television blared.

"I'm Sheriff Canaday. Are your parents at home?"

The girl's eyes traveled the length of him and settled on the old Colt on his hip. She cocked her head to one side and put on a pert smile, as if it were something she practiced.

"Are you that new sheriff who used to teach at the high school?"

"That's right. It's important that I speak to your parents."

She shrugged. "They're out."

Harte waited, but she offered no more. "As in 'asleep' or 'away from home?' "

She shrugged again. "They're out doing whatever it is they do when they go out."

"When do you expect them back?"

Another shrug. This she practiced a lot, too.

Harte pointed to the turnaround. "How many cars should be out there?"

She frowned. "What do you mean?" She stepped out so she could survey the parking area. "Looks like they took the Lexus."

"Can you get hold of them?"

She stepped back into the doorway and frowned again. "You mean, like, now?"

"Yes."

She widened her eyes. "I could call Mother's cell phone, I guess."

"Is there anyone else here with you?"

She inserted the ice cream in her mouth and shook her head.

"Whose is this?" Harte said, pointing to the mud-caked trail bike.

Her face wrinkled with disapproval of a new order. "My brother's." She pointed to the four-wheeler. "And that, too. He's at a party somewhere." She gestured behind her with the ice cream. "I gotta, like, stay *here*." She rolled her eyes and worked on the ice cream some more.

"What's your name?" Harte said.

She made some kind of cryptic smile that Harte imagined was her automatic response to any male who asked her name. "Lindsay."

"Lindsay what?"

"Balfour," she droned, pronouncing the word as if it were an admission of guilt.

"Your brother's the basketball player?"

She rolled her eyes again. "Like that's a big deal. I mean, *duh*! He's just tall . . . so what?"

"Lindsay, is there anyone you can call to come get you? I need you away from your house."

She had started sucking on the bare ice cream stick but stopped as if it had impaled the roof of her mouth. "Why? I mean, you can't just kick me out of my house, can you?"

"I'm not kicking you out. I just need—"

She took a quick step back and slammed the door between them. The lock tripped, and Harte was left staring at the tarnished brass door knocker. The static of the shoals behind the house was like the taunting whisper of a trickster god.

He took out his cell phone and Googled for the Balfour phone number in Copper Estates. The ringing in his ear matched the one he heard through the door. The TV shut off, and then a tentative voice ventured a hello.

"Lindsay, this is Sheriff Canaday," he began. "Look, I want you to call your parents now. If you can't get hold of them, I'll have a female deputy come over to be with you. Right now I want you to lock all your doors and windows and keep the house quiet so you can hear things. I'm going to be walking around on your property, okay?" When she said nothing, he added. "I'm here to keep you safe. But I want you to call your parents . . . let them know I'm here."

A long pause followed. Harte wondered if she had already hung up her phone.

"Keep me safe from what?" she said, her voice sounding small and distant.

Harte studied the tiered beds of shrubs as he considered his choice of words. "I'm looking for a man in this general area. He's Hispanic, lean, about five-eleven, a hundred-seventy pounds."

Another pause. "Why are you looking for him? Is he, like, dangerous?"

"Yes, he is. I think he'll be looking for a car to steal. How close are your nearest neighbors?"

The longest pause yet.

"I don't know," she said, giving her words a rise and fall melody that suggested she should not be expected to know such an answer.

"Can you call your parents for me, Lindsay?"

"Okay," she sighed, exasperated. "I'll try."

Walking the drive to the side of the house, he checked the three cars. Only the sleek model under the tarp was locked. Harte judged it to be a Jaguar. Behind the house a field-stone patio jutted from a flank of sliding glass doors, all shored up by a six-foot retaining wall of railroad ties. Under the flood of a security light the land sloped steeply to the river. All of the laurel and most of the trees had been removed, providing a scenic view of the shoals. Harte walked to the back of the house.

Santiago would not chance the roads. He would follow the river, the only part of the forest where starlight could illuminate his way. From the edge of the patio Harte descended the hill and from the top of the riverbank looked down at an eight-foot-wide strip of sand along the shoreline. The surface of the sand was unblemished, as if God had recently smoothed it with an angel's wing.

Glancing behind him he saw the Balfour girl standing in full view in a huge bay window that exposed much of the main room on the middle floor. Behind her a sliver of TV screen glowed with bright colors. She backed away, and soon two ceiling-high curtains advanced in jerks from the sides and met in the middle. Harte moved upstream toward the woods.

Just uphill he found a hard-packed trail wide enough for the four-wheeler. It led down toward the shore through a stand of blackberry, wild sunflowers, and goldenrod, all fading in color and showing signs of the coming season. He took the trail, stepping twice into the weeds to avoid spider webs etched out of the dark by the house security lights.

At the shore, he once again found a smooth, pristine surface of sand. Harte moved back up the hill into the weeds to make a plan. An engine started near the house. Abandoning all stealth, he started back for the Balfour home in time to see the Jeep's taillights burn red as it backed in the turnaround. Through the translucent vinyl window, Harte could make out the outline of Lindsay Balfour's curly hair. He stopped and watched the Jeep lurch in fitful starts and stops up the incline until it went out of sight.

He had just returned to the top of the trail when he saw something bulky moving at the shoreline, a dark silhouette contrasted against the lighter sheen of the water. Harte drew his pistol and dropped to one knee. Peering over the tops of the weeds he saw a man struggling with a large bag slung over one shoulder. It was Santiago.

Behind him Harte heard the downshift of a vehicle's gears whining down the driveway. Headlights caught him squarely in their beam and remained there as the engine idled in place. The Jeep had returned and carved him out of the night like a black silhouette target at a shooting range.

"Is that you, *Senor* Sheriff?" Santiago's voice seemed an extension of the river's sibilant whisper. "I suggest you stand up with empty hands before we turn this rich man's backyard into a war zone. People can get hurt, no?"

Staying low, Harte tried to wave the Jeep away. The engine kept running as the lights burned down on him like a spotlight on a stage.

"I finally reached my parents," Lindsay Balfour called out. "They're sending my brother and we're supposed to stay here until they get home." Three long seconds ticked by. "What are you doing down there?"

Unable to see her for the glare, Harte took in a deep breath and cupped his hand beside his mouth. "Go inside and lock yourself in, Lindsay! Now!"

He listened for a reply, but there was nothing but the purr of the engine.

"I will send the first bullet her way," Santiago said quietly. "Stand up with your hands high."

Harte holstered his gun and rose with his hands climbing to the height of his hat brim. He could see all of the Cuban now. The automatic shone like quicksilver in the beam of light.

"If you knew you could hit me from there," Harte said, "you'd have already done it."

Santiago hesitated long enough to let Harte know that his hunch was probably right. When Santiago started toward him, Harte eased to his right to place his shadow squarely on the trail.

"I do not wish to kill you, *señor* . . . I wish only to leave your little town. But if you try to stop me, make no mistake, you will die here."

With all the scattered light coming from behind him, Harte could see what Santiago could not. When the Cuban was one step away from the tallest of the weeds, Harte threw out a distraction.

"If you're not going to kill me, what are you going to do with me?"

As the Cuban began his reply, he stepped into a spider web that engulfed his face. By reflex, he blinked and turned his head away as he dropped the bag to swipe at his face. Harte shifted quickly to his left, taking his shadow off Santiago's face. Cocking the old Colt, he brought it before him until the light from the Jeep shone like a laser along the top of the barrel. When he squeezed off the shot, the air filled with the roar of both guns.

The Colt bucked in Harte's hand, and he cocked it again by the rote mechanics inculcated into him from his youth. But he didn't need a second shot. Santiago was falling back into the weeds, his arms floating out from his sides as though searching blindly for something to support him.

When he saw no movement, Harte moved down the trail with his gun extended before him. With his free hand he sliced through the first glistening spider web and closed the distance to the body. Santiago lay still, his eyes open, as if being granted one last view of the world. Harte knelt, picked up the automatic in the weeds, and parted the lapels of the Cuban's coat to inspect the wound. By the spread of blood that soaked the front of Santiago's shirt, Harte saw all the man's cleverness, his scheming, and his disdain for the law as a meaningless anomaly wasted on the world.

Santiago's face appeared peppered with grit. Harte realized he was looking at powder burns from Ash's gun. When the man's lips moved, Harte leaned closer.

"Fuck-ing cow-boy," Santiago whispered and angled his eyes to Harte. Then the lids slowly closed, and the sound of the river seemed to whisper an immutable truth, one never to be reversed.

Harte pressed his fingertips beneath the man's pronounced jawline. Santiago was gone.

Harte stood and holstered his gun. Far upstream he heard the sound of baying hounds mixing with the constant rush of the shoals. Just downhill he opened doubled trash bags that must have held over a hundred pounds of powder. Turon Santiago had been a determined man.

Harte made his way down to the edge of the riverbank, stuffed his hands into his pockets, and looked out over the water, content to watch the current slide steadily by like a clock marking time. And there he waited, trying to let the weight of the night lift from his shoulders.

When the sound of the hounds became clearer, he turned to see two men at the bend in the river. By the time the trackers were within twenty yards of him, the two dogs were frenetic, howling, and straining at their leashes. The man in front leaned back as the hounds pulled him along the sandy beach. Cody ordered him to stop, and it was all the man could do to hold back the baying animals.

"It's me . . . the sheriff!" Harte yelled over the yelping of the dogs.

Cody climbed up the bank and approached alone. When he saw the body of Santiago, he lowered his weapon and assessed the volume of blood covering the Cuban's chest.

"You okay, Sheriff?" Cody called out over the canine yammering.

Harte nodded and gestured toward the tracker on the sand. "Can he quiet those dogs?"

Cody stepped to the edge of the bank and yelled something. The man tugged his dogs farther down the narrow beach and led them up into the lighted backyard. The baying continued, but the distance took the edge off their mournful howls.

A battered pickup truck came rattling down the lane and braked in the turnaround next to the Jeep. A carrying cage of slapped-together planks was bolted into the bed. The driver stood in the doorway and waited as the hounds were coaxed to the back of the truck. In the middle window of the second floor of the house, Lindsay Balfour's silhouette stood watch over the commotion in her drive.

"Send us a bill, Walter!" Cody yelled to the truck, as it turned around. The horn beeped twice, and the pickup climbed the hill, taking the wailing of the dogs with it. "How'd this go down?" Cody asked quietly.

Harte nodded toward the corpse. "Pretty much what you see. I shot him."

"Did he resist arrest?"

Harte took in a lot of air and eased it out like a prayer. "He had the drop on me."

Cody's brow lowered over his eyes. "So, how'd you get off a shot?"

Harte nodded toward the tallest weeds. "Spider web. He walked into it."

Cody stared down at the body. "So, he had the drop on you. Were your hands up?"

When Harte nodded once, Cody splayed his hands on his hips.

"So, your gun was holstered?"

Harte gave Cody a sidewise glance that suggested he lay off the interrogation.

"Damn, Mr. C, I think maybe you were born about a century and a half too late."

Harte looked toward the river. "Jim Raburn used to tell me that."

Cody pursed his lips, looked down at Santiago, and considered the face of the dead. "One thing's for damned sure: the world will be a better place without this man. He was poison."

Harte stared down at the Cuban. "Maybe there's a little poetic justice in this night."

Cody's head came up. "How do you mean?"

Harte nodded back up the trail again. "Spider web."

Cody's face turned thoughtful. "Yeah, but spiders aren't supposed to get stuck in their own webs, are they?"

# Chapter Thirty-Six

It was well after dawn when Harte stepped into the dispatch office. Talking on the switchboard phone, Maxie-Rose raised a finger to stop Harte before he could disappear into his office.

"Your undercover man is gonna be fine, Sher'ff," she said, sliding the radio headpiece down to her neck. "He's got a mild concussion, but his signs look good. He might need a day in the hospital for observation." Maxie barely suppressed a smile. "Fortenberry and I found the three Hispanic women. Immigration already came by and picked 'em up. They had the old man, too." She picked up her coffee cup but paused before drinking. "Oh . . . and Family Services came by to pick up the Harliner boy, but when I called Miss Seagrave, she asked if she could keep him another day. Turns out the boy is into herbs, and she wants to work with him a little. County says their facilities are full-up, so they're gonna let her keep 'im as long as she wants." When Harte made no reply, she continued, "Speakin' o' full-up, Childers is upstairs in the holding cell. He's been pretty quiet."

Harte started for his office but stopped in the doorway. "What about the driver of the semi?"

Carrying her coffee, Maxie followed him into his office. "His name is Aaron Porter, independent trucker outta Jacksonville, Flor'da." She raised one eyebrow and winced. "Hospital says he's gonna be walkin' with a wide straddle for a while. Joe-Joe says he's a hard case who has learned how to whimper. Says he'll prob'ly spill his guts in court."

Harte squinted one eye. " 'Spill his guts?' "

Maxie shrugged. "I know . . . I watch too many cop shows on the TV."

Harte found the blue kettle full and turned on the burner. Maxie came in and closed the door.

"Sher'ff, that recording device is still working down there in the cellblock. Maybe we ought to let Childers spend some time down there with McAllister. Could be interestin'."

Harte hung up his hat. "I like that idea. Let's switch Varley to the holding cell."

In the front room the switchboard buzzed, and Maxie turned to go.

"Maxie," Harte said, stopping her. "No calls for a while. And close the door."

"Yes-sir-ree-bob-tail, Sher'ff." She continued to stand in the doorway. "You did mighty good last night, Sher'ff. You made us proud."

"We all did well last night, Maxie. You included."

She scowled and cocked her head to one side. "Well, ever'body but Ash. But I guess he got his comeuppance." She shrugged, and her face went all business again. "I looked up his next of kin. Closest relative was an ex-wife in Charlotte, so I called her. She didn' have much to say. I don't think any o' this surprised her."

"Where's his body, Maxie?"

"In the basement of the funeral home. The coroner will make his report later today."

"Who do we have on duty this morning?"

"Just me and Fortenberry. And Cody, I guess. He's over at the Raburn house. Ever'body else was like the walkin' dead. Prob'ly sound asleep at their homes."

The kettle began to rattle, and Harte spooned out portions of coffee and cocoa into his blue speckled cup. As Maxie waited, the switchboard continued to buzz. Harte poured water and stirred.

"I want Fortenberry to go by the funeral home and pick up Ash's weapon and badge. Bring them both to me." He looked up at her. "Got that?"

"Yes'r," she said, backed away, and closed the door.

Facing out the window, Harte heard her answer the call. He sipped his drink and thought about the events of the night. Within seconds a light knock sounded at the door, and Maxie leaned back in.

"Sher'ff, excuse me for interrupting. Captain Nesmith would like to meet with you at your usual conference site at half past noon. I figured you'd want to know."

Harte sipped his drink and gazed out the window. "Tell him I'll be there."

\*\*\*\*\*

Billy Nesmith sat at the same table under the albino deer mounted on the wall. Drinking a glass of water, he looked no different than last time Harte had seen him, his manner self-contained, his suit and tie impeccable, his eyes taking in everything in the room. He watched Harte approach.

"Busy night," Nesmith said. "You ought to be tired."

Harte nodded. "Probably got more than a full day ahead of me."

Nesmith smiled. "It'll hit you around two o'clock. My money says you'll go home by three."

Harte smiled, but he saw no reason to tell Nesmith that the sheriff's office was his home. He took off his hat and set it in a side chair as he sat across from the state captain.

"I hear you lost a deputy . . . and another one injured," he said. "Sorry to hear that. How is the one who survived?"

"He's good. The one we lost was Ash. Remember him? Opened up on the Moody brothers with a shotgun?"

"And killed your jailor," Nesmith finished.

Harte's face hardened. "Ash was working for the other side."

Nesmith frowned. "How does that figure?"

Harte lowered his gaze to the flatware and napkin on the table before him. "Some snakes eat their own kind," he offered and raised sober eyes to the captain.

Nesmith drank half of his ice water and set down the glass. "We tracked the driver's route. He drove from Miami. They've got small boats bringing in drugs through the Everglades. That's going to put this whole thing into the lap of the feds. Pretty soon you'll have enough FBI agents in your county to support the local economy for a year." Nesmith cracked a dry smile. "I think the feds are impressed. They always like it when you get the bad guys *and* a heap of product."

A waitress with flaming red hair appeared beside them and set down a glass of water before Harte. "The high stakes chess players," she sang in a sultry melody.

Both men turned to the familiarity of her voice, but her hair held them in check.

"Well, what do you think?" She smiled and turned her face in profile.

"Lorraine," Nesmith said. "Your blonde hair caught fire."

"Ooh, you remembered me! Maybe I should go back to blonde." Her eyes flashed at Harte for only a moment before returning to Nesmith. Then she put on her dead serious act. "Let's see," she said, pointing her pencil at Harte, "he orders and then you say you'll have the same, right?" She waited in an exaggerated pose of anticipation, her pencil poised over her pad.

Harte nodded toward Nesmith. "I'll have what he's having."

Lorraine frowned at Harte. "He hasn't ordered yet."

Straight-faced, Nesmith played along. "I'll have the usual," he said.

She smirked. "You think I can't handle the likes of you two?"

"I guess we'll find out," Nesmith said.

Without writing she flipped the top of her pad closed and swished away.

Billy Nesmith leaned forward. "All right, I want to hear about it." He raised his chin to Harte. "You and Santiago and the shootout down at the river."

Harte turned his head to the front window and watched a tow truck pass by on the highway. He took in a deep breath through his nose and then looked at the state captain and considered shrugging just like Carter Harliner did.

"Come on," Nesmith prodded. "I know you're not going to give it to the papers . . . and you're not going to talk about it to your friends. But cop-to-cop . . . I want to know."

Harte sat back and crossed a boot over one knee. He brushed at a piece of lint on his pant leg. When he looked up, Billy Nesmith was waiting with his elbows propped on the table.

"I got to the nearest home before Santiago, and I set up. But when he arrived, a girl who lived there pulled up in a Jeep, and the tables turned just like that." Harte snapped his fingers. "The Jeep's lights were behind me, and the girl was in the line of fire, so Santiago got the drop on me. I had to raise my hands, empty. I think he would have shot me right away but for the headlights shining in his eyes. As he approached for a closer shot, the Cuban walked into a spider web. That gave me the moment I needed, and the ball opened. Both of us fired. He missed. I didn't." Harte spread his hands to signal the story was over.

" 'The ball opened?' " Billy Nesmith said.

Harte shrugged. "It's just an old expression."

"Did he die right away?"

Harte shook his head.

"He say anything?"

Harte looked back at the front window again. The only traffic was a man in faded bib overalls bicycling away from town in the middle of the north lane. Harte realized it was Mel Saine.

"He called me a 'cowboy.' " Harte checked the customers nearest him, dropped the propped boot to the floor, and leaned closer to Nesmith. "Actually, it was a 'fucking cowboy.' "

Nesmith smiled, lifted his hands from the table, and turned them palms up. "Well?" he laughed, insinuating the obvious.

Lorraine returned and set down Nesmith's iced tea. "Unsweetened," she said and placed a glass before Harte. "And sweetened." She struck a pose. "How am I doing?"

"You're batting a hundred," Nesmith said. When Lorraine walked away, he raised his chin to Harte. "Okay . . . what about these girls?"

Harte kept his face a blank page. "Looks like they might have been hostages."

Nesmith pursed his lips and nodded. Leaning forward, he stared at the palm of one hand. "One was Sheriff Raburn's daughter, correct?" His eyes came up to fix on Harte.

"That's right," Harte responded matter-of-factly.

They sat in silence for a time until a work crew came into the room for lunch, the group boisterous with one voice booming louder than the others. Harte turned and saw Streak Pendergrass and his Appalachian Landscaping buddies crowding into two booths by the window. Burt "The Bear" Harliner was laughing so hard at something that his cheeks shone red.

Lorraine arrived with a tray. She set down Harte's plate first—a perfect replication of his previous meal at the Rainbow: trout, creamed corn, green beans, and rolls. Nesmith's plate was presented with a little flourish, as if Lorraine might say *voila!* But she only propped her fists on her hips, cocked her head to one side, and put on a saucy smile.

Billy Nesmith looked at Harte and raised an eyebrow. "One of us ought to hire this girl," he said and then turned sly eyes on the waitress. "Can you handle a gun?"

Lorraine didn't blink. "I can probably handle anything you got."

When she sashayed away, Nesmith looked back at Harte, filled his cheeks, and let the air rush out from his tightened lips. "Or maybe we'd better let her waitress career blossom."

Harte spooned up corn and talked around a mouthful. "We have a wire in the cellblock. I think Layland Childers will give us—" He stopped as someone approached his table. Streak stood beside him with a smile stretched across his thin face.

"How ya doin', Mr. C?"

Harte wiped his hands with his napkin, and they shook. "How's the landscaping business?"

Streak shrugged. "I'm just, like, taking off a year before I think about college, you know?"

"Make a little money, huh?" Harte said.

The boy shrugged again. "College is damned expensive."

"It is," Harte said and nodded across the table. "This is Billy Nesmith, a friend of mine." Harte gestured toward Streak. "This is one of the students that made me decide to quit teaching."

Streak laughed and shook hands with Billy Nesmith, but his attention quickly returned to Harte. "Hey, I heard about what happened at Donnie Balfour's place. Damn, Mr. C, you're gettin' a hellava reputation." Streak bobbed his eyebrows. "Kinda like Wild Bill, you know?"

Harte acknowledged the compliment with a doubtful look. "Just try-ing to get the job done, Streak . . . pretty much like I did in the class-room."

"Hey, did you ever get that article on Hickok published?"

Harte shook his head. "I put it on hold. I expect I'll get around to it."

"Hey, Pendergrass!" It was Burt Harliner's big voice filling the room. "We're leaving here at twelve-thirty sharp. You want me to eat your goddamned food for you while it's hot?"

The restaurant grew quiet except for the clang of pots from the kitch-en. Every face in the room had turned to the landscapers' booths, and then one by one the customers glanced at Harte.

Looking casually at the landscapers, Harte watched Harliner snatch a handful of French fries from the plate across from him where no one sat. He did it again and then smiled broadly as he chewed with his cheeks full. At the adjacent booth, the men there—all Hispanic—looked up with impassive faces to stare at Streak. Harte wiped his mouth and laid his napkin on the table. When he stood, Nesmith set down his fork and half-turned with one arm propped over the back of his chair.

Harte walked up the aisle past the Hispanic workers and stopped three feet from Harliner's outside seat in the booth. "The Bear" was still smiling, but now there was malice in his eyes as he glared at the sheriff. Harte turned his head and looked across the room where the owner stood at the cashier's counter looking back at him, frozen in the middle of a transaction with two middle-aged women. Like the others in the room, the two women stared indignantly at Harliner.

"Jerry," Harte called out in the quiet of the room, "is this man upset-ting your clientele?"

Jerry frowned and licked his lips. "Yeah, I guess so," he replied meekly.

Harte looked Harliner in the eye. "You're too loud and too crude for this restaurant."

"The Bear's" eyes glanced at Harte's hip. "What are you gonna do, shoot me?"

"The owner does not like your language," Harte said. "Neither do I."

Harliner lost the smile and thrust his chin forward. "What . . . now you're gonna harass me in a fuckin' restaurant? It's not enough that you took my son from me?"

Harte hitched his thumb upward with a quick jerk. "Get up."

"I'm havin' my meal, so get outta my face," Harliner said and took a huge bite out of his burger. As he chewed he looked down at his plate, trying his best to look nonchalant . . . and failing.

"Are you going to get up?" Harte said.

"Hell, no!" Harliner mumbled with his mouth stuffed. "I'm eating!" He took another massive bite of the burger.

Harte looked at the man next to Harliner. "Mind if I borrow your salt there?"

Surprised, the man looked down at the salt canister and frowned. "Yeah, sure."

Harte waited for Harliner to sink his teeth into his burger again, and then he stepped forward and reached across the corner of the table, bumping Harliner's glass of ice tea into the man's lap. As Harte stepped back, "The Bear" growled something unintelligible and hurriedly stood with the burger still in one hand. The front of his trousers dripped with tea and pieces of ice.

"Wha' tha fawk!" he said through a mouthful.

Harte set his hand firmly on the butt of his gun and nodded toward the door. "Now that you're up, step outside with me."

Harliner threw what was left of his burger on the table, pieces of it flying onto others' plates.

"You slimy sonovabitch. You don't get to push people around just because you think you're the Lone Ranger or something."

"When they offer resistance, I do."

Harliner glanced down at Harte's grip on the Colt and worked up a snide smile. "That's your gun blowin' all that hot air. You wouldn' be much without that hardware strapped on your hip."

Harte nodded toward the door. "Why don't you come outside with me." He unbuckled his gun belt and shifted his attention to the foreman seated against the wall. "He comes alone . . . nobody else . . . understand?" Without waiting for a reply, Harte walked down the aisle and out the door with the holster swinging from his hand. He knew Harliner would have to follow.

Harte crossed the lot to his cruiser, unlocked it, and tossed gun and holster into the passenger seat. Then he unpinned the badge and dropped it next to the gun. Without checking the faces in the front window of the restaurant, he walked around to the side of the building by the Dumpster, out of sight of the customers.

Harliner swaggered across the gravel lot, his long arms flared from his sides, stiff and barely swinging. When the big man stopped two yards away from Harte, he widened his stance.

"What's the catch?" he growled. "After I beat the shit outta you, are you gonna arrest me?"

"I don't want to fight you, Mr. Harliner. I want to talk."

"The Bear" snorted a dry laugh through his nose. Ice still clung to the wet stain on his pants.

"I was right," Harliner sneered, "you got nothin' without the gun and badge." He huffed a laugh and shook his head. "So why the big show of puttin' it all away?"

"I figure it's the only way you'll listen to me."

Harliner raised his chin to Harte. "How 'bout I whip your ass anyway?"

Harte kept his voice level. "I can't stop you from trying."

Harliner spewed air through his lips. "'Tryin'? I'll beat your ass six ways to Sunday."

"Like I said," Harte replied quietly, "I can't stop you . . . but—"

" 'But' nothin'! I will stomp—"

"Where is Carter's mother, Burt?" Harte interrupted in a quiet, placating tone.

Harliner's face darkened. "None o' your fuckin' business."

"Is she alive?"

The big man glared at Harte. "She ain't none o' your fuckin' business! That bitch is—" He caught himself from saying more and breathed heavily, his rage like an engine.

"So she is alive," Harte said. He watched the man scowl at the sparse traffic on the highway and at all the world that lay behind it. When Harliner turned back to continue his glare, Harte kept his voice steady and quiet. "I want you to listen to me. Drop all the macho bullshit and hear me out. I think you're a man close to the end of his rope."

Harliner held a hard mask of anger on his face, but there was something in his eyes that had not been there before. Harte nodded toward the bench that ran along the side of the building.

"Let's sit," he said and, without waiting for an answer, walked to the bench and sat.

Harliner stood his ground as a pair of heavy motorcycles rumbled by on the highway.

"I'm asking you to sit with me," Harte said. "It's about your boy."

After another ten seconds, the big man scuffed across the lot and sat heavily three feet away. Leaning forward, he propped his thick forearms on his thighs and stared out into the lot.

"Nobody knows the full story between a man and a woman . . . except the man and the woman. I know there are always two sides."

Harliner turned to show his resentment. "You said this was about my boy."

Harte nodded. "I'm getting to that." Leaning forward, he matched Harliner's bent-forward pose and spoke in a voice more wistful than he had intended. "I just got divorced myself."

Harliner looked quickly at Harte, as though trying to catch him in a lie.

"Look," Harte continued, "I'm not going to pretend I know your circumstances, but I do know something about your history."

"Oh, yeah? And how do you know that?"

"Part of your history is on record," Harte said flatly. "And I've had run-ins with you twice now. You seem to think that pushing your weight around makes you a better man. It doesn't. It makes you look small." Harte half-expected the cork to pop then and there, but Harliner just stared out into the trees with his jaw jutting forward as if he wanted to take a bite out of the forest.

"People are afraid of you. You seem to take some pleasure in that."

Harliner showed his teeth in a baleful smile. "Yeah . . . well . . . the world is full of bastards, and I'd rather have them afraid of me than thinking they can run over me."

Harte let a few seconds pass, as he reminded himself not to sound judgmental. "That include your wife and boy?"

Harliner said nothing. He only stared out at the trees.

"How old are you, Mr. Harliner?"

The big man shook his head and contrived a pitying laugh. "What the hell has that got to do with a damned thing we're talking about?"

"Well," Harte said and ran his left thumb along the lifeline of his right palm, "you get to a certain age in your life when you begin to realize that about all you've ever really had of value are your friends, the people you love, and the ones who love you. Everything else . . . is just a line of road signs along the highway." Harte turned to face him. "Seems to me you've mostly made enemies. And now you've pushed your son out."

Harliner's anger flared, and he jabbed a finger at Harte. "*You* pushed my son away. You're the sonovabitch who got Family Services climbing up my ass."

Harte's voice remained calm. "You pushed him away. You weigh what . . . over two-twenty? And Carter can't be a hundred pounds. What kind of man beats a kid like that? What's that supposed to teach him?"

Harliner sulked. "I dunno . . . to change his behavior? It's how my father trained me."

Harte wanted to say, 'And look how that turned out,' but instead he spoke in a kind tone. "Did you love your father?"

The question seemed to dismantle the man's hostility. His eyes flinched, and he made a raspy sniff through his nose, as if the sound might cover his vulnerability.

"He was just my father. You know how it is. They run your show until you get old enough to handle it yourself."

"He still alive?"

Harliner shook his head. "Naw . . .died about five years ago."

"Your mother?"

Another head shake. "She left long before he died."

"So he died alone?"

Harliner frowned. "He was in a hospital. Plenty of people there . . . doctors, nurses."

Harte watched doubt play over the man's face. "But he died alone," Harte confirmed.

Harliner looked toward the highway, forcing Harte to talk to the back of his head.

"Carter might be your last chance to have something . . . someone . . . and you're sabotaging that . . . and you're denying him the father every boy needs to have."

He expected Harliner to turn with some explosive denial to that accusation, but the man continued to hide his face. After a few seconds Harte stood. He did not know if their conversation would be a catalyst for reconciliation or an excuse to see the world as still being full of bastards. He turned to stand in front of Harliner and waited for the man's eyes to meet his own.

"Don't lose Carter," Harte said. "He needs you, and you need him."

When Harliner's head lowered, he seemed to be studying the gravel between his work boots. Harte walked back around the corner of the building and into the restaurant. He stopped at the cashier's counter, where the owner eyed him with open curiosity.

"I want to pay for the landscapers' lunches, Jerry."

Jerry looked past him at the booths. "The Mex, too?"

"All of them," Harte said. "And take a new iced tea to the Anglo booth, will you?"

"The *what*?"

"Streak Pendergrass's booth. "You'll need to take a rag down there, too."

When Harte returned to his table, Billy Nesmith was enjoying a cup of coffee, smiling. A small plate by his elbow showed a scattering of crumbs from a pie crust.

"Well, looks like you survived," he remarked blandly.

Harte sat. "How's the pie?"

"Damned good. It was cherry. But I'm pretty sure there was an underlying message in it. I asked Lorraine for a scoop of ice cream. I got three. You want some? It's my turn to pay."

Harte shook his head and pushed away his half-eaten plate of cold food.

"So how'd it go out there, Lone Ranger? He's not wearing your gun now, is he?"

Harte raised his eyebrows like a shrug. "We had a talk. Or, I talked. I think he listened."

Nesmith wadded his paper napkin and dropped it on his dessert plate. "So, you think we've got this drug ring in your county wrapped up, Sheriff?"

Harte idly brushed aside a few crumbs on the tabletop. "I don't think we've cut off the head of the monster yet. I figure Santiago was invited in, and I think Layland Childers was assigned to show him around."

Nesmith frowned. "What makes you say that?"

"The girl with Lauren—Jen—she mentioned somebody they call 'The Toad.' I want to find out who that is." Harte grabbed his hat. "I'm going to have a talk with Layland?" He stood and picked up the check. "I've got this. I owe you for coming up this morning."

"Ah . . . the white man's gnawing guilt for all the broken treaties. Too little, too late. But I accept." Nesmith stood. "I'm on my way to interview the driver at the hospital." He buttoned his suit coat and then raised his eyebrows. "Then I thought I'd talk to the two girls. You okay with that?"

Harte stared out the window for a time before replying. "Can you hold off on that?" Neither man blinked for the few seconds it took a flock of motorcycles to grumble past on the highway.

"You know Lauren was using," Nesmith said, not phrasing the words as a question.

Harte softened his voice. "I know she needs help. And . . . I know she'll get it."

Billy Nesmith narrowed one eye. "She was your best friend's daughter."

Harte nodded. "Still is," he said.

Nesmith pivoted his head to stare out the front window. "Maybe I'll wait on the girls." He started to rise but hesitated. "Oh, about your deputy . . . Ash . . . how is it he—"

"Ash was ordered to stay put. He disobeyed that order and tried to kill Santiago, probably as an insurance policy to keep the Cuban from talking if captured."

Nesmith frowned. "I'm told he shot five or six times and missed from point blank range."

Harte stared out the front window for a time before responding. "I couldn't trust him. His gun was loaded with blanks."

Now it was Nesmith's turn to gaze out the window. The room filled their silence with the *clink* of silverware and the steady crosscurrents of conversations.

"You put that in your report?" the captain asked.

Harte shook his head. "Not yet."

Nesmith nodded. "Who else knows about this?"

Harte looked his colleague in the eye. "No one."

Nesmith looked down at his hand and studied his palm for a time. "Well," he said, stretching out the word, "everything doesn't always make its way into a report, Harte." He stood and pushed his chair to the table. "You ask me . . . Ash was a poor shot with a handgun." Nesmith's eyes were hard as obsidian.

As the two lawmen stared at one another, Harliner reentered the restaurant, crossed the room, and sat in the booth with his white coworkers. Both tables went quiet.

Nesmith offered his hand. "Adios, Kemosabe. Keep me posted."
They shook, and the state captain walked to the cash register.

# Chapter Thirty-Seven

In the cruiser, Harte called Emmanuél's cell phone. When Manny's voice answered, Harte heard a flurry of trumpets and strumming guitars behind the greeting.

"Where are you?" Harte asked.

Emmanuél covered the phone and spoke to someone, and the background music faded. "I am at a friend's. Putting on the rings for your pistons."

"Keep tabs of your hours," Harte said. "I'm going to pay you the same as I'd pay the best auto shop in town. How's your head?"

"Like your Liberty Bell, I think," he chuckled. "A little cracked but still ringing with a memory. The doctor says it will be okay."

"Don't worry about any hospital bills. The county will take care of them." When Manny made no reply, Harte got down to business. "When you were inside Santiago's circle, did anyone mention someone called 'The Toad?' "

"Si, Jen. I ask her who that is, but she no want to talk. Maybe if the right person ask."

"And who would 'the right person' be?"

"Cody," Manny said without hesitation.

"Why him?"

After a time Emmanuél answered in a somber voice. "She care about him."

Harte frowned. "I'm talking about Jen. It's Lauren that Cody is with."

Emmanuél paused for only a moment. "*Si*, I know he love Lauren, but—" His voice softened with certainty. "The love does not go both ways, *señor*. Jen . . . she love Cody."

Harte took the news at face value and felt his heart sink. "Does Cody know all this?"

"*No, señor* . . . he is blind to both parts."

Harte thought about where this left Lauren. Alone with drugs, it would seem. And where did it leave Cody? Harte had seldom seen such dedication from a man toward a woman.

"He won't give up," Harte finally said.

Emmanuél's voice came back with quiet confidence. "Until he does," he said.

From the background arose an unmistakable equine whinny.

"Where did you say you were?"

"At the *rancho del caballo* with your truck and my *aprendiza* for the changing of the rings."

"Your apprentice?"

"*Si*, Collette," he said.

"You're at Cherokee Rose?"

"*Si*. We take apart your engine here by the trailer. I have it ready for you in a few days."

"Emmanuél, as long as I'm sheriff . . . or until I decide to go to Montana, if I do . . . that truck is yours. When you decide to wear a badge for the long haul, you'll have your own cruiser."

Harte heard Collette talking in the background. He pictured her by the fence with her trio of equine fans. Kenneth Fallon was probably nestled in his lawn chair under layers of blankets.

"I will think about that, *Señor* Harte," Emmanuél promised.

A few minutes later, when Cody answered his phone quietly, Harte heard two females arguing in the background. "Hang on, Sheriff," Cody said. Soon a door closed and the yelling was replaced by the sound of a moving car, a leaf blower, and a dog barking in the distance.

"I guess you're at Lauren's," Harte said.

Cody made a dry laugh. "Yeah, she and her mother are having one of their discussions."

"How much does Lauren's mother know?"

"Only about the drugs. Joe-Joe, bless his lying heart, told her it was me who arranged to get her home without an arrest. First time the mother ever thanked me for anything. Must'a been like swallowing a razor blade."

Harte kept his voice casual. "Is Jen there?"

"Oh, yeah," Cody hummed. "She's always here, seems like. She's in the kitchen."

"Eventually, Captain Nesmith from the state will be coming by there to question both of the girls. You might want to suggest they retain lawyers before they start talking."

"Yeah. I already called Sharon Spader. Said she'd represent Lauren if her mother agreed. Plus, she'll take on Jen gratis. Jen barely scrapes by, you know. Had a pretty tough life."

"Are you on pretty good terms with Jen?" Harte asked, edging toward the purpose of his call.

The line was silent for several seconds. "Sure . . . I guess," Cody said.

"Can you ask her something? It's important."

"Okay," Cody said. "Shoot."

"Ask her who 'The Toad' is."

For five long seconds the leaf blower whined over the line. "I'll call you back," Cody said.

In his office Harte and Maxie gathered at the laptop as she loaded the newest surveillance disk. The laptop screen lit up, and the sound graph materialized.

"This is from early morning, Sher'ff. I think Layland Childers has fried his own egg. And McAllister's a-sittin' in the fryin' pan with 'im."

For the next five minutes they stood absolutely still and listened to the recording. Layland's mewling voice droned on and on, trying to coax advice from McAllister. Finally, McAllister, worn down by questions, snapped at Layland in a short, choppy whisper.

McAllister: *"Shut up, goddamnit! You'd better learn to tough it out until our lawyer can get us outta this pig's sty. Keep up this moanin' an' cryin' an' somebody's gonna think you might'a spilled your guts to the law. You hear what I'm sayin'?"*

Childers: *"But we were both caught at a drug exchange. How're we gonna beat that?"*

McAllister, laughing: *"I was at a public bar. They found nothin' on me. You were caught with a truckload of powder, two whores, and a Cuban with the mentality of a wolverine."*

Childers: *"Now wait a minute! If you think—"*

McAllister: *"Figure your own damn way out of this, Layland! You're the one who thought he could deal with this big shot Cuban! You try to drag me down with you and I will sing a blue streak. That'll include arson up in Union County to push the Bullochs out of our county."*

Childers: *"That fire was your idea! You said 'burn the cretins out of business!' Remember?"*

McAllister: *"Yeah, but you paid me to do it. Re-mem-ber?"*

Childers: *"I brought in Santiago to make us more money. I didn't hear you complain."*

McAllister: *"Yeah, well, if I had been in on the details, I might not have advised stepping up the quantity so fast. Overnight you went from a flatbed carrying a coupla dozen bags of cocaine inside cinder blocks to a few thousand kilos in a tractor-trailer."*

Childers: *"Yeah, it was my idea. You think big, you get somewhere! That's the way business works!"*

McAllister, snorting: *"Yeah, and look where it got you."*

Maxie shut down the playback and locked eyes with Harte, the corners of her mouth curling into a hard smile. "How'll that do for evidence, Sher'ff?"

He stared at the frozen graph on the screen. "That's going to be hard to misinterpret, I think, even for a clever lawyer." He began to nod. "Maybe it's time to let McAllister know we found his money with his prints on the bag. He might want to start singing that blue streak."

"Can I be the one to tell 'im, Sher'ff Harte," Maxie asked. "I'd love to see that smirk wiped off his face."

"Be my guest. But first bring Childers to me. Cuff him behind."

Harte stepped to the window, turned on the hotplate, mixed coffee and cocoa into his blue cup and waited. Two blocks away people moved about the square as they always did, mostly tourists with their pamphlets and cameras as they milled about the gold museum. Brown, desiccated leaves littered the streets beneath the big sycamores that lined the square, but to Harte the town appeared clean. A lot of trash had been removed from the county in the last six hours.

By the time he was sipping his drink at the front of his desk, two knocks sounded at the door. At his command, Maxie ushered Layland Childers into the room and closed the door behind her. And there she stood like a sentry to bar entry or exit.

"Well, hey, Harte," Layland began, exhuming a trace of his good-old-boy routine. He approached slightly bent forward in a beseeching posture, his hands manacled behind him, his face slack with surrender in his need for mercy or absolution. "I've been wanting to talk to you. There is a big misunderstanding about my place in all this."

Harte set down his cup and with the same hand held up a palm. "Save it, Layland." He pointed to the straight-backed chair across from his desk. "Sit," he ordered.

Layland sat. Harte motioned Maxie over and gestured to the laptop. "Run this back a little bit and turn it on."

"What's this?" Layland said, managing a smile but unable to hide the fear in his eyes.

Harte set the video program on his cell phone and propped it against the lamp on his desk. "You don't mind if I record this, do you?"

In his peripheral vision Harte watched Layland squirm in the chair, but when he looked directly at the prisoner, Childers stared at the phone as if it had spoken to him. When the sound crackled on the laptop, Layland's whining voice was easily recognizable.

*"I brought in Santiago to make us a lot more money. I didn't hear you complain."*

*"Yeah, well if I had been in on the details, I might not have advised stepping up the quantity so fast. Overnight you went from a flatbed carrying just twelve bags of cocaine inside cinder blocks to ten thousand kilos in a tractor-trailer."*

*"Yeah, it was my idea. You think big, you get somewhere! That's the way business works!"*

When Harte shut off the playback, Layland began shaking his head frantically. "Let me explain what I meant," Layland pleaded.

Harte held the hand up again. "Do you know what prison life is like for a man like you, Layland? If I were in your shoes, I might be hoping for the death penalty."

"Death penalty!" Layland said, coughing up a strained laugh. "What for?"

"For Arthur Meeks," Harte said, barely above a whisper. "Ash took orders from you."

Harte sat on the edge of his desk and watched Layland swallow. The room was so quiet, the wet *tick* in his throat was like the snap of a small stick.

"It's going to get worse. The FBI is getting involved. You brought in those drugs over a state line, Layland."

"Now wait, Harte. I never asked anyone to hurt Meeks. I had nothing to do with that."

"Probably true," Harte said and let his eyes go stony. "Ash thought Meeks was me."

"Harte! I would never—"

"Tell me about the girls," Harte interrupted. "Lauren and Jen."

Layland closed his mouth to swallow again, and the *tick* chimed in on cue. When his lips parted again as if to talk, he only breathed as though, for once, speech had failed him.

"Did you forget that Jim Raburn was your friend? And that Lauren was underage?"

Layland's eyes burned with desperation. "I was never with her, Harte. I swear it!"

"Jen is underage, too," Harte reminded.

Any hope that might have flickered in Childers's face now died.

"Who is 'The Toad,' Layland?"

The skin on Layland's face tightened. "What?"

"Who is part of your crowd that calls himself 'The Toad'?"

Layland's hangdog face turned to the window, and he seemed to be searching for something among the buildings around the square. He opened his mouth to speak but then closed it when Harte's cell phone rang. Seeing Cody's name on the screen, Harte answered succinctly.

"Hang on a minute," he said and lowered the phone. "Maxie," he said, pointing to Layland, "put him in the holding cell. He and McAllister have had enough talking time."

"Now, wait, Harte!" Layland mewled. "What if I could tell you some things? Could it help me in my situation? Would you be willing to do some horse-trading?"

Harte fixed his gaze on Layland. "Who is 'The Toad'?"

Layland tried for a frown of regret. "Maybe there are other things I can tell you, Harte."

Harte gave Layland his stoniest glare. "I might be willing to work with you, if you can find a way to keep these girls out of the story."

Layland's face brightened. "I can do that! Hell, yes!" He shifted on his feet. "So what can you do for me in return?"

"We'll talk about that later." Harte signaled Maxie with a hitch of his head. "Get him out of my office." Turning to the window, he waited until the door closed, and then he put the phone to his ear. "I'm here, Cody. Did you hear that? That was Childers groveling in my office."

"Yeah, I heard," Cody said. When his voice came back, it was muffled as if his hands were cupped around his phone. "I talked to Jen, Sheriff. 'The Toad' is some fat dude with a sour smell. Childers used to drive Jen and Lauren to a motel somewhere—they don't know where. Childers made them wear something tied over their eyes before they got there. Then this degenerate called 'The Toad' banged both of them in the dark. Jen said he had disabled every light in the room. She never saw him. But she smelled him. Jen says that's how she and Lauren got their drugs. Then Jen got off the stuff . . . and off 'The Toad.' But Lauren—" Cody didn't finish.

"Do you have an idea who he is?"

"All I know is . . . the sonovabitch has got warts. That's why they call him 'The Toad.' "

Harte felt an electric tingle run across his shoulders. "Where?"

" 'Where' what?"

"Where are the warts? Where on his body?"

"Hang on, Sheriff."

Harte waited, feeling his grip on the phone tighten. "On his stomach, Sheriff. The bastard's got warts on his stomach."

# Chapter Thirty-Eight

It was four o'clock in the afternoon when Harte drove through the gate at Cherokee Rose and coasted to a stop next to the drive-through garage, where Jan's big six-wheel pickup filled the space beneath the aluminum canopy. Wiley's black Jeep was parked under the oak on the grass behind the lower level of the house. Just as Harte turned off his engine, the radio crackled and Maxie's tinny voice came through the speaker.

"Sher'ff Harte, we got us a problem up on the Cooper Gap Road."

"I'm busy right now, Maxie."

"We've got a full-size school bus that tipped off the road about a mile up the mountain. A front wheel slipped down a gravelly spot and the bus just slid downhill into a big buckeye tree. They're from the Methodist church, Sher'ff. Apparently they've got a new driver who thought he could shave off some miles. They've got a Bible Camp goin' on and twenty-two kids were headin' over the mountain to go to the gem mine in Gaddistown."

Harte cursed and slid his key back into the ignition. "When was this?"

"Sher'ff Harte, don't ask me how, but nobody was hurt. Looks like this joker lookin' for a shortcut at least had his kids in their seatbelts. It happened about two o'clock, but it took one o' the counselors a coupla hours to walk to where he could get phone service. Fire and Rescue is already there, and I just sent out Burns and Joe-Joe to the scene. The staff had plenty of food and water, so there's no problem with dehydration."

Harte relaxed his grip on the key and sat back deeper in his seat. "What about a wrecker?"

"Taken care of, Sher'ff. Bud Ramsey is already up there with his tow truck, but it's gonna take a while. They're sayin' a few hours. Bud's broadside in the road, winchin' the bus back up a inch at a time. The road will be closed for a while."

Harte could picture the operation—Bud hauling up the bus like a hooked whale, the children watching as if it was the greatest show on Earth. "Sounds like it's under control, Maxie."

"Yes'r. I just wanted you to know in case you were headin' up that way to your old camp site." Maxie hesitated a moment. "Betty-June Ferribee told me she saw you drivin' out that way, so—"

Harte eyed the Haversack house and spoke quietly into the mic. "I'll be back in twenty minutes. I need to see a man about something."

"Copy that, Sher'ff." A long pause followed before Maxie cleared her throat. "You wanna tell me where you're headed . . . just so I know?"

The side door of the house opened, and Jan stepped out talking non-stop on a cell phone. So animated was she in her conversation that she didn't notice the cruiser. Harte watched her reach behind the passenger seat of her truck, grab a clipboard, and go back inside the house.

"Maxie," Harte said into the microphone. "I'm—"

"Sher'ff, I'm gettin' piled up with phone calls . . . prob'ly about the church bus. I know the mayor will be wantin' to know what the bus was doin' on the Cooper Gap Road. I'll hold down the fort here and see you in twenty minutes."

Harte stepped out onto the gravel, quietly pushed his door shut, and checked the loads in his Colt. Deciding to keep the Jeep in sight, he walked down the hill to the back of the house where a bright creamy light burned behind a window curtain.

For a full minute he listened, hearing nothing more than the wind rattling leaves in the oak behind him. He removed his hat, cupped his hand to the window, and peered through the glass to see a storage room shelved with cans of food. A long top-opening freezer ran across the far wall. Brooms, mops, and other long-handled tools, and two pairs of well-worn boots stood in a corner. Above these hung two work coats. A pair of fluorescent lights illuminated a counter, where someone had laid a bridle with a bit-ring that had worn through the leather.

Then came a surprise. The familiar sound of a dispatcher's radio crackled from the other end of the room, and the monotone of Maxie's professional voice reached him through the glass. Following Maxie's message came a louder voice that Harte recognized as Bud Ramsey's. Maxie spoke again and then the radio went dead.

Harte thought back to the night of the cinder block fiasco and imagined Wylie here listening to the police band over his radio, orchestrating the removal of the truck like a chess master leaning over the playing board. When he moved past the door to the next window he heard the start-stop tapping of a computer keyboard. When the radio came alive again with Maxie's voice, the volume was suddenly lowered to a fraction of what it had been.

"Dumb sonovabitch!" someone said from behind the window, and only after the words were spoken did Harte recognize Wiley's surly voice. "Run a fool bus off the Cooper Gap Road! What an idiot!"

Harte fitted his hat to his head, stepped back to the door, and knocked. Through the door he heard Wylie mumble something unintelligible. A lock tripped. When the door cracked open, Wylie's face flinched and quickly glanced back into the room where he had been working. When he turned back to Harte, he tried for an indignant look.

"What do *you* want?" he said, edging the question with insult. Wylie was dressed in his trademark stained white undershirt and loose gray sweatpants.

"I want you to step outside," Harte said. "I need to search you."

" 'Search' me?" Wylie smiled. "What the hell for?"

Harte kept his face expressionless as his eyes held Wylie in place. "Warts."

Wylie closed his mouth, and his breathing made faint whistling sounds through his nose. "I've had my fill of you. Go away and stop harassing me."

The radio came to life again, and the canned voice of Burns reported that three vans had arrived to cart off the stranded campers. Wylie disappeared behind the door, and the radio clicked off. When he reappeared, he manufactured something between a cough and a laugh.

"Shouldn't you be up there at the gap, helping out or something?" When Harte made no reply, Wylie worked up an impatient frown. "Look . . . if this is about the Devereaux girl—"

Harte reached out and pushed the door open wider. "Lift up your shirt, Wylie."

Wylie's expression sobered to a dead-eyed glare. "What the hell for?"

Harte took a fistful of Wylie's soft cotton shirt and, jerking him forward, raised the tee-shirt, exposing Wylie's beer gut. The rounded swell of flesh was dotted with dark tufts of hair rising from more than half a dozen discolored bumps. The sour acid stench of wart-remover rose from his skin like the fumes from a big city storm sewer.

"Let go of me!" Wylie whined and swatted at the sheriff's hand.

Harte pulled Wylie closer. "Did you know the girls call you 'The Toad'?"

Wylie seemed frantic. "What?" When he jerked himself free, the shirt tore beneath the collar. Stepping back to the threshold, Wylie scowled. "I've always had warts. So what?"

Harte almost smiled. "I'm betting it'd be an easy connect-the-dots in court. Like reading braille. Jen and Lauren could probably draw the pattern from memory." He let that sink in as he watched Wylie squirm. "Almost as good as fingerprints," he added.

Wylie's eyes were like two hot coals. "Who the hell are Jen and Lauren?"

"Step outside here and keep your hands where I can see them," Harte ordered.

A cold stillness settled over Wylie. "You got a warrant?"

"No warrant," Harte said. "But I've got compelling evidence . . . and I've got a boot."

" 'A boot'?" Wylie snorted.

Harte planted his foot in the doorway.

"You can't come in here," Wylie snapped and pushed on the door until it wedged against Harte's boot. "Get your foot out o' my god-damned house!"

"You're under arrest, Wylie. You can either come out on your own or I can assist you."

"Arrest!" Wylie croaked. "Look, I don't have time for this right now, so go away." He pushed the door again, but it didn't budge. Wylie jerked the door open enough to show the full outrage building on his face. "Move, goddamnit!"

Harte stepped back quickly and kicked the door with the sole of his boot. The wood made a splintering sound, and the door swung open a foot, sending Wylie stumbling back into the long freezer. When his hip caught the corner of the appliance, he twisted and hit the wall. Crouching there, he brought up both hands like a partially opened book but stopped short of touching his face. Blood dripped steadily into his palms.

"You broke my fucking nose!" he screeched, his complaint nasal and hollow inside his steepled hands. "What the hell's the matter with you?"

"Resisting arrest has consequences. You want to step outside now?"

"What the hell're you arresting me for? I told you that Devereaux girl was lying! And besides, I haven't even seen the little—"

When Harte stepped quickly inside, Wylie shut up and drew his arms over his head. "You'd better choose your words carefully tonight, Wylie," Harte said in a whisper of warning.

While Harte looked around the room, Wylie looked at his blood-smeared hands. "God . . . damnit! You can't just push your way inside a man's home!"

Harte cocked his head. "You opened your door to me, Wylie. We're old school buddies, remember?" He nodded toward the radio on the shelf. "Maybe you didn't hear about the drug bust at McAllister's equipment yard. We kept a radio silence most of the night. And you've probably had a hard time getting through to anyone by phone. Santiago is dead. Ash is dead. Childers is in jail."

Wylie's bloodied face froze like a Halloween mask as he breathed heavily through his mouth. Each tooth that he bared was framed in red.

"Who is Santiago and what the hell's Layland Childers got to do with me?"

"Your world is coming apart, Wylie. Your business associates are not feeling too loyal with these charges laid in their laps. Layland is singing like a rooster at dawn."

Above the hands steepled over his nose, Wylie's brow lowered over his eyes. He leaned back against the wall, and Harte took the opportunity to look at the lighted computer screen on the desk. A list of names ran down the left margin. After each name was a number entry: "100," "200," or "300" . . . and so on. The third column contained dates and abbreviated descriptions of locations: road intersections, bridges, subdivisions, and landmarks around the county. The final column showed dollar figures with a wide range up into the thousands.

The names were in alphabetical order. Harte, scrolled to the C's. Layland Childers's last entry showed yesterday's date, ten-thousand kilos, and the note: *"McA, Copper Tr., with T.S."*

"T.S.," Harte read aloud. He turned to watch Wylie pull himself up by the freezer. "Turon Santiago."

Wylie said nothing. With his hands folded over his nose, he glared over his fingertips.

"Wylie!" Jan called from the top of the stairs. "What the hell're you doing down there?"

Harte stepped into view at the bottom of the stairwell. "It's Harte Canaday, Jan."

Later he would not remember what else he had said, only that his skull had been replaced by a great iron bell that clanged once, its massive peal lingering inside him like a permanent echo . . . that and a bright yellow light that had flashed behind his eyes. Then came the void.

*****

Someone's fingers probed his hair, and then he heard the tearing of paper. By the fusty smell of the basement, he remembered where he was, but he didn't know how much time had passed. When he opened his eyes he could only focus on the ceiling, where a black pipe ran beneath the main level's floor joists and bare insulation. The dark shadow that moved across his field of vision finally stilled, and he felt something both soft and firm press to the back of his head. He squinted at the silhouette until the face floating above him came into resolution. Jan Haversack's short hair framed her head like a golden halo under the stairwell light. Her pinched eyes suddenly filled with relief.

"Thank God, Harte! I thought you were almost dead. I've already called nine-one-one."

He tried to sit up, but she pressed a hand to his chest. "Wait for the ambulance, Harte."

The pressure on his skull relaxed, and she showed him a gauze compress with a broad blot of blood. "You took a hit to the head. What in the world happened?" Her voice trembled, and he thought her fear had more to do with what he might tell her than the state of his bleeding head. He rolled over and got to his knees.

"Where's Wylie?" he said, his voice like sandpaper.

"Harte, you probably have a concussion."

He paused on all fours and turned to look at her. "Where is he, Jan?"

"I don't know. He just left and took the Jeep."

"How long was I out?"

"Maybe ten minutes. You were talking to me up the stairs, and the next thing I hear is this loud *whang* like a horse kicking a bucket. Then I saw you fall."

Harte stood and steadied himself by the freezer. Jan picked up his hat and offered it to him. The hat's crown was dented and the brim buckled in back.

"What's all that?" Jan said, pointing to a spattering of blood on the floor near the freezer.

"Door hit Wylie's nose," he said and studied the tracks of blood-stained shoe prints that led out the backdoor. A heavy spade shovel lay on the floor. "That what he hit me with?"

"Lord, God, Harte! Why would he do that? Is this about the girl . . . Collette?"

Through the open backdoor Harte looked at the open space under the oak where the Jeep had been parked. "That . . . and a lot more. Jan, does Wylie own a gun?"

"We keep a shotgun upstairs. Why?"

"Is it still up there?"

483

Jan's brow lowered. "I think so. He didn't go upstairs. He just left out the back."

"Anything else? A pistol, maybe?"

Her eyes cut to the empty drawer pulled open in Wylie's desk, then she frowned and shook her head. "Not that I know of, Harte. But I'm not sure what I know about Wylie anymore."

"Go check on the shotgun, would you?" Harte asked.

When she went upstairs, Harte moved to the desk and opened the drawer all the way. A single cartridge rolled in a circle, making a reso-nant sound in the hollow of the drawer. When it quieted and stopped, he picked it up. It was a revolver bullet, .38 caliber. Nothing else was in the drawer. Pulling out his cell phone he dialed his office and caught Maxie in a high gear.

"Sher'ff," she began without a greeting, "it's under control up at Cooper Gap. Bud has 'bout got the bus hauled up onto the road. His wench locked up for a bit, but he's got it goin' now."

"Maxie, I want you to get word out that the Lumpkin County sher-iff's department is in pursuit of Wylie Haversack. Call the Highway Patrol, state police, and all the surrounding counties. He's in a black Jeep, license number HK 3931. Probably armed. Possibly dangerous."

Jan came back down the stairs and stopped at the door with a look of intense concentration on her freckled face. Harte removed the phone from his ear and waited for her report.

"He didn't take the shotgun," she said. "What is this about the state police?"

Harte held up an index finger and made a quarter turn away. "Maxie, I want road blocks at every outlet from Cooper Gap: Grassy Gap Road, Tritt's Store, Gooch Creek, and Three Forks. And I need a warrant for the computer in the Haversack's basement. I've seen evidence on it linked to the drugs we impounded last night."

Jan walked stiffly to the desk, where her face paled in the glow of the computer screen. Leaning in, she scanned the data that was displayed and then straightened with one hand pushed partway back through her short hair.

"Harte, what is all this?" she said flinging a hand toward the computer.

Harte pocketed his phone. "It's drug distribution . . . and prostitution with minors." He nodded toward the shovel. "Now, add to that: resisting arrest and assaulting an officer."

Jan slowly closed her eyes. "The idiot!" she said, her voice hard and unforgiving.

"Where would he go, Jan? Does he have someplace where he might hole up?"

She looked out the window. "He drove off toward the back end of the property."

"To the trailer?"

She shook her head. "The other way. I think I heard the Jeep climbing up the old logging road that runs past the Moss Cemetery. He's never done that before."

"Can he get all the way to the ridge on that?"

She thought for a moment. "I've done it on horseback. I don't see why the Jeep couldn't."

Harte looked northwest to the mountains. "He would have heard about the Cooper Gap Road being blocked by the bus. That logging road would bypass the tangle and get him all the way to the gap. From there he's got dirt roads to Ellijay or to Suches or to Gaddistown." He turned to Jan. "I want you to go to a motel or a friend's for the night. Can you do that?"

"What are you going to do with Wylie?"

"I'm going to bring him back."

485

Jan frowned. "You can't drive that old road in your cruiser, can you?"

Harte shook his head. "I'll need a horse. Can I take the paint?"

Without hesitation she nodded. "Take it," she said.

Harte eased his hat over the knot on his head. "Do you have a topo map for the gap?"

"There are maps in the tack room." She began sidling past him. "Come on. You saddle the paint, and I'll find the map."

In the barn the paint mare nickered and stamped her front hooves in the soft-powder dirt of the stable floor as Harte outfitted her for the ride. A siren wailed in the distance, and soon a squeal of tires marked the sharp turn into the Haversack driveway. The siren cut off, but they could hear the popping of gravel beneath tires.

"That's the ambulance," Jan called from the tack room. "You should let them look at your head." But when she brought out the map, Harte was already in the saddle. "After the cemetery," she said, "leave the road and follow Ward Creek up to the top. With all the washouts he'll need to straddle, you might be able to get to the gravel road west of Hogback before he does." She folded the map, stuffed it into his saddlebag, and closed the leather flap. Looking up at him, her face was as earnest as he had ever seen it. "Don't kill him, Harte."

The sentiment surprised him. "That'll depend on him. If he has a gun—"

With a worried look, Jan pulled in her lips. "I know," she conceded. Then she turned and took a raincoat off a wall peg. As she lashed it behind his saddle, she appeared resigned to anything that might come. She met Harte's eyes once again and then stroked the horse's neck. "Supposed to rain tonight," she said.

Harte nodded his thanks. "I'll probably lose phone service once I'm up there in those coves. Would you call my dispatcher, Maxie-Rose, and let her know which way I'm headed? And let her know where you're staying tonight."

"I will," Jan said and stepped back. She looked down at the ground for a moment, and then her eyes met his. "Harte, you take care of yourself, do you hear me? But, please, don't kill him." With that she turned and walked purposefully toward the strobe of red and blue lights flashing around her house.

Harte prodded the paint with his boot heels and leaned forward as the horse lunged into a smooth and powerful gallop toward the rear of the property. The mare flew across the meadow as if her hooves were touching only the tips of the grass blades. When she splashed through the creek and plunged into the shadows of the forest, she showed no signs of wanting to slow.

The road was passable for a four-wheel drive vehicle as it wound its way northwest, continually folding back upon itself like the trail of a giant serpent. The Jeep's signs were blatant, the road being so rutted and thick with saplings. The stop-starts and grinding of the tires left fresh broad scars and the lingering smell of torn earth. Countless young pines were scraped of their bark on the downhill side, and the scent of fresh sap was pungent in the air. The tracking was easily done from the saddle, and so the only task was to keep the horse moving faster than the Jeep.

After the Moss Cemetery the ruts grew to gullies, and the rock and dirt showed more aggressive signs from the Jeep. At Ward Creek, Harte left the road and led the horse upstream, staying in the middle of the bed to avoid the rhododendron leaning out from the banks. When the stream broke into a long series of small cataract falls, he pushed his hat tighter on his head and made his way through the undergrowth onto the flood plain and wove his way as best he could through the tangle of branches.

As the crow flew, he knew, the gap lay two more miles to the northwest. Harte figured that, with the endless switchbacks, Wylie's route had to be double that . . . and full of problems. With each gain in altitude the temperature dropped, and the change seemed to empower the horse with renewed enthusiasm. He posted in the stirrups, complementing the paint's gait and felt the animal giving her best to the impromptu mission.

At a trickling ribbon of tributary creek, Harte dismounted and fed out the reins as Piper lowered her head to drink. He watched her guzzle water for ten seconds, until a low celestial grumble rolled overhead. The paint's head came up, walleyed and alert. She nickered, and water dripped from her muzzle like glass beads. Harte looked up at a leaden sky.

"Just a little thunder, girl," he whispered. He stood in front of her and stroked the flat-plated muscles of her cheeks. "I need you to keep it together for me." The paint nickered again, and Harte made a single breathy laugh. "Hell, you just want to run, don't you?"

He mounted, and the horse thrashed through the underbrush in powerful strides. The next thunder shook the earth, and rain began to tap the leaves. Piper struggled to break into a faster gait, but he held her back with low reassuring sounds as they angled slightly to the west. On the move he unfurled the raincoat and bundled up against the rain, thankful that the garment was oversized enough to cover his thighs. The temperature had dropped significantly. His breath plumed before him in a gray mist that came apart in the rain.

After fifteen minutes, a logging road appeared high on his left, and Harte coaxed the paint up the bank to a road bed full of pine saplings, wet and glistening from the rain. The paint sucked in air in deep doses and exhaled in twin curling jets of fog, the sound like a steam engine. Finally she leapt with nervous energy onto the level space of the road.

Thunder crackled across the sky. Harte dismounted and stroked the mare's neck, speaking to her just as she stutter-stepped and jerked against the pull of the reins. When she began to settle, he listened to a sound far down the cove. The faint whine of an engine rose and fell as it struggled up the mountain in a low gear. Another boom of thunder rolled across the sky—this one drawn out and troubling, like boulders tumbling down a wooden hallway. Rain began to fall in earnest, drumming on Harte's hat with a steady hum. Piper danced in place, and Harte coaxed her uphill into a holly thicket where he tied her to a wrist-sized trunk. For a time he stared at the knot he had made in the reins. Then he slipped the knot and rewrapped the leather in simple loops around the tree.

"If this goes south on me," he said to the paint, "don't want you stranded on this mountain."

By the time he returned on foot to the top of the road-cut, the rain had let up, and a thin bank of fog rolled in like a gray tsunami washing slowly through the trees. The sound of the engine remained muted, until the black Jeep rounded the bend below him and came into view, its headlights glaring like two angry eyes in the darkening forest. With jolts and snarls, the Jeep came on doggedly, its engine revving in spurts, the tires tearing at the rocks and dipping into the road's ruts.

Stepping behind the thick trunk of a chestnut oak at the lip of the road-cut, Harte slipped his gun from his holster and waited, rippling his fingers on the Colt's handle to bring life into his cold fingers.

He could make out Wylie's head bobbling with each buck of the vehicle. When the Jeep was ten yards away, it straddled a deep ditch, its left wheels riding high on the bank on which he stood. When it came alongside him, the Jeep's wheels spun and started to slide backward until Wylie braked. Harte took two quick steps down the mud bank and pulled open the Jeep's flimsy door. Wylie turned a shocked face to the muzzle of Harte's Colt.

"How the hell did you get up here?" he barked, his surprise now turned to a vicious scowl.

Suddenly the tires slid sideways into the trench, and the Jeep settled, its open door knifing into the bank and its axles jammed into the ground. Harte skated a foot but kept his balance.

"Shut it off!" Harte commanded.

Wylie wore a purple, puffy jacket that billowed around his body like an inflated life jacket. On the passenger seat beside him was an unzipped, bulging athletic bag. Wylie's face turned to rage, made all the more savage by streaks of blood running from his nose, over his lips, and down his chin. His jacket front was dappled with red. Like a petulant child he shut down the engine and glared out the windshield. Cursing, he slapped the steering wheel with his hands.

Harte extended his free hand. "Give me the key and get out."

Wylie glowered, and tightened his grip on the wheel. His knuckles turned white as quartz. Exhaling in a rush, he extracted the keys and slapped them into Harte's hand. Then he clasped the wheel again, showing no indication that he would exit the vehicle. Harte grabbed a fistful of Wylie's coat and hauled him out onto the wet red clay of the road-cut. Right away Wylie's flat-soled shoes went out from under him, and he slid down the bank on hands and knees until his backside banged against the Jeep's running board.

"Ow!" he yelled and looked up angrily at Harte. "That hurt, god-damnit!"

Harte steadied the Colt on Wylie's chest. "Stand up!" he ordered. "Take off the coat!"

"What for! It's cold as hell up here."

Harte gestured with the gun barrel, and Wylie got to his feet. After peeling off the coat, he threw it at Harte, who caught it without altering the aim of his revolver. Harte searched the pockets as Wylie hugged his arms across his stained undershirt.

"Lift the shirt," Harte ordered and threw the coat onto the hood of the Jeep. In the fading light, the hairy warts that dotted Wylie's rounded belly were like a colony of tufted parasites. Harte could see no weapon. "Turn around and lean on the Jeep."

Wylie turned awkwardly on the slope and leaned into the Jeep's roof. As Harte began frisking, working his way down the legs, he felt Wylie lean deeper into the cab. Choosing the nearest point of vulnerability, Harte pressed the Colt's muzzle up into the soft flesh below Wylie's buttocks.

"If there's anything in your hand," Harte said, "your day is going to go from bad to worse."

Wylie's body stiffened, but he managed to muster enough indignation to snap at Harte. "There's nothing in my hands, goddamnit!"

"Raise them and make me a believer," Harte instructed and right away his lower boot lost purchase on the slick bank. Sliding toward the ditch he felt one leg bend behind him in a semi-split.

With surprising quickness, Wylie turned only to slip and fall himself. As they hit, Wylie's full weight pinned Harte's gun arm to the bank. Wearing a maniacal grin, he raised a small, black pistol, and, before Harte could react, Wylie jammed the gun into Harte's gut and fired.

The sound of the gunshot bloomed between them and echoed down the valley. The acrid smell of smoke and cordite diffused into the air. With the explosion so close and with the raw shock of being on the wrong side of gunfire, Harte took the impact with an immediacy that stopped time. The shot had come at point blank range, delivering a driving force that Harte felt to his core.

Blinking and open-mouthed, as if surprised at what he had done, Wylie kept the revolver trained on Harte's chest. "Let go of your gun," Wylie ordered.

When the Colt slid into the ditch, Wylie got to his feet and backed away a step. Then, almost as surprising as the gunshot itself, he laughed one loud and triumphant note.

"The great Harte Canaday! Our gunfighter sheriff!"

Harte looked down at himself. With the raincoat open, a neat hole in his black coat smoldered red at its edges like a ring of cigarette ash. He slapped at the glowing circle and rubbed it out. The shock of being shot was nothing like he had imagined. There was no screaming pain, just a stunned coldness spreading from his belly. He watched Wylie pick up the Colt by its barrel and heft it in his hand.

"You were always an odd one, Harte, but for the life of me I can't figure why in hell anybody would want to lug around this old cannon." He heaved the gun over the Jeep, sending it in a low arc until it thudded into the wet leaves below the road.

Wylie backed away and assessed the tilt of the Jeep. "Shit!" he said and leaned to inspect the undercarriage. "Damned thing's sittin' on the chassis!" He straightened and curled his lip as if he might spit. "Wrong fuckin' time to put my winch in the shop." He straightened and frowned as he studied the road illuminated by his headlights.

"So, how the hell did you get up here?" Wylie asked, his face now sharp with interest.

"Cruiser," Harte lied. "Just up the hill."

Probing for bodily damage under his coat, Harte worked his fingers between the buttons of his shirt until his fingertips found the bare skin and trail of hairs below his navel. The moisture he found there was minimal, just a film of sweat.

Wylie extended his free hand palm up. "Gimme your keys."

When Harte hesitated, Wylie leveled his gun at Harte's head. "Or I could just be done with you and take the keys off your corpse."

When Harte checked his hand, it was blood-free. Hiding his surprise he reached into the coat's flap pocket, dug out his keys, and tossed them to Wylie. Wylie swatted at the keys with his free hand but missed. The ring of keys made a *chink* sound as they hit the ground beyond the Jeep. Wylie spewed an impatient blast of air through his lips and worked his way around the Jeep to shuffle through the leaves. The rain started again and pattered the ground around them.

Harte sat up and waited for the wound to double him up in pain, but all he felt was a residual tingling in his abdomen. Digging into his clothing he craned his neck forward and saw a twisted lump of dull gray embedded in the old badge on his belt buckle. He touched its rough surface and felt the mangled bullet loosen then tumble free.

The rain escalated, coming down now in a steady downpour. Through the drumming of water on the Jeep's hood, Harte heard a jangle of keys, and then Wylie appeared at the passenger side of the cab, working the strap of the athletic bag over his shoulder. From there he moved to the front of the Jeep and jerked his damp jacket off the hood.

"Thanks for bringing me a backup vehicle, Sheriff," Wylie crowed. "I'll enjoy listening to your deputies on your radio." Then something occurred to him and he frowned. "Are you carrying one of those mobile radios on you?"

"In my cruiser," Harte said. "I was in a hurry and forgot it. You'll see it on the seat."

Wylie's eyes narrowed as he smiled again. "Let's just see."

He worked his way around the Jeep and pressed the gun into Harte's chest. Harte kept one hand pressed to his stomach, as Wylie fumbled at Harte's hips to frisk him.

"Stupid mistake, Sheriff. How're you gonna get help before you bleed to death?"

Pushing away from Harte, Wylie moved to the front of the Jeep and stood in the headlights as he worked his arms through the glistening sleeves of his wet coat. The loft of the coat was diminished, flattened by the rain. His thinning hair was plastered to his skull. Wylie snorted a laugh as he waggled the gun before him like a taunt.

"Maybe someone will find you, Harte," he said and widened his sadistic smile, ". . . in a few weeks."

"How do you expect to get away in a sheriff's cruiser?" Harte groaned.

Wylie laughed. "Who's gonna know?" he said. "Besides, if I wanna switch to something more anonymous, what better than a sheriff's cruiser to pull somebody over to make the trade?"

Harte let his head lie back in the red clay, the back of his hat brim folding like a pillow. He closed his eyes and tried for a believable performance of a man living his last few seconds.

"Go away and let me die without having to look at you, Wylie."

Wylie showed his teeth, turned, and ran up the road, the wet pine saplings swishing against the nylon shell of the jacket. When he was out of sight, Harte rose and hurried to the slope below the Jeep, where he went down on all fours and began searching the hillside, sweeping his hands back-and-forth in wide arcs as he felt for the Colt.

He caught a glint of reflected light in the leaves and spotted the curve of the Colt's cylinder. Grabbing the gun, he carried it to the front of the Jeep and examined it in the beam of the headlight. Setting the hammer at half-cock, he rotated the cylinder and listened to five crisp clicks. Then he eased down the hammer. The action was smooth.

The paint tensed at his approach but soon calmed. The reins were held now by a single turn around the holly. After swinging up into the saddle, he urged the paint down to the old road and turned to follow

Wylie's trail, the Jeep's headlights shining on his back and throwing the shadow of man and horse before him.

Harte did not bother to look for signs. He knew that Wylie would be desperate to get to the car he believed waited ahead. Wylie was intent on escape . . . not an ambush.

He broke out into the openness of the dirt-gravel road sooner than expected. The paint seemed to gather energy from the newfound space and communicated this with a series of snorts and jerks of its head. A stiff breeze funneled under the overarching trees, pushing the rain into a slant and chilling the right side of his face. The wet blustery air was bracing here, the cold so immediate that Harte fastened the top button of his coat and pushed his hat tighter on his head.

Looking left then right, he could see no farther than ten yards either way down the dark road. He figured Wylie would head for the gap and the small parking lot where the Appalachian Trail crossed the road. He reined the mare into the softer dirt of the shallow drainage ditch and, with a light touch of his heels, he started the paint west.

The temperature dropped radically, and the rain turned to sleet. It rattled on his hat brim and hit the ground around him with a sound like plastic beads tumbling steadily from a bottomless bag. After half a mile of cutting through the storm, the horse shied at something in the trees off to their left. Harte struggled to get the paint under control as he tried to make out a dark shape attached to the base of a big sawn stump.

When the horse settled, Harte recognized the slump of Wylie's body and the athletic bag lying next to him. Wylie's arms were wrapped around his shins as his whole body trembled in violent spasms. Ice crystals clung to his bare head. The sweat pants were sodden, and the saturated jacket now hung heavily on him. Clutched in one hand, the revolver trembled with him.

"Y-you're s-s'posed to be bl-bleeding your guts out b-back there," Wylie stuttered.

Harte eased his pistol out and leveled it at Wylie's chest as he backed the paint away to the far side of the road. "Drop the gun, Wylie."

A jolting shiver ran through Wylie, causing his head to bobble on his shoulders. "S-s-sonova-b-bitch," he sputtered and scowled at the paint. "Th-there's no car, is th-there?"

"There'll be one up here soon enough . . . to take you into town."

Wylie's breath came now in broken gasps. "I n-need y-your coat. I'm fr-freezing."

"I'm not coming over there to help you until you toss that gun aside."

Through his misery, Wylie managed to smile. "I d-don't think so."

He moved faster than Harte would have thought possible, throwing the athletic bag at the horse's feet. Even as the paint reared, Harte saw Wylie raise the revolver. As the horse wheeled left, two shots broke through the sound of the falling needles of ice, the explosions coming so close together that Harte knew Wylie was jerking wildly on the trigger.

As the paint reared and thrashed its front hooves at the sound of thunder so close, Harte twisted and leveled the Colt at Wylie and fired off a single round. When the horse came back to ground, the Colt was cocked for a second shot, but there was no need. Wylie was out of the fight. He lay on his back beside the stump, the sleet falling on his exposed face. His legs had flattened to the wet earth, and his arms sprawled out like a human crucifix. The black pistol lay several feet away.

Harte dismounted, tethered the paint off the road, and approached Wylie. After picking up the gun, he knelt, unzipped the sopping jacket, and found the wound positioned precisely where he had aimed—just under the collarbone of the right shoulder. He tried to imagine Jan

Haversack's face when he told her that Wylie was still alive. Her last words had been puzzling, but they had stayed with him.

"D-damn you, Harte Ca-Ca-Canaday," Wylie groaned. "Why aren't you d-dead?"

Harte reached under his two coats and pulled his shirt tail free. Gripping the hem with his teeth, he made a tear and then completed the rip with his hands. After folding the cloth three times, he worked it under Wylie's coat and pressed it against the wound. Pulling the shivering body toward him, Harte checked for an exit wound.

"The bullet is still in you. Just hold this compress in place right here. Press it hard."

Wylie's trembling hand made its way to the wound. "Y-you sh-should'a k-killed me."

Harte arranged the wet jacket over Wylie's chest and sat back to see the man suffering against the pain and the cold. "You just about killed yourself coming up here dressed that way. If I hadn't gotten to you, you would have died a miserable death up here with this stump as your grave marker."

Wylie's palsied face took on a look of bottomless self-pity. "H-Harte, f-finish me. I tr-tried to k-kill you! For G-God's sake, k-kill me!"

From the west a vehicle's light shone through the darkness, and soon the sound of the tires on ice could be heard. A curtain of ice crystals fell through the cone of high beams like a shower of diamonds released from the black sky.

"You've got a debt to pay, Wylie. And there are a lot of people who will want to know you're paying it."

As Harte's old truck slowed to a stop next to the paint, the window came down and Emmanuél's face was etched out by the light of the dashboard. "You okay, Sheriff?" he said, studying Harte's torso. "I hear your gun speak last. I figure you have the final say."

"I'm all right," Harte said and gestured toward Wylie. "We need to get him to a hospital."

Manny left the engine running, stepped out, and slipped into a raincoat. He faced the direction from which he had come and let out a shrieking whistle into the dark. Soon someone appeared in a hooded raincoat. Harte could hear running footsteps crunching in the ice.

"Is Collette," Manny explained. "I leave her until I see the situation here."

"Why did you bring her up here," Harte asked, a little anger in his voice.

"In case I have to track you," Manny said. "She drive the truck."

Emmanuél pulled a flashlight from his pocket and shone it on Wylie. "Good thing we find you. Not a good night for tracking. The ice comes down heavy. I think maybe you have a protector who hovers near you, *Señor* Harte. Do you believe in such things?"

Harte felt the dented badge on his belt buckle. "After this night . . . I just might."

Emmanuél's smile spread to his eyes. "*Santa Colta*, perhaps?"

The wind surged and almost blew away Harte's hat, but he caught the crown and pushed it tighter on his head. "How'd you know to come up here?"

"We see you ride off to the old road. *Senora* Haversack tell us what happen."

Collette came around the truck through the beam of the headlights. Bundled up against the falling sleet, she approached and studied Harte from hat to boots.

"You're all right, Mr. Canaday?"

"I'm fine," he said. When her inspection turned to the horse, he added. "Piper's fine, too." He pointed to where Wylie trembled in the dark. "But Wylie needs a hospital."

The two men handled the weight of Wylie's inflated torso as Collette lifted his feet. When they had settled the prisoner inside the cab of the truck, Harte turned up the heater and repeatedly tried to fix Wylie's shaking hand to the wound. Each time the hand fell away. Putting his shoulder into Wylie's ribs, Harte pushed with his hands against Wylie's ample hips until they spanned the space between the seats. Wylie groaned but remained as unmoving as a side of beef.

"Get behind the wheel, Emmanuél. I want you two to take him to the hospital." Turning to Collette, Harte gently laid a hand on her shoulder. "I'm going to need you to keep pressure on that wound all the way. Can you do that for me?"

Collette eyed Wylie as if he were a disease. "Yes," she said, "I can do it."

Harte lightly touched her cheek and turned her face to him. "You saved my life tonight."

She frowned and watched him spread the front of his coats. Clasping his dented belt buckle, he angled the old badge for her to see. Then he showed it to Emmanuél.

"She gave this to me," Harte explained. "*Santa Colletta.*"

He smiled at the girl and pulled her closer, embracing her thin body as she stood as passively as a bag of tent poles. "Thank you, Collette," he whispered and stepped back from her.

When she climbed into the truck, Harte buttoned up his coat and zipped the raincoat. "Mr. Canaday?" she called. Harte stepped closer to the window. Against the shattering sound of falling ice and the blow of the truck's heater fan, her quiet voice barely made its way to him. "I think you saved my life, too."

After a respectful time, Emmanuél leaned over a comatose Wylie and put his face nearer the window. "What about you, Sheriff? Ride in the back?"

Harte shook his head. "I've got a horse to return to its owner."

Emmanuél nodded and handed Harte a small flashlight. "When we get phone service, I'll call in for a deputy to escort you. Maybe they bring you some gloves and a thermos of coffee."

Harte lifted his eyebrows. "Call Maxie-Rose, the dispatcher. She knows my style of coffee."

The truck made a checkmark turn and headed back toward the gap. Harte stood until the taillights disappeared down the road, and then he clicked on the light and walked to the paint. All the tracks around him were filling with ice. Untying the reins, he watched the mare endure the weather with hooded eyes . . . but otherwise resigned to the cold. Ice clung to her mane and tumbled off her long face. Without thunder, he decided, she was a trooper.

"I think maybe you're the hero on this night." He stroked her flat cheeks and brushed at the crystals clinging to her forelocks. "Thank you."

He swiped ice from the bow of the saddle, mounted, and walked Piper downwind on the road. He turned up his coat collar to encircle his neck and crumpled the hood of the raincoat like a shield for the back of his head. Sleet tapped on the brim of his hat in a continuous drumroll. Together man and horse made their way west, the wind howling at their backs, and the sleet pushing them along.

It was, seasonally, the earliest storm of his memory and probably, ironically, a symptom of global warming. The trees were now covered in ice, the hardwoods standing erect in frosty armor and the evergreens bowing with their accruing weight. The forest had become a crystalline palace, and its voice was a steady, sibilant, shattering sound, like an applause erupting around him to honor the fickle turn of the weather.

The cold touched his face with a light sting, but inside his cocoon of wool and waterproof nylon he was warm. The rhythm of the horse beneath him carried the comfort of a mother rocking her child in a cradle. The frozen world seemed to breathe new life into his lungs. He felt a dozen years younger. All around him the ice-rimed trees stood as a colorless masterpiece through which, it seemed, at least on this night, he alone had been selected to witness all its beauty. Despite his hurried ascent of the mountain . . . despite being shot . . . and despite shooting another man . . . Harte felt some kind of grace descend upon him. It was as though an unexpected alignment of the spheres was trying to send him a message encrypted in wind and ice.

"I'm home," he whispered aloud, knowing that this was probably as close as he would come to interpreting the message.

# Chapter Thirty-Nine

Harte was sipping his morning coffee in the office when Maxie came in. She laid down a folder on his desk and canted her head to one side.

"You're looking pretty pleased with yourself," she laughed. "And you damn well oughta be."

Harte raised his cup to her. "I think I finally figured out the perfect ratio of cocoa to coffee."

Maxie let her head tilt to the other side. "Well, I guess it's the little things in life," she said. "Mrs. Haversack called and said the horse you borrowed is doin' fine. She thanks you for rubbin' 'er down. That's the horse, I mean."

Harte turned to the window, taking in the view of the mountains to the west. He couldn't see Hogback Mountain from there, but the eidetic image of that frozen high country would always be etched into his mind.

"Maxie," he said, "I've got a new project for you when you get the time." He turned to gesture with his cup toward the Montana print on the wall. "Think you can find me a print of *our* mountains to slip in that barn-wood frame?"

She carried her look of surprise to the hanging artwork. "The Appalachians?" she chirped. "Yes'r, I can." Then her face sobered. "That mean you don't want the Montana picture now?"

Harte studied the picture. "We'll keep it underneath the new one . . . just in case."

Maxie frowned. "Will we be needin' a horse and rider in this one, Sher'ff?"

Harte kept gazing at the picture. "Sure, and if you can find it, maybe some ice."

"Appalachians on the rocks," she said. "I'll get on it today." She handed him a folder.

"What's this?" Harte said.

"Forms from Family Services for you to fill out. There's a Mr. Harliner put you down as a reference. He's tryin' to get his son back." Maxie raised an eyebrow. "The county people are confused that the man who raised the complaint is listed as a reference." She waited, but Harte just nodded and sipped his coffee. "Sher'ff, how'd Mrs. Haversack handle ever'thing 'bout her husband?"

Harte set down his cup. "She handled it. She knows what Wylie is."

"How come she didn't know before, Sher'ff Harte? I mean, don't it make you wonder 'bout what's going on around us all the time? I've always thought of our county as a special place, you know? Removed from all the filth and crime you always hear about in the big cities."

"Probably why somebody here thinks he can get away with pulling off something like this. Maybe a criminal can feel invisible out here in God's country."

Maxie hissed through her teeth. "Makes me mad is what it does, Sher'ff Harte. People like that are guilty of more'n what we're charging 'em for."

Harte looked up at her. "You mean, like treason?"

Maxie pointed at him. "That's exactly what I mean." Her brow pushed low over her eyes. "It's one thing to have somebody move in here and bring their nasty habits with 'em—like that Santiago fellow . . . and Ash . . . and McAllister, wherever he comes from. But Wylie and Layland, they were born here. Seems to me they got no reason to turn out so rotten."

"Everybody's got to come from somewhere, Maxie." Harte sat in his chair and shook his head. "People are always going to be people. They say Cain killed Abel. Look where *he* came from."

Maxie thought about that until they heard the front door open. She marched out of the room, and Harte heard her greet someone in her official voice. In a moment she was back, leaning through his open doorway, wearing an expression of supreme deference.

"It's Captain Nesmith, Sher'ff."

"Send him in, Maxie," Harte said and turned on the switch under the hotplate.

Nesmith wore an immaculate blue suit and a faint smile as he entered the room in his slow economical walk. Maxie quietly closed the door, and the state officer draped his overcoat on the sofa and took a seat in the chair across from Harte's desk.

"Looks like you had another busy night," Nesmith said. "I see you came out unscathed."

"Got a horse and a belt buckle to thank for that." Harte rose enough to display the buckle.

Nesmith softly whistled a sliding note. "Centuries ago my people believed that a horse's spirit and its rider's spirit entwined like the roots of two neighboring trees." He nodded toward the bullet-dented shield on the buckle. "Good thing they made that one the way they used to. You knew him, right?"

"Haversack? We went to school together. Turns out I didn't know him at all."

"Do we ever really know anybody?" Billy Nesmith mumbled. The way he said it, he could have been alone in the room.

With the kettle rattling on the burner, Harte turned off the switch. "Coffee?"

Nesmith shook his head. "If you have no objection, I'm taking McAllister and Childers to Atlanta and hold 'em until the Feds want 'em. Childers says he's ready to spill the beans on the lot of them—Ash, McAllister, *and* Haversack. Not that we need it, but it'll play well in court. I think he's more likely to talk to us than to you. I don't think he's feeling too popular in your county."

"Take them all," Harte agreed. "I'll consider it part of a new county purification project. Just don't promise Childers too much in return. He fancies himself a real deal maker."

Nesmith smiled without a trace of humor. "Won't promise anything. What he *thinks* we might do for him is more important." He snorted a little laugh. "He's an optimistic bastard." He crossed one leg over the other, and his face went all business. "As far as Meeks's murder goes, we're going to push for conspiracy to murder," Nesmith said. "Add to that the drugs and illegals, Childers is facing a lot of time."

"How much?"

Nesmith pursed his lips. "He'll be an old man when he gets out. If he gets out."

Harte stood and finished his drink by the window. In the exercise yard, Layland stood unmoving in his orange jumpsuit, staring through the chain-link fence toward the square. Harte almost felt sorry for him. In prison, Layland would likely believe he had descended into the lowest rung of Dante's inferno. He would be lucky to survive it.

Billy Nesmith cleared his throat. "My men were over at the Haversack place this morning. Got the computer." He made an expression that approached disbelief. "It's a gold mine. This guy, Haversack, was pretty loose with his evidence. Kind who thought he'd never be found out. I'm surprised his wife didn't know." He kept his eyes on Harte. "You think she could be in on it?"

Harte shook his head. "They lived separate lives. She loathed him. I think she knew about Wylie's sexual proclivities but couldn't prove it. If she could, Wylie would have gotten worse than what I gave him. Maybe a pitchfork to the gonads."

Billy Nesmith pursed his lips and winced. "Too bad. Could'a saved you that ride up that mountain and that dent in your buckle."

Lowering his gaze to his papers, Harte absently squared the folder with the desktop. "What about the girls? Can we keep a low profile on them? This is the kind of hole that can be hard to climb out of. They're just kids . . . seventeen."

Nesmith rubbed at a spot on the shoe propped on his knee. "They've got a good lawyer. We'll see what she can work out with the D.A." He began to nod. "See no reason to ruin their lives."

They did not speak for a time, until finally Nesmith stood and offered his hand. "Well, Sheriff, nobody's going to call you a 'one-night wonder' ever again. You be careful, now. A reputation can be a heavy load to carry."

The two lawmen shook hands. "I'll be careful. You do the same."

Billy Nesmith picked up his coat, ambled to the door, and turned. "That horse you rode last night . . . sounds like a good one."

Harte smiled. "She is. And I told her so."

Nesmith put on his earnest expression. "The Comanches talked to their horses. The animals may not know the words, but they understand the message."

Harte smiled down at his boots for a moment, but when his head came up he kept his face expressionless. "Hoka hey, it was a good day to die."

Billy Nesmith smiled, his handsome face belonging on the plains of a forgotten time. "The phrase is Lakota, but I've always appreciated the sentiment." Nesmith opened the door and hesitated. He tapped his own belt buckle and smiled. "Maybe today is a good day to live."

Harte nodded. "Maybe the two ideas are not all that different."

Nesmith smiled so broadly that years seemed to melt from his face. He pointed at Harte.

"I may have to speak to the elders about taking you into the tribe."

"Better let me figure out my own tribe first," Harte said but waved his thanks. When the door closed, he started mixing another perfect blend of his special brew, thinking of this second cup less as an extravagance than as a celebration.

For the next ten minutes he sipped his just reward for a good night's work and read the treatise that Burt Harliner had written to Family Services about why he wanted his son back and how he would alter his parental behavior. When he had finished the heartfelt piece, Harte put his signature on the line labeled "filer's advocate" and finished the last of his coffee.

He was looking longingly at the fold-out sofa when his phone rang. "Sher'ff," Maxie said, "Mrs. Haversack called and said you'd better get out to Cherokee Rose right away. She didn't say why." After a beat, as if reading his mind, Maxie added. "I can ask Joe-Joe to go if you wanna get some sleep."

Harte gave up on his plan for a nap and closed the folder. "Thanks, Maxie. I'll go."

\*\*\*\*\*

Jan met him outside before he had turned off his ignition. Without a greeting she waved him to follow her around the side of the house to the rear door, where she dipped under the yellow crime tape and entered the basement space where Wylie had run an office. When Harte followed her inside, he found the desktop empty with a dust-free rectangle where the computer had been. Blood stains still dappled the floor.

"The state police were here for hours," Jan said. "They told me not to move anything, but I told them I was going to get this blood up because I was sick of looking at it. They didn't argue."

Harte was quiet, waiting.

Jan pointed to the floor beside the freezer. "So I was down here cleaning . . . a place I haven't been in ten years. Wylie's orders," she added sarcastically. "And I was sloshing around with a mop down there, and the bottom of the freezer fell down. I got a flashlight to look under there." She picked up the flashlight lying on the freezer top and offered it to him. "Have a look."

Harte took off his hat and knelt with the light. Lowering his head to the concrete floor he peered under the freezer and saw a collapsed metal tray angling down to the floor. Dried blood dotted the interior of the tray and several small pieces of paper lay along one side. Reaching into the opening, he pulled out three one hundred dollar bills and one curled brown band of paper that had probably packaged a stack of money. Turning back to Jan, Harte waited to see what she might say.

"There's no telling how much he was hiding down here," she said, her voice full of spite. "That little hideaway could hold hundreds of thousands." She hissed air through her teeth. "I've been pinching pennies all these years while my business is going down the toilet." She flung an arm toward the freezer. "And the son of a bitch was down here sitting on all this."

Harte returned the bills and band to the tray. "Let's leave it just like this, Jan. I'll get the state investigators back out here."

Harte stood and placed the flashlight on the freezer top. "He was carrying close to eight hundred thousand in a satchel."

Jan's eyes widened. "Eight hundred thousand!" With the harshness in her voice hanging in the musty air of the basement, she closed her eyes, shook her head, and offered a contrite smile.

"Sorry. I'm just so angry at him."

Harte pushed up the brim of his hat and felt the sweat band rake over the lingering bump on the back of his head. "Yeah . . . well . . . you've got a right to be angry." He watched the tightness in her face give way to fatigue. "I'm angry, too. For a lot of reasons. Did you know he shot me?"

Her face compressed into a web of wrinkles. "Shot you?" Her eyes narrowed and panned up and down the length of him. "Where?"

He opened his coat and tapped the buckle. "I was lucky," he said and let the coat fall in place.

Jan stared into his eyes. "What about Wylie? Was he lucky, too? Getting shot in the shoulder? Or was that you being noble?"

Harte pursed his lips and watched her wait intently for an answer. "I remembered what you'd said . . . about not killing him. I guess I just reacted with that in mind."

Her face seemed to compress. "Which endangered you, didn't it?"

Harte shrugged. "Maybe. But it worked out okay."

Without speaking, Jan studied Harte's face, her eyes seeming to soak up his features the way an artist might memorize an image for a future portrait. "You're a good man, Harte Canaday." She lowered her gaze to the floor and shook her head. "I should never have said that to you . . . about not killing him. It put you in danger. I'm sorry."

When Harte made no reply, she turned and walked up the stairs, her footfall slow and weary. When the door upstairs closed, Harte pictured her alone in the house. There was, he knew, more distance to travel down this bitter trail. The legal aftermath of Wylie's secret life would be a long and punishing ordeal for her. She would have to appear in court, face a slew of reporters from local and Atlanta papers, and deal with the fallout for Cherokee Rose Stables.

He quietly exited the basement and eased the door shut. Then, striding across the yard into the meadow, he made his way down the double tracks where Emmanuél was working alone in front of the trailer, putting a shine on Harte's truck as he quietly half-sang half-whispered something in Spanish. When he saw Harte approach, he stopped the singing but continued to work with his hands.

"How's Collette?" Harte asked.

"She is good. She sleeps inside. It was a long night for her." Emmanuél shook his head. "That not bother her. It was leaving her father for so long at night. But he ees okay."

To change the subject, Harte nodded at his truck. "How's she running?"

The young Mexican considered the old pickup, his eye gleaming with pride. "She purr like the mountain lion soaking up the Sonora sun."

Harte raised an eyebrow. "You're a poet, too?"

Emmanuél smiled and beckoned Harte to follow. "I show you something." The young Mexican led the way around to the back of the trailer, where Santiago's BMW sat dormant on the grass. Beside the rusted trailer propped on cinder blocks, the dark shining car looked like something that had landed here from another planet. "You know how Collette have to borrow the lady's truck to get her father to the doctor? I figure she can use this." He shrugged. "Santiago say he give me a car." The boy held up a ring of keys. "I help him keep his promise. Now I pass it on to Collette."

Harte chuckled. "I assume he made that promise before he knew you worked for me."

Emmanuél shrugged again. "A promise is a promise, *señor*."

Harte nodded. "How'd you get this? The county usually confiscates vehicles taken in drug raids."

"Cody," Emmanuél said. "He bring it by. He say an impounded car sits around for months while someone handles the paperwork. Not good to let these expensive cars sit idle." He smiled.

Harte laughed. "I'd have to agree. I'll see if I can take care of that paperwork. I'm known to be very slow."

Emmanuél's eyes ran the length of the car. "She take good care of it. I help with that."

When they returned to the front of the trailer, Harte saw that the usual trio of horses had gathered at the fence to watch them. He moved toward them in a slow walk and rested his arms on the top rail, letting the horses come to him in their own time. Emmanuél hung back and watched.

In a casual manner the animals gathered around Harte and nosed his head and shoulders. When he began to scratch the ears of one mare, the other two crowded in for their share.

Turning his head toward Emmanuél, Harte softened his voice for the sake of the animals. "Did Collette talk to you about Wylie Haversack?"

Emmanuél approached the fence and held out a hand to one of the horses. The animal rested its chin in his palm, and the boy gently stroked the soft tissue under the mouth.

"*Si*. She tell me all about it last night at the hospital."

He spoke so quietly that Harte shallowed his breathing to hear every word.

"I tell you something, Sheriff." Emmanuél turned, his handsome features now sharpened by the intensity of his thoughts. "It ees good for him that you are the one to find him . . . and not me. I would send him straight to hell."

Harte checked the trailer and then leaned in closer. "Well, think of it this way: maybe prison will be worse than hell."

"Maybe," Emmanuél said and watched the horses nose the tufts of grass clustered at the base of the fence posts. As the silence drew out, Harte could almost feel the thoughts turning in his deputy's head. "Collette ees private person. She has shed enough tears for a lifetime, yes? I'm hoping she won't have to testify."

By the flicker of light in Emmanuél's dark eyes, Harte knew that the boy was asking this one favor—an act of kindness that he prayed Harte could grant.

"I'd like to keep all these girls out of this, if I can."

Emmanuél's face smoothed out like the surface of a placid pond. "Ees good idea."

Last night's cold front still put a chill in the air. Harte slipped his hands into the pockets of his coat and turned to watch the clouds in the west take on a fine red edge, like a scalloped wire heated to incandescence. Then the red disk of sun descended through the lowest stratum of clouds, and the grass seemed to catch fire with the color. The horses suddenly moved away together and broke into a gallop. They ran out into the rolling meadow like a living portrait of freedom.

To a horse, Harte thought, Cherokee Rose was the source of everything that was needed: forage, water, space to move around, shelter from the weather, and the companionship engrained into an animal with a herd-mentality. The simplicity of it was tempting to admire, but he knew ultimately that it was not enough for people. People always demanded more. Often, too much more.

He imagined what Wylie had been like when he had started the ranch with Jan. There must have been something good and promising in the project . . . some kind of shared hope they had talked about. At what point, he wondered, did Wylie give all that up to follow the bent path that would destroy so many lives . . . including his own?

Harte spun around to admire his truck, and Emmanuél turned with him. "The truck is yours for as long as you need it . . . or until I do."

Emmanuél nodded. "I take good care of it."

Harte smiled to himself. "Hell, you're already taking better care of it than I did." He turned to face Emmanuél. "Will you stay on as my deputy? You seem to be good at it."

Emmanuél adjusted his gaze to the trailer. "I talk with Collette about that."

Harte clapped his hand to the boy's shoulder. "Good answer. Let me know."

The Mexican smiled, nodded once. As if by some tacit signal, they walked away from one another, Emmanuél heading for the trailer and Harte walking toward the barn.

When Harte reached Piper's stall, he rested his forearms on the gate and waited for his eyes to adjust. The paint nickered and moved toward him, its long piebald face bobbing and then settling as the nostrils blew.

"I figure I owe you plenty," Harte whispered. The mare nuzzled his ear with the velvet of her nose. "I'll start by bringing you a couple of apples. How does that sound? Then, soon as I can get around to it, let's have a day up on the mountain without someone shooting at us."

Pied Piper nickered, and the soft flapping from her nostrils was a song to his ears. He scratched her head and then walked toward the west end of the property toward Bella's orchard. The dark was coming on and the temperature was dropping faster. He picked up his pace, scissored through the wood rails next to the section of barbed wire, and walked around to the front of the cottage.

A few seconds after he knocked, the porch light clicked on, and Bella opened the door in her well-worn jeans and gray plaid flannel shirt. Neither of them spoke, and the silence seemed just right. She reached back inside and the light clicked off.

"Those are snow clouds, aren't they?" she asked.

"They are," Harte said. They stepped to the edge of the porch and admired the sky.

"Brrr," she said. "And it's only November." She smiled at Harte. "Water is on. How about some hazelnut coffee?"

He followed her into the kitchen and set his hat on an apple crate. She pulled down two mugs from a cupboard but lost her smile when she frowned at his midsection.

"What happened to your coat? That looks like a burn."

He craned his neck down to examine the hole. When he looked up at her, she had carried her frown to his hat on the crate. The brim in back was permanently creased from Wylie's shovel.

"My favorite hat and coat," he said. "They haven't fared well in the last twelve hours."

She studied his face for what he was not saying. "Is that a bullet hole in your coat?"

He unbuttoned the coat and fanned it open. "Remember the gift my students gave me?" He tapped the buckle with a finger. She stepped close and touched the dent. "Favorite belt, too," he said.

She leaned to examine the back of his head. Gently, she probed the swollen lump there.

"Wylie Haversack," Harte said, answering the question on her face.

Bella shrank with a pale sickened look. "Oh, Harte," she whispered. "He tried to kill you?"

He nodded, removed the coat, and draped it on a chair. Lifting his eyebrows, he gave her a look meant to imply that, sometimes, people just had to swallow the ineffable ways of the world.

"Is he—?" Bella stopped short of saying the word.

"No, but he'll probably wish he was dead."

She poured him coffee and left the room. When she returned, she set down a wicker sewing basket on the kitchen table and lifted his coat from the chair.

"Sit," she said and sat across from him with his coat in her lap. As she squinted at a needle she was threading, she said, "Tell me."

He sipped his drink, set it down, and told her the story as she closed the hole with repetitive passes of the needle and thread. When it was done, they sat in the silence of the house for a time. The thermostat clicked, and a low breath of warm air pushed from the vents. Bella stood and hung the coat back on his chair. When she sat again and stared at Harte, he leaned to inspect the repair.

"Thank you," he said quietly.

"I'm not sure about the hat. Maybe some steam. But I'll be no help with the belt buckle."

Harte looked down at the gouge in the badge. "I'll keep it just as it is. It's a good reminder."

Bella pressed her lips into a tight line. "Was it hard to shoot someone you knew?"

Harte shrugged. "Didn't have time to think about that. Things happen too fast when someone is shooting at you." He leaned his forearms on the table, and looked directly at her. "But I have been thinking about something you said." He looked around the room and then settled on her receptive eyes. "You once reminded me there's good and bad in everybody. But if a man is shooting at me, I have to believe he is evil incarnate so that I can put him down. Like with the Bullochs the night Jim was killed. In my mind, they were demons. These thoughts didn't run through my head the way I'm telling it to you now. It was more reflex. So I shot for center mass. To end it. To end *them*."

"What does that mean . . . 'center mass?' "

Harte tapped a finger just below his sternum. "You shoot for the middle. That way if you're a little off, you've still got a hit. All that stuff we saw on TV as kids, the hero shooting a gun out of the villain's hand, that's fantasy. You can get killed trying that. You miss that shot and you've missed entirely. The idea is to hit a man somewhere . . . get him off balance . . . stun him. You can always shoot again while he's disoriented." Harte waved away that thought. "The thing is, with Wylie, I shot to wound. I took a chance."

"Why?" Bella said.

He spread his hands palms down on the table. "Not sure. Partly for what you said, and partly for Jan, I guess. She asked me not to kill him." Harte narrowed his eyes. "I knew how much she despised Wylie, and somehow that took the decision away from me. If she could show him mercy, seemed like I had to."

Bella nodded thoughtfully. Her face showed lines of worry.

"I had a lot of reasons to hate Wylie," Harte continued. "Maybe more than any other man I've known in this county. But I've known him most of my life. It's funny . . . I saw him staggering up the mountain trying to get away from me, him breathing like a freight train, and it took me back. I'd seen him play basketball in school. Then later, maybe fifteen years ago, I watched him haul a neighbor's cow out of a mire with his tractor. For just that flash of a second when he had left me to die—or so he thought—I saw that he was more than what I hated about him. And this was even after he had shot me."

Bella propped her elbows on the table and gripped her hands together into a double fist beneath her chin. "Now you make me worry, Harte. What if you had missed? I don't want my words to put you in danger."

"Well," he said, "it's done now."

They stared at one another. The heat clicked off, and the house was still. Bella lowered her forearms to the table and slid forward, craning her neck to better see his eyes.

"I think we need to establish a rule, Sheriff Canaday. When someone is shooting at you . . . or about to . . . you shoot at that center mass! Do you hear me? You follow your instincts, Harte."

Both her hands enveloped one of his. Her skin felt cool and smooth. A beatific smile spread across her face. Then her head turned to the window, and her eyes took on the sharpness of a bird of prey. She stood and walked to the backdoor, staring out the glass panes at the dark.

"It's snowing."

He stood and moved behind her. Looking over her head he watched flakes as large as poker chips tumbling down on the angle of the wind. They landed in the grass as gently as white downy feathers. The endless falling somehow served to underscore their aloneness in the house, as if the snow had afforded them a new remoteness. Harte slipped his right arm around her, just under her chin, and gently gripped her left shoulder. Both her hands came to his forearm and gently held on.

"Do you think it's snowing in Montana?" Bella asked.

"If it is, it can't be any better than this."

The flakes came down so thickly now that the whiteness almost completely blocked out the black of night. "Where is your car?" Bella asked.

"At the Haversack house."

She was quiet for a time, but Harte could sense the wheels turning in her head. "I don't know how you can make it there in this storm," she said in a deadpan voice.

Harte smiled. "Looks treacherous," he agreed.

She turned inside the circle of his arm. "I have an emergency bed. I keep it on hand for young boys in need of a refuge . . . and for wayward sheriffs out lost in the night."

"How *was* your time with Carter?"

"You mean 'Lance'?" she said and smiled. Then she tilted her head. "He's a good kid. But I'd like to take a pair of pliers to that jewelry in his nose."

"I think his father is set on improving himself. He really wants the boy back."

She frowned. "That doesn't usually work that way, does it?"

"I don't know. But if it does, that would be the best outcome. I guess we'll see."

She looked up at him, and he brushed a loose lock of hair from her forehead. "Will you stay with me tonight?" she whispered.

As she waited for his answer he looked over her head through the panes of glass at the snow clinging to the bare branches of the orchard trees. "In the old West . . . back in the eighteen hundreds . . . it was common practice for people all over the remote territories to take in a stranger for a night. It was an unwritten code. Officers of the law could count on a roof and a hot meal when they were in pursuit of outlaws. But outlaws could expect the same."

Bella nodded gravely. "In that case, you'd better make sure you start all your sheriff-like pursuits in this direction."

He gave her a look. "What about the outlaws? Will you take them in too?"

Bella pushed out her lower lip and pretended to think about it. "Oh, I might give them coffee and directions . . . but that's about it."

"Does that mean I get the hot meal?"

Bella nodded. "I can't refuse the sheriff, can I? But it won't be a handout. You've got to help." Taking his hand, she pulled him toward the cutting board, where she had laid out onions, peppers, and carrots. When Harte didn't follow, Bella turned, surprised.

"Before we get into that, I need to ask you for a couple of apples."

"Apples?"

He nodded. "Just two."

She stared at him for a time, all the while a smile playing at her lips. When Harte seemed prepared to wait indefinitely, she released him and rummaged through the nearest crate.

"These look like good ones," she said.

He took them from her and turned them in his hands. They were firm and dusty red with a scattering of dark spots. He smelled them and nodded.

"These will do fine."

Bella cocked her head. "What's this about?"

Harte slipped into his coat and dropped an apple into each pocket. "A promise," he said quietly and nodded to her coat on the wall peg. "Wrap up and walk over to the barn with me."

When they stepped outside, the orchard was lit up with the glow from the back porch light. The ground was covered in two inches of immaculate snow, and the flakes were coming down still.

"Goodness," she said. "This could be Montana!"

Harte looked at her. The cold wind had already brought out some color to her cheeks. Her smile was contagious, and he felt something warm settle inside his chest, much like the sensation he had experienced when Emmanuél had walked back to Collette's trailer.

"Maybe even better," he said and tugged down on the brim of his hat as they started for the barn.

# Coming Soon!

# A TALE TWICE TOLD
## BY
## MARK WARREN
## AWARD WINNING AUTHOR

This permutation of the Robin Hood legend (set in modern times) is a tribute to the powerful bonds that can exist between tried and true friends. Who is to say that souls cannot recycle and return for another go at life? And, when "blood is in the bond," could not a handful of comrades make that journey back together?

**For more information**
**visit:** www.SpeakingVolumes.us

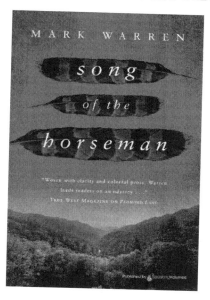

# On Sale Now!

## SPUR AWARD-WINNING AUTHOR
## PATRICK DEAREN

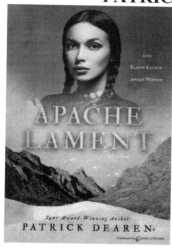 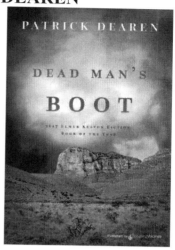

### For more information
### visit: SpeakingVolumes.us

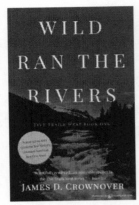
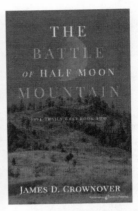
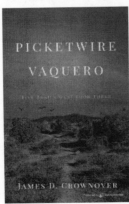
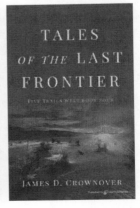

Made in the USA
Columbia, SC
25 April 2025

57137046R20317